Amy Cross is the author of more than 100 horror, paranormal, fantasy and thriller novels.

The Ghosts
of Lakeforth
Hotel

AMY CROSS

First published by Dark Season Books,
United Kingdom, 2017

ISBN: 9781520732091

Also available in e-book format.

www.amycross.com

CONTENTS

Part One
ANNIE HAYES
PAGE 1

Part Two
BETH HAYES
PAGE 21

Part Three
MAURICE MECKLETHORPE
PAGE 69

Part Four
RUTH MAYWHISTLE
PAGE 111

Part Five
ELLEN NASH
PAGE 169

Part Six
JOBARD NASH
PAGE 225

Part Seven
STEVE CULSHAW
PAGE 281

Part Eight
STEVE CULSHAW
PAGE 339

Part Nine
BETH HAYES
PAGE 345

Epilogue
PAGE 397

THE GHOSTS OF LAKEFORTH HOTEL

PART ONE

ANNIE HAYES
TODAY

AMY CROSS

ANNIE HAYES
TODAY

"WELL, YOU DIDN'T *HAVE* to come," Beth replies, as the car continues to bump along the dumpy old dirt road. "You could have stayed at home for the week and hung out with all your fabulous friends."

"Nah," I mutter, still filing my nails on the back seat. "They'll be there when I get back. Besides, your brain-dead boyfriend has been going on about this place so much, I just *had* to see it. His taste is so lacking in other areas, after all."

Glancing at Beth, I smile as soon as I see the scowl on her face.

"Joke," I add silently. "Still, I don't really have high hopes. I'm gonna bet this turns out to be the crumbiest, most rundown hotel in the whole of England."

"Is it much further?" she asks, turning to Steve, She's doing that thing she always does when she's

3

annoyed. She pretends to ignore me, even though I know she's seething. Honestly, my sister is so easy to read. Sometimes, I wish I had another hobby, but winding her up is just so much fun!

"We should be there by now," he replies.

"Maybe you took the wrong turning," I suggest.

"I know the way, Annie. I came here every summer when I was a kid."

"But you said there should be a sign. I didn't see a sign. Beth, did you see a sign? The lack of a sign seems like a sign to me that maybe we're on the wrong road."

"Did you see the sign?" she asks him, still studiously avoiding looking at me.

"This is definitely the right way," he replies, although he sounds a little annoyed now. Steve and Beth are such a good couple. They're so alike, which is why it's so easy to annoy them both at the same time. Even now, as the car rumbles along the road, they're still muttering to one another about turn-offs they might have missed, or routes that might have changed over the years. I swear, they're starting to sound like some lame old couple.

Sitting up, I look out the window and see nothing but a dirty old forest spreading to the horizon on either side of the road. The trees don't even look very healthy, with pale, leafless branches reaching up as if they're trying to scratch the dull gray sky. I never thought any part of England could be more depressing than Sittingbourne, but I've got to give my sister and her boyfriend a little credit. They've actually managed to find an even worse cesspool.

"Where the hell are we?" I ask finally. "I thought you said this hotel was, like, cool and chic. I mean, I didn't believe you for a second, but you still said it. Defend yourself, man."

"There!" Steve says suddenly. "See it?"

Turning, I see that there's a large building up ahead, barely visible behind a line of dead trees. I open my mouth to tell him that it looks like a dump, before suddenly realizing that 'dump' might actually be too flattering. In fact, as the car rounds the bend and the hotel looms fully into view, I'm shocked to see that the place looks like it's falling down. I was expecting to be able to make fun of this hotel, but I thought I'd at least have to work a little. Instead, I think Steve might actually have driven us all this way, only to find that the fabled Lakeforth Hotel is closed for business.

I can't help grinning from ear to ear.

"Honey," Beth says cautiously, "are you *sure* this is it?"

"What the hell happened?" he mutters, bringing the car to a halt at the edge of the cracked, leaf-strewn driveway.

"I don't see any signs," Beth points out. "This doesn't look like a hotel at all. We must've taken a wrong turn."

"This is definitely it," he replies, unbuckling and climbing out of the car.

Beth finally turns to me, and my grin somehow gets even bigger.

"Don't!" she says firmly.

"What?"

"Just don't! You know how much this trip means to him!"

"Just because something means something to someone," I reply, "doesn't mean it's worth doing."

"Annie! Stop!"

With that, she gets out of the car and goes over to join Steve, who's standing dumbstruck at the foot of the steps that lead up to the grand main door. I watch them for a moment, still unable to stifle a faint smile, and then I open the door and clamber out of the car. I've been curled up on the back seat for so long, my legs are stiff, and I'm starting to get a little hungry. Stretching my arms out wide, I let out an exaggerated yawn that I just *know* will bug my sister.

Now that I'm out of the car, the first thing I notice is that the air is clean, the kind of clean that people always bang on about whenever they're pretending to enjoy getting away from the city. Those people are so tiring and over-enthusiastic about everything. And the second thing I notice, to my absolute delight, is that the large sign for Lakeforth Hotel has not only been knocked over, but there are actually vines growing across its surface.

This place has blatantly been abandoned for years.

As my grin broadens, I finally raise my hands and start a slow, sarcastic clap.

"Stop that!" Beth hisses, turning to me. "Annie!"

"It's a ruin," I reply, putting my hands on my hips. "I mean, I was probably going to say that anyway, but I figured I'd be exaggerating a little. But no, this hotel is an actual, real ruin. It looks like it's on the verge of falling down. Didn't you even double-check that it was still running before you drove us out here? I mean, hello? Ever heard of the internet, guys?"

Ignoring me for some reason, Steve steps forward and starts making his way up the steps, as if he still can't quite believe what we've found. He's a cute guy, earnest but fun to be around sometimes, and I actually feel a little sorry for him. I mean, he's been bigging this hotel up for so long, and one might even say that he staked his reputation on it being the most fun place in the history of the world. Now we're here, and it's blatantly clear that the owners packed up and moved on a long time ago.

The whole trip is a joke.

"Well this is fun," I say as I wander over to join Beth. "I am *so* glad I let you talk me into coming."

"*You* talked *me* into *letting* you come," she whispers. "Can you at least stop grinning like that? Steve's going to be really upset."

"Why? We can just hit the road again and find a motel somewhere. Preferably one with a bar attached."

"You know why he wanted to come here," she replies, turning to me. "Believe it or not, Annie, some people actually have real human emotions. They care about things."

"Blah blah blah."

"Of course you don't understand. You don't care about *anything*, do you?"

"Ouch," I reply, raising a skeptical eyebrow. "If

7

I didn't know that you knew better, I'd be tempted to think you're trying to make me feel bad."

"It's open!" Steve calls out suddenly.

Beth and I both turn to see him standing at the top of the steps, holding the front door wide open to reveal the gloomy interior.

"Yay," I mutter, rolling my eyes.

"Maybe there's someone around," he continues. "I'll go check."

With that, he heads inside, leaving the door to slowly and creakily swing shut again. I guess that'll probably be the last we see of him. He'll probably be, like, eaten by hillbilly cannibals while he's in there, or slaughtered by the ghost of some long-dead serial killer.

"So we're leaving soon, right?" I ask, turning to Beth. "Promise me we're getting the hell out of here."

Sighing, Beth makes her way up the steps. I guess it's only natural that she's going to follow her darling Steve into the building. After all, they've been practically joined at the hip ever since they started dating last year. Beth's a sucker for a guy with a tragic backstory, and Steve ticks all her boxes. In fact, finding this place abandoned probably makes her love him even *more*. She can dote over him, and try to make him feel better, and tell him he's not being a total wimp. And then they'll get all lovey-dovey and...

A shudder passes through my chest, and I swear I actually feel a little nauseous.

"I'll just go take a look around outside, then!" I call after them, even though I doubt they can hear me. Still, the idea of hanging around with those two right now is enough to make me want to vomit. "I'll probably get raped and murdered, but hey, who cares? Right?"

I wait.

No reply.

Wandering toward the far corner of the building, I can't help noticing that the entire area seems overgrown and abandoned. Like, this hotel has clearly not been in use for several years, and I actually have to be careful as I pick my way through the weeds. When I get to the corner, I spot a large patio area, complete with rusty old metal furniture that looks to have been just left behind by the previous owners. There are thick knotty weeds growing through the gaps between the patio's paving slabs, and some of those slabs feel loose as I make my way over to take a look at the swimming pool.

There's a pale gray cover over the pool itself, although it's not particularly secure and I can see water bobbing under the edge. I shiver slightly as I think about how cold this pool must be right now, and a moment later I see that there's something floating in the water. Leaning down a little and squinting, I see that the object in question is a dead wasp.

"Lovely," I whisper. "Who *wouldn't* want to go for a dip?"

Still, as I look around at the vast, deserted expanse of the hotel's garden, I guess I can see how this place might have been nice once.

Years ago.

Years and years and years ago.

Before it became a gross trash heap.

"What a dump," I mutter, heading around to the

far end of the pool. "I am *not* staying here a moment longer than I have to."

Glancing back toward the main building, I see nothing in the windows except the gray afternoon sky reflected back at me. I guess Beth and Steve are in there somewhere, and she's probably telling him how everything's going to be fine, and how he's a strong, sensitive guy who's in touch with his feelings and blah blah blah.

God, I really *do* feel sick.

Stopping at the edge of the paved area, I look toward the trees and see the lake glittering just a few miles away. There's no sign of life out there, of course, but at least the area has *some* potential. I mean, I could get behind some speedboat action, maybe some jet-skis, that sort of thing. Maybe I could go for a topless swim, let some guys check me out, see if any of them have the balls to make a move. Not that there are any guys around right now, but I reckon it'd be possible to hold a decent party out here. Not with Beth or Steve around, though. They're just -

"Ow!" I hiss, suddenly feeling a stinging sensation on my right leg.

Looking down, I see that I've brushed against a thick patch of nettles.

"Piece of shit!" I mutter, rubbing the patch of skin as I glance around, hoping to find some of those plants you can use to soothe the sting. I don't remember the name of them, but -

Suddenly I let out a gasp as I spot a face staring back at me from the forest. I tell myself I must be wrong, that I'm imagining things, but my heart is pounding and as I stare at the face I realize that it's real.

A little girl.

There's a faint, cold breeze blowing over my shoulder, ruffling the overgrown grass and causing the trees to rustle. The girl, meanwhile, looks to be no more than seven or eight years old, and she's standing completely still as she stares right back at me from her vantage spot about fifty feet away.

I wait for her to turn and run, or for her to just do *something*, but she just seems happy to stand there like some kind of idiot.

"Are you okay?" I call out finally, trying to force a smile even though I'm officially feeling 100% weirded out. Like, maybe even 1,000% or more.

Of course, the girl doesn't reply. She just keeps staring at me, and now I can't help noticing that she looks very pale. Whatever the hell's going on with her, she seems totally dedicated to the creepy little girl act, to the extent that I really just want to turn around and leave her alone.

At the same time, I'm not exactly the easily-upset type, and I figure this kid could give me some valuable intel that I can use to screw with Beth and Steve.

"Hey!" I yell, waving at the girl before using my hand to shield my eyes from the sun. "Come over here!"

I wait, but she's still just staring at me.

"Oh great," I mutter, realizing that *I'm* going to have to go to *her*.

Well, I guess I could not bother, but it's not like I have anything better to be doing.

The overgrown grass isn't so bad, although I'm really not liking the mud and nettles. Still, as I make my way slowly and carefully toward the treeline, I tell myself that this might all be worth it. If the girl can tell me some juicy tidbits about what really happened here at Lakeforth Hotel, I can dangle those details over Steve and really make him sweat. It's not as if I've got anything else to do while we're at this dump, and maybe I can even expedite our departure a little. In fact, by the time I get all the way through the grass and stop just in front of the little girl, I'm starting to think that I'm the only person around here who actually has a hope of getting to the truth.

"Hey dude," I say with a cautious smile. "So what's up? Do you know why this hotel is, like, all closed and stuff?"

As I wait for her to reply, I can't help noticing that she really *is* pale. Like, she doesn't really have very much color to her skin at all, just a tinge of very faint yellow to offset the white tones. She seriously needs some sun, maybe even a few tan jobs.

"Do you speak English?" I ask finally. "Am I making any sense to you at all?"

She's starting to really piss me off now, and I'm also wondering whether maybe she's retarded somehow. Still, I step closer, until I'm just a couple of feet away. Figuring I might still be able to get some info from her, I crouch down until we're face to face, and now I can't help noticing that her eyes are very dark, with smudged, smoky patches that form deep bags. Frankly, for someone her age, she really could use some skincare lessons, although I'm totally not in the mood to help her out right now. Instead, I'm actually starting to think I should have just ignored her and gone to find Beth and Steve.

"Do you know why the hotel closed?" I ask, speaking very clearly and very carefully, in case she's a bit slow. "My friends and I thought it'd be open, but it's closed. Do you know what happened?"

Still staring at me, she shows no sign that she might actually answer.

I open my mouth to ask again, but suddenly I realize that there's a really kinda foul smell here. Sniffing slightly, I can't help noticing a scent of... I don't know what it is, exactly, but it reminds me a girl from school who used to stink of pee all the time, although there's something else added to this particular mix, like something damp and rotten. The girl's clothes look old and pale, with a few rips in the fabric around her left shoulder, and I'm starting to think she must be from some family of hicks who live in the area. She's probably never seen someone like me before, someone well-dressed and wearing properly-applied make-up. For a little girl who lives in a shack, I must be just way more beautiful than anyone she usually bumps into.

Poor little thing. She probably thinks I'm, like, some kinda god or something.

"Okay then," I say finally, getting to my feet and taking a step back. "I'm gonna leave you alone, and me and my friends are gonna head off. I'm sorry if we disturbed you in any way."

I hesitate, just in case she might actually reply,

and then I turn and start walking away, back toward the pool area.

"Not that you're not disturbing on a whole different level, kid," I mutter under my breath. "Rude little piece of -"

Suddenly hearing a rustling sound over my shoulder, I turn and find that the girl has actually started following me. I've got to admit, I let out a faint gasp of surprise as I take another step back, and this little prick has actually managed to properly get my heart racing.

"I don't have anything for you," I tell her. "Okay? I don't have any money on me, if that's what you're after. Just go back to your inbred family and leave me alone."

I wait, but now she's just staring at me again.

Reaching into my pockets, I feel my apartment keys and a bottle of nail-polish I must have forgotten to put back into my make-up kit. I hesitate for a moment, feeling a little bad for the kid, and then finally I take the bottle out and hold it up for her to see.

"Did you ever see anything like this before?" I ask, forcing a smile. "It's a real pretty red color, huh? I bet you don't get quality items like this out here in the sticks."

I watch her face carefully, searching for any sign that she's impressed. At least she's looking at the nail-polish bottle now, instead of continually gawping at me, so I guess the color has caught her attention.

"You can have it, if you want," I tell her, figuring that I might as well be generous. "I'm sure the color'll really suit you."

I wait for her to take the bottle, but after a moment she raises her gaze and looks at me again.

"Don't you want it?" I ask. "What's wrong? Too fancy for you? You don't wanna show it off to your friends?"

Her stare is really starting to piss me off now.

"Don't you have any friends?"

Again, the prissy little princess doesn't even bother to reply.

"Fine," I mutter, shoving the bottle back into my pocket. "You wanna be ungrateful? Go for it. At least I tried to be nice, but then again I guess there's no point. I mean, what would you do with *one* bottle of the stuff, anyway? You could play dress-up, but you'd never be able to look really nice." I hesitate for a moment, giving her one final chance to show some frickin' emotion, and then I turn to walk away. "Whatever you -"

Suddenly I gasp as I feel an ice-cold grip on my left wrist.

Stopping, I look down and see the girl's pale hand holding me tight, and then I slowly turn and look at the girl's dark, staring eyes.

"Seriously?" I continue, flinching a little as I realize that her skin feels really cold. "That's actually uncomfortable. Also, for your information, in some states grabbing someone like that can be classed as assault, so I really think you'd better let go of me right now."

I wait for her to respond, but she's still staring at me. Before I can tell her again to let go, however, I notice that there seems to be a little color coming to her

15

cheeks, as if the hint of yellow is being joined by a greenish patch. The effect is very subtle, but it seems to be spreading down onto her arm and hand, too, and I quickly start trying to pull myself free of her grip. After all, if she's sick, I really don't want to catch whatever's left her looking so awful.

"Seriously, kid," I mutter, twisting my hand in an attempt to get loose. "I've tried being nice to you, but you're going too far now. You have to let go of me right now or I'm going to be officially pissed off."

The little prick doesn't respond at all, so I reach down and start trying to force her icy fingers away from my wrist. She's holding me pretty tight, and after a moment I realize that maybe I'm going to have to be a little tougher. I mean, sure, she's a kid and all, but that doesn't mean she gets a free ride to jerk me around.

"Okay," I says firmly, grabbing her wrist and squeezing tight, hoping to make her realize she has to let go, "two can play at that game."

I start twisting her wrist, figuring that she has to get the message, but she doesn't respond at all.

"Come on, kid," I grumble, "this is literally too much!"

Her hand feels colder than ever, cold enough to start hurting a little, and her fingers remain wrapped around my wrist as I try to wriggle free. I really don't want to be a bitch, but she's starting to get seriously annoying, so finally I apply more pressure to her wrist, in an attempt to make her let go.

"Seriously!" I hiss. "Enough's enough! Stop -"

Suddenly I hear a loud cracking sound coming

from her wrist, and at the same time I feel a crunching sensation as the flesh around the base of her hand ruptures. Startled, I let go and take a step back, and I'm shocked to see that her wrist has begun to break away, leaving her hand still clutching me. I pull back a little further, and her hand comes completely away from her own wrist, leaving a black, rotten stump.

Looking down, I see her severed hand still holding me tight.

"What the..."

Something wriggles in the fleshy stump, and to my horror I see that there are a couple of thick, juicy white maggots poking their way out from the meat.

"What the hell?" I stammer, taking a couple more steps back with the girl's icy hand still gripping my wrist.

Turning to look at her again, I see that she's calmly watching me, apparently completely untroubled by the fact that her goddamn hand just tore away. The stump around her wrist is glistening but not bleeding, and after a moment I see that there are maggots in that patch of flesh too.

"Get it off me!" I shout, trying again to pull the hand loose before finally turning and starting to run back to the hotel. "Don't -"

Before I manage another step, however, I feel the ground give way beneath my feet. Looking down, I see that I've run past the edge of the pool and onto the pale gray cover. Before I even have a chance to react, however, the loose covering crumples beneath my feet and I fall forward, slamming against the side of the pool with enough force to shatter several teeth before I bump down and slip into the gap between the pool covering and the edge itself. Plunging into the icy water, I quickly start sinking into the darkness, and I turn and look up through the dirty water just in time to see the pool covering slipping back into place.

A thick cloud of blood is rising from my mouth.

Trying to scream, I let out a mass of bubbles as I swim back up and try to push the covering aside. I can see a thin sliver of daylight running along the pool's edge, but for some reason I can't seem to make the covering open again. Desperately trying not to swallow any water, I slip my fingertips around the covering's edge and try to push it up, and then I try to pull it down, and then I try to scream again as I realize I can't get out.

The little girl's rotten hand is still clinging to my wrist as I struggle furiously to make a gap, but I'm already running out of breath.

And then I freeze as I realize another hand just grabbed my ankle from below.

Looking down into the depths, I can just about make out my own legs treading water, but it takes a moment longer before I see that a pale, rotten hand is reaching up from the darkness and holding my ankle tight. I try frantically to kick the hand away, but its hold is firm and suddenly I feel myself being pulled down.

I turn and reach up, trying to grab the pool's edge, but I'm sinking faster and faster and finally the side of the pool is simply a long, thin light line that's too far above for me to reach.

Turning, I look down into the darkness as I feel

something grabbing my waist. This time, when I try to scream, icy water comes flooding in through my open mouth.

PART TWO

BETH HAYES
TODAY

CHAPTER TWO

"WHERE'S ANNIE?" I MUTTER, peering out the window and looking at the hotel's barren, overgrown garden. The place clearly hasn't been tended for years, and there's no sign of my sister anywhere.

Still, I guess I shouldn't be *too* keen for her to join us inside. After all, she can be annoying at the best of times and she's really been on top form during this trip.

I could definitely do with a break from her.

Hearing a clanking sound nearby, I turn and look back across the deserted dining room, toward the door at the far end and the corridor a little further off. The sound continues, echoing slightly, and I can't help thinking that this is how a haunted house would sound, if a house *could* be haunted. A moment later, however, I hear Steve muttering something under his breath, and finally he steps into view.

"Find anything?" I ask.

"Nope. What about you?"

Stepping toward him, I make my way between the old chairs and tables. There's something very old-fashioned about this place, and I can't help feeling that the furnishings must have been a little faded even when the hotel was open for business. There's dust everywhere, of course, and a table at the far end of the room bears a set of crystal decanters. Evidently the Lakeforth was a little stuck in a rut, although I guess the place has a certain charm. It's probably the kind of place where the owners had a very high opinion of themselves, despite the small cracks that run through the plaster on the walls.

Looking up, I see a huge chandelier hanging high above us.

"I think we have to face facts, honey," I tell Steve as I reach him and puts my arms around his waist. "The Lakeforth isn't taking reservations anymore."

Sighing, he looks past me as if he expects to see some sign of life in the dining room, but I can tell he's begun to accept the inevitable.

"I can't imagine what happened," he mutters. "I know the Lakeforth wasn't exactly the most modern hotel, but it was always popular. Not everybody wants flashy decorations and state-of-the-art facilities. The Lakeforth was dependable, there were people who came back year after year. Hell, there were even people who lived here. I don't get why anyone would just shut the place down and leave it like this."

"Maybe the regular guests just died off," I reply. "If they were pretty old anyway, it makes sense that there'd be fewer and fewer people coming each year. If the hotel's management team didn't manage to attract new clients, maybe the place went into a spiral and became unprofitable. Things do change, you know. Over time."

"Still, they should have been able to keep going."

Slipping away from me, he makes his way across the dining room. I swear, his inability to face the truth is kind of charming, and I've got to admit that I feel bad for him. I know those childhood vacations at the Lakeforth are among his most treasured memories of his parents, and he's been talking for so long about one day coming back here. At the same time, he seemed reluctant, and I really had to talk him into finally biting the bullet and making the journey. Even when he failed to get through to the hotel and book a room, I suggested we should just pack our bags and drive out anyway. And now that we're here, I'm honestly not sure whether this was a good idea or not. Is he finding closure, or just reopening old wounds?

"We used to sit over there," he says suddenly, pointing toward the far corner. "The same table, three times a day for breakfast, lunch and dinner. It was that kind of hotel."

"It must have been really grand," I reply, heading slowly over to join him beneath the chandelier. "I really wish I could've seen it when it was still up and running. Do you have any photos?"

"There was a piano at the head of the room," he continues, turning and pointing past me. "They used to have this guy who impersonated a different famous musician each evening. On Mondays he was always Elton John, on another night he was Liberace, and I remember he was Billy Joel once too."

"Sounds... interesting," I say as I reach him.

"I know it was kitsch," he admits, "but it had a certain kind of charm. The people who stayed here weren't worried about being cool. They just wanted to relax and -"

Suddenly there's a loud bang somewhere in the distance, as if a door was slammed in another part of the hotel. We both turn and look out toward the corridor, but now the entire building has fallen silent again.

"It's probably just Annie," I say, turning back to Steve. "Would you rather she was here in this room instead? Going on and on, complaining about everything?"

"I guess it was dumb to think things would have stayed the same," he replies, and I can see a hint of sadness in his eyes as he looks around at all the empty chairs and abandoned tables. "That's not how the world works, is it? Things change, people leave, and all that's left behind is a bunch of ghosts. We should have gone somewhere fun instead, somewhere near the beach. I should have listened to the guys."

"Steve -"

"Let's do it!" he continues, turning to me with a sudden flush of enthusiasm. "Screw memory lane! Let's get back in the car and head south. We can be at the beach this time tomorrow, and we can spend almost a whole week in the sun."

"But you really wanted to come here," I point out.

"I came here and it's dead. We can't exactly check in when the place isn't even a hotel anymore. Maybe this is a sign from the gods, maybe it's fate or destiny telling me that I need to stop thinking about the past and start looking to the future." He hesitates, before placing a hand on the side of my face and running his thumb against my chin. "I should never have dragged you here. Come on, there's one more thing I want to check out while we're in this dump, and then we should hit the road. Go tell your sister the plans have changed. I doubt she'll complain too much."

"Are you sure?" I ask.

He nods, before leaning closer and planting a brief kiss on my lips.

"I *did* pack my bikini," I say with a smile, "and frankly, the pool here looks a little unwelcoming."

"I'll meet you out front in twenty minutes," he replies, stepping past me and heading out into the corridor.

"Where are you going?"

"It's nothing big!" he yells back to me, as I hear him hurrying up a flight of stairs. "There's just one thing I really want to check, to see if it's still here! See you out front!"

"See you out front," I mutter, turning and looking around at the large, deserted dining room. To be honest, it's hard to see a plus-side to this place, and finally I head over to the door. As I walk, I run a fingertip across the surface of a nearby table, quickly gathering a thick crown of dust. "Beach, here we come."

***

"Annie!" I yell, raising my voice louder than ever, with my hands cupped around my hands. Turning, I look back across the garden and toward the main building. "This isn't funny! Where the hell are you?"

Hearing a creaking sound, I glance at the front door and spot Steve hurrying down the steps, carrying what looks suspiciously like a large framed photo.

"What have you got there?" I ask, raising a skeptical eyebrow.

He turns the photo around, revealing an old, faded photo of a man and a woman. They look very formal, as if they're taking their portrait very seriously.

"I used to see this thing every time we came," he explains as he reaches me, "and I figured, if nobody wants it anymore, I might as well take it. Don't you think it'll look good in my room at school?"

"Sure," I mutter, even though the faded, sepia-colored photo gives me the chills. Taking the photo for a moment, I see some text at the bottom, in sloping, old-fashioned handwriting. "Jobard and Ellen Nash," I read out loud. "Were they the owners?"

"I think that's the guy who founded the hotel. This photo was hidden away next to the elevators on one of the upper floors. I always wondered about it, but I never got around to asking anyone. I guess they look like a pair of stuck-up aristocrats, huh?"

Staring at the woman in the photograph, I can't

help noting a hint of real sadness in her eyes.

"Pair of freaks," Steve mutters. Taking the photo back, he pauses for a moment as he stares down at the two faces. "Or is it morbid for me to take this? Am I being a bit weird?"

"You should take it if you like it," I tell him, amused by his eclectic taste, while secretly resolving to hide the photo when he and I eventually get our first apartment together. "First, though, we have to actually get out of here, which is gonna be difficult until my idiot sister shows up."

"I heard you calling her. What's wrong, did she flounce off after an argument again?"

"I can't find her," I explain with a sigh, looking toward the garden and still hoping that she'll suddenly make an appearance. "I checked inside, I checked outside, I checked by the pool, and I can't figure out where the hell she went."

"Damn," he replies, before hesitating for a moment and then grinning. "Oh well, I guess we'll just have to abandon her here. Shame, but if that's how it has to be, I can live with the peace and quiet. She'll be fine, she'll just live out the rest of her days here, living off the land and eventually marrying some passing yokel. Quick, let's hit the road before she comes back."

"Nice try," I say as he heads around to the other side of the car, "but Annie has the keys."

He stops and turns to me. "Please tell me you're not serious."

"She must've taken them when we arrived. You know how possessive she gets about this car. So until we find her, I guess we're stuck here."

"Seriously?"

"Seriously."

He stares at me. "*Seriously* seriously?"

"Sorry, babe. Looks like she's stranded us here."

Sighing, he puts his hands around his mouth and turns toward the hotel.

"Annie!" he yells, so loud that I flinch and take a step back. "Get your sorry ass back here right now!"

I swear, his voice actually echoes slightly, but the only reply is silence.

"She can't have gone *that* far," I point out, "so she must be able to hear us. Which means she's deliberately pissing us off. Can you try your cell? I don't have service up here."

He takes his phone from his pocket and checks the screen.

"Me neither," he mutters. "What's wrong with that girl? Seriously, why does she have to do the most annoying thing possible at every opportunity? It's a skill. It's, like, almost impressive how irritating she can be. Sorry, I know she's your little sister and I shouldn't say that, but right now I could put my hands around her throat and..."

He pauses, before smiling.

"Well," he adds. "You know what I mean. I wouldn't *actually* strangle her. She deserves it, though."

"Annie!" I shout, stepping around to the front of the car. "A joke's a joke! We're ready to head off and go to the beach now! There'll be guys at the beach! And alcohol! And parties! Does none of that appeal to you?"

I wait, but now the only sound is the faint rustle of nearby trees as a cold wind blows in front the lake.

"Well, she'll come back," Steve mutters. "I mean, she has to. The more we yell her name, the more she'll enjoy pissing us off. So I vote we just head back inside, chill for a bit, and wait for her to grow the hell up. She's probably hiding in a bush somewhere, watching us and finding the whole thing hilarious. Then again, I could always try hot-wiring the car. *That'd* show her."

"It's a nice thought," I reply, patting his arm as I head back toward the steps, "but we can't *actually* leave her here."

"We can pick her up on our way home!" he calls after me.

"Tempting," I mutter with a sigh, making my way up the steps. Frankly, I'm so angry at Annie right now, I feel like I want to finally say some of the things I've been keeping bottled up over the past few years. I get it, she thrives on attention now that Mom and Dad live separately, but there comes a point when I actually need to be able to rely on her. I work two jobs to get myself through school, and a week off is a rare and valuable privilege. I want to hang out with my boyfriend and have fun, not run around after my whiny, self-indulgent little sister.

As I reach the hotel's large, bare reception hallway, I stop and listen to the silence, hoping against hope that I might hear some hint of movement far off in the distance. All I hear, however, is Steve coming through the door behind me a moment later, and when I turn to him I can't help seeing the frustration in his eyes.

"I'm really sorry about my sister," I tell him. "Please don't hate me."

"Forget it. She won't hold out for long. She's not the only one who can mess with people's heads." Stepping closer, her puts his hands on my waist, and I can tell he's planning something. "I guess that's settled, then," he announces loudly, clearly putting on a show for the benefit of anyone who might be eavesdropping. "We're going to stay a night at this place. It might be cold and empty and creepy, but I'm sure one night won't kill us. There's no turning back now."

"Steve," I whisper, "what are you -"

"It's to freak her out," he replies, grinning mischievously. "We're staying the night!" he says loudly. "I mean, if we can't drive away, we have no choice! Right?"

We stand in silence for a moment.

"She won't fall for this," I tell him.

"Well, I'm sure she'll come running soon," he mutters, setting the framed photo on a nearby table before putting an arm around my shoulder and leading me toward the grand staircase that leads up to the hotel's upper floors. "So shall we go and choose a room, my dear? I hear the presidential suite is absolutely delightful. Assuming the mattress hasn't been devoured by bedbugs."

As we head up the stairs, I can't help glancing over my shoulder and looking back down at the reception area. I'm not superstitious and I don't believe in ghosts, but I have to admit that this hotel is genuinely a little unnerving. If I *did* believe in ghosts, I'm sure I'd be much less willing to even set foot in the place.

CHAPTER THREE

PULLING OPEN THE DOOR, I find myself at the top of a set of steps that seem to lead down into a dark basement. It doesn't look very inviting down there, although I kind of like the idea of exploring a spooky old hotel. After all, Steve's off checking the upper floors, so why shouldn't I do some poking about of my own?

So, reaching into my pocket, I take out my phone and use the screen to light my way as I head down the stairs. The air at the bottom is noticeably much colder than in the main part of the building, although I guess that's due to the bare brick walls. Still holding my phone up, I look around and see nothing but an empty room with a dusty concrete floor and an open doorway at the far end. I guess the basement must run beneath the entire building, and it's definitely creepy to think of all this dark, abandoned space.

"Hello?" I call out, enjoying the buzz of excitement in my chest. "Any ghosts around?"

There's no reply, of course, so I make my way across the room and look through the next doorway. Tilting my phone, I see another bare room, although this one at least has some old metal pipes running along one of the walls. Still, the excitement is starting to fade a little and I'm not sure I want to go exploring empty room after empty room. It's not as if I believe in ghosts, and I'm not too keen on the amount of dust in the air. Or the cobwebs that are hanging down from the arches.

"Okay, then," I mutter, turning and heading back to the stairs. "If that's your -"

Suddenly I hear a faint scuffing sound over my shoulder, as if something is being dragged across the dusty floor of the next room. I turn and hold my phone up high, but the sound immediately stops and there's no sign of anyone or anything. I head back to the doorway and take another look in the room, just to make absolutely certain that I'm alone down here, and all I see is a cracked, dirty concrete floor with a few dubious dark patches.

I wait.

Nothing.

"Hello?" I whisper.

Silence.

"Annie," I continue, "if that's you, I want you to know that every second you waste here is another second we lose at the beach. Is that seriously what you want?"

No reply.

Either Annie is hiding somewhere close by, trying not to laugh, or I'm talking to myself.

"Okay. Whatever."

Turning, I head back to the stairs again, although I half expect to hear the sound again. This time, however, the basement remains silent, and I tell myself that I'll go crazy if I try to track down the source of every unexplained noise in this crumbling old building. And the last thing I want is to amuse my dumb-ass sister and reward her stupid antics.

Making my way back up the stairs, I can't help smiling as I think back to how I briefly let myself get creeped out just now. All I heard was a very faint sound, but at the back of my mind some part of me was just very slightly scared. This place would definitely be a ghost-hunter's paradise.

Once I'm at the top of the stairs, I head out through the door and then push the door shut. I think I should probably leave the exploring to somebody else. Right now, I'm cold and tired and hungry and thirsty, and I *really* hope Steve has managed to sort out somewhere for us to take a rest. Or, even better, maybe my dumb-ass sister will show up and we can get out of here.

***

"It's going to be dark soon," I mutter, staring out the window and watching as the sun's light breaks through the tree-line. "What if she calls our bluff? Annie can be stubborn sometimes. What if she won't give up until we break and beg her to come back?"

Turning, I listen to the sound of Steve still

banging about in the en-suite. A moment later, he comes back into view and stops in the doorway.

"The toilet doesn't work," he announces. "None of the plumbing does. I guess all business has to be conducted outside, if you know what I mean."

"I'm getting seriously pissed off with her now," I continue. "She's wasting our vacation time! Like, this time is actually valuable to me!"

"She has to show up soon," he says as he comes over to join me at the window. "It's freezing in this place. I mean, we've got each other for warmth, but what's she got? Maybe she found some moldy old duvets hidden away somewhere, but your sister seems like a girl who likes her creature comforts. As soon as she finds there's no running water, she'll be begging us to leave."

Staring out the window, watching the light of the sunset as it glitters on the lake, I can't help thinking that this time Annie has *really* gone too far. She's always had a sense of humor, and she's always delighted in pissing people off, but there have been occasions in the past when she's gone way overboard. Once she even left home for the entire summer, refusing to tell anyone where she was going. I eventually discovered she was staying with a friend across the street, camping out in a spare room and watching our house while Mom panicked. Now she's done a runner again, and I'm worried she's trying to make some kind of point.

"She won't keep this up all night," Steve tells me, before kissing my shoulder.

"She might," I mutter. "You don't know her. Not like I do."

"Well, then maybe we should give her a taste of her own medicine."

"How?"

"That lake looks pretty inviting, and it's only about a mile away. Why don't we go for a sunset swim?"

"It's probably cold."

"So? You'll soon warm up, and it might do Annie some good to be left alone for a few hours. That way, she'll realize how boring this place is, and she'll probably decide it's time for us to leave. Like I said earlier, we have to beat her at her own game."

I pause for a moment, before figuring that he might be right. Just as I'm about to agree to his plan, however, I remember a stumbling block.

"The car's locked," I point out.

"So?"

"So our stuff's in the car. I can't get my bikini out."

"It's a deserted lake in the middle of nowhere," he continues, kissing my shoulder again. "Who said anything about needing a bikini?"

***

"Argh!" Steve screams as he races naked into the water, splashing wildly. "It's cold! It's cold! It's so -"

Suddenly he dives forward, crashing against the lake's surface and disappearing in a shower of spray. A moment later he comes back up, gasping for air and holding his arms across his bare chest, rubbing his shoulders. Splashing about, he's really breaking the silence of this vast, deserted place.

"It's really cold!" he shouts. "Like, really *really* cold! Get in!"

Dipping a toe into the water, I realize he's right. The water's icy, and I'm not even sure I can bring myself to go all the way in. Looking out across the lake for a moment, I see the hills beyond the farthest shore, silhouetted black against the darkening blue sky. There's something very calm and peaceful about this place, and I honestly don't know that I've ever been so far from civilization, but I'm still not certain that I want to swim in such cold water. Turning, I see an old wooden jetty just a couple of hundred meters away, and I'm tempted to just go sit there and watch while Steve swims.

"It'll be fine once you're in!" Steve calls out to me. "Take off the rest of your clothes and come in!"

"I'm not sure I -"

"I did it! Now it's your turn!"

I pause for a moment, before realizing that I can't exactly chicken out now. The last thing I want is for Steve to tease me *again* about not being fun and spontaneous. I'll show him. Well, within reason, anyway.

"Turn around," I tell him.

"Why?"

"Turn around!"

He laughs. "It's nothing I haven't seen before."

"Turn around or I'm not doing it!"

Sighing, he turns his back to me. Figuring that it's now or never, I quickly slip out of my underwear, and then once I'm naked I start making my way into the water. At the same time, I keep my hands in strategic places, covering my modesty just in case somehow somebody can see me. The water is so cold, each step sends a jolt through my system. Finally I tell myself I need to take the plunge, so I dive forward and plunge deep beneath the surface. To say that the cold is a shock would be an understatement, and by the time I come back up for air a moment later I feel as if every muscle in my body has suddenly tensed.

"You'll get used to it," Steve says as I smooth my hair back. "Besides, it's good for you."

"Is that right?" I ask as I swim slowly toward him. I'm still freezing, but I guess I have to be more patient.

"The cold gets your pores exercised or something," he continues. "Makes them open, or close, or it just helps your heart-rate. I don't remember the details, but this is definitely healthy."

Turning, I look back toward the hotel and see the main building silhouetted at the top of the hill. The place is pitch-black against the darkening blue sky, and it's strange to think of Annie up there all alone. Then again, I've got a sneaking suspicion that she probably followed us down to the lake. I thought I heard a few twigs snapping behind us as we walked through the forest, and it wouldn't surprise me at all if my sister is lurking in the bushes, watching us right now as we swim.

"Come here," Steve says, placing a hand on my waist under the water. "Is that warmer?"

"Slightly," I admit, turning to him.

"And how about this?"

I feel him place another hand on my side, with

his wrist brushing against the curve of my left breast.

"Steve..."

"And this?"

Leaning closer, he kisses me on the lips. I try to just kiss him back and pull away, but he clearly wants more, so the kiss quickly becomes fuller and deeper, with his tongue slipping into my mouth. Losing the will to resist, I put my arms around him and let my inner thigh bump against one of his legs, and I know it's only a matter of time before I feel a different part of his anatomy brushing against me. I'm really not sure how far I want to go here, but the kiss feels good and overdue so I let it continue, and finally he moves one hand fully onto my breast and the other down to my hip.

"What if someone's watching?" I whisper, as he starts kissing the side of my neck.

"Lucky them," he replies, his hot breath making my shoulder shiver against the cold water.

"What if *Annie's* watching?"

"Then she's a pervert."

"But -"

"Just relax, Beth," he continues, kissing the side of my neck again. "Please, for once, don't over-analyze everything. Empty your mind and listen to what your body wants."

I open my mouth to protest again, but it's very clear that we're past the point of no return here. Steve and I haven't made love in a long time, so I guess any time now he's going to want to go back to the shore and seal the deal. Telling myself that I'll probably get more in the mood once we've started, I place the side of my face against his bare shoulder and focus on the feel of his touch as he runs a hand across my breast and down onto my belly. Another hand is curling across my inner thigh, edging higher, and I swallow hard as I feel a knot of anticipation starting to tighten in my chest. As one hand slips its fingers around my ankle, I kiss Steve on the side of the neck, enjoying the feel of his thumb against my nipple, and the soft stroke of his fingers running up my thigh toward my -

"Wait!" I gasp suddenly, pulling back as I feel a rush of shock.

Steve pulls his hands away, and the hand on my ankle also slips loose and drops into the depths.

Looking down at the surface of the water, I try to figure out exactly what just happened. Steve had one hand on my breast, another on my thigh, and another on my ankle, but that doesn't make sense. I tell myself I must have been mistaken, but my mind is racing and I feel as if something's wrong here. It's almost as if there was someone else, someone reaching up from the depths.

"Babe?" Steve asks. "Are you okay?"

"Can we go to the shore?"

"Why?"

Turning, I look around at the calm, smooth lake, but there's absolutely no sign of anybody else. Of course there isn't. Even if Annie was nearby, there's no way she'd start pranking us while things were getting hot. I mean, my sister's sick, but she's not *that* sick. At the same time, I can't help feeling deeply uncomfortable, and finally I realize that I really just want to get back on dry land.

"Doesn't this place seem quiet to you?" I ask. "Like, completely silent?"

"Is that a problem?"

I pause for a few seconds, and I really don't hear anything at all. Like, not even the kind of faint background buzz or hum that you usually hear during moments of supposed silence. It's as if there's nothing for miles around, not so much as a bird hopping along a branch or even an insect scurrying across the ground. Just absolute, complete silence, the kind that seems to almost dare you to break it. The kind it feels *wrong* to break.

"You're letting yourself get freaked out, aren't you?" Steve asks after a moment. "I can see it in your eyes. Come on, I told you, you need to shut your mind off and let your body make decisions for a while."

"I just thought -"

Stopping myself just in time, I realize there's no way I can tell him I thought I felt three hands touching me while we were making out. One on my breast, one on my thigh, and one on my leg. Steve'd just think I'm losing my mind if I told him, and he'd probably make fun of me for the rest of the trip. I'm sure it was nothing, but at the same time I really just want to get out of the water.

"Let's head to dry land, yeah?" I say, turning and start to slowly swim ashore. "There's nothing out here."

"Why would there be anything out here?"

Not really wanting to stop and talk about it, I swim to the shore and then make my way up, ruing the fact that I don't have a towel. I don't like the idea of getting dressed while I'm wet, but at the same time I *definitely* don't like the idea of standing around naked while I wait for the cool evening breeze to dry me. Reaching down, I grab my clothes and start slipping into my underwear, and then I turn and see that Steve is still out in the lake, watching me.

"Hey, come on!" I call out to him, watching his silhouette against the rippling water. "We can do stuff, but not in the water. Sorry, I just got freaked out."

I wait, but he doesn't respond at all. He seems to be just staring at me, although after a moment I furrow my brow as I realize that his silhouette seems a little -

Suddenly there's a loud splashing sound just a few feet away, and I let out a startled gasp as Steve bursts up from beneath the surface and clambers ashore, laughing as if he thinks he's hilarious. Shocked, I look past him, but now the silhouetted figure is gone and the lake looks completely calm. I have no idea how Steve managed to do that, and I can't help staring at the spot where – just a few seconds ago – there was a figure in the water. If the silhouette wasn't Steve, then who was it? I wait, in case Annie shows up, but the ripples in the water quickly fade away, leaving the surface clear and calm again.

"No jokes about shrinkage," Steve says, dripping wet as he comes and places his soaking hands on my shoulders. "There's no rush to get back to the hotel, is there? Let's just have some fun down here."

He kisses the side of my neck.

"Have you ever done it outside?" he asks,

dropping his voice to a whisper. "I have. It's kinda fun, looking up and seeing the sky as you -"

"Let's get back to the hotel," I reply, pulling away from him and grabbing the rest of my clothes. I don't want him to know that I'm freaked out, but at the same time I really just want to get back to the car, find Annie, and get out of here. "I'm sure my dumb-ass sister has decided to stop being an idiot."

"Are you okay?"

"Of course. Why wouldn't I be?"

"I thought we were getting in the mood for something. Come on, you're -"

"Don't tell me I'm over-analyzing things again!" I reply. "Please, Steve, I'm sick of that."

Already dressed again, I turn and see him standing naked, dripping just a few feet away. It's very clear that he's ready for some fun, and I feel like I definitely owe him. If we were anywhere else, I'd go right over to him and give him what he's after, but the shore of the lake just feels like the wrong place.

"I guess the cold water doesn't do it for me," I tell him, forcing a smile in the hope that he'll get the message. "Tomorrow we'll be somewhere warm, and we'll send Annie out to get drunk at the beach, and we can make up for lost time. I promise. Please, Steve, just... Let's get out of here."

"But -"

"What do you think that was?" I ask, pointing toward some charred wooden posts that are rising up above a patch of high grass just a little way along the shore.

"Beth, seriously -"

"Fine," I continue, turning to him and realizing that my attempt to distract him was a bust. "Can we please just not let things get all stressy right now? I'm really not feeling this place, and I know you're trying to make the best of it, but I just want to get it over with. Can you try to understand that?"

He hesitates for a moment, before sighing and heading over to his clothes.

"I'm sorry," I add, already feeling like I've let him down. Our sex-life has been non-existent for weeks now, and I'm sure he's starting to have doubts. The truth is, Steve always seems to want to try new, adventurous things, whereas I kinda prefer to keep things simple and safe. Even doing it outside seems too risky for my tastes, but I guess eventually I'll have to experiment a little.

Just not now.

Not here.

As Steve continues to get dressed, I look down at my ankle, at the spot where I swear I felt a third hand touching me in the water. To my surprise, I see that the flesh is very slightly discolored, as if I've developed a faint bruise. Reaching down, I touch the sore spot and feel a flush of soreness. Whatever touched my ankle, it definitely can't have been a hand, but it sure was real.

Looking back out across the lake again, I see that the water is so completely, utterly calm. Already, it's as if we never disturbed the surface.

CHAPTER FOUR

"HEY ANNIE, YOU PERVERT!" Steve yells as he drags a rotten old mattress into the room. "We're calling your bluff here! If you wanna stay the night, that's fine by us! You're the one who's gonna be shivering all alone! This is your last chance to admit you're a lying little bitch!"

"Hey, don't call her that."

"Sorry, but... You know what I mean."

"I'm worried about her," I reply, holding my phone up so that we at least have a little light. "She should've come back by now."

"You said it yourself. Your sister takes pranks too far."

"But -"

"And the more you worry, the more you play right into her hands."

He throws the mattress down, and we both stare at its worn, moldy fabric. There are tufts of foam poking out through several holes, and even from here I can smell a faintly fusty odor.

"We can't sleep on this," I tell him.

"Not posh enough for you?"

Turning, I shine the phone's light around the room. We're up on the top floor of the hotel, in what I guess must have once been one of the larger bedrooms. There's no electricity, of course, and the sun has finally set, so the place is pitch-black except for the light from our two phones. There's no heating, either, and I genuinely can't imagine how we're going to get through a night here. Unfortunately, since we came back from the lake, there's still been no sign of Annie, and it seems she really expects us to endure a night in this place.

"I'm going to kill her," I mutter under my breath.

"She'll be fine," Steve replies. "She has the car keys, remember? Once she thinks we're asleep, she can sneak in there and make herself nice and cozy. She'll be out there in the morning, laughing it up about our night in the hotel. She's gonna think she's so funny."

"What if she's not playing a prank, though?" I ask, unable to ignore the niggling doubt in the back of my mind. "What if something happened to her?"

"Like what?"

"Maybe she's hurt."

"Then she'd yell for us."

"Maybe she can't."

"Then we'd have found her when we took a look around the place."

"Maybe she's outside."

"Maybe aliens came and took her," he says with

a sigh. "Or maybe, like you said at the start, she's playing a joke on you and she knows how to push all your buttons. Come on, Beth, seriously, you have to beat her at her own game. If she wants us to spend the night here, let's make the best of it and try to have a good time. The last thing I want is to let her see that she's getting what she wants. She wants us to be miserable, and she wants us to argue. Let's not give her that."

"But -"

"Wait right here. I have something to show you, something that'll make your eyes light up."

With that, he heads back out into the corridor, and a moment later he comes back with a big bundle of sheets.

"Where did you get those?" I ask cautiously.

"They were in a closet." He dumps them next to the mattress. "They smell a little old, but I think they're clean. And there are a couple of pillows, too. I swear, we're gonna camp out here in this room overnight and we'll be warm and comfortable. If Annie thinks she's gonna give us a crappy night, she's got another thing coming, because we're gonna make the best of this. And one day, we'll look back on the whole experience and laugh."

He puts an arm around my shoulder, but I can't help feeling as if something might be wrong. No matter how much I try to tell myself that this is just Annie being Annie, I have this underlying worry that she might actually be in trouble. I guess I just can't help worrying about my little sister.

"What's wrong?" Steve asks after a moment.

"Never spent a night in an abandoned, haunted hotel before?"

"It's not a -"

I pause, before turning to him.

"Haunted?"

"Just kidding," he adds, kissing the side of my head. "Well, maybe. I mean, I have to admit, the place is pretty spooky. You know when I was searching for mattresses and sheets just now, all alone and going from empty room to empty room? I've gotta admit, I glanced over my shoulder a few times, just to make absolutely certain I was alone. And I'm a rational, level-headed kinda guy, so it's not like I was pooping myself every time I heard a creak or a bump."

"You heard creaks and bumps?"

"Just one or two. But it's an old place. It's gonna be a little noisy."

He hugs me tighter, but I still can't help feeling uneasy. I've heard a few creaking sounds myself since we got back from the lake, and at one point I even thought I heard a door swinging shut nearby while Steve was off in another part of the building. I've been putting those sounds down to the place being ancient and unloved, but each and every unexplained noise adds another little ounce of weight to my worries. Then again, I can't say anything about that, not to Steve, because then he'll just make fun of me the whole night. And as I keep reminding myself, ghosts aren't real and it'd be crazy to let this place get to me.

Besides, if Annie *is* listening to us right now, I wouldn't be surprised if she's planning to try freaking us out during the night.

"Let's just get this bed sorted," I mutter finally. "It's cold over by the window, so we should drag the mattress to the wall over there. I just want to get this night over and done with."

By the time we've made the bed and climbed under the covers, I've just about managed to start ignoring the fusty smell. Steve's body heat keeps me a little warm, although it's hard to focus on what he's saying as he tells me all about what we'll do when we get to the beach. After all, I keep expecting Annie to come bursting into the room. I'm seriously worried about her, but Steve starts trying to initiate sex again and I feel bad for rejecting him earlier. So finally I give in and try to fake some enthusiasm, and he doesn't seem to notice that I'm not really in the mood as he climbs on top and whispers in my ear about all the things he wants to do to me.

***

"What?" I gasp, sitting up suddenly with the bed-sheet clutched to my chest. My heart is pounding, and I swear I was woken from a light sleep by some kind of noise, but now the room is dead silent again.

I wait, shivering slightly in the cold air, and it takes a moment before I remember exactly where I am. Looking around, I can't make out anything at all in the darkness, except for the faint dark blue rectangles of the windows on the room's far side. For a few seconds, I find myself waiting to see a figure pass in front of those windows, but of course no figure appears. Still, I wait a little longer, just in case.

I heard a noise, though.

Something definitely woke me. A distant bang, maybe, or more of a brief rattling sound.

Reaching down, I fumble for my phone and tap the screen, before using the light to take a look at Steve. He's fast asleep, no doubt exhausted after his exertions a couple of hours ago, and I know from experience that it'd take a runaway train crashing through the room to wake him after we've had sex. I should probably -

Suddenly I hear it again.

A rattling sound, as if someone is trying to open a locked door out in the corridor. The sound continues for several seconds before stopping as abruptly as it started, but this time there's absolutely no doubt.

I know what I heard, and I also know there's only one person who can possibly be to blame.

Even though the room is freezing cold, I climb out of bed and get dressed, and then I grab one of the sheets, wrapping it around my shoulders for a little extra warmth. Part of me wants to just stay in bed, close to Steve, but I feel like this nonsense with Annie has to stop right now. Checking my phone again, I see that it's a little after midnight, which means that my plan to just sleep through the misery seems not to be working. Apart from Steve in his post-coital daze, I honestly don't get how anyone could sleep in a place like this.

Annie has to be just as miserable as I am right now.

Shuffling over to the door, I lean out and hold

my phone up, but the light from the screen only casts a faint glow over the nearby wall. I know there's a long corridor running both left and right from this room, and there's a window at each end. Looking each way, I'm at least able to tell that there doesn't seem to be anyone nearby. After all, I'm pretty sure I'd be able to see them silhouetted against the window, unless they're crouching down to hide.

I wait, but the place is silent.

"Come on, Annie," I whisper, as my teeth almost chatter in the cold. "Give me a clue. Where are you?"

A moment later, as if to answer me directly, I hear the rattling sound again. This time, I can tell that it's definitely coming from somewhere on this floor, although not particularly close. I know the hotel has a maze of corridors, and I'm not entirely sure of the layout, but as the rattling sound stops I'm pretty sure it was coming from somewhere past the end of the corridor to the left.

I open my mouth to call out, to let Annie know that I heard her, but at the last moment I decide to hold back. Why should I warn her that I'm coming? Better to sneak up on her, so she can't run away again.

Making my way along the corridor, with the sheet still wrapped around my shoulders, I'm already starting to shiver by the time I get to the next closed door. I keep going, however, with my phone raised so that I can at least see a few feet ahead. This whole situation feels ridiculous and I've already decided that I'm never, *ever* inviting my stupid little sister anywhere again, but I tell myself to stay focused so that I'm able to sneak up on her. Once I've tracked her down, I'll confiscate the car keys and go back to wake Steve, and then we'll get out of here straight away. There's no point waiting until morning. We're leaving Lakeforth Hotel as soon as possible.

By the time I get to the end of the corridor and look around the corner, I haven't heard the rattling sound for several minutes. I look along the next corridor, seeing yet more closed doors on the left, while the corridor's right side has several windows overlooking the grounds of the hotel. Stepping over to the nearest of those windows, I look out and see the moonlit patio area below, along with the pale rectangular shape of the covered swimming pool. The cover itself is rippling slightly, so I guess there's a breeze out there, but the thought of heading outside and taking a closer look isn't exactly appealing. It's cold enough *inside* the hotel.

Turning, I head along the corridor again, although I stop a moment later when the rattling sound returns.

It's closer.

Much closer.

In fact, I think it might even be in this corridor.

Thanks to the moonlight that's coming through the windows, I'm not entirely reliant upon my phone. Lowering the screen, I look along the corridor, but there's definitely nobody here. The rattling sound stops a moment later, but I'm convinced it was really close. So close, in fact, that I can't work out how I didn't see whoever was making it happen.

Stepping along the corridor, I keep my eyes

fixed on the open doorway at the far end, just in case there's any sign of Annie. I'm managing to stay pretty quiet, so at least she won't be able to hear me as I approach, and I'm determined to sneak up behind her and make sure she doesn't get away. If I scare her senseless in the process, then maybe she'll finally learn from getting a taste of her own medicine. I won't even feel bad. In fact, I *want* to terrify her.

Suddenly there's a brief rattling sound right behind me, lasting for just a fraction of a second.

Turning, I look at the closed door I just passed, and I swear this is where the sound must have come from. After staring at the handle for a moment, I step closer and give it a try, and I find that the door opens easily. The hinges creak loudly as I push the door all the way, and then I raise my phone to shine a little light into the room beyond, which turns out to have a window on its far side.

A window, and nothing more.

Tilting my phone, I'm just about able to see that there's no furniture in here at all.

Not even a bed.

I guess the hotel's owners must have cleared most of the rooms when they left, although I can't help taking a step forward and looking around. If the sound was coming from in here, then it must have been caused by *something*, although there's not even so much as a mouse-hole in the walls. The window's shut, too, so I doubt the rattling sound was caused by a gust of wind, and I'm starting to think that maybe I simply got the wrong room. Either that, or Annie's set up a far more elaborate prank than I expected. Maybe I'm just letting myself get easily tricked here. Reaching the window, I look out and see the empty courtyard at the front of the hotel, and I stare for a moment at the car parked out front.

I swear, if I knew how to hot-wire an ignition, I'd be sorely tempted to go out there right now and get that damn thing running.

Sighing, I turn to head back to the door.

And then I freeze as I see the silhouette of a little girl standing in the doorway, no more than ten or twelve feet in front of me, blocking my exit from the room.

I open my mouth to ask who she is, but somehow the words catch in my throat. I can't see her face, all I can see is the pitch-black outline of her shape against the window out in the corridor, but I can tell that she's definitely staring straight at me. I can also tell, without a shadow of a doubt, that this little girl is definitely not Annie.

I wait a moment, hoping against hope that she'll turn out to be a shadow, but with each passing second I'm more and more certain that she's real.

"Who are you?" I stammer finally, tilting my phone but still not managing to get any light onto her face. "Where did you come from?"

I wait, shivering in the cold air, but the girl doesn't respond at all.

"Where did you come from?" I continue, struggling to stay calm. "Did Annie send you? Is this some kind of joke?"

Again I wait, and after a moment it occurs to me

that the girl might be some kind of mannequin. She hasn't moved since I spotted her, and I guess it's possible that Annie might have found a mannequin in one of the rooms and decided to use it to freak me out. I should step closer and check, and I'll probably find that the girl is made of plastic or wood, but I can't quite bring myself to move.

And then, slowly, the girl disproves my theory entirely by starting to hold her left arm out toward me.

I stare at her outstretched hand for a moment, but there's no way I'm going to touch her, not just yet.

"What do you want?" I ask, and now my teeth are starting to chatter. "Who are you? Where did you come from?"

When she still fails to reply, I realize I'm going to have to step closer. From the shape and size of her silhouette, it's clear that she can't be more than eight, maybe nine years old at most, and she's still holding her hand toward me. I mean, it's not like a little girl can actually hurt me.

Finally, swallowing hard, I take a step forward and reach out to take her hand.

"Beth?" Steve yells suddenly, from far off in the building. "Where are you?"

Immediately, the little girl turns and runs, vanishing from view as she hurries along the corridor. Startled, I step through the doorway just in time to see her disappearing around the far corner.

"Beth?" Steve shouts. "Babe! Come on, what's going on here?"

I hurry to the corner and look along the next

corridor, but all I see is Steve coming this way with his phone held up for light.

"Where did she go?" I ask.

"Where did who go?"

"There was a girl," I continue, as I feel my heart pounding in my chest. "She ran right this way, you can't have missed her!"

"Do you mean Annie?"

"No, a little girl! She ran this way, she must have gone right past you! Either that, or she went into one of the rooms, but I didn't hear any doors opening."

"Are you okay?" he asks, coming over to join me. "When I woke up and you were gone, I kinda figured maybe you'd gone to find Annie."

"I heard a noise," I reply, slipping past him and opening the nearest door, only to find another empty room. I try a couple more doors, but there's still no sign of the girl and finally I turn back to Steve. "She must have run right past you! I know it's dark, but how could you have missed a little girl running past you?"

"Uh, maybe because a little girl *didn't* run past me? Babe, I'm pretty sure I'd have noticed something like that."

"I'm not making this up!"

"I never said you were."

"And I didn't imagine it!"

"You're under a lot of stress," he replies, sounding as if he's trying to be diplomatic, "and this place probably gave you nightmares."

"I didn't imagine her," I mutter again, heading to yet another door and pushing it open, only to find myself staring into another empty room. "I know what I saw," I continue. "Don't tell me to doubt myself. That girl was as real as you are. It's like she wanted something, but then your voice scared her off."

Turning to him, I raise my phone, and I immediately see the doubt in his eyes.

"So what do you want to do?" he asks finally. "Check every room in this place until we find her?"

"I want you to tell me you believe me!"

"Fine. I believe you."

Staring at him, I realize he's just humoring me. He obviously thinks I'm cracking up, that a few hours in a creepy old hotel was all it takes for my mind to fall apart.

"I'm not staying here," I tell him.

"Beth..."

"I'm not spending another minute in this place!" I hiss, storming past him and heading back to the room where we put together our makeshift bed. "I'll sleep outside, by the car."

"Beth, you're overreacting," he says as he follows me. "So you thought you saw a spooky little kid, so -"

"I don't *think* I saw anything! I saw a little girl, and since I don't believe in ghosts, the only explanation is that you and my idiotic sister are somehow in on this together. I should have known something was up when you claimed you hadn't bothered to check the place was still open before we drove all this way. Nobody'd be that stupid!"

Stepping around the mattress, I look for my bag,

before realizing that it's under a pile of Steve's clothes. Reaching down, I pull the clothes aside, only for a familiar set of keys to slip out of his pants pocket and land on the bare floorboards.

"Beth, let's talk about this," he says, standing behind me as I pick the keys up. "You're over-analyzing everything again."

These are Annie's keys, the set for the car, but if Steve has had them all this time...

Slowly, I turn and hold the keys up for him to see.

He opens his mouth to say something, but I can see from the look in his eyes that he knows the game is up.

CHAPTER FIVE

"YOU'RE A DIRTY, LOUSY, goddamn stinking liar," I say slowly, my voice simmering with rage. "You let me think Annie had the keys all along, when they've been in your pocket."

"Beth..."

"Why would you do that? What possible reason could you have?"

"Beth, listen..."

"And now you're going to lie again? You're going to claim they were planted there, is that it?"

He hesitates for a moment, before sighing. "No, I'm not going to claim that. I've been an idiot, and I can only ask you to forgive me. If you'll let me explain, you'll see that I -"

"Where's Annie?"

"I don't know, she -"

"Where's Annie?" I hiss, taking a step toward him. Right now, he's goddamn lucky I'm not the type who hits people, because I'd love to wipe that lying mouth clean off his face. I don't think I've ever been this angry with anyone before, not in my entire life.

"I don't know where Annie is," he says, holding his hands up as if somehow that'll make me believe him. "I swear. I took the keys and pretended I didn't have them. I admit that. I know it was dumb, but I wanted us to spend one night here. I swear, Annie running off is nothing to do with me. I can only assume she's playing some other kind of game, but I promise, it's nothing to do with me. I don't even like her! Why the hell would I plot something like this with her?"

"You *wanted* us to spend a night here?" I ask. "Why?"

"There's something here I wanted to check out."

"There's *nothing* here," I reply. "Look at the place, it's a complete dump. It's empty!"

"I wasn't lying when I said I wanted us to come and stay," he explains. "Then, when I found out the hotel had shut down, I figured we could make the trip anyway. I've been waiting ten years to get back here, but I never dared, not until recently. You make me stronger, Beth. You make me feel like I can face anything, and now I want to face whatever I saw, or thought I saw, when I stayed here all those years ago."

He reaches out to touch the side of my face.

"Beth, you make me stronger and -"

"Don't!" I hiss, pushing his hand away.

He hesitates for a moment, as if he's worried about saying any more.

"There's something here," he tells me finally.

"What do you mean?"

"There's something at the hotel," he continues. "I'm not talking about furniture, or even about people. I'm talking about something else, something I think I saw ten years ago. Something that most people *don't* see while they're here. If I could explain it any better than that, I wouldn't have had to come all the way back here to figure it out properly, but I promise you, there's something in this hotel that only lets itself be seen when it *wants* to be seen. And for some reason, ten years ago, it wanted to be seen by me."

Staring at him, I can't help feeling that he's completely lost his mind. That this kind, fun, handsome guy I've been dating is actually insane.

"You're talking about a ghost," I say finally. "Seriously?"

"I think so, but I don't know for sure. Maybe." He hesitates for a moment, as if the ridiculousness of these claims is sinking in. "You have to understand, Beth, that I came back here because I need to know for certain. I've spent ten years wondering whether she's real, or whether -"

"She?"

"The little girl. But if you saw her too, then -"

"I didn't see a ghost!" I say firmly, feeling a rising sense of anger at the realization that this whole trip has been one long manipulation. "I saw a little girl, but she was real! So if you -"

"Her name is Ruth."

I open my mouth to reply, but I can tell that he really, truly believes this. Turning, I look back toward the dark corridor, but there's no sign of anyone and I certainly don't intend to stick around while Steve goes chasing after bumps in the night. I want to scream, I want to tell this bastard exactly what I think of him, but after a moment I realize that there's no way I'm going to let myself fall apart. I can cry later, when I'm alone, but not right now.

"Here's what's going to happen," I say finally. "I'm going to go outside, and I'm going to sit in the car and wait for Annie to come back. And then she and I are going to leave."

I wait for him to reply, but he simply stares at me.

"Just promise me one thing," I add. "Please, *please* promise me that Annie didn't know about any of this, and that you and her weren't conspiring to -"

"Of course not."

"And you don't know where she is?"

"I swear. I'm sure we were right earlier. She's just messing with us."

"She's not the only one," I reply, before turning and heading to the door.

"Beth, wait!" he calls after me. "Can we at least finish the night here?"

"You should have been honest with me from the start," I tell him through gritted teeth, as I use my phone to light the way to the top of the staircase. "I don't like liars, Steve. You had hundreds of chances to tell me the truth, and you know I'm a reasonable person. I wouldn't have laughed at you. But you've been lying this whole time, and that means I can't ever trust another word that comes from your mouth."

"Wouldn't you want to know?" he asks. "If you'd met a ghost when you were younger, wouldn't you want to come back and see if she was real?"

I hurry down the stairs, not even bothering to look back at him. I can't believe that not only did I let him lure me into a so-called haunted house, but I even slept with him in one of its rooms. I've been completely humiliated.

"Beth!" he shouts. "What if -"

"Go to hell!" I yell, turning and seeing him at the top of the stairs. There are tears in my eyes now, and the sight of him makes me feel nauseous. "And in case you haven't figured it out yet, we're through. Annie and I'll drop you at the first town we come to, but after that we're going our own way. You can go home alone."

"I was scared to come by myself," he tells me. "You make me stronger, Beth. This hotel -"

"I don't care," I say firmly. "What you do is none of my concern, not anymore. Just be glad that we're willing to give you a ride at all. A lot of people would just dump you here and let you walk back to civilization."

With that, I turn and hurry out through the front door and down the steps, before making my way toward the car. I'm starting to cry properly now, but there's no way I want James to see me when I'm upset. By the time I reach the car and start fumbling for my keys, my hands are trembling and I feel like I'm going to break down completely, but I tell myself there'll be time for that later. As I unlock the car, I glance back toward the hotel and see that at least Steve isn't coming after me, and then I turn back to the car.

Suddenly I spot something in the corner of my eye. Looking toward the patio, I see a familiar silhouette standing next to the swimming pool.

Finally!

"Hey!" I yell, waving my hands at her. "Annie! We're getting out of here!"

I wait for her to reply, but she's just standing by the pool, watching me.

"Annie!" I shout, cupping my hands around my mouth. "We're leaving! Right now!"

When she still fails to respond, I can't help sighing. Even now, my dumb little sister apparently thinks it's fun to pull some kind of stunt, so I march around the car and hurry past the hotel's far corner, heading toward the patio. I'm freezing cold and there are still tears in my eyes, and all I can think about is that I want to get as far away from this crumby hotel as possible. In fact, I never want to even *think* about the stupid Lakeforth again.

"Annie, it's freezing!" I continue as I get closer to the pool. "Aren't you cold? You're wearing next to nothing! Where the hell have you been for the past ten hours?"

Stopping at the pool's edge, I see that Annie has her back to me. She's watching the pitch-black forest, and I can't help thinking that she's *still* engaged in whatever dumb game she's been planning all night.

"I'm so not in the mood for this," I tell her, taking a step closer. "Annie, please, Steve's turned out to be a total asshole and I really need you to just come with me. I just broke up with him, and I feel like everything's going to hell right now, and for once I need you to see things from my point of view and just stop playing this game, okay?"

I wait, but still she doesn't turn to me.

"You got us good," I continue, edging toward her. "Okay? Is that what you wanted to hear? We were freaked out when you disappeared, and you really inconvenienced us, and it's all very impressive. But you're my sister, and I need you to understand that I'm really hurting right now and I just want to get the hell away from this place. Please, you can prank me again once we get to the beach, but I'm begging you, just make this easy. Let's go."

Nothing.

No reply.

The only sound now is the rustling of the trees.

"Seriously?" I continue, stepping up behind her and reaching out to put a hand on her arm, only to find that her flesh is wet and ice cold. "You're going to get pneumonia if you stand out here like this. Come on, let's blow this dump and go somewhere with soft beds and warm showers. For once in my life, I actually *want* to just hang out and party and forget my worries. I might even drink more than one beer. Please, can you do this for me?"

I wait, and this time she slowly starts turning to me. As soon as I see the side of her face, however, I can tell that something's wrong. Her eyes look very pale, almost glassy, and her mouth is hanging open with a steady trickle of water running down onto her chin.

"Annie?" I ask, trying not to sound like I'm *too* freaked out right now. "Did you go in the lake? What's wrong?"

She turns a little more, until finally her eyes are staring straight at me, but the expression on her face seems really off. I want to ask her again what's wrong, but I'm not even sure she's capable of hearing me, She looks completely stoned, as if she's out of her mind, and I can't help noticing that more and more water is dribbling from her mouth and running down her chin.

And her eyes are milky white.

"Annie..."

"Annie had a little accident," Steve says suddenly, from right behind me.

I turn to him, but he quickly grabs me by the shoulder and pulls me back. At the same time, I feel a sharp pain slicing between my shoulder-blades, and a moment later the tip of a knife bursts out of my chest, just below my collarbone. Gasping, I stare down at the bloodied metal.

"I'm sorry, Beth," Steve continues calmly, "but I really need you to stay."

PART THREE

MAURICE MECKLETHORPE
1915

CHAPTER SIX

"LOOK AT HER!" FATHER hisses, grabbing me by the shirt collar and dragging me across the room, before forcing me to my knees and placing his hands on either side of my head. "Look of your own free will, boy, or I'll make you look!"

With my eyes still squeezed tight shut, I try in vain to end my miserable shivering. I've been working to hide my fear, but my body betrays me and now Father is pushing his hands against the sides of my head as if he means to crush my skull. I tell myself to be calm, to be a man, but my heart is racing out of control and I feel as if fear incarnate has taken control of my limbs. I cannot stop shaking.

"Look at her!" he sneers, leaning so close that I can feel his hot breath against my ear. "I'm telling you, boy! If you want to join me in the family business, you're going to start by looking the old bitch in the face!"

I know I should open my eyes, but I cannot bring myself to witness this horrific sight. I caught a glimpse of Grandmother's body earlier, through a crack in the door, and it was enough to strike terror into my soul. Perhaps Father is right, perhaps I *am* too weak, but the thought of seeing her again, this close, is too much to bear and -

"Look at her!"

Suddenly Father places his dirty, calloused fingertips against my eyelids and works to force them open. I struggle, even though I know better, but Father slips one fingertip beneath the lid of my left eye and raises it up. For a fraction of a second, I see Grandmother's face on the bed before me, but I immediately try to look away, only for Father to put an arm around my throat and start squeezing tight.

"Look," he whispers, spraying my ear with hot saliva, "or so help me God, I shall slice off those eyelids of yours and make it so you can never look away from anything again. No son of mine is going to live as a coward! How do you ever expect to make it as an undertaker, if you can't even look at a corpse?"

"But it's -"

"I don't care!" he shouts. "Look!"

I know he means it. I've seen Father do worse things to people before, and I have no doubt he'd slit my eyes open as soon as look at me. Slowly, I force myself to focus on the fear of Father's retribution, and this is enough to make me open my eyes and look at the twisted, gnarled dead body that has been laid out on this bare little bed in this gloomy, stinking backroom. As soon as I see Grandmother's face, with her eyes wide open and her mouth locked in a dead scream, I feel my chest starting to shudder. At the same time, she does not look quite as frightful as I'd imagined.

"Look at the foulness before you, boy," Father continues. "She appears, does she not, like some worm spewed up from the soil in Hell."

I open my mouth to tell him I agree, but my lips are trembling and I don't think I can get any words out.

"That's what a life of wrongdoing does to someone," he mutters. "Your mother's mother was not a good woman. I wouldn't say this in front of anyone else, of course, but you and I, Maurice, we know. Aye, we see it, don't we? Tell me you see the consequence of evil on her wretched face."

"I see it," I stammer.

"Say it again."

"I see it." This time, my voice sounds a little firmer.

"One more time. So I know you mean it."

"I see it."

Looking at Grandmother's hands, I see that they are locked in a kind of curled rictus. Each finger looks like the branch of an old and rotten tree. As I continue to stare, I feel Father letting go of me, until I am kneeling of my own accord at the side of the bed. For a moment, the room falls utterly silent, save for the faint flickering of a candle that burns on the bedside table.

I am no longer trembling.

I believe I have conquered my fear.

"The body cannot hide the evils of the soul,"

Father says finally, still standing behind me. "Sins live in the flesh, Maurice. There's no escape. None at all. Watch, I shall show you something."

He walks around the bed, before leaning over Grandmother and using a knife to tear the fabric at the shoulder of her dress. Although I do not wish to see such a thing, I force myself to keep watching as he pulls the dress away, revealing her mottled, pale old chest. A moment later, Father carves the knife's tip against the flesh at the breast's edge, but no blood runs from the wound, even as he cuts deeper. Tossing the knife onto her belly, he slips his fingertips into the wound and starts peeling the flesh back to reveal dark red meat beneath.

"Do you see the sin?" he asks.

Staring at the wound, I try to work out exactly what he means.

"Do you see the sin, boy?"

"I..."

"It's not a trick question. The sin has accumulated beneath her flesh. Do you see it or not?"

I swallow hard. "Yes," I say finally, even though it's a lie. "I see it."

"And what does it look like?"

I shall have to be careful here. If I give the wrong answer, I'll surely be beaten.

"Rotten," I say cautiously. "Rotten like bad meat, but more so. Festering and ruined."

I wait, but evidently he thinks I'm not finished yet with my description.

"Almost devilish," I continue. "It's clear that you are right, Father. Grandmother was indeed a cruel and cursed woman, and it shows in her flesh."

Again I wait, hoping against hope that Father won't ask me to comment any further. I have no idea what he thinks I should see, but I see only meat and bone.

"Aye," he says finally, still holding the peeled section of flesh back. "I reckon you're onto something there, boy. Maybe you're not as hopeless as I'd come to think, although you still look puny. We're gonna have to toughen you up, but that shouldn't be too difficult, not now it's just you and me in the house. You'll be spending more time in the workshop, and you'll be learning what it really means to be a man. And then by Christmas, you should be ready to pull your own weight. God willing, at least."

Suddenly Grandmother turns her head and looks straight at me.

Startled, I let out a gasp and fall back, slamming against the wooden floor and staring in horror as her dead, sunken eyes watch me with a hint of yellow at their edges.

"What is it, boy?" Father asks. "You look white as a sheet."

"She..."

My heart is pounding, and all I can do is stare at Grandmother's eyes. Her mouth is still wide open, and now I think I can hear a faint hissing sound coming from her throat.

"What's up with you?" Father continues, letting go of the flap of skin and stepping around the bed. Stopping in front of me, he obscures my view of

Grandmother's face, but now I can see her curled fingers slowly starting to move, accompanied by a growing creaking sound. Father seems oblivious, but Grandmother is most certainly starting to rise from the bed.

"She's moving," I stammer. "I thought you said... Father, you said she was dead! You said she died last night!"

"Aye, she did. She made quite a palaver of it, too. Why?"

I flinch as I hear the hissing sound getting louder.

"Then why is she moving?" I ask, feeling as if my heart is about to burst from my chest. "Father, look!"

"Have you been on the vapors?" he replies, kicking my right leg hard. "Up with you, boy. You're acting out of sorts."

I stare in horror at Grandmother's hands, which are still slowly moving. Although I still can't see her face, since Father is standing in front of her, I can hear the sound of her bones creaking and bending, as she continues to sit up on the bed. After a moment, her face peers at me from behind Father, and I see her sunken eyes watching me.

"Father, look!" I shout, stumbling to my feet. "Father, she's alive!"

Grabbing my shoulder, he steps around me and forces me toward the bed. I let out a cry and hold my arms up to protect myself, but suddenly I realize that not only is Grandmother once again flat on her back, but her face is looking up toward the ceiling and it is as if she never moved at all, not even once. I watch her carefully, looking for any hint that she might yet be animated, but she seems truly still. Did fear drive me to momentary insanity?

"I saw..." I start to say, before realizing that I cannot possibly tell Father what I think I saw. He'd have me dragged straight to the madhouse.

"You saw what, boy?"

"Nothing," I continue, taking a step back. I continue to stare at Grandmother for a moment, before turning to find that Father is eyeing me with suspicion. "Honest. I didn't see anything. I think I must have just been overcome for a moment."

"You're a strange lad," he replies cautiously. "I think I might yet have to toughen you up a little. Of course, it'll take me a little while to think of something, but when I do..."

His voice trails off for a moment, and then suddenly he grabs my collar, pulling me toward the doorway.

"We'll keep the old woman's death between the two of us," he mutters. "If it gets out, I'll have to give her a proper burial in Christian ground. The expense isn't worth it. She'll be lucky if I can find an old coffin to put her in, and then we'll stick her in the yard."

"But won't she..."

Again, my voice trails off.

"Won't she what, lad?"

"I heard it said once," I continue cautiously, "that if a body isn't destroyed, and if it isn't buried in sanctified ground, then it can rise again. The ghost will...

I mean..."

Father starts chuckling as he puts an arm around my shoulder and starts leading me out of the room.

"You mustn't believe in old superstitions, boy. A body is just a lump of meat and bone and hair, and nothing more. I've been an undertaker all my life. Don't you think I'd have noticed if the dead had any way of coming back?"

Once we're out of the room, he pulls the door shut and then turns to me. I stare down at my shoes, but I know that he wants me to meet his gaze, and finally I look up at him and see a strange expression in his eyes. I'm used to him seeming disgusted by me, but this time he almost seems amused at the same time. I wait, and it's as if he's pondering something, and finally he starts nodding.

"Aye," he says as his grin broadens. "I know how to toughen you up. You fear ghosts, do you? Well, I've got just the thing."

"What's that, Father?" I ask.

He starts chuckling. "Never you mind for now, boy. I want you to go to Sutton Street and buy a bag of coal. Carry it back here, and make sure you're quick."

"Of course," I reply, turning to head toward the back door. Any chance to get away from the workshop is too good to turn down. "I'll get the cart and -"

"I need the cart!" he says firmly. "You'll carry that bag of coal over your shoulder, like I did every day when I was your age. You're fourteen years old now, Maurice. It's time you knew what it means to do a proper day's work. You might be too sick and feeble to go off to war, but you can sure as hell drag a bag of coal home. Otherwise, what use are you to anyone?"

"Yes, Father," I stammer, hesitating for a moment before turning and heading toward the front door. I honestly don't know if I can carry a bag of coal all the way home from Sutton Street, but I suppose I can manage it if I really try hard. Besides, I have no choice. Father's already laughing at me, and I know he's planning to pull some kind of trick that'll most likely leave me humiliated. All I can do right now is fetch that coal and carry it all the way home, and make him see that I'm not as weak as believes.

Already, the sky is darkening and smog from the nearby factory has begun to settle in the cooler air. Coughing, I set off for the coal merchant's shop.

CHAPTER SEVEN

"ARE YOU ALRIGHT?" A man asks, hurrying over to help me up. "Boy, did you hurt your back?"

"No!" I gasp, struggling to push the bag of coal aside so that I can start getting up. I feel a sudden twinge of pain at the base of my spine, but other than that I'm uninjured. Wincing slightly, I accept the man's hand and allow him to help me up, and then I look down and see the bag waiting to be carried again. It's getting dark now, and I'm sure Father will be waiting for me. The coal is a test.

As the man steps back, I see that he's wiping his hand on a handkerchief. Evidently my coarse, dirty hand left some marks on his smooth flesh.

"I'm sorry," I tell him. "I didn't mean to..."

"You can't possibly bear all that weight," the man continues. "Don't you have a horse, or at least a cart of some kind?"

"I'm fine," I stammer, although I feel as if the

pain in my spine is getting tighter and tighter. I'm embarrassed by the rags I'm wearing, and I just want to slip away.

"You certainly don't look fine," he replies. "How far are you taking that bag? Surely there's somebody who could help you."

Although the street is dark, I can just about make out that he's a well-to-do gentleman wearing a proper suit, and I realize that he must be upper class. I don't even know why he bothered to stop and help me, but I suppose he must have simply felt sorry for me as I collapsed under the weight of the coal bag. I'm used to proper people ignoring me.

"I'll be okay," I tell him, standing up straight and feeling the pain in my spine starting to fade. "I'm not far from the yard. Thank you for your help, though."

"I'm afraid I haven't been much help at all," he says, rather unnecessarily, as he finishes wiping his hands. "I can only wish you good luck on the rest of your journey. And try to have a cart with you next time, I'm sure it'll make all the difference."

"I'm sure it would," I reply as he turns and walks away. "Thank you. Thank you again. Thank you."

Taking a deep breath, I tell myself that I just need to haul the sack back up and get going. At the same time, I'm worried that I might collapse again, so I decide to spend just a couple of minutes recovering from the pain. Turning, I look along the darkened street, and I realize that this shortcut has brought me into an unfamiliar part of town. I usually avoid this area, since the people around here tend to have money and I know my place. I should just get out of here, so finally I turn to grab the bag of coal.

And then I see the lights.

Just past the next corner, there's one particular building that's splendidly lit up. In fact, it's like nothing I've ever seen before. I should turn away and continue my journey, but I can't help stepping over to the corner and taking a closer look at what turns out to be a large hotel. I've seen such places before, of course, although this is the first time I've ever been quite so amazed. The lights are sparkling in the night air, and I can see a vast, beautiful chandelier on the other side of one of the windows.

"Moorchester Hotel," I whisper, dazzled by the huge, bright sign above the entrance.

Unable to help myself, I check both ways to make sure that nobody is coming, and then I hurry across the cobbled street until I'm right outside the hotel. I can honestly say that the sight of this place is beguiling, and I head over to the nearest window in something of a trance. I swear, I can feel the warmth of the hotel's lights as they shine out and fill the street. Setting my dirty fingertips on the edge of the window, I have to stand on tiptoes in order to see inside.

There are people in a dining room, dressed in the finest clothes and eating food that looks as if it was made by the gods themselves. Waiters are moving from table to table, delivering pots of tea and glasses of wine, and I can hear the most beautiful music drifting from some other part of the room. A man at one of the tables is sipping from a glass of whiskey. Craning my neck, I finally spot some musicians over at the far end of the dining room, and I can't help but think that this is the most sumptuous, luxurious sight I've ever witnessed.

This is what life should be like. This is how real, proper people live. If I could step into a place like this, just for one moment, and walk in such graceful light, I think I'd be transformed. I don't belong in Father's yard, helping him stuff common corpses into poorly-built coffins. I belong here, among the rich, but I know it's too late for me. I was born into poverty, and at fourteen I'm already too old to find a way out. I shall simply -

Suddenly a woman screams at one of the tables, and I'm shocked when I see that she's looking straight at me.

"I'm sorry," I stammer, taking a step back from the window, "I -"

"Get out of here!" a man yells, rushing from the hotel's brightly-lit front door and swinging a broom at me. "Go on, clear off! You're upsetting people!"

He hits me on the shoulder as I turn and run, but fortunately I'm able to get away quickly enough. When I reach the other side of the cobbled street, I stop and look over my shoulder. The man is still outside the hotel, watching to make sure I don't go back, but at least the woman has stopped screaming. Her horrified voice is still echoing in my mind, however, and I feel utterly ashamed that I caused her such a great deal of distress. After all, she was simply trying to enjoy her dinner, and I intruded by putting my dirty, lower class face at the window. It was probably the most horrific thing she'd ever seen in her life, and I don't blame her for screaming.

Not at all.

Turning, I head back over to the sack of coal and haul it onto my shoulder. I feel another tightening pain in my spine, but I suppose there's no point delaying things. I just have to walk the final half mile until I get home, and then hopefully Father will leave me alone for the rest of the evening.

***

"What's the matter?" he asks, his voice sounding a little slurred and drunken as he holds the bottle of whiskey toward me. "Too good for you, boy? Get it down your throat!"

"But -"

"That's expensive stuff," he continues. "I don't offer it to just any old Tom, Dick or Harry. Drink, Maurice. It'll put some hair on your chest and make a man of you! I'm sick of having a weakling for a son."

I raise the bottle to my lips, although the foul smell gives me pause. I don't want to become a ferocious drinker, I don't even want to touch the stuff, but he's watching me intently and I'm worried about what he'll say if I refuse. Knowing his temper, he'll most likely hold me against the floor and pour the stuff down my throat. After taking a deep breath, I swallow a sip of whiskey, while taking care not to look too disgusted.

"Aye, and more," he mutters, clearly not satisfied. "Drink more, boy. Go on."

"I thought whiskey was to be savored," I reply, "not -"

"Only the good stuff," he replies, as he starts chuckling. "What you've got in your hands there is good old-fashioned home-brew. It's for rinsing, not for sipping. Now get a quarter-bottle down and stop faffing around like an old maid. Believe me, after a hard day at work, there's nothing wrong with taking a drink. Not that you'd know much about hard work, but you will soon enough."

"Is this the whiskey that Grandmother brewed?" I ask. "I think I saw it in a bathtub."

"At least she was good for something."

I hesitate, before swallowing some more of the foul stuff. I swear, I can feel a burning sensation at the back of my throat, and a moment later I realize my gut seems to be shuddering slightly. I honestly don't think that this whiskey agrees with me.

"How many times did you fall over," Father mutters, "while you were carrying that coal home?"

"None."

He laughs. "Be honest, boy."

"None. I didn't fall once."

"Aye, if you say so. Be warned, though. You're not a good liar."

Realizing that there's no point even trying, I take another sip of whiskey. The taste is still foul, as is the burning sensation, but I'm starting to notice that the whiskey at least takes a slight edge off my fear. With each fresh sip, I feel as if Father somehow becomes less threatening. I'm fourteen years old, soon to be fifteen, and it's high time that I started thinking about getting out of here. Taking another sip of whiskey, a longer sip this time, I watch as Father picks the dirt from beneath his fingernails, and I feel more certain than ever that I'll find some way to leave this old bastard behind. I might not ever become rich, but at least I don't have to be an undertaker.

"Getting a taste for it, are you?" he mutters, casting an amused glance toward me.

I don't reply.

Instead, I simply take yet another, even longer sip, and this time the burning sensation actually feels good. Perhaps whiskey has its uses, after all.

"Every boy needs a shock," Father continues. "Did you know that, Maurice? Every boy, when he's young, needs a shock that brings out his true nature. There's no need to be scared of the world. You're lucky, you're too sick to be shipped off to the trenches. There are people who think this war'll never end, but mark my words, it'll be over some day. And when it is, there'll be opportunities for the likes of you."

I drink some more whiskey from the bottle. "What kind of opportunities?" I ask.

"That's for you to figure out. But the world is changing fast, and it'll change faster in years to come. The smart ones, the ones who make money, will be the ones who can keep up."

"Maybe the war'll last long enough that I *will* get to go and fight," I continue. "I wouldn't mind that. It seems wrong for me to be left behind."

"Aye, well, they'll have to be getting pretty desperate if they call up someone like you. With your gammy leg and all those illnesses you've had, you'd be the first to drop and get ground into the mud."

"You don't know that," I mutter darkly, instinctively taking another sip.

He smiles.

"You don't!" I hiss.

"Getting confident now, are you?"

"Maybe I'll go and fight anyway," I tell him. "Maybe I can use a false name, and maybe I can hide my bad leg and my poor lungs, and maybe I can get to the trenches in France and fight!"

He starts laughing. A deep, rumbling belly laugh.

"Maybe I'll go and do it tomorrow," I continue, feeling as if signing up to fight might be my only way out of this place.

"You will, will you?"

"There can be nothing nobler than to fight for your country," I point out. "You're not *so* old, Father. Why aren't *you* fighting? You're not even sick, so -"

Suddenly Father bursts from his chair and lunges at me, grabbing me by the collar and hauling me up. He lets out a grunt of anger as he slams me against the wall, and then he crashes his knee into my belly so hard that I cry out. Pulling me back, he shoves me to the floor, and then he stands over me as I roll onto my side.

"What was that?" he asks breathlessly. "Were you questioning my honor, boy? Were you calling me a coward?"

"No!" I gasp, wincing as I feel a tightening sense of pain in my chest. "I swear!"

"Oh, I'm going to teach you," he continues,

picking up the spilled bottle of whiskey and pouring the last dregs down his throat. "You're getting cocky, are you? You think once you're a real man, you'll be able to put your old man in the shade." He looks at the bottle for a moment, before walking over to the fireplace. Stopping, he peers at his own reflection in the dusty, scratched mirror. "When I told you to grow up, boy, I didn't mean for you to lose respect for your betters. You're stuck here with me, like I was stuck here with my father, and like he was stuck here with his father before him. You're too stupid to find a way out."

"Of course, Father," I whisper, wondering whether it's safe for me to try getting up yet. "I'm sorry, Father."

"Don't apologize," he replies, eyeing me carefully. "This is your last night as a boy. Soon, you'll be a man. Do you know how the great change will take place?"

"I..."

My voice trails off. I swear, my heart is pounding so fast, I fear it might suddenly fail.

"I don't know," I stammer finally. "Father, I carried the coal. You gave me that job, and I did it. Perhaps I wasn't quick enough, but I shall carry a sack of coal every day until it feels almost weightless, and then I shall start carrying two sacks a day, then three, then four until -"

"Shut up!" he sneers.

I open my mouth to continue, but now Father is once again examining the empty bottle.

"People don't change in gradual steps, Maurice,"

he says eventually, with a heavy sigh. "No, they change in sudden jolts. Some never experience one of those jolts, of course, while some change several times in a lifetime. You haven't changed yet. In your fourteen years, you've more or less stayed the same. Maybe I'm wrong, maybe there's no hope left for you. You're my only son, so I've clung to hope, but now I realize that I was wrong. You have no potential, Maurice. You'll never amount to anything more than a disappointment, not unless I force the issue."

"But -"

Suddenly he storms across the room, heading straight for me. As he does so, he raises the empty whiskey bottle, and I quickly realize what he intends.

"Father, no! I -"

Before I can finish, he smashes the bottle against the side of my head, knocking me out cold.

***

It's the smell that wakes me.

The foul, rotten stench. Filling my nostrils, filling my mouth too. Even before my eyes have opened, I feel my stomach tighten with nausea, and the air somehow seems moist and cold. Once my eyes *are* open, however, I find myself in pitch darkness, although something is pressing hard against my left shoulder. I immediately try to sit up, only for my head to bump hard against some form of low wooden board.

"What -"

Reaching out, I find that my right hand hits

another board, while my left hand brushes against some kind of fabric. I turn and try once more to get to my feet, but I seem to be in some form of tight, enclosed space. Turning again, I hear a close, hollow bumping sound as my shoulder hits the wooden sides, and already the air in this place is becoming much thinner. I cannot fathom where I am, although a moment later I feel a throbbing pain on the side of my head and I remember Father hitting me with the bottle.

"Father?" I stammer, fumbling for some way out of this space. Perhaps I am in a wardrobe, or the drawer of a dresser, or -

Suddenly my left hand brushes against a human face.

I freeze, with my fingers lifting from the face and holding in the cold air for a few seconds. My heart is beating faster than ever as I slowly move my hand down and feel the face once more. My fingertips brush against cold, gummy flesh that has lines of wrinkles running in every direction, and a moment later I feel what seems to be the edge of an open mouth. As the smell becomes increasingly sweet and pungent, I feel the cold grip of fear in my chest as I start to realize where I have woken.

"Grandmother?" I stammer, before reaching out and feeling the sides of the coffin. "No, please..."

I push against the wooden above my head, but it budges not one inch.

"Let me out of here!" I scream, filled with a sense of pure panic. "Father! Help me!"

CHAPTER EIGHT

DESPITE THE PAIN IN my ankle, I cannot stop myself. I continue to kick as hard as I can, and I think that perhaps the wood is finally starting to split. I cannot see, of course, not in this dark interior, but finally I reach down past Grandmother's dead feet and run my fingers against the coffin's lower end.

I was right!

After kicking so hard for so long, I have finally managed to start breaking the coffin apart.

"Help me!" I shout, even though my throat feels sore and bloodied. "Father!"

I start kicking again, unable to help myself. I have felt panic in my chest before, of course, but never for so long all at once. Even now, as I continue to try forcing my way out of the coffin, I can feel myself pressed close to Grandmother's corpse, and I cannot help but brush against her cold flesh. There are tears in my eyes, and I know that Father is most likely standing outside the coffin and laughing at me. We are probably in his work-shed, and he means to teach me a lesson. This is what he was planning last night, while he was trying to get me drunk. This is his way of turning me into a man.

His coffins are usually poorly made. This one, however, must have been strengthened for my benefit.

Finally I feel the wood split again, this time with more force. Although I cannot fully turn around in this confined space, I manage to reach down, and sure enough I quickly feel that the wood is damaged. I start pulling splinters away, desperately waiting to see some sliver of light, but a moment later I feel something cold and moist running between my fingers like crumbs.

Soil.

No, it cannot be soil.

Soil would mean...

Forcing my fingertips between the sections of broken wood, I feel more soil on the other side, packed tight. I try to dig some away, but all I feel is more dirt. This time, I cannot hold back the fear and panic in my chest, and I start kicking harder and harder.

"Let me out!" I scream. "Father, let me out of here!"

Pausing, I realize that my voice sounds so hollow and constrained.

"Father!" I cry out again, as tears start running down my face. "Please!"

And then I freeze as I hear a faint guttural rasping sound. Turning my head in the darkness, I cannot see anything, but the hissing persists and I am certain it must be coming from somewhere near Grandmother's face. A moment later, the hissing falters slightly, as if it might stop altogether, but then it returns as a kind of slow, twisted groan. At the same time, I feel a cold sweat break out across my entire body as the sound seems to fill the darkness all around me.

I wait, telling myself that some other explanation will surely arise. I am sure that dead bodies, even when they have been dead several days, can make certain noises as gases are released. It will stop soon.

Yet the sound continues, stuttering a little but refusing to die away.

"What are you?" I whisper, even though I am beginning to feel very short of breath. "Why -"

No.

No, I must not let my mind fill with fear.

Any sound I hear is just some normal process caused by her body breaking down.

"I am not a fool," I say out loud, trying to keep myself strong. "I will not -"

The sound suddenly becomes choked, as if the air is struggling to escape. Despite the absolute darkness of this confined space, in my mind's eye I cannot help but see Grandmother's dead face with her wide-open mouth, and I am certain that this sound must be coming from her throat.

"You're dead," I continue, hoping to conjure up some hidden strength from deep within my chest, even as tears gather in my eyes. "You're dead, Grandmother, you -"

Suddenly she lets out a louder sound, like a kind

of hacking cough. I instinctively pull back, only to bump against the side of the coffin, but all I can do now is listen as the sound continues. I remember the long weeks of Grandmother's illness, when she seemed at times to be choking on her own saliva, and I also remember the sudden sense of peace and calm that filled the house once she was dead. Now her death rattle has returned, several days after she drew her final breath, yet I know that such a thing is impossible.

"You're dead," I remind her, as if she might realize I'm right and fall silent. "I saw you, you died and -"

Her cough suddenly becomes louder, and I swear I think I even hear her trying to form words. At the same time, her body briefly shuddered.

"No!" I shout, filled with a sudden rush of panic. "You're dead!"

I try to pull away in the darkness, yet there is nowhere for me to go. And then, just as I feel certain that my pounding heart must be about to rip itself to shreds, the coughing sound stops and I find myself once again in absolute silence.

I wait, not daring to move.

Grandmother's corpse is silent and still.

Eventually, once I start to believe that maybe the sound was just some imagined thing, I realize that I need to focus on getting out of here. I refuse to accept that Father simply threw me down here in a grave with Grandmother for no reason, so there has to be some method to his madness. Reaching around, I try as much as possible to avoid touching Grandmother's body, while also taking care to check the coffin for some kind of tool that I might be able to use. After all, if Father truly means for me to prove myself, he must have left me a chance. He might be a cruel man, but he is not without reason.

Yet there is nothing.

I check again, but still I can find nothing that might prove useful. The air is getting thinner and thinner, to the extent that I can feel myself becoming short of breath, and I tell myself that panicking will only make me suffocate faster. At the same time, I cannot help but think of the crushing weight above me, and of the fact that I cannot possibly crawl my way out of a full, six-foot grave. Perhaps in his drunkenness, Father decided to do away with me entirely, and now he sleeps in a stupor while I am left to die down here. Even if he relents once he's sober, I might not last long enough.

A moment later, as I shift my weight again, I realize I can feel something small and hard in one of my pockets. I reach down, and to my surprise I find that a small box of self-igniting matches has been left for me. Feeling a rush of hope, I immediately slip one of the matches out and strike it against the box's side, and to my immense relief the match brings a bright flame that casts flickering light throughout the coffin.

Hope turns to horror, however, as soon as I see Grandmother's dead, veiny bare feet at the coffin's far end. I cannot stop staring at her toes, and at the nails that seem to have grown significantly since her death, until suddenly the match burns to my fingertips and I have to quickly blow it out.

Once again in darkness, I contemplate striking another match, yet I hesitate as I realize that I would have to see Grandmother's body again. At the same time, I feel that perhaps Father left me the matches so that I might find some way out of here, so I force myself to be strong and I light another mother before turning and looking toward the coffin's other end.

I cannot be a coward. Not this time.

A shudder passes through my chest as soon as I see the match's warm glow flickering against Grandmother's dead face. Her eyes are wide open, albeit having sunk deeper into their sockets, and her mouth is agape. I know I should use the light to search for a way out of here, yet I cannot help staring at Grandmother's features until I feel the match burning down. I blow the flame out, and then -

At the very last moment, just as the light dies and I'm plunged back into darkness, I see Grandmother's head turn slightly, accompanied by a brief creaking sound.

Holding my breath, I wait, but now the coffin is once again dark and silent.

She can't have moved.

I must have imagined the whole thing, yet I feel certain that at the very last moment I saw her shift slightly. Taking another match from the box, I find that my hands are trembling terribly, but I know I must have a little more light so that I can be *sure* Grandmother did not move. I must banish that fear. I cannot quite bring myself to strike the match, however, and a moment later I hear the creaking sound once again, for just a fraction of a second before it stops.

Did she turn to me again in the darkness?

"No!" I say firmly, trying to calm my racing heart. "I am not weak! I shall not surrender to foolish delusions! I know you're dead! I know you're..."

My voice trails off as I stare into the darkness and imagine her sunken eyes staring back at me.

Perhaps this is what Father meant. Perhaps he is testing me, and I am failing as wild, impossible visions flood my senses.

The creaking returns for a few more seconds, before stopping once more.

"Give me strength," I whisper. "Let me prove that bastard wrong."

I hesitate, before striking the match.

Grandmother's face is staring straight at me, and her shoulders are raised slightly, as if she began to turn in my direction. I pull back against the coffin's side, and at the same time the match falls from my hand. Too shocked to even think straight, I look into Grandmother's dead eyes, and it takes a moment before I realize that the fallen match has set light to her white dress.

I quickly pat the flames out, and now I am in darkness again. Still, in my mind's eye I can see her awful, shriveled face looking straight at me. There is no doubt, no doubt in my mind at all, that she has begun to rise.

And then I hear another faint creaking sound, coming from just a few inches away.

"No!" I say again, as if somehow my words might force her back. "Stop! No!"

The creaking continues for a moment, before fading to nothing.

"This isn't real," I continue, as tears stream down my face. "It's an illusion, or a trick, or a dream."

Even as the words leave my lips, however, I know that I do not believe them.

"It's not real," I say again, hoping to get my thoughts under control. "It can't be!"

I wait in silence, too scared to light another match, too scared to do *anything* except listen for the merest hint of movement. No matter how hard I try to focus on rational thoughts, and how fervently I tell myself over and over that my senses must be deceiving me, I cannot help but think of that wretched face still staring at me through the darkness. I want so desperately to feel strength in my heart, to really believe that my senses have betrayed me, yet I cannot force the lingering doubt from my mind.

What if Grandmother has really returned?

So I wait.

Silence.

Please, let it not be true.

For several minutes, I barely even dare breathe. I simply stay completely still, listening to the silence and waiting in case there is any hint of movement. Even the slightest creaking sound would set my mind racing again, but the ongoing silence is actually starting to become a little comforting. If I have regained control over my senses, I can begin to think of some other way out of here. I just have to wait a little longer, staring into the absolute darkness, so that I can be absolutely sure there is nothing to fear.

Silence.

Utter, blessed silence.

And then slowly, I feel a set of wrinkled fingertips press against my face.

CHAPTER NINE

SUDDENLY A VAST, FREEZING shock rushes against my face. Opening my eyes, I see a kind of shimmering pale light, accompanied by a flood of bubbles. A moment later, something tugs hard on the back of my head, and I am pulled back from the barrel and sent crashing to the muddy ground as Father laughs heartily.

"Whatever will become of you next, eh?" he asks, as I smooth my soaking wet hair away from my face.

Looking up, I see Father framed against the gray morning sky, and his features are red with excitement.

"She's coming for me!" I stammer, filled with panic. "She wants me! She's alive! She's going to get me, she's trying to -"

Before I can get another word out, Father slams his knee against the side of my face, sending me crashing down against the muddy ground. This, at least, makes me shut up, and I take a moment to check that my jaw isn't shattered.

"You should have heard yourself," he continues, "screaming like a woman, ranting about the old bitch coming back to life and clawing at your body. I was tempted to leave you down there a while longer, but I began to worry what the neighbors might think."

Turning, I see that the coffin is down in a shallow grave, its lid no more than a couple of feet from the surface. With the lid open, Grandmother's body is exposed to the light, and her dead eyes still stare at me. Startled, I pull back, terrified in case she moves again. I'm shaking with fear, and all I can think about is the sensation of her hand touching my face in the darkness, and then...

And then what?

I barely remember what happened next. It's as if my terrified mind was unable to retain the memories. I know I screamed, and I know I lit more matches, and I know Grandmother's dress began to burn. I know I saw her face in the flames, and I felt her hands grabbing at me, and I heard Father yelling as he tore the lid off the coffin, and then...

I remember the sound of my own horrified, rambling voice as Father dragged me to the water trough.

"You didn't have to set fire to her," he mutters, stepping around to the other side of the grave and peering down at her. "Good job I got you out when I did, or the pair of you might have burned down there. I trust you've learned your lesson now, at least. No son of mine is going to live a life ruled by fear. You're a wretched lad, to be sure, but we'll make a man of you yet. Whatever you think you saw and felt down there, I hope you know it was all in your head."

"It *was* a test," I stammer, as my whole body shivers in the cold morning air. I stare at Grandmother for a moment longer, before looking up at Father again. "You did that to me on purpose!"

"Aye, and I'll do it again if you're not careful." Still grinning, he seems to find me highly amusing. "In all seriousness, let this be a lesson to you. There's no point letting your fears run out of control, because they'll only deceive you further. If you truly thought the old woman was coming back to life, you only have yourself to blame. It's a weak mind that perceives such things, Maurice, and you must be stronger. Promise me you won't get like that again."

"You put me down there with her," I whisper, feeling a rising sense of anger in my chest. After a moment, I start getting to my feet, and I swear I have a new strength in my chest. I am no longer scared of Father. Instead, I hate him with a passion. "You fooled me."

"You can't fool a man if he's not already a fool," he replies smugly. "Still, at least you *are* a man now. I hope so, anyway. If you're not, there's nothing more I can do for you. You won't make much of an undertaker if you're scared of the dead."

With that, he turns and walks away, leaving me standing at the edge of the grave. I cannot help staring down at Grandmother's body, and I still feel certain that she truly moved while I was trapped with her in the coffin. The mind might be a powerful thing, but it cannot possibly conjure up such horrors.

"Come on, lad!" Father calls out. "We've got work to do!"

***

"Will he even fit in that thing?" I ask, as I wheel the next body through. "He's a big man, and I'm not -"

"Don't be stupid," Father replies with a chuckle, leaning under the table and pulling out an ax. "Now you're working with me full-time, I can let you in on a few tricks of the trade. First things first, you don't waste time building a large coffin for a man like Henry Corner. Hell, his family can barely afford to pay for him to be buried in the first place. All you do -"

He swings the ax down, cutting Henry's left arm clean away and letting it fall to the floor.

"All you do is prune the man down until he fits the coffin," he continues, heading around to the far end of the table. "He was a tall bastard, wasn't he?"

He hesitates, before raising the ax and then chopping one of Henry's feet off. He does the same to the other foot, and then he kicks them both across the room as he steps around the table. "That oughta do it, don't you think? We'll give him a try and see."

Staring in horror at the severed body parts on the floor, I feel a sense of nausea rising once more in my gut.

"You're not still thinking about those few hours

you spent in the coffin, are you?" Father asks. "You need to get over it, my boy. That was just an initiation into the family business, so to speak. Don't take these things so seriously. My father did something similar to me once, and I turned out alright."

He starts laughing, as he sets the ax aside and drags Henry Corner's body to the side of the coffin.

"Are you gonna help, or what?"

Figuring that I have no choice, I head around to grab Henry's feet, only to remember at the last moment that his feet are no longer attached to the rest of him. I hesitate for a moment, before grabbing hold of his stumpy legs and helping Father haul the corpse into the coffin.

"In America," he mutters, "they've taken to having the coffins open at funerals. Can you believe that? People actually want to see the faces of the dead bodies. God help us if that ever catches on in England." He grunts as we squeeze the body into the coffin. With his left arm missing, and both feet cut away, Henry just about fits. "See?" Father continues. "Problem solved. And now for your second lesson of the day."

Reaching down, he picks up the feet and arm and tosses them unceremoniously into a crate.

"You'll be taking those down the street in a bit," he explains, "to old Warner's place."

"The butcher?" I reply, shocked by the suggestion.

"You don't seriously believe his cheapest lumps of meat are all from pigs and cows, do you?" he asks with a grin. "Why do you think I always said never to buy the mincemeat from that place? Half of it's from rats, and the other half's from... Well, let's just say we don't waste anything around here. And frankly, I'm starting to think we should send the whole bloody body over to Warner. It's not as if anyone's gonna check who or what is getting lowered into the ground in these boxes."

"You mean people are eating..."

My voice trails off as I realize exactly what he means. I've never trusted Mr. Warner, and I always suspected that he was passing off vermin as decent meat, but now my stomach turns as I come to understand the truth. Feeling a little dizzy, I lean against one of the tables and try to get my head straight, although after a moment I become aware that Father is watching me intently. Turning to him, I can't help worrying that he might be contemplating another lesson that I need to learn, and I think I might have had enough of those for one day.

"You look sick to the gills," he mutters.

"I'm not," I reply, swallowing hard. "Honest."

"I almost believe you. Now make yourself useful and fetch some more coal. I won't be cold this afternoon. And drop those chunks off at Warner's on the way, and mind that you bring back what I'm owed. He'll take one look at you and try to cheat you, seeing as how you look like a vacant string of piss. I want half a crown off him, on account of him owing me from last time. See that you get the lot."

I stare at the body parts for a moment, before turning to him.

"Well?" he continues. "What's confusing you, boy? You know your job. Get to it."

"Of course," I stammer, heading over to the other table and picking up the crate. It's surprisingly light, considering the body parts it contains, but I have to focus in order to keep from vomiting as I carry the crate toward the door.

"And don't take too long!" Father calls after me. "I'll be waiting, boy!"

By the time I get out into the yard, I'm starting to feel dizzy. I can't bring myself to look down at the arm and feet in the crate, but at the same time I can't stop thinking about them. I think I can even smell the pale, dead flesh and the congealed blood, and I once again feel as if my head is spinning. Reaching the gate at the yard's far end, I hesitate for a moment before grabbing some rags and placing them over the body-parts. At least that way, passersby in the street won't see what I'm carrying.

"Get moving!" Father calls after me. "There's still plenty of work still to be done when you're back!"

"Of course," I mutter, slipping out into the alley and then making my way along the street. The idea of ever going back to the workshop, of even hearing Father's voice again, is profoundly nauseating, yet at the same time I know I have no other options. I am destined to work for Father, and then to one day take his place as head of the family business, and then perhaps even to become like him. One day, I might have a son of my own, and I might be equally harsh and cruel.

By the time I'm getting close to the butcher's

back door, I can't shake the feeling that nothing I ever do will be enough to rise above the squalor and filth of this world. If we are born in the mud, we can never entirely rinse ourselves clean. Lost in these thoughts, I make my way along the alley, trying to avoid eye contact with a beggar who sits hunched next to one of the walls. Just as I pass the foul old man, however, I trip against a broken cobble, and I drop the crate as I crash to the floor.

In an instant, the beggar lunges forward, pulling the rags from the crate and grabbing the arm and feet.

"Stop!" I shout, but it's too late and he makes off with his prizes, scampering along the alley and quickly disappearing around the corner.

Getting to my feet, I feel a sharp pain in my ankle, but I still run after the old man. There's no sign of him in the next street, or the next, and I'm about to give up when finally I spot him huddled in the shadows at the side of a public house. I clench my fists, ready to go over and demand that he returns what he stole from me, but then my stomach turns as I see that he has already begun to chew on one of the feet.

For a moment, I feel as if the rest of the world has disappeared entirely, and all that is left is this gruesome scene. I can't even look away as the old man uses his teeth to tear loose a strip of flesh, or as he sucks the meat into his mouth and starts chewing. Somehow fascinated by this vile display, I feel a sinking feeling in the pit of my stomach as I realize that I have been wrong all along.

It's not just Father.

The whole world is miserable and foul, and yet...

And yet there is one beacon of decency and honesty.

Turning, I stagger back along the street, making my way toward the lights in the distance. With each step, I become more and more aware of my own stench, as if the smells of the workshop have become entangled in my clothes. Even though I'm now only a few corners from the spot where the beggar sat chewing on a stolen foot, already the buildings around me are starting to look grander and more stately, and I can't help noticing that the people seem much better dressed. It's almost as if I've reached another world.

Finally, stopping at the next corner, I look across the street and see the vast, blazing lights of the Moorchester. I know it's just a hotel, but somehow this place represents the best that the world has to offer. It's so close, and yet at the same time I feel I cannot approach.

Men in suits and women in beautiful dresses are dining on the other side of the windows. I don't go too close, not this time, since I would rather not disturb such elegant people. Still, I can't help but watch as a horse-drawn carriage pulls up outside the main entrance, and as a smartly-dressed man steps out before helping a woman down. They look so perfect and so graceful, and I can't help thinking that I belong in their world. I belong among the upper classes.

I must find a way to reach them. Either that, or I shall die trying.

***

"Is that you? Boy? Are you finally back with the coal?"

I can hear Father stomping through the house, heading this way, but I don't bother turning. Not yet. Instead, I continue to go through the box on the dresser, picking out anything that looks like it might be valuable. I know there's not much here, but there has to be at least *something* I can pawn. These items belonged to Mother and Grandmother, so I feel they're as much mine as Father's now. I don't need much money, but I need a small sum so that I can get far away from this wretched place.

Far away from London, even.

"Boy! What are you doing?"

Hearing the door crash open, I realize that Father is going to want answers. I wait until he's right up behind me, and then I feel his hand on my shoulder.

"Where's the coal?" he asks. "What -"

Before he can finish, I turn and punch him square on the side of the face, sending him crashing back until he slams down against the floor. I step toward him, ready to hit him again, but I quickly see that I managed to knock him out cold with my first strike. My right hand hurts a little, but I can move the fingers well enough, and I cannot help but feel rather satisfied that I managed to cut him down so easily. Perhaps I am more of a man than he realized.

"I'm getting out of here," I stammer, turning back to the jewelry box and scooping out everything I can hold, quickly shoving the various rings and necklaces into my pocket. "I was born in the wrong world, but I can find my way to where I'm supposed to be."

With that, I step over Father's unconscious form and head toward the door. I don't know where I'm going, or what I shall do when I get there, but I am sure of one thing.

One day, I shall be a great man. The world will bow down before the great Maurice Mecklethorpe.

PART FOUR

RUTH MAYWHISTLE
1935

CHAPTER TEN

"I'M NOT SELLING THIS land!" Pappa shouts, slamming his tool-bag against the kitchen table as he marches through to the other room. "Jobard Nash will own this plot over my dead body!"

"Why's Pappa so angry?" I whisper, turning to Mamma.

"Quiet," she replies, keeping her voice low. She's scared. I've seen her scared before, but usually only when Pappa has been drinking. This time, he's sober and she's still scared. "Ruth, perhaps you can go and play with your sister for a little while."

"But -"

"Go to your sister!" she says firmly, and I can tell that something's really wrong.

Without even waiting to make sure that I leave the room, she hurries to the counter and grabs a glass, and to my horror she pours Pappa a whiskey. Her hands are trembling, and she's muttering to herself under her breath.

"Please don't give him that!" I stammer. "Not when he's already mad!"

"It might help this time," she replies, before turning to me. "Go!" she shouts. "Now! Don't you dare answer back!"

She takes a moment to adjust her dress, and then she makes her way cautiously through to the next room, where Pappa seems to be still stomping about in a fury. This isn't the first time he's been angry about Mr. Nash, but it *is* the first time he's flown into such an absolute rage, and it's *definitely* the first time Mamma has looked like she's scared of him while he's sober. I want to believe that Pappa would never hurt Mamma, but deep down I worry about these fits he's started to get. It's almost as if he's slowly losing control of his temper.

At the same time, he brings less and less back each time from his hunting trips.

"I won't speak of it!" he shouts suddenly from the next room. "There's no discussion to be had! Get out of my sight!"

"What was the offer?" Mamma asks him, as I watch the empty doorway. I can see their shadows on the far wall, and it sounds as if Pappa has at least stopped storming about. "If it was enough for us to buy a house in town, perhaps we should at least consider the -"

"Are you on his side?" Pappa snaps, loud enough for me to flinch slightly. "Did he come to you while I was out working? Did he persuade you to work on me?"

"Of course not! I'm simply saying that it's been several years since we've been able to make this land really pay. I don't know what's wrong, but -"

"I've told you what's wrong!" he yells. "It's that cursed hotel that Nash built up the hill. Ever since he first broke ground on the place, the soil down here has been dry as bone. That man single-handedly made all our land infertile, and now he thinks he can swoop in and buy us out for a pittance!"

"What does he want our land *for*?" Mamma asks.

Even though I'm scared, I step closer to the open doorway.

"I didn't even bother to listen," Pappa mutters darkly. "Evidently he aims to expand his hotel, hoping to lure more unsuspecting customers. The man would be better off shutting that place down, tearing it apart, and going to seek his fortune somewhere else. This land was fine before he showed up, and it'll be fine after he's gone."

"You don't know that," Mamma replies. "The damage might be irreparable, at least in our lifetimes."

"You don't have a clue what you're talking about. And now, to add insult to injury, he says that he's rescinding my hunting rights! He wants to starve us into submission! You should have heard the way he talked to me! He said he was running out of patience, and that soon he'd have to take matters into his own hand. The man actually threatened me!"

"How much did he offer, Charles? I'm not saying I *want* us to leave our home, but times change and perhaps we must simply -"

Suddenly there's a loud slap, and Mamma falls silent. I take a step back, my heart pounding as I tell myself that there's absolutely no way Pappa would have struck her, but a moment later Mamma steps into view and I see that not only does she look pale and shocked, but she's holding a hand to the side of her face, as if she's in pain.

"Go to your sister!" she shrieks suddenly, as soon as she spots me. "Get out of here! Go!"

I hesitate for a moment, and suddenly she steps toward me with a hand raised, as if she's about to strike me about the face. I turn and hurry through to the next room, and then to the next, and then I push open the door to Mary's room and slip inside, before slamming it shut again. For a moment, I stay completely still, in case Mamma comes after me, but now the house seems to have fallen silent again.

And then I hear a faint creaking sound over my shoulder. Turning, I see that Mary is over on her bed, resting against a pillow. She looks paler than ever, almost waxy in the candlelight, and so very weak. Still, her eyes are fixed on me, and I know there's no point trying to keep the truth from her.

"They're arguing again," she groans, her voice sounding weak and damaged. "Why?"

"It's about Mr. Nash," I tell her, feeling a little breathless. Before I can continue, I hear more raised voices from elsewhere in the house, and it's clear that Mamma and Pappa's disagreement isn't over yet. "He wants to buy Pappa out of this land, but Pappa doesn't want to do it. I think Mamma wants him to reconsider."

"He never will," Mary gasps. "He's too proud."

"I wish he *would* agree to sell," I reply, making

my way across the room and then sitting on the side of my sister's bed. "We could go and live in the city, or at least in a town. Anywhere would be better than this place, down at the bottom of the hill, next to the lake, with that horrible hotel so high up against the sky."

"I wouldn't let Pappa hear you say that."

"I won't. Don't worry."

"He'd take it as a betrayal, Ruthie."

I nod. "It's not, though. It's just being sensible about things."

She starts to say something in reply, but she quickly breaks into another coughing fit. She leans forward and I immediately step around behind her and start hitting her hard on the back, hoping to help her out a little by dislodging some phlegm from her chest. She coughs for several more seconds, and it sounds as if she's getting worse and worse, but finally she holds up a hand to let me know that she's okay. Stepping back around the bed, I watch as she leans once more against the pillow. She forces a smile, but I have to grab a cloth from the bowl and wipe the edges of her mouth, to take away the strings of yellow pus.

"How are you feeling today?" I ask.

Her smile falters slightly, and I can see that she doesn't want to answer, nor to lie.

"Mamma says you'll be better soon," I continue. "You have to be."

"Do I?"

I nod.

"And why's that?" she asks.

"You just do, that's all. You're only young,

Mary. I was your age a couple of years ago, and *I* didn't get sick. So why should you be suffering like this?"

"Different bodies," she groans, before letting out another brief, gurgling cough.

"If we lived in the town," I continue, "you could see a proper doctor. If only Pappa wasn't so stubborn, we could have left by now. Mr. Nash wants this land very badly, and the only thing stopping us is Pappa's insistence that the Maywhistle family should never leave the farm." I pause for a moment, feeling a ripple of fear in my chest as I realize that Pappa will likely never change his mind. Or maybe it's not fear. Maybe it's anger. "It's not even a farm, anyway," I add. "Not really, not anymore. It's just a house by the lake and a little patch of land that won't grow anything."

"It means the world to Pappa," she gasps.

"That doesn't mean we have to stay," I point out. "If we voted equally, the four of us, we'd -"

"He'll never allow that."

"I know." Falling silent for a moment, I can't help noticing that Mary's eyes seems to have become a little sunken, almost as if they've started to retreat into the hollows of her skull. I don't want to see these things, but I can't help myself. Deep down, I don't believe Mamma is telling the truth when she says Mary will ever be well again.

"Why are you looking at me like that?" she asks suddenly.

"Like what?"

"Like you think I might die at any moment."

I shake my head. "I'm not."

"Yes you are," she whispers, her voice almost fading to nothing. A moment later, she reaches out and takes my hand in hers, and I feel her cold flesh squeezing against mine. "When I'm gone, Ruthie, you must be strong. It'll just be you with Mamma and Pappa, and that won't be easy."

"You're not going anywhere," I tell her.

"We both know I am."

I open my mouth to tell her she's wrong, that she can't die, but something about the look in her eyes makes me realize that I can't lie to her. Instead, I feel as if I'm on the verge of bursting into tears. Forming a fist with my right hand, I dig my fingernail into my palm, hoping that the pain will keep me strong.

Suddenly hearing the door starting to open, I turn just in time to see Mamma peering into the room. She has tears in her eyes, too, and she looks rather shaken.

"Ruth," she says, her voice faltering slightly, "I need you to fetch some water from the well."

"I fetched some earlier."

"I need you to fetch more. Please, don't argue with me. Just do it."

"But -"

"There's a good girl. The sooner you get going, the sooner you'll be back. Remember what I told you the other day. You have to help out more."

With that, she steps away from the door, and it's clear that she expects no further argument from me.

"You'd better go," Mary tells me, letting go of my hand. "You know what'll happen if we run out tonight. Pappa will blame Mamma, and with the mood he's been in of late, I wouldn't be surprised if he wallops her good and hard." She hesitates for a moment. "When you get back, we can read together. If you like, anyway. I think I'm strong enough for that. Not like last night."

"Are you sure?" I ask with a smile.

"You must hurry," she gasps, trying to offer a smile in return, even though I know she's in the most agonizing pain. "I won't want to stay up too late."

The well is a good couple of miles from our home, so once I'm outside I quickly grab a bucket and make my way along the edge of the lake. It'd be slightly shorter to go through the forest, but I don't much fancy climbing that wretched hill, so I stick to the low land. Glancing up toward the trees, I see the large, hulking shape of Mr. Nash's new hotel set against the skyline of the setting sun, and deep down I can't help but curse the day that place was first built. I'm sure that if Mr. Nash had placed his hotel elsewhere, Pappa would be much happier and perhaps Mary wouldn't be so ill. And we could be happy.

By the time I get to the well, darkness has almost fallen, but I've done this job so many times that I don't really need light at all. I lower the bucket and collect some water, and then I turn and start making my way home. I hope Pappa will have calmed down by the time I get there, else this evening is liable to be tense and strange. Then again, Pappa has been angry very often of late, so I don't hold out much hope that everything will be okay. I shall simply have to sit with Mary and hope that I'm not called out to perform any further chores until morning.

Fortunately, sitting with Mary is my favorite thing to do in the whole world. Sometimes I feel that I don't need Mamma and Pappa, not really. Mary and I would be quite alright on our own, although I suppose that's a wicked thing to think. Still, the only thing I'm looking forward to right now is the chance to sit on Mary's bed with her and read from one of our books. As long as I have Mary, I can put up with anything else.

Stopping suddenly, I spot flickering flames in the distance, beyond the trees that line the curve of the lake. They seem to be coming from home, and I watch as thick black smoke rises into the darkening sky. Telling myself that something else must be burning, I take a couple of steps forward, but then I realize I can hear the sound of crackling, burning wood in the distance. And something else, too.

Cries and screams.

And one of those screams is Mary.

Dropping the bucket, I race along the lake-shore, desperately trying to get home before the entire house burns to the ground. By the time I get there, however, I'm shocked to see that the flames have really taken hold, roaring through the timbers with the roof having already partially collapsed. Struggling forward as I hear Mamma and Pappa and Mary screaming from within, I have to hold my arm up to protect my face from the heat, but I feel I shall burn to a cinder if I get too close.

"Mary!" I shout. "Where are you?"

Suddenly there's a crashing sound nearby, and I spot something moving in the flames. A moment later, a blackened figure stumbles out with flames rushing from its body. All the hair on its head has been burned away, and I don't recognize the figure at all until suddenly it turns toward me and lets out an agonized cry. As it drops to the ground and falls still, I realize the figure is Pappa, and now the fire is burning through his charred corpse.

Mamma and Mary are still screaming inside, but a moment later I spot movement nearby and I turn to see that several men have run down from the hotel to help.

CHAPTER ELEVEN

"BRING HER IN HERE!" a voice shouts in the distance. "Let me see her!"

Before I can react, a hand grabs the back of my dress and hauls me along the corridor so fast that I can barely keep up. I try to pull away, but the hand's grip is too tight, and a moment later I'm dragged through a doorway and shoved forward with such force that I trip and fall to the floor, landing hard on my knees. Letting out a cry of pain, I wipe tears from my eyes before sitting up, and then I let out a gasp as I find myself staring at Mr. Jobard Nash himself.

He's sitting on the other side of the desk, watching me with a furrowed brow.

"This is *her*?" he asks, sounding highly dubious. "She's rather smaller than I expected."

"She put up quite a fight," the other man explains. "She was screaming while we put the flames out, and then she fought tooth and nail when we tried to bring her up here. I had to strike her a few times around the face, just to get some sense into her. If you ask me, the scrappy little thing is mostly feral."

"She certainly looks uncivilized," Mr. Nash replies, tilting his head slightly while keeping his eyes fixed on me. "Then again, if she was raised by that brutish man and his wife, I suppose she hasn't had much of a chance at life. There is, perhaps, hope for her yet. Have you ascertained the fate of her family?"

"Her parents and sister are dead. There's no doubt of that."

Sobbing, I try to get to my feet, only for the man to put his hand on my shoulder and force me back down. There are so many tears in my eyes, I can barely even see Mr. Nash properly as he continues to watch me with suspicion.

"This one name is Ruth Maywhistle," the man behind me continues. "She's the oldest daughter of that disagreeable bastard who refused to sell you his land."

"Mind your language, please," Mr. Nash replies calmly. "This is a child, after all, and it would not do for her to hear such things. She's no longer in crude company. She must be given a chance to better herself."

The man behind me mutters something under his breath.

"Well, get up," Mr. Nash continues. "Come on, girl, you can't spend the rest of your life cowering on the floor in my office, can you? Somebody is liable to trip over you. You must stand and offer an account of yourself, and mind that it's good. This is going to be my first impression of you, young lady. First impressions are everything."

Not daring to move, yet not daring to break his gaze, I remain in place. After a moment, however, I realize that I'm trembling with fear.

"What's wrong?" he asks. "Cat got your tongue?"

"Answer Mr. Nash," the other man says, kicking me slightly from behind.

I flinch, but I'm still too scared to speak.

"It was a nasty business," Mr. Nash continues finally. "What happened to your family, I mean. I suppose we shall never know what caused that fire, but the house was burned to the ground and your parents perished, along with your sister. I suppose that means, Ms. Maywhistle, that you are the last member of your family left alive. That gives you a certain degree of responsibility."

"We really thought she'd died," the man behind me adds. "She should have been in the house when it went up."

"Then we can only give thanks for this blessing," Mr. Nash continues, getting to his feet and making his way around the desk. "Tell me, child, what do you think I should do with you? I have no need for a child here. I do not even like children. So in what manner am I expected to find you useful?"

Still not daring to speak, I stare up at him with a dreadful feeling of fear in my chest.

"Did your father not teach you to speak?" he adds, raising a skeptical eyebrow as a faint smile crosses his lips.

"She was screaming enough when we cornered her," the other man explains. "We caught her near the new pool area. Took three of us to get her down. She might be young, but she knows how to scratch and claw at a man."

"No doubt," Mr. Nash mutters, before reaching toward me with a black-gloved hand. "You don't need to be afraid, child. I might have a reputation as a hard-nosed man when it comes to my empire, but I assure you that I am not in the business of causing harm to orphans. Please, get up off the floor and perhaps we can come to some kind of arrangement. After all, I can't leave you running around in the forest, can I? You'll scare my guests."

I stare at his gloved hand for a moment, before cautiously reaching out and accepting his help. As I get to my feet, however, I can't shake the feeling that this is a man I must never trust. Before I'm standing properly, I pull my hand free of his, and I regret taking his help in the first place.

"You may leave us, Silas," he says, chuckling as he turns to the other man. "I don't think I'm in any danger here."

Not even daring to turn around, I hear footsteps heading out of the office, followed by the sound of a door swinging shut and then silence. I can tell, even without looking at him, that Mr. Nash is staring down at me, and a moment later he starts walking slowly around me, as if he wishes to see me from all sides. I remember the way Pappa used to examine a pheasant or a rabbit he'd newly shot; he'd examine it physically, of course, but he'd also stare at it for a while, as if he was searching for some deeper truth. As Mr. Nash now continues to walk around me, I think I know how those dead pheasants or rabbits must have felt.

"You have my sincere condolences," he says finally, stopping next to me left elbow and staring down (I assume) at the top of my head. "I know what it's like to lose one's family at an early age. There is potential for great sorrow in such a predicament. Still, it doesn't do to let oneself slip into mawkish sentiment. You must seize the opportunity that has been presented to you, and move forward with determination. Obviously, you have no choice but to come to live and work here at the hotel. As I'm sure you're beginning to understand, I'm a very generous man to those who have not wronged me."

Suddenly he crouches down, and I turn to find his eyes peering at me.

"Or would you prefer to be returned to the wild?" he asks.

Too scared to speak, I wait for him to continue.

"Should I send you out to the forest?" he whispers, as if he's lost in thought. "I could arrange to have scraps of food left out by the kitchen's rear door. You'd be able to forage, to come close to the building from time to time. I'd have my cooks try to chase you away, but I'm sure you'd grow inventive and resourceful over time. It might be instructive to observe your progress as you grow up, changing from a savage and primitive little girl to a savage and primitive young woman. Perhaps you'd barely even have a command of language. You'd communicate mostly by grunts, and you'd be wearing no clothes, and you'd come to see the hotel as a kind of temple or..."

He pauses, and then he lets out a faint, moist trilling sound that seems half like a sigh, and half like a groan.

"Light," he mutters. "Tell me, from out there in the darkness, did you marvel at the lights of my hotel?"

"I..." Pausing, I realize he wants an answer. "Not really."

"You didn't?"

"I mean... I don't think so."

"Then again," he replies with a sigh, "you're more or less savage already. To you, the corridors of the hotel are probably like a jungle, and you have the eyes of a wildling. Not everybody has the potential to rise above their station. I think I should ignore my baser urges and keep you closer. Domesticated. You might become something phenomenal."

Reaching out, he tucks a strand of hair behind my ear, as if he wants to see my face a little more clearly. The thought of working at the hotel sense a shiver through my chest, but I don't suppose I can turn him down. After all, where else am I to go?

"One thing must be made clear right away, however," he continues, suddenly getting to his feet and heading around his desk, where he stops and turns to peer at me once again. "You must not grow up to be in any way like your father. He was a most disagreeable man. Why, just the other day I made him the most generous offer for his land, and for my trouble I had him screaming the most frightful things at me, right here in this room. To say that I was unimpressed would be an understatement. I am not sorry that the man is dead, but obviously I extend my sympathies for the loss of your mother and sister. They were awful, *awful* collateral damage."

He picks up a piece of paper from the desk and reads it for a moment, before setting it back down and holding a pen out toward me.

"Come here, child."

I hesitate, not wanting to get any closer to him. He smells of tobacco.

"I told you to come here," he continues. "Don't make me say it again."

Realizing that I have no choice, I step forward and take the pen.

"I want you to sign this document," he tells me. "It's nothing important, it simply relates to some land. Since you're the only surviving member of your father's family, I shall need you to write your name at the bottom, in the spot that I have indicated."

Standing on tiptoes, I take a look at the piece of paper, which certainly contains a great deal of writing.

"Here," Mr. Nash continues, grabbing my wrist and placing it next to the paper, before taking hold of my hand and forcing me to scrawl a few lines. "That should do it," he continues, taking the pen from me and then examining the signature. "Now, we can get on with more important matters. My dear, you shall be put to work in the rooms. It will be hard work, with long hours, but in return you shall receive board and lodgings, including three meals a day. I hope you realize how generous I am being here. Most men would fling you outside to die."

I know I should thank him, but I feel as if maybe I shouldn't have signed that piece of paper after all. Still on tiptoes, I try to see what the paper says.

"I think we shall become good friends, Ruth," Mr. Nash says after a moment, stepping back in front of me and placing his hands on my shoulders, so that I have no choice but to look up at him as he towers above me. "If you work hard, you'll be rewarded. And believe me, this hotel is only going to grow and grow in popularity. Why, one day soon, Lakeforth Hotel will most likely be the grandest and most famous hotel in the civilized world! What do you have to say about that, eh?"

When I start to move my lips, I find that they're slightly stuck together, since it has been so very long since I last spoke.

***

"You see the shit on this one?" Mrs. Crandall asks, holding up a white sheet with brown stains smeared in the fabric. "This means it needs washing before the next guest comes. You can't just turn it over like I showed you with the others. You'll get complaints if you do that, because the shit shows through from the other side."

She shoves the sheet onto the trolley and then grabs another, tossing it onto the bed. As she does so, she lets out a long, exhausted sigh.

"Sometimes I wonder about the animals who come and stay in this place," she continues finally. "Shit, blood, vomit, and that's just the things I want to admit I recognize. Anything you can think of, sooner or later you'll come to change a room and find someone's left it wiped on the bedding. Or, even worse, on the drapes. There are some filthy beasts in the world, child, and nobody ever went broke underestimating the common man's propensity for vulgarity. Now grab the other side of that thing and help me make this bed."

I take hold of the sheet and help her unfold it, and then she shows me how to fit it to the bed. There are tears in my eyes, so I try to look away so that Mrs. Crandall won't be able to see me properly, but I can tell she's watching my every move. In my mind's eye, I keep imagining myself running from the hotel and going to live in the forest, but I know that I'd only end up starving to death.

"That won't do any good," she says suddenly.

I try to sniff the tears back. "What won't?" I ask.

"Turning into a sniveling wreck. No-one'll respect you, and you'll just get laughed at. If you want to last around here, you'll need to toughen up, which you're more than capable of doing if you just buckle down." She pauses. "You're from that family that used to live in the house down by the lake, aren't you? The house that burned down the other day."

I stare at her, hoping that she might not talk about what happened.

"Terrible business," she continues. "We heard the screams from up here. Must've been trapped inside for a while, until they were overcome by the smoke. Did you have a sister, by any chance?"

I nod.

"That's what I thought. I was sure I heard a little girl's voice screaming from the flames. Her screams seemed so much louder than the rest. Closer, even."

I flinch at the thought of Mary, confined to her bed and shouting for help. I heard her at the time, and I tried desperately to get to the house so I could save her, but the fire was far too strong by the time I arrived. The house burned so fast, it's hard to believe a single candle could have caused such destruction in less than an hour. My face is still a little sore from the heat.

"You're lucky, though," Mrs. Crandall says after a moment. "Mr. Nash'll see you right, provided you show him some respect in return. A man like him is exactly what this area needed. Someone with ambition, someone with drive and determination. Someone who won't take no for an answer." She hesitates, and now there's a very faint smile on her lips. "He *never* takes no. Not ever. There are plenty of people who've learned that the hard way. In fact, I wouldn't be surprised if..."

Her voice trails off for a moment, and she watches me as her smile grows.

"Well," she adds finally, "there's no need to talk about that, is there? What's done is done, and it's men like Mr. Nash who prosper. You'll see soon enough, child. This hotel'll be the talk of the world, and people'll flock here from other countries. When a man like Mr. Nash sets his mind to something, he simply refuses to fail. The possibility just never enters his head. And the rest of us? We're just the lucky ones who get to hang onto his coat-tails. Sometimes, I wonder if maybe one day he'll actually speak to me. I can't imagine how happy that would make me."

She hesitates for a moment, watching me intently, before stepping closer and crouching down in front of me. To my surprise, she puts her hands on the sides of my face.

"Never forget that fact," she continues, her eyes bright with excitement. "We're lucky to be here. Mr. Nash is the most perfect man in the whole world."

***

Later in the evening, after I've finished my first day of work, and after I've eaten bread and jam in the kitchen for dinner, and after I've made up my bed in the corner of the storeroom next to the kitchen, I finally manage to sneak away from the hotel and hurry past the edge of the gardens. I know I'm not supposed to leave the estate, but there's one thing I have to see for myself.

When I get closer to the lake, I find that Mr. Nash was telling the truth earlier when he said work would begin immediately. Already, the burned and ruined timbers of the house Pappa built have been partially torn away, and there are tools propped against nearby trees. With the sun setting in the distance, casting sparkling light across the lake's surface, I edge closer to the ruins of the house, and I can't help remembering the screams I heard on the night of the fire. Although I saw Pappa's body falling from the flames, it's Mary I think of the most as I stand here.

"Mary?" I whisper, daring her ghost to come to me. "Are you here?"

I make my way around the side of the ruins, but Mary's ghost doesn't appear, nor does she say anything.

"Pappa? Mamma? Are you here?"

The only sound comes from the trees as they rustle nearby.

"Mary, please," I continue, close to tears. "Can you come back as a ghost? Can you give me a sign? It doesn't have to be anything big, but just one sign would do, so I know you're close."

I wait.

Nothing comes.

I spend a few more minutes exploring the ruins, and for a while it occurs to me that I really *could* try to run away from the hotel. I could find a road and follow it, and who knows what I'd come to? I might even make it all the way to London if I really walked fast. Then again, I might die horribly, and I can't do that. I think I'm the only person in the whole world who remembers Mary, which means she only exists now in my head. So I have to try to stay alive for as long as possible, and that means staying at the hotel.

At least for now.

Finally I head back up to the main building and go to my bed in the storeroom. I cry for a long time, as I listen to the sounds of people working in the rooms above me. A hotel is a noisy place, as it turns out, and I don't manage to sleep until well after midnight. Even then, once most of the sounds have died down, there's a faint and very distant banging that persists for several more hours. I don't know exactly when I finally fall asleep, but the respite is all too brief. I don't even dream of Mary or Mamma or Pappa, at least not that I remember. And after what seems like no time at all, I open my eyes and find that morning has come, and all the noises have started up again.

"Come on!" Mrs. Crandall yells, pushing the door open. "Get up, girl! We've got more work to do!"

She sets me to work in the dining room, putting out plates and cups for breakfast. A few guests watch me as they come down, and they smile at me as if they think I'm being good.

CHAPTER TWELVE

"I'M GOING TO SHOW you why you should trust me!" Mr. Nash says, grabbing my arm and dragging me across his office. He stinks of whiskey, and he seems a little unsteady on his feet as he pushes me against the wall and then steps back. "I can see it in your eyes. You doubt me."

"No, I -"

"Don't disagree with me!" he yells angrily. "Don't ever disagree with me! I'm always right!"

Swallowing hard, I watch as he stumbles back over to his desk, where his unfinished lunch has been left on a tray. I'd have thought he was a neat and tidy man, but he's left crumbs all over the desk. I expect he has someone else to clean those up for him.

"Mrs. Crandall said I'm to go back and help with the rooms as soon as possible," I tell him cautiously, hoping against hope that he'll let me go. "It seemed very important."

Instead of replying, he simply mumbles something under his breath as he takes a tea cup, pours its contents onto the floor, and then comes stumbling back toward me.

"I want you to hold this," he slurs.

"But -"

"Don't argue!"

He shoves the cup into my hands, so firmly that I'm surprised it doesn't break.

"Hold it up," he continues, taking hold of my wrist and forcing me to hold the cup high above my head. "Now don't move. Don't move a muscle, is that understood? Stay still!"

Turning, he makes his way back toward his desk, where he stops for a moment to go through the various drawers. I don't know exactly what he's doing, but I remember seeing Pappa get drunk like this. Of course, Pappa always used to pass out in his armchair before he became too loud, whereas Mr. Nash just seems to get more and more agitated. Even now, he's muttering to himself, and I flinch slightly as he pulls a drawer out from the desk and tosses it to the floor, sending papers and other items all over the place.

"There!" he says suddenly, triumphantly holding up a revolver.

My eyes widen with horror, but I don't dare run to the door.

"Now hold that cup up high," he continues, closing one eye as he struggles to load some bullets into the chamber. "The higher the better. It's for your own benefit."

He hiccups, and this seems to amuse him. He laughs.

I open my mouth to ask again if I can be excused, but at the last moment I tell myself I'll probably only make him angry. Instead, I watch as he fumbles with the bullets, and finally he drops several and seems unable to get down and pick them up. Still, he managed to load two, I think, and he closes the chamber before stumbling toward the far window and peering out.

"Look at them down there," he mumbles. "My guests. They look like ants from here."

He pauses, before suddenly turning to aim the gun directly at me.

I immediately flinch.

"Hold still!" he sneers, and I watch as the gun trembles in his shaking hand. "What's wrong with you, girl? Don't you trust me? You will. You'll learn to. Soon, you'll see why men all across the -"

Suddenly the gun fires, blasting a chunk of plaster loose from the wall about two feet to my left. I flinch, almost dropping the cup, but I don't dare turn and run. The door is only a few steps away, but I know he'd only insist that I come straight back.

"Nearly," he mutters, with one eye closed as he tries to aim the trembling gun at the cup. "Nearly, nearly..."

He falls silent for a moment, still struggling to aim properly. After a moment, he grabs his whiskey bottle and takes another swig, before setting it down and returning to the business of aiming the gun at the cup.

"How old are you, Ruth?" he asks.

"I'm eight," I tell him, and for a moment I'm tempted to ask if I can leave now.

"You'll make somebody a very fine wife one day," he continues, watching me with a faint smile as the gun continues to shake in his hand. "Very fine indeed. You're lucky to live where you do, my dear. You could be married in as little as another seven years, perhaps even less if nobody is paying too much attention. Perhaps you might even marry a great man, such as myself. In fact, if I am still in need of a wife in a few years' time, you shall perhaps marry the greatest man in the country. I'm sure you know to whom I am referring. I'll tame the savagery out of you."

I think he's talking about himself, but I hope I'm wrong. Mr. Nash is an older man, surely in his late forties or early fifties at least, and I can't imagine any girl ever wanting to spend time with him unless she is forced to do so. In fact, I wonder if perhaps -

Suddenly the gun fires again, blasting a hole in the wall just inches from me and causing me to drop the cup. I look down, shocked, as the cup hits the floor and smashes, and then I hear Mr. Nash starting to laugh. Looking over at him, I see that he has set the gun on the desk, and he's chuckling to himself.

"See, my dear?" he laughs. "Second time lucky!"

Realizing that he thinks he hit the cup, I decide it would be unwise to tell him otherwise. It would also be unwise to ask if I might leave now, so I simply stand and wait as he slumps into his chair and continues to laugh. I tell myself that he has to stop laughing soon, that he might even pass out. Yet his laughter continues, going on and on, and all I can do is stand and wait and hope very much that soon I shall be allowed to leave.

I just have to wait for him to stop laughing first.

***

"The sheets are at the end of the corridor," Mrs. Crandall told me a few minutes ago, as she sent me down here to the bowels of the hotel. "Don't be a difficult child, just go to the basement, go to the end of the corridor, and take as many fresh sheets as you can carry. And bring them up here as quickly as possible."

The task sounded simple enough at the time, but now I'm down here and there's absolutely no sign of any sheets at all. I've found some shelves, but they're entirely empty and I don't much like the idea of going any further into the basement. The place is so horribly dark, with just a few electric lights placed high up on the bare bricks walls, and the air all around me is very cold. At the same time, I know Mrs. Crandall will be furious with me if I return empty-handed, so I force myself to be brave and to head further along the corridor, going deeper into the darkness.

Suddenly I stop, listening to the sounds of the guests' footsteps in the rooms above. There seems to be another sound nearby, a little closer than all the others, as if somebody is weeping.

"Hello?" I call out cautiously, and the weeping immediately stops.

I wait, but now all I hear is laughter from upstairs. I think I'm directly beneath the dining room, and lunch is in full swing. There are so many people up there, laughing and talking and eating, and the noise almost drowned out the sobbing that I briefly heard.

Almost, but not quite entirely.

"Hello?" I continue, stepping forward toward a doorway that opens into a pitch-black room. "Is somebody down here? I heard a -"

Stopping suddenly, I realize that perhaps the sobbing came from somebody else who works at the hotel, perhaps somebody who was upset by Mr. Nash. I suppose I shouldn't interfere, so I hesitate for a moment before turning to go back.

"Ruthie?" a whimpering voice calls out suddenly.

I freeze for a moment, before turning to look into the darkness again.

"Ruthie, is that you?" the voice continues. "Oh Ruthie, please, say it's you!"

I recognize that voice.

It's Mary, but I know it *can't* be her, not really. I must be going completely mad.

"Ruthie, help me," she sobs. "Ruthie, I'm so cold down here, and it hurts so much. Ruthie, please, do you have something I can eat?"

I step closer to the doorway again, but I still can't quite believe what I'm hearing. I know, with absolute certainty in my heart, that Mary died in the fire. After all, I heard her screams. Yet as I take a step through the doorway into the colder air of the next room, I'm quite certain I can hear her breathless sobs. I've heard Mary cry many times over the years, and I swear I'm not wrong.

"Please, Ruthie," she continues. "I'm in so much pain."

I hesitate, convinced that this has to be some kind of illusion or trick.

"Why don't you say anything?" she asks. "Do you hate me? Has he turned you against me?"

"Who?" I stammer.

"Mr. Nash, of course. Please, Ruthie, I haven't been given anything for my burns, and the pain is so very awful. I can barely even think, the pain drowns all my thoughts. I can't walk and my skin... I'm still burning, Ruthie. The flames are gone but I can feel the heat still in my flesh, all the way to the bone."

"Mary?" I whisper, staring ahead into the darkness.

"Help me!" she gasps, and suddenly I hear a rustling, dragging sound, as if fabric is being pulled across the bare concrete floor.

Coming closer.

"Why won't you help me?" she sobs. "Ruthie, it's me! It's Mary! Why are you just standing there like that?"

The dragging sound continues. Although the room ahead of me is completely dark, there's a very faint patch of light at my feet, cast by an electric light behind my shoulder. Staring down at the concrete floor, as the dragging sound comes closer and closer, I feel a rising sense of dread in my gut, but I know I can't turn and run. I can't leave Mary, even if...

Suddenly she lets out a gasp of pain, and the

dragging sound stops.

"I can't," she sobs. "Help me..."

Stepping forward, I move past the patch of light and into the dark, cold room. I can still hear Mary crying, and I follow the sound through the darkness until finally I feel that I must almost be standing on top of her. I stop and listen again, and then I crouch down and reach my hands out in the dark.

"Where are you?" I whisper. "Ruthie, I -"

Suddenly I feel something.

A shuddering, sobbing shoulder, barely covered by scraps of torn fabric. As my fingertips brush the shoulder, however, I'm horrified to feel charred, torn flesh that seems horribly dry and burned in some places and wet, almost sticky in others.

"Do you have something for my burns?" Mary cries. "Please, Ruthie, anything to make the pain stop..."

Still convinced that I must be imagining the whole thing, I run my hand along her shoulder until I reach the side of her neck. Her entire body seems to be convulsing as she continues to sob, but now I can feel her damp, matted hair between my fingers, and I force myself to touch the side of her burned face. At first, I feel a faint flutter of relief as I realize that here at least her flesh feels soft and undamaged. After a moment, however, my fingertips brush against some kind of rippled edge, and I realize that part of her flesh has burned away entirely, leaving me touching the meat and muscle beneath.

"Ruthie, help," she sobs. "Don't leave me down here. Get help, or..."

Her voice trails off for a moment.

"Make the pain stop," she continues. "One way or another, make it stop hurting. Ruthie, please..."

"You're not real," I whisper. "You died in the fire."

"Help me..."

"I heard you. I heard you as you were dying, Mary."

She tries to reply, but her voice breaks into a series of shuddering, breathless sobs, and I can feel her body shaking as my hand rests on the side of her face. I try telling myself that this is all in my head, that the shock of the past few days has caused me awful visions, but I'm feeling a rising sense of panic in my chest and finally I realize that I can't just walk away. Whatever has happened to Mary, I have to help her.

"Wait here," I stammer finally. "Just wait right here. I'll go and find someone."

"Don't leave me!" she gasps.

"I have to go and get help!"

Stumbling to my feet, I turn and hurry back to the doorway, although I hesitate for a moment as I hear Mary's wretched sobs getting louder and louder. At the same time, I can hear chair legs scraping against the floor of the room above me, and the sound of laughter in the distance. I want to turn back and go to Mary again, but deep down I know she can't be real. Either she has sprung unbidden from the deepest traumas in my mind, or she's some kind of spirit that has come back to the world and stopped to rest here in the basement.

"Please," she groans, as if she's getting weaker

and weaker. "Ruthie, help me..."

"I will," I whisper, before hurrying along the corridor and then making my way up the stairs. As I reach the door and push it open, I tell myself that I shall have to find somebody who knows better than I what to -

"And where have you been?" Mrs. Crandall sneers, as I almost slam straight into her.

"I was in the basement!" I stammer, stepping back and bumping against the wall.

"And where are the sheets you were supposed to fetch, young lady? I've been waiting upstairs in room nine for so long, I began to worry that you'd puffed out of existence entirely."

"I found..."

My voice trails off as I stare up at her. She looks so angry, but at the same time I can't think of anybody else in this entire hotel who might be able to help me.

"My sister," I say finally. "I think I found my sister down there."

She raises a skeptical eyebrow. "Your *what*?"

"My sister Mary," I continue. "She's crying in one of the dark rooms and -"

"Your sister Mary is dead, dear," she replies, interrupting me. "You were told that, were you not? She died tragically in the fire."

"But I..."

Again, my voice trails off.

"I found her," I add finally, trembling with fear. "I heard her voice, and I felt her. She's in the room at the far end, under the dining room. I know it sounds like it can't be true, but she's really there!"

"She is, is she?" Mrs. Crandall mutters, clearly very unimpressed as she steps past me and heads down the stairs. "We'll soon see about that. Wait up here while I go and check for ghosts. And I suppose I shall have to find the sheets, while I'm at it. God forbid that you might have some gumption."

She continues to grumble and complain as she heads down into the basement, leaving me standing completely alone. A moment later, hearing footsteps nearby, I turn and see a man and a woman leaving the dining room, heading toward the reception area. They're dressed in very fine clothes, and suddenly the woman turns and looks at me. I see the disgust in her eyes, as if the mere sight of me is repulsive, and she quickly hurries to keep up with her husband as he makes his way around the far corner.

Hearing someone coming up the stairs, I turn just as Mrs. Crandall emerges from the basement.

"Well, we'll have to find some sheets from the laundry room," she tells me, quickly closing and locking the door. "I suppose someone forgot to put them in their usual place. Come along, Ruth."

"Did you look in the room at the end of the corridor?" I ask, as she turns and starts walking toward the staff stairwell.

"There was nothing there," she replies, not even bothering to look back at me. "Of course there wasn't. Don't fill your head with such nonsense, girl. We're busy enough as it is, without the likes of you imagining this, that and the other."

As she starts going up the stairs, I look down at

my hands. To my surprise, I see that my fingertips are glistening with traces of wet blood. Pressing my fingers together, I expect to find that the blood is another illusion, but instead I find that I'm able to smear it against my own flesh. I'm still quite sure that my encounter with Mary in the basement must have been some moment of madness, but I don't understand why I seem to have some of her blood on my hands. Actual, real blood.

"Girl!" Mrs. Crandall shrieks from the stairs. "Come! At once!"

Fearful of being beaten, I hurry after her.

CHAPTER THIRTEEN

FLAT ON MY BACK in bed, I stare at the dark ceiling and listen to the sound of the cooks finally getting ready to leave the kitchen next door. They've taken forever, and it must be past midnight by now, but I don't dare go out until they're all gone. For one thing, some of them have leering eyes, and I really don't want their attention. And for another, they might ask why I'm up and where I'm going, and I can't possibly tell them.

Eventually I hear the kitchen door click shut, and I wait a few more minutes until I'm certain that there's nobody in the next room. Finally, I climb out of bed and pick my way carefully across through the darkness, taking care not to trip on any of the sacks of flour that have been left on the concrete. I know I should be well-behaved and stay in bed, but my mind is racing and I don't think I'll ever be able to sleep again, not until I know for certain whether my sister's ghost is really in the basement.

Even if she's dead, Mary might still need me.

***

"Hello?" I call out cautiously, trying not to shout too loud just in case anyone hears me. "Mary? Are you here?"

I wait, holding a candle up to cast flickering light across the doorway in the basement. All I see in the next room is darkness, and so far there's been no hint of movement. I haven't heard so much as a whisper, and deep down I'm already starting to think that the whole thing must have been a figment of my imagination earlier. After all, why would Mary's ghost be in the hotel, and why would she be begging me for help?

"It's me," I continue. "It's Ruthie. Mary, are -"

"Ruthie?" a faint, weak voice gasps suddenly. "You came back?"

I take a deep breath, forcing myself to stay where I am instead of turning and running. The air is so cold down here, and I fear that I must be going completely mad.

"They didn't bring anything for me," she whispers. "A woman came and looked at me, but she wouldn't help. It hurts so much, Ruthie. Why are they doing this? You have to get me out of here."

I wait.

Silence.

"Ruthie?" she continues finally. "Are you still here? Ruthie, please -"

"I'm still here," I tell her, feeling a knot of panic

in my chest. "I promise."

"Can you come closer? Do you have food?"

Reaching into my pocket, I take out the piece of bread I wrapped in a napkin. I don't know why I bothered, since I'm sure ghosts can't eat, but I suppose I just felt that I had to bring something. Stepping forward, I make my way through the doorway, and then I realize that I've inadvertently lowered the candle. Perhaps I just don't want to see whatever state my dear sister might be in, but slowly I force myself to raise the candle again, and then I gasp as soon as I see Mary's bloodied, burned and near-naked body shivering on the bare concrete. Curled into a ball, she's staring up at me, her eyes bright white against the charred black and red of her face.

"Help me," she shudders. "Ruthie, please..."

Forgetting all my fear for a moment, I hurry forward and drop to my knees. Setting the candle next to her, I hold the piece of bread out and watch with horror as she reaches up and takes the food with her burned, reddened hands. I swear I can hear her flesh crinkling as she moves the bread to her lips, and she flinches as if the merest touch is enough to cause excruciating pain. She doesn't stop eating, however, and she seems to be wolfing the bread down as if it's the first thing she's eaten in days. As she does so, I can't help noticing that some parts of her left hand have been burned so badly that patches of bone are showing through around the knuckles, while several of her fingers appear to have been completely torn away.

"Water," she gasps finally, once she's finished the bread. "Give me water."

"Wait!"

Hurrying back out of the room, I fetch a cup of water from the kitchen. By the time I get back down to Mary, I find that she's tried to prop herself against the wall, leaving a smeared trail of blood and loosened skin on the concrete floor. Figuring that she's probably too weak to hold the cup properly, I lift it to her lips and pour the water into her mouth, and I hear the sound of it flowing down the back of her throat. Finally, once the cup is empty, I set it down on the ground.

"I'll fetch more," I tell her, although for a moment I can only stare at her ravaged face. "Do you feel better now, Mary? Did the food help?"

"We have to..."

She pauses, as if she can barely get the words out. If I didn't know better, I'd swear that she seems weaker than before. The more I look at her, the more I find it hard to believe that she's a ghost, but I know deep down that she's definitely dead.

"We have to get out of here," she manages finally. "We have to... go before he comes back..."

"Before *who* comes back?" I ask.

I wait for an answer, but she's simply staring at me as if she expects me to know already.

"Do you mean Mr. Nash?" I continue. "Has he been down here? Does he know about you?"

Her lips move slightly, but all that emerges is a faint sigh.

"But you're a ghost," I point out. "You don't have to just sit here like this. You can't even be hurt, can you? All you have to do is get up and walk through a wall and go somewhere else. You can probably even move your legs again!"

She stares at me, and now her eyes have opened a little wider, as if she's shocked by what I said.

"You *know* you're a ghost, don't you?" I continue, with tears in my eyes. "Mary, our house was burned down. Mamma and Pappa and you died, and I managed to survive because I was off getting water from the well. Are Mamma and Pappa down here too? Did *their* ghosts come back?"

"Ruthie," she whispers. "Ruthie, please, it hurts so much..."

"You can't feel pain!" I tell her again. "Look, I'll prove it!"

Reaching out, I place a hand on her bloodied arm, but she immediately lets out a searing, agonized cry and I instinctively pull back. Sobbing now, she turns her head away from me slightly, and I see that her bottom lip is trembling.

"That can't have been real," I continue, although when I look at my palm I see that some of my sister's charred flesh has come away from her meat, sticking instead to my hand. "I don't understand, I can't -"

"They pulled me out," she groans, her voice trembling with sorrow. "Right out of the flames, Ruthie. They reached through the window and pulled me out. Mamma and Pappa was screaming, but they left them to burn and they took me out and brought me here. And then they just left me in the dark."

Slowly, she turns to me with a hint of anger in her eyes.

"Mr. Nash comes down twice a day," she sneers, "and does things to me in the dark. He says he doesn't want to see me, so there can't be any lights. He talks about such strange things, about making me live in the forest as some kind of wild thing. He stinks of whiskey and he hits me. It hurts so much, Ruthie. The last time, I just wanted him to kill me, but he wouldn't even do that. He'll be back again soon, I know it, and then he'll hurt me some more. I can't even scream, because he puts something over my mouth. Sometimes I hear people above, laughing and talking in one of the other rooms, and I'm down here trying to cry out but I can't! My throat is burned!"

She breaks into a series of convulsing sobs, and for a moment I can only stare in shock at her ravaged features. If she's really alive, then I have to get her out of here right now, even though I don't have a clue how to start. There's nobody I can ask for help, nobody I can trust at all, but it's the middle of the night so I might be able to sneak her out. She can't walk, though, and I don't know if I'm strong enough to carry her, so I'm going to have to find some kind of cart or wheelbarrow. My mind is racing as I try to come up with a plan, but then I gasp as Mary reaches out and puts a hand on my wrist.

"Either get me out of here," she whispers, "or kill me. I don't mind either. Just promise you won't leave me down here alone."

"I promise," I stammer, "I just... I don't know where we can go."

"Anywhere. Anywhere that means we're away from him."

"I'll figure something out," I tell her. "It's only just gone midnight, so if we leave now we can be far from here by the time the sun comes up. Hopefully that should give us a head-start, and then they won't be able to catch us. And then we can find someone and tell them about this place, and Mr. Nash'll be arrested and we can live somewhere else."

"Hurry," she groans. "There's not much time. I don't want to die down here."

"I'll go and find something to put you in," I reply, starting to get up, only for her to grab my arm again. Turning, I see fear in her eyes. "I *have* to go," I continue, "just for a few minutes. I'll be back really soon, I promise, but I have to go!"

She stares at me for a moment, before slowly letting go of my arm.

"Don't leave me too long," she says cautiously. "And leave the candle. Please, I don't want to be in the dark again, in case... I just don't want to be in the dark, Ruthie. I'm scared I might never see light again."

"I'll be back soon," I reply, turning and heading out the door. I still don't know where I'm going, not really, but I figure I'll work something out. Hurrying up the stairs, I push the door open, and then I stop for a moment as I try to come up with a plan.

The garden.

There's a shed out there, where the hotel's gardener keeps all his tools. If I can get ahold of his wheelbarrow, I can use it to carry Mary far from here. I know the plan isn't perfect, but it's all I have right now, so I hurry along the corridor and around the next corner, determined to -

"There you are!" Silas says suddenly, grabbing my arm and twisting me around so hard that I slam against the nearest wall. "I've been looking for you, young lady! Mr. Nash has requested the pleasure of your company!"

CHAPTER FOURTEEN

"THE SWIMMING POOL IS key to all of this," Mr. Nash mutters drunkenly, as he peers at the model on his desk. "Once the pool is in place, and once people hear about the marvelous improvements I've made, we'll be packed to the rafters throughout the season. I'll order the men to stop their other projects by the lake and focus on the pool."

He makes his way around to the other side of the desk, still examining the model. He's holding a bottle of whiskey in one hand, and it's clear that he's been drinking for most of the day. I know from experience with Pappa that it's best not to interrupt a man when he's drunk, and that it's quite possible Mr. Nash will completely forget that I'm here. Although he's been talking for the past few minutes, he seems to be talking mostly to himself, and he hasn't glanced at me for a while now, or at Silas.

If Silas leaves, then perhaps I can slip away.

"I am a great man," he continues after a moment, stepping back from the desk and swaying for a moment as he stares at the model. "Like all great men, however, I find myself forced to operate in a world of fools. There must be some way to make them recognize all the work I've done here. It's my money that built this hotel, and my money that paid for the road that leads here. I can only suppose that, like all great men, I shall have to be patient while I wait for the world to recognize my achievements."

I wait, but now he seems lost in thought.

All I want is to get out of here and go to find a wheelbarrow, so that I can get Mary out of this place. There's a part of me that wants to scream at Mr. Nash, to tell him that I know he had my sister brought here, but I know there's no point making him angry. So long as he doesn't know that I found Mary, it'll be much easier for me to steal her away from the hotel. I just have to be smart about this.

Mr. Nash is mumbling about something now, but I can't make out any of the words.

Glancing to my right, I see that Silas is still standing by the door. He'll try to stop me if I make a move to leave.

"The average man is an idiot," Mr. Nash says suddenly, getting down onto his knees and squinting as he examines the model. "If the world were filled with men of my standard, oh..."

Again, his voice slips into a mumbled whisper, before he suddenly reaches across the desk and picks up his revolver. Clearly struggling to even see properly, he checks the chamber to make sure there are bullets, and then he pauses as if he's suddenly shocked by something. In his drunken state, he seems almost to be hearing voices in his head.

I have to get back to Mary.

I promised I'd be back soon.

She must be wondering where I am.

Suddenly Mr. Nash mumbles something unintelligible and struggles to his feet, grabbing a paperweight from his desk and bringing it over to me. Still muttering under his breath, he slips the paperweight into my hands and then forces me to hold it up, and I immediately realize that he means to try another bout of target practice.

"They mock me," he mutters, shuffling back past his desk and then stopping in front of the window and turning to aim at the paperweight. "Can you believe that? They have the temerity, those pathetic and insignificant wretches, to mock and -"

Suddenly the gun fires, and I flinch as a shower of plaster rains down on me from above. When I dare to look up, I see that the bullet hit the wall several inches from the paperweight.

Still muttering under her breath, Mr. Nash leans against the desk for a moment, as if he might be about to pass out. I wait for him to try shooting the paperweight again, but now he almost seems to have fallen asleep. Staying completely still for a few minutes, I tell myself that I have to be patient, although eventually I start wondering whether Silas might let me leave.

"The other one," Mr. Nash mumbles finally,

lifting his head and looking over at Silas. "Maybe you should bring the other one up here."

"She can't hardly walk," he replies. "I haven't checked on her for a while. She might even be dead by now."

"Well, go and take a look. If she's got a pulse, bring her up here. And use the back stairs, so none of the guests can see."

Sighing, Silas turns to leave the room.

"Leave her alone!" I shout, panicking at the thought that he might be going to fetch Mary. "Please, don't hurt her!"

As soon as those words have left my mouth, I know I've made a terrible mistake. Turning to Mr. Nash, I can already see that I've piqued his curiosity.

"You've seen her, have you?" he mutters with a faint smile, before aiming the gun at me again. "You shouldn't go poking about, young lady. That's a sign of bad character."

"Leave her alone," I stammer again, still holding the paperweight up. "Please, I'll do -"

Before I can get another word out, the gun fires for a second time. I squeeze my eyes tight shut, just as a loud blast fills my ears, and the paperweight falls from my hand. As I open my eyes again, I see the paperweight hit the floor and roll, although it doesn't break. At the same time, Mr. Nash is laughing hysterically, and I turn to see that he's slumped back down in his office chair. He seems vastly, vastly amused by something, although I'm relieved to see that he's set the gun down, and a moment later Silas steps over to the door and leaves the room.

"Can I go?" I ask, once I've been left alone with Mr. Nash.

He doesn't reply. He doesn't stop laughing. Finally, after a couple more minutes, I dare hurry to the door. Behind me, Mr. Nash is laughing louder than ever.

***

"I'm back!" I shout, hurrying through the darkness until I reach the room where I left Mary earlier. "I'm sorry I was so long, but I'm back now!"

Stopping in the doorway, I see to my immense relief that she's still where I left her. The candle has burned down quite considerably, but at least it still casts a flickering light as Mary keeps her eyes fixed on the opposite wall. She hesitates for a moment, and I can see a hint of fear in her eyes, but I can't blame her for that. She must be in immense pain, and she probably thought that I'd abandoned her.

"Mr. Nash was drunk again," I explain, stepping forward. "I haven't had time to find a wheelbarrow, but I'm worried he might send Silas down to hurt you, so we're going to have to move right now! I'm going to take you to the road, and from there we're going to walk and walk until somebody finds us. I know there's a chance we'll be brought straight back here, but we just have to hope for the best. If we meet somebody who's kind, everything might be alright again!"

I wait, but Mary doesn't look at me. She hasn't even acknowledged me since I returned, so I kneel next to her and place a hand on her shoulder.

"Mary!" I hiss. "We have to go!"

Suddenly she turns and looks down at her shoulder, as if she's shocked.

"Mary!" I continue, glancing briefly back through the doorway to make sure that there's no sign of Silas coming down to fetch her. When I turn back to my sister, I find to my relief that she's finally looking at me again. "You have to listen to me! You have to believe me! It's not safe for us to stay here! Silas will come down soon, and then there'll be nothing else we can do, so we have to move!"

I wait, but she's just staring at me.

"Mary -"

"Ruthie?" she whispers.

"I'm right here," I tell her, worried that she might be slipping away. She seems dazed, perhaps even a little confused. "Do you think you can walk?"

She hesitates for a moment, before slowly shaking her head.

"I'll carry you," I continue, even though I'm not sure I'm strong enough. Nevertheless, I reach my hands under her burned body, and then I start to lift her from the concrete floor.

She immediately lets out an agonized cry, and I pull back. She's gasping now, clearly suffering, but I don't know how else I'm supposed to get her out of here. My mind is racing and I keep telling myself that there has to be a way, but I'm not very smart and I'm worried I'll let my sister down. Just as I'm about to start really panicking, however, I remember that Mrs. Crandall showed me some laundry trolleys earlier in the day. One of those, filled with sheets, would be much better than a wheelbarrow.

"I know what to do!" I stammer, getting to my feet and hurrying back to the door. "Wait here!"

"Ruthie..."

"Just wait!"

"Ruthie, look at me!"

Stopping in the doorway, I turn to her.

"Is it really you?" she whispers, her voice trembling as if she's more afraid than before.

"We don't have time!"

"But are you really there?" she continues. "Ruthie, my darling Ruthie..."

I wait for her to finish the sentence, but she seems almost to be falling asleep.

"I'm going to find a trolley," I tell her, terrified that Silas might arrive at any moment. "There'll be time for us to talk later, but right now I have to get you away from here!"

Turning, I make my way back to the stairs and up to the main part of the hotel. This time, I'm much more careful to make sure that Silas isn't lurking anywhere, and I manage to make it all the way to the laundry room without seeing another soul. I fill one of the trolleys with sheets, before wheeling it out into the corridor and pushing it toward the door that leads down to the basement. My arms are already aching, and I still don't know exactly where I'll take Mary once I get her outside, but I'll figure that part out later. I still have hope, and I know that anybody we meet on the road has to be kinder than Mr. Nash.

Right now, I just have to make sure Mary doesn't scream when I carry her up the stairs. I might have to put my hand firmly over her mouth, but if that's what it takes, then that's what it takes.

"I'm back!" I tell her as soon as I get back down the stairs. "I know it's going to hurt, Mary, but I have to take you up to the next floor. And then -"

Stopping suddenly, I see that the candle is no longer burning in the next room.

"Mary?" I whisper, stepping forward into the cold air. "Where are you?"

When she doesn't reply, I reach down to the spot where I left her. Although my hands quickly find the candle, which has been knocked over and snuffed out, there's no sign of my sister, not even when I fumble in the darkness and check the rest of the room. In the few minutes I was gone, she's somehow disappeared entirely.

"Mary!" I hiss, starting to panic. "Mary, where did you go?"

It takes me several more minutes to check the room without any light, but finally I'm certain that there's no sign of her. Heading back toward the stairs, I look for any hint that she might have tried dragging herself to safety, but it's almost as if she simply disappeared without a trace. Finally, I make my way back up the stairs and into the main part of the hotel, but I don't even know where to begin looking. I can't call out, because then other people would realize that something's wrong and Mr. Nash might decide to punish us. Instead, I make my way through all the rooms near the top of the stairs, while telling myself that whatever she decided to do, Mary can't possibly have managed to get very far.

Reaching the dining room, I hurry between the tables and stop at the window, looking out at the patio in case there's any sign of her. At first, I don't see anything at all, but after a moment I realize I can see movement out in the trees, as if someone is in the forest and heading toward the lake.

"Mary?" I whisper, trying to figure out why she'd do such a thing, before realizing that she might be delirious. Filled with panic, I take a step back, before turning and running back out of the room. "Mary!"

It takes a few more minutes until I manage to get out to the patio, and then I hurry past the chairs and tables and run into the forest. I can't see anyone now, of course, and the entire forest is pitch-black, but I can just about make out the moonlit shimmering lake far off in the distance. I can't quite believe that Mary is apparently able to move so quickly, and after a few more paces I start wondering whether perhaps I was mistaken, but then I spot a silhouetted figure far off between the trees.

It's not Mary.

It's a man, and he's carrying something.

He's carrying a girl's body.

"Mary!" I scream, racing forward between the trees. Silas must have gone down to the basement and carried her out, and I have to stop him before he reaches the lake. As I continue to run, however, I feel as if I'll never catch up, and I lose sight of the silhouette a few times before finally I burst out from the tree-line and find myself on the lake's shore.

I look both ways, and I quickly spot Silas standing at the end of the little wooden jetty. Staring at him, I'm horrified to see that he's wrapped Mary's body in blood-stained sheets, and he's using ropes to tie rocks to her feet and neck.

"Mary!" I scream, racing toward them. "Stop!"

Before I can reach the jetty, however, I see Silas shoving the body over the edge, sending her crashing into the water.

"Get her out of there!" I yell. "She'll drown!"

Scrambling along the jetty, I rush past Silas as he walks the other way. When I reach the end, however, I look down into the moonlit water and see nothing but darkness.

Behind me, Silas is whistling as he wanders back toward the forest.

"Help me!" I scream, turning to him as I break into a series of desperate, breathless sobs. "You have to help me get her out of there! Please!"

Ignoring me, and still whistling, Silas strolls out of view, leaving me to turn and look back down into the water. After a moment, realizing that there might still be a chance, I swing my legs over the side of the jetty and drop down, crashing into the water and finding that it's much deeper than I'd expected. My feet aren't even touching the bottom of the lake, and I tread water for a moment before diving down in a desperate attempt to find my sister.

After searching for almost a minute, I come back up for air, but I know I don't have any time to lose. I have to find her soon, so I dive down again, swimming deeper and deeper into the darkness, reaching out and hoping that my hands will finally feel her somewhere in the depths.

CHAPTER FIFTEEN

BY THE TIME MORNING comes, and rays of sunlight reach across the still, glittering lake, I've finally given up the search for my sister. I know it's too late, that she's been down in the water for a couple of hours now, and that she must surely have drowned.

And perhaps she was dead even before she was dropped down there. Perhaps Silas and Mr. Nash killed her before she was taken from the basement.

Sitting on the edge of the jetty, sobbing as I think of how close I came to saving Mary, I feel for a while as if I might never be able to move again. Part of me wants to put rocks in my pockets and jump back into the water, to sink down and join my sister so that we can be together forever. Before I do that, however, I know that I have to make sure that the people who killed her are forced to pay for their crimes. And as I stare down at the water, I feel a slowly rising sense of anger in my chest, before finally I turn and look up at the hotel high on the hill.

I'm going to go to Mr. Nash. I'm going to kill him. And I'm going to do it right now.

PART FIVE

ELLEN NASH
1945

CHAPTER SIXTEEN

Dear Mother and Father,

I am writing this letter from my own private desk in my own private bedroom at the Lakeforth. This is no exaggeration, nor is it intended to sound boastful. I merely wish to assuage your concerns, and to assure you that Jobard Nash is taking great care of me. I cannot imagine that any other newly married woman has ever been so looked after by her husband.

Jobard is frightfully busy with the business of running the hotel, of course, so I don't see him very often. Some days, I'm lucky if he can spare time for dinner. Even then, I can tell his mind is elsewhere, but this is simply how life must be when one's husband is such a busy, successful and ambitious man. I know you had reservations, but I can honestly say that I cannot imagine a better husband. Jobard Nash is a magnificent man, and strong as an ox. Our life together here makes me very happy.

I shall write to you again soon, hopefully with some good news about our endeavors in the family department.

Yours with love,

Mrs Ellen Nash
July 23rd, 1945

***

"You mustn't be too hard on yourself, my darling," I say with a sigh, as I stand in the doorway and watch Jobard pacing back and forth past the window, as if something out there is bothering him. "It takes time to gain the recognition you deserve. You've already achieved so much, far more than any other man could have managed. This hotel is utterly magnificent."

I wait for a reply, but he seems utterly absorbed by his own thoughts. I have long known that Jobard is a rather intense man, and truly I love him for this quality. Lately, however, I have begun to feel that he could lighten up just a little. It wouldn't kill him to take a day off work, or even an evening, yet here he is once more in his office well past dinner. If this is how things are when we have only been married for two weeks, I cannot imagine the course of the rest of our lives.

He hasn't even spared time for a honeymoon.

"Are you scared?" I ask.

Again, he doesn't look up. "Of what?"

"Of losing it all. Of going back to -"

"Don't talk nonsense!" he mutters. "I built this place up from nothing! How could I possibly lose it?"

"Perhaps you should come downstairs with me, then," I tell him, forcing a smile. "To the dining room. Just for once. The Sawards are almost done, and I'm sure they'd like to speak to you before they retire for the night."

"The who?"

"The Sawards. Mr. Bernard Saward is an eminent travel writer. He and his wife are currently enjoying a tour of the shires, and I feel sure that if you were to spend some time with him, in return he would -"

"Go and entertain the man," he replies, interrupting me. "That's what you're good at, after all. It's one of the reasons I knew I had to take a wife. It's your job to play the hostess, Ellen."

I open my mouth to tell him that I'm sure this isn't the *only* reason he married me, but something causes me to hold back. Instead of arguing with my husband, I make my way across the room and join him at the window. Looking out, I see the well-lit patio arranged around the new swimming pool, with several of the hotel's guests having already made their way out there after dinner. The scene is quite delightful, and I shall go down myself and mingle soon enough, but I haven't quite given up hope of persuading Jobard to come with me. After all, he works far too hard.

"My darling," I say finally, "what troubles you

so?"

Stopping next to me, he stares out at the scene for a moment.

"Do you see her?" he asks after a few seconds, his voice tense with concern.

"See who?"

I wait for a reply, but now he seems once more to have turned inward. Sometimes, I can be standing right next to him and yet I feel that he has no idea I'm even in the room.

"I see two ladies out there," I continue, forcing a smile. "One wearing a frightful turquoise dress, and the other wearing a rather more tasteful number in pink chiffon. The one in turquoise is Mrs. Saward, I'm afraid, but one simply can't buy taste. Mutton dressed as lamb, if you ask me."

Again, I wait.

Again, Jobard says nothing.

"My dear," I add, "is -"

"You see nobody else?" he asks, interrupting me again. "You have seen nobody else at all, nobody at the edge of the light? Not even a -"

He stops suddenly, as if some desperate inner trouble has briefly risen again and filled his mind.

"You have not seen her once," he continues, "since you arrived at the Lakeforth?"

"Seen who?"

I look at him, watching his face for some hint of a clue, but finally I turn and look back out at the patio. At first, I simply watch the bright lights and the guests who are down there, but a moment later my gaze is drawn to the darkness beyond the patio, where the grass runs toward the vast, dark forest and the lake. I know I am perhaps being a little foolish, but I can't deny a very faint shudder as I think of such a huge, untamed plot of land. Sometimes, I almost feel that this hotel is surrounded by a kind of darkness that watches us all.

"You should flatten that forest," I say finally, as another shudder passes through my chest. "You should put electric lights up, all the way to the lake."

"I should," he whispers.

"Well, why don't you?"

"I don't know that it would be enough," he replies. "Ten years ago, I acquired the last part of the lakeshore that was not already mine. I meant to make use of it, but some of the workmen flat out refuse to work in the forest."

"Why?"

"I suppose they are too superstitious."

"What do they fear?"

His lips move, but I don't quite hear what he says.

"Well, then you should replace them," I point out. "The only thing they're *truly* scared of is hard work, and there are plenty of others who would gladly take their jobs. Now that the war is over, we're all going to have to straighten up and focus on improving our lot in life. Jobard, it's most unlike you to accept anything other than the best. If I didn't know better, I'd be tempted to say that you're..."

My voice trails off.

Perhaps I should not finish that sentence.

Perhaps, after only two weeks of marriage, I should refrain from accusing my husband of cowardice. I would be wrong, after all. Everybody in the whole of England knows that Jobard Nash is the bravest, fiercest and most admirable man who ever lived.

"I'm sure you'll do what's best," I tell him finally. "You are, after all, the man who built this place, so clearly you know exactly what you're doing. I should not even dare offer you advice."

He mutters something under his breath, but he's still staring out at the dark forest, almost as if he expects to suddenly spot something moving between the trees. A moment later, the door behind us creaks slightly, and Jobard turns so fast that he gives me a fright. I watch his face, marveling at the fear in his eyes, and then I turn and look back at the door, which has simply creaked open of its own accord. Such things happen, of course, yet evidently Jobard is very jumpy tonight.

"Perhaps I should leave you to calm your thoughts," I tell him, leaning closer and kissing him gently on the cheek before making my way around the desk and heading to the doorway. "Do come down when you feel better, though. I rather fear some of the guests might start to wonder why you so rarely make an appearance. And the Sawards are very influential, so it would be wise to get on their good side. Why, one decent write-up from them in their paper, and this place could be heaving with guests. That's what you want, isn't it?"

"It's your job to socialize, my dear. It's one of your responsibilities here."

"You make it sound like a business deal," I reply, "more than a marriage."

I wait for him to reply, but he is once again looking out the window. Sighing, I realize that there is precious little chance of him coming down to join the guests this evening, but at least I tried. I watch him for a moment longer, feeling a very faint tinge of disappointment in my chest, and then I head out of the room.

By the time I'm at the far end of the corridor, I've managed to put the disappointment out of my mind.

By the time I'm halfway down the stairs, I've remembered to ensure that my posture is perfect.

By the time I'm in the reception hallway, I'm smiling the smile I practiced so carefully before I arrived at the Lakeforth.

And by the time I'm at the door to the dining room, I feel utterly composed, and all my concerns about Jobard have been pushed aside.

And then I spot her.

Glancing toward the smaller staircase at the far end of the corridor, I see a young girl standing next to the door to the basement. She's staring at me with a very calm expression, and she seems to exhibit none of the usual exuberance one would expect from a child. She can't be more than eight or nine years old, yet there is something rather striking about her appearance, perhaps even mournful. The more she watches me, the more I feel extremely uncomfortable, as if tiny prickles are running beneath my flesh.

I hesitate for a moment, before remembering that

I should put on a good face and be kind to the child.

Forcing a smile, I start walking toward her.

"Are you lost?" I ask. "Can't you find Mummy and Daddy?"

The girl doesn't respond. She simply stares at me as I get closer, and now I see that her eyes are dark and shadowed.

"Whatever's the matter?" I continue. "Did you -"

"Mrs. Nash!" a voice calls out suddenly from behind me. "There you are! We were starting to worry that we were going to be left all alone this evening!"

Turning, I see that Mr. and Mrs. Basingstoke are coming over to greet me. I smile at them, before glancing back toward the door and seeing that the strange little girl has suddenly and quite inexplicably vanished. I suppose she must be here with her parents, staying at the hotel, but she seemed a rather strange child and I can't help hoping that I shall not chance upon her again.

"Left alone?" I say with a smile, turning back to the Basingstokes. "Why, of course not! How could you contemplate such a ghastly thing? I'm afraid my husband is frightfully busy, but you simply must let me show you the view from the patio! Can I interest you in a glass of champagne?"

With that, I sweep into the bright, candlelit room, and I join the throng of the crowd. I soon forget all about the strange little girl, and I feel that all is well with the world.

CHAPTER SEVENTEEN

DEAR MOTHER AND FATHER,

I am dreadfully sorry that I did not write to you last week. You must understand, however, that Jobard has given me a set of great responsibilities here at the hotel. He values my opinion on matters of fashion and decoration, and I have barely had time to sit down or take a cup of tea. Such is the life of a woman who is married to this whirlwind of energy and brilliance that we call Mr. Jobard Nash.

The hotel is becoming more and more splendid with each passing day. My newest project is to renovate the basement, which is at present a rather dark and foreboding set of dusty rooms. I am spending a great deal of time down there, supervising the refurbishment of this part of the hotel, and I shall endeavor to send photographs with my next letter, showing you the improvements I have made.

I am so excited, and so happy. Marrying Jobard was the most wonderful blessing, and I feel that the Lakeforth shall eventually stand as a testament to his strength. I am so lucky to be his wife. Give me best to Eve, and tell her I hope she will some day find such a man. Although, as I constantly tell the employees around here, Jobard is utterly without equal. Just between us, I am confident he will be Sir Jobard Nash before too long. What will that make me? Lady Nash? I do hope so!

Yours as ever, with love,

Mrs Ellen Nash
August 10th, 1945

***

"What's that smell?" I mutter, stepping across the dark, dimly-lit room. "You smell it, Mrs. Crandall, do you not? Whatever can be causing it?"

"I can't say I have any idea, M'am," she replies, sounding as useless and dull as ever. "I gave it a scrub last night, just like you told me to."

"Are you sure?"

"I was on my knees for hours."

"Well, clearly you didn't scrub hard enough," I continue, turning to her. "Smell the air. Doesn't it seem fusty and dirty? Why, it's almost as if something died down here. I want you to come down again tonight and clean it for a second time, and make sure that you don't stop until the air is sweet and delightful. You must take pride in your work, woman. It's not enough to simply go through the motions. You should not stop until you're absolutely certain that you're done."

"Of course," she replies, even though it's clear that she dreads such hard work. "Will that be all for now?"

"Are you busy?" I ask, raising a skeptical eyebrow.

"Well, I've got rooms to make up," she explains, "and seeing as I don't have any help, it'll take me a while."

"Have you never spoken to my husband about hiring someone to assist you?"

"I've never spoken to your husband at all, M'am," she continues. "Not directly. He's never seen fit to really look at me very often, but I understand that he's very busy. I don't expect him to notice me."

She hesitates for a moment, and I can't help noticing that she looks rather uncomfortable.

"What?" I ask finally. "Spit it out, woman."

"It's nothing really. Just... I had some help once, briefly. A little girl. I think Mr. Nash put her to work with me personally. She only lasted a day, though. To be honest, I found her rather creepy. I think I'd prefer to work alone, rather than have the likes of her around again."

"Get on as best you can," I tell her, "and I shall speak to Jobard personally about the matter this evening. Perhaps if you had some proper help, the hotel would be a little cleaner."

"Yes, M'am," she replies through gritted teeth, turning and heading toward the stairs. "Thank you, M'am."

Once I'm left alone, with just a single electric light to break the darkness, I make my way to the far end of the room and try to open the metal door that I find in the corner. It's locked, of course, so I suppose I shall have to ask Jobard for a key when I see him later. Honestly, I don't know what he expects me to do with this place. The basement has no windows, precious few doors, and very little air. It *does*, however, possess a set of pipes running along the wall, and their heat is rather oppressive. On top of that, I can hear the sound of people in the dining room directly above this wretched little warren of rooms, and I'm starting to think that the basement is beyond salvation.

Perhaps it ought to be used merely for storage, after all.

"Fine," I mutter with a sigh, turning to head back to the stairs, "I shall -"

Stopping suddenly, I see a figure standing in the doorway. It takes a moment, but finally I realize that I have seen this particular individual before.

It's the same little girl I first saw a few weeks ago. Even though that was our only encounter, her features have remained etched on my mind, and I have thought of her once or twice. Truth be told, until today I had noted several times how thankful I was not to have run into her again. I suppose I assumed she and her family had departed.

"Who are you?" I ask. "What are you doing down here? This part of the building is not for guests."

She stares at me for a moment, before looking down at a bare patch on the floor.

"Did you hear me?" I continue, feeling more than a little irked by her reappearance, while struggling to maintain an appearance of utter calm. "You're to run along at once."

"Have you seen her?" she replies, her voice sounding frail and scratched.

"I beg your pardon?"

She stares at the floor for a moment longer, before turning to me again.

"Mary," she continues.

"What?"

I wait for a reply, but now she's simply watching me with those dark, shadowed eyes.

"Mary?" I continue. "Is that your name? Mary *what*?"

"I..."

She pauses.

"I'm looking for my sister," she continues finally, and now she sounds rather confused. "I thought she'd be here, but I can't find her anywhere. I thought she'd come back here."

"There's certainly nobody else in the basement," I tell her. "You must run along now and go back to your parents."

"Parents?"

"You've been here for a while now, have you not? When are you leaving? I thought most people only stayed a week."

She stares at me as if she doesn't understand at all. In fact, I'm starting to think that perhaps she is a little simple in the head.

"Do you realize who I am?" I ask, stepping toward her. "My name is Ellen Nash. That's Mrs. Jobard Nash to you, my dear. Soon, one day, to be *Lady* Nash. I am the wife of this hotel's proprietor and I am not somebody to be trifled or fooled with. I demand that you go upstairs at once."

"Nash?" she whispers, still staring at me. "That name..."

"Or would you like me to tell your parents that you've been poking about?" I continue. "If they're any kind of parents at all, they'll be thoroughly ashamed of you, and I imagine they'll punish you in some way. A smacked behind, perhaps, or the withholding of your allowance for a few weeks. Is that what you want?"

"Nash?" she says again, as if the name means something to her. "Mr. Nash?"

"My husband, and a great man. You should feel very lucky that your parents brought you to the Lakeforth. And now I think it's time for you to go and rejoin them."

I wait for her to obey my command, but she simply stares at me for a moment longer before turning and looking past me.

"Is Mary here?" she asks finally. "I thought..."

Her voice trails off for a moment, and frankly she seems a little confused. In fact, I'm starting to feel increasingly certain that the infernal child is damaged in the head. Really, if her parents insisted on bringing her to such a fine establishment, they should at least have had the good grace to keep her under control. It's simply not right to let her wander loose like this.

"Mary was gone," she continues, with a hint of shock in her voice. "Wait, I followed the man who had Mary. He was taking her to the lake. I remember now..."

"Whatever are you talking about, child?" I ask, stepping closer to her. "This nonsense -"

"He threw her into the water," she stammers, taking a step back as if suddenly she's gripped by fear. "I tried to save her, but there was nothing I could do. I went down again and again and again, always searching for her, but I never found her! And then..."

I wait for her to continue, but she seems genuinely shocked by some realization. After a moment, before I can tell her to get out of here, I see that a considerable amount of water seems to be seeping from one corner of her mouth, dribbling down onto the concrete floor.

"What *is* that?" I whisper, peering closer.

"I should have saved her!" the girl gasps, taking a step back and then turning away from me. At the same time, she places her hands over her face and starts weeping, as more and more water runs down over her wrists and dribbles to the floor.

"Whatever is the matter with you?" I ask.

When she fails to reply, I find myself torn as to what I should do next. On one hand, I would prefer to go upstairs and fetch somebody else to deal with this situation. On the other, I have very little experience with children, and I feel that perhaps I should test my maternal skills on this odd, unlikely girl. After all, I hope to have a first child of my own within the next year, so finally I take a deep breath and step up behind the girl, before reaching out and carefully placing a hand on her shuddering shoulder. I don't feel at all maternal, but perhaps I can force something to stir in my soul.

Before I can say a word, however, I'm shocked to feel that the fabric of the girl's dress is both soaking wet and ice cold.

"Perhaps we should find your parents," I tell her, flinching but forcing myself to make an effort. "Let's go upstairs together. Do you know where your parents might be at this hour? Taking a walk, perhaps? Or enjoying some time by the lake?"

"I should have saved Mary!" she sobs, as a veritable torrent of water starts running from her face, flowing down her neck and splattering against the floor. "If only I'd been quicker or smarter, she would have been alright!"

"I'm sure you..."

Taking a deep breath, I try to think of something I can say that might make the girl feel better. Before I can even try, however, something small, fat and glistening slips down from behind her hands and lands on her shoulder, and then it drops to the floor. Staring down in horror, I see that it appears to be some kind of bloated, yellowish maggot. I watch as the foul thing wriggles on the floor.

"Child," I whisper, "I think -"

"Where's Mary?" she screams, suddenly turning

to me and lowering her hands to reveal a discolored, rotten face. "What did you do to her?"

Startled, I step back, but the girl lunges at me. I pull away, tripping at the last second, and I stumble across the concrete floor before falling and crashing against the bottom of the stairs. Feeling a sharp pain in my wrist, I nevertheless start forcing myself up, and then I turn to see that the girl is limping toward me with a furious expression on her face.

"Where is she?" she groans, as thick, juicy maggots wriggle in the flesh of her rotten face. Worms are slipping out of her mouth, squirming with hooked tails as they rolls down her chin and fall to the floor, while some kind of tube-shaped creature appears to be curled in her left eye, having chewed a hole straight through the pupil. Finally, as she opens her mouth and tries to speak again, a rush of more worms, maggots and other creatures comes flooding out, splattering to the floor just inches from me.

"Get away from me!" I shout. "Don't touch me!"

"What did he do to me?" she gurgles, as a thick, bloody hole begins to open in her forehead. "Help me!"

Screaming, I pull back and cover my face with my hands. A moment later, I feel a set of icy, wet fingers grabbing my wrist.

CHAPTER EIGHTEEN

DEAR MOTHER AND FATHER,

All is well here, and I am having the most marvelous time. In the week since I wrote to you last, I have been working mostly in the dining room, trying to ensure that our guests have an enjoyable experience while they eat. I have also been taking an interest in the kitchen, trying to encourage Chef to liven up the menu a little. Honestly, I have been so busy, I don't think I have been alone for even one moment.

Jobard continues to be very busy, working every hour of the day and often through the night as well. He assures me that he plans to take a holiday at some point, but in truth I am not too worried. He is a great man, and great men are always consumed by their work. The important thing to remember is that everything is perfect here at the Lakeforth and nobody could ever wish for a more perfect home. I know I am blissfully happy.

That said, I am considering coming to visit you for a few weeks soon. Please reply by return of mail, advising me if you are amenable to putting me up next weekend. Do not delay. In fact, I might just set off anyway. I'm sure you'll be pleased to see me.

Yours with the greatest love,

Mrs Ellen Nash
August 18th, 1945

***

"Just a week," I stammer, trying to force a smile even though I feel sick to my stomach. "Two at the most. You could spare me for two weeks, could you not? I just feel that, after last week's events, I should rather get away for a while. I'm sure you'll understand."

I wait for a reply, but Jobard doesn't even look up from his papers. I know I should remain silent until he's ready to speak to me, but I'm still feeling rather restless, and it is only twenty-four hours since I dared rise from my bed again. I feel certain that I shall be much better once I have been away from the Lakeforth for a few weeks, but first I need Jobard's permission to travel and he seems resolutely determined to keep me here. I suppose he simply doesn't understand my suffering.

"Jobard, please -"

"Is this because of that business last week?" he asks suddenly, setting his pen down and looking up at me.

"Jobard -"

"Because if it is, I must caution you that you're being utterly weak. When Silas found you screaming at the foot of the stairs, you had simply been overcome by the stresses of your recent routine. You were gabbling away about some frightful vision you believed you'd encountered, but I'm sure by now you must realize you were entirely mistaken."

"Jobard -"

"*Entirely* mistaken," he says again, much more firmly this time, while fixing me with a stern gaze. "There was not a jot of truth in the whole thing!"

"Of course," I reply, affecting a degree of certainty that I honestly do not possess. "I was just being weak and foolish, and -"

"So there is no need for you to go and visit your parents," he adds, interrupting me. "Whatever would people think, Ellen, if they learned that you had left the marital home just a few months after your arrival? You must consider how these things appear to the outside world, and you must remember that one of your duties as my wife is to stand by my side, no matter what. You know that I am too busy to entertain our guests at the moment. Therefore, you must be here to take my place and show them that we are good hosts."

He hesitates, before looking back down at his papers.

"I simply cannot spare you at the moment," he

continues, and it's clear from the tone of his voice that he will brook no further argument regarding the matter. "Now, if there's nothing else, I would ask you to leave my office. This paperwork grows tiresome, yet it never seems to end."

"Of course," I reply meekly, taking a step back. In my heart of hearts, I still want to beg him to let me leave, even for a few days, but I know I have no right to do so. I must stay here, by his side, and put any superstitious thoughts out of my mind.

"And don't forget," he adds, "that we are having our portrait taken later."

"Of course," I say again.

Taking a deep breath, I tell myself to stay strong.

Still, when I reach the doorway and step out into the empty corridor, I suddenly flinch at the thought of walking all the way to the stairs without anybody to accompany me. I have rather expertly avoided being alone over the past week, ever since I encountered that frightful little girl, while I have taken pills to thoroughly knock myself out every night. Now, even though I can hear voices in the distance as guests make their way across the reception hallway, I shudder at the thought of walking alone even for thirty seconds or less.

"Shut the door after you," Jobard mutters. "There's a good woman."

Since I cannot possibly argue with him, I do as I am told, and then I find myself standing alone in the corridor.

All alone.

I turn and look over my shoulder, but there is no

sign of anyone behind me. Too scared to move a muscle, lest I might cause a disturbance and perhaps summon that terrible spirit one more time, I hesitate for a moment before telling myself that I must simply stop being so silly. Why, my nerves are getting so bad, I fear I am actually starting to break out into a cold sweat.

Taking a deep breath, I finally hurry along the corridor, walking faster and faster as I make my way toward the top of the stairs. I feel certain that the girl is right behind me, that I shall see her if I turn, or that I shall feel her cold, wet hand on my shoulder. Each step I take feels as if it lasts a thousand years, and by the time I reach the stairs I am quite sure that the girl is directly behind me. Turning, I see no sign of her, but that only means she is trying to fool me. Looking down the stairs, I see several guests near the main desk, and finally I breathe a sigh of relief.

The girl cannot come to me now, not when I am in the company of others. Of that, I am quite sure. With that thought in my mind, I hurry down to join them.

***

"Are you ready?" the photographer asks cheerily, peering through the lens of his device. "Smile for the camera, please!"

"You must smile," Jobard whispers, nudging my arm. "Ellen, you look terrified."

"I have never had my portrait taken before," I reply. "I have never been photographed at all."

"You know how to smile, do you not?"

I try to smile, but deep down I still feel dreadfully out of sorts and afraid. I can't help looking past the photographer, toward the doorway at the far end of the dining room. That wretched girl could appear at any moment, and I am sure I can feel her presence somewhere nearby.

"Stay still now!" the photographer instructs us. "I'm about to start!"

"Smile!" Jobard hisses.

Doing my absolute best, I force a smile that feels utterly unnatural. I can only hope that I am a better actress than I realize, because I feel sure that no smile in all the world could hide the horror I feel in my chest. Then again, perhaps a camera cannot pick up such things. A smile is a smile, and so long as I appear happy in the portrait, that is all that matters.

***

"On the contrary," Major Barton says with a haughty laugh, "I am quite sure of it. There shall never be another war, not like these last two. The human race has learned its lesson. And if I am wrong, then we deserve everything we get."

With that, he takes a swig of wine, and the other men at the table murmur in agreement while the ladies all remain silent.

Glancing over my shoulder, I look back across the patio and toward the doors that lead into the dining room. Once again, Jobard has failed to come down from his office, leaving me to entertain our guests this evening. I suppose I should not be in any way surprised, and I am certainly accustomed to playing the role of host, but tonight I do wish he might have shown his face. I do not quite understand what he does up there every evening, but as I look up toward his office window, I see that the light is still on and that his shadow is still visible against the closed drapes.

Are his shoulders becoming a little more hunched these days?

"And what about you, Mrs. Nash?" Mrs. Dawley asks suddenly. "Do you think our sons and daughters will one day have to go off and fight again?"

Turning to her, I feel momentarily startled by the question.

"No," I stammer, "I mean... Yes, no, I..."

Hesitating, I realize that the others seem terribly amused by my indecision. In fact, I have evidently become the center of attention, with all the faces at the table turned to me. Swallowing hard, I resolve to give a firmer answer.

"I should hope not," I continue. "So many died over the past few years. Surely, we are due a period of peace?"

"Not in the age of the machine," Mr. Plum mutters darkly, sitting at the far end of the table. "The machines need to be fed, and they won't eat other machines."

"What *will* they eat, then?" his wife asks, affecting a bright, amused giggle.

"Soil," he replies. "And mankind."

"You must excuse my husband," Mrs. Plum

says, turning to each of the rest of us in turn. "He takes a frightfully pessimistic view of the world sometimes."

"Mark my words," he continues. "One hundred years from now, machines will rule the world. In the year 2045, the human race will be reduced to the role of scurrying, pathetic vermin, while the machines will make every decision, implement every plan, and redesign the world so that it better suits their needs. Why wouldn't they? The day the first machine gains an understanding of its own nature, is the day the human race begins its inevitable slide into oblivion. And the crowning irony will be the fact that we are the ones who will create the machines in the first place."

As Mr. Dawley offers a counter-argument, I rather start ignoring the conversation. I feel a strange, unsettled sensation creeping up my spine, and a moment later the hairs on the back of my neck seem to shift slightly. Reaching back, I scratch the affected patch of skin, and then I glance around to make sure that nobody is watching me from the darkness at the edge of the patio. In the back of my mind, I suppose I expect to see that wretched girl again, although I keep telling myself that she won't appear while I am with others.

Sure enough, there is no sign of her.

Yet that unsettled feeling persists.

Turning the other way, I look past the far end of the table, but all I see is darkness. I know the forest is out there somewhere, and the lake beyond, but I feel certain that something is watching me right now.

Watching, yet unseen.

"Are you alright?" Mrs. Walsh whispers,

nudging my arm. "You look rather pale, Ellen."

"I'm fine," I reply, trying to smile even though I feel sick to my stomach. I continue to look around for a moment longer, before turning to her again. "Please, pay me no attention. Lately, I have simply allowed myself to be overcome far too easily. That's all."

"I know the feeling," she mutters, as the others continue to talk. "Married life is never easy, especially at the beginning. One must simply fumble along as best one can, mustn't one? Until one gets into a rhythm, I mean."

I nod, supposing her to be right, and then I try to force myself to focus on staying calm. Taking a deep breath, I look at the others around the table, before glancing back up toward Jobard's office window.

And then I freeze, as I see that there is now a second shadow cast against the drapes. Jobard's hunched shadow is where it should be, writing at the desk, but next to him there is another, shorter shadow, as if a young girl is standing next to the desk and watching him.

Staring for a moment, I keep telling myself that the girl must simply be a trick of the light, yet still she persists.

"Ellen?" Mrs. Walsh says after a few seconds, nudging my arm again. "What is it?"

"Do you see that?" I ask, unable to stop watching the window.

"See what, my dear?"

"At the window! Up there! Do you see a little girl?"

"Well... Yes. Of course. I mean, I think so. It's rather difficult to be sure from here. I'm afraid I don't have my glasses with me."

Getting to my feet, I keep my eyes fixed on the window. Jobard appears not to have looked up from his desk, but the shadow of the little girl is just a few feet from him. I want to call out, to scream so loud that he'll hear me and realize that something is in the office with him, but at the same time I worry that the girl might do something awful if she realizes that she has been spotted. Torn by indecision, I can only manage to watch the window with a mounting sense of horror.

And then, quite suddenly, the girl steps toward Jobard and reaches out, and the shadow of her hand falls upon the shadow of his shoulder.

"No!" I shout, rushing around the side of the table and hurrying across the patio, heading back into the building. I honestly have not a single sensible thought in my head, but I know I must get to the office at once and warn my husband that some spirit or creature of the next world has materialized in his presence.

Almost tripping as I start making my way up the stairs, I push past a couple of guests who are coming down the other way, and I'm quite sure that they must be disturbed by my wild, frantic rush.

"What's wrong with *her*?" an unimpressed voice mutters behind me. "Why's she racing about like a madwoman?"

"Jobard!" I shout, unable to hide my desperation a moment longer. "Jobard, get out of there!"

Reaching the top of the stairs, I hurry along the

corridor until I reach the door to his office, which I immediately fling open as I throw myself into the room. As soon as I do so, however, I see that Jobard is sitting quite alone at his desk, still working at his papers, although he quickly looks up at me with a hint of irritation in his eyes.

"Ellen?" he says cautiously. "Whatever is wrong with you?"

"She was here," I stammer. "Did you not feel her touch? She placed her hand on your shoulder!"

"I beg your -"

"She was right here!" I hiss, hurrying over to the desk and then stopping to look around at the rest of the room. The girl is not here now, but this time I know what I saw and I refuse to let anybody tell me I'm crazy. "You must have at least sensed her. Even a spirit cannot pass through a room without leaving some trace of her presence."

Turning to him, I see that he clearly has no idea what I mean.

"She was right here!" I scream, with tears rolling down my cheeks as I point to the spot next to him. "I saw her shadow from the patio! You can't possibly tell me that you weren't aware, not when she was standing right next to you!"

Rushing around the side of the desk, I place my hand on his shoulder.

"There!" I shout. "You feel that, do you not?"

"Ellen -"

"So how could you not have felt *her*?" I sob, dropping to my knees as I feel great, convulsing waves of horror bursting through my chest. "Tell me, Jobard! How could you not know that the horrid little creature was right here in the room with you? Did you not hear the water running from her mouth? Did you not feel the air getting colder? Please, tell me you've seen this girl!"

He says nothing. All I see in his eyes is a sense of utter bewilderment.

"Why am I the only one?" I whimper, collapsing in a heap as I hear Silas hurrying into the room. "Why does she appear to me, but to nobody else? Why must I be haunted by that pale, rotten little face?"

CHAPTER NINETEEN

DEAR MOTHER AND FATHER,

I shall be on the train that arrives at noon tomorrow. You must excuse the suddenness of the visit, but it cannot be helped. I look forward very much to seeing you both again.

Yours with love,

Mrs Ellen Nash
August 21ˢᵗ, 1945

***

"And what did Jobard say when you told him you'd be coming back to us for a few days?" Mother asks as she brings a cup of tea into the parlor. "I'm surprised he was willing to let his young wife leave the marital home so swiftly."

"He was surprisingly amenable to the idea," I reply, forcing a smile even though I feel sick to my stomach. "He agreed that it might be for the best, since..."

My voice trails off.

Since what?

There is no way to adequately explain my sudden departure from the Lakeforth. I have told Mother and Father that I simply wished to come and check on them, but I can tell that they're not entirely persuaded by that argument. Fortunately, they are far too polite and respectful to press me on the matter, so they have focused instead on making sure that I am comfortable.

I wish I could say the same for Eve, however. My younger sister is watching me like a hawk, and I know that she'll press me for details as soon as she and I are alone together.

"You'll be heading back after the weekend, I assume?" Mother says as she sits in her usual chair by the window. "You can't leave a married man alone for too long, Ellen, or he'll start regressing into bad habits. Men are like dogs, you know. They need training, and they need repetition."

"I shall go back to the Lakeforth very soon," I tell her. "You mustn't worry about that. Are you not pleased to have me home?"

"Of course we are," she replies, getting to her feet and heading to the door. "I forgot the sugar. Just wait right here."

I almost get up to go with her, but at the last moment I decide to remain seated. That quickly proves to be a mistake, however, as I realize that now I am alone in the room with Eve, and it's quite clear that she has many questions. I might be able to pull the wool over the eyes of my parents, but Eve knows me far too well. Besides, she always seems to take a devilish delight in asking questions that she knows will irritate me.

"So?" she says finally.

I turn to her. "So *what*?"

"So what's the real story?" she continues, keeping her voice low. "The way you rode off to your wedding, I didn't think you'd *ever* set foot in this house again. And now here you are, clearly upset by something. If I didn't know better, I'd be wondering whether you ran away from the hotel. Did Jobard hit you?"

I shake my head.

"Are you with child?"

Again, I shake my head.

"Have there been arguments?"

"It's nothing," I tell her. "I have simply been missing home a little, that's all. Can't you believe that I wanted to see all of you again?"

"Honestly?" She eyes me with suspicion for a moment. "No, I can't believe that. Something happened at the Lakeforth, something that sent you scurrying back here. You'll return to the hotel, of course, because you know you have no choice, but you're dreading it. The only question in my mind is about *what* could have upset you like this."

"Eve..."

"Everything about you is different," she continues, clearly warming to her theme. "The way you hold yourself, the way you talk, the way you look at people, the way you sit, even the way the muscles rest on your face. It must be something profound to have changed a person like that. I don't think I've ever seen anything of the like, at least not since old Father Joe claimed to have seen an angel at the church and -"

She stops suddenly, as if she's had an idea.

"Did you see an angel at the Lakeforth?" she asks excitedly.

"Don't be ridiculous!" I mutter.

"Then what *did* you see? A ghost?"

Flinching, I look over at the door and find myself wondering why Mother is taking so very long in the kitchen.

"You saw a ghost!" Eve continues, clearly greatly enthused by the idea. "You saw some kind of spirit, and you came rushing home because you were scared to stay at the hotel! Well, I can't say I blame you, and I suppose Jobard isn't exactly the type to indulge in such speculation. Still -"

"It's nothing," I reply, interrupting her. "Please, I'd really rather not talk about it, if that's alright."

"Of course it's not alright! What did you see?"

I shake my head.

"You're going to tell me eventually, Ellen, so you might as well spit it out now!"

I pause for a moment, and I can't deny that she has a point. Eve always wears me down whenever I have a secret, and this situation is unlikely to be any different.

"I do not believe in ghosts, as a matter of course," I say finally. "I still don't, not really. But I believe in what I have seen, and I have seen a child at the Lakeforth. A little girl who appears to me, and seemingly *only* to me. She's most horrid, with rotten flesh and dark eyes, and I can't imagine what she wants. I have seen her several times now, and I know everybody there thinks I am going quite mad. Jobard expects me to return fully rested, and for there to be no more talk of such things, but..."

My voice trails off.

"But you know," she says cautiously, "that you'll see the girl again, as soon as you return to the hotel?"

"What am I to do?" I ask. "The Lakeforth is my marital home, I am expected to live there and to raise children of my own, yet I cannot even bear to be alone for one minute in any of the rooms. I dread going back, Eve. Truly, I am filled with the most horrendous sense of dread when I think of setting foot once more in that place. What would you do, if you were in my shoes?"

"I believe in ghosts," she points out. "I always have done. Remember?"

I nod.

"You're right," she continues. "You *do* have to go back. But perhaps you can help the ghost, and make it go away."

"Help it?"

"If it's a lost spirit, it must still be roaming the mortal world because it has some unfinished business. If you help it to complete that business, the spirit will be freed and you'll never see it again. You must simply find out what it wants, and then you must endeavor to satisfy this need. Once you have done that, the spirit will not be seen again. Tell me, do you know anything about this girl?"

"Only that she mentioned her sister," I reply, grateful to Eve for taking this matter seriously. "A sister named Mary, I believe. I asked Jobard, but he refused to even discuss the matter. Evidently he believes me to be utterly insensible, perhaps even a lunatic."

"Is her sister alive or dead?"

"I do not know."

"Clearly she's the key to all of this, Ellen. Somebody at that hotel must know the truth. I'd wager that Jobard knows more than he's letting on. I always thought he was shifty, but I doubt he'll confess all to you now. You'll have to talk to the other people who've been there for a while. Mention this name Mary, mention the little girl and her sister, and perhaps somebody will be able to help you. It's the only way."

"Perhaps," I whisper, although I still dread the idea of ever going back to the Lakeforth. At the same time, I know I have no choice.

"Stay a few days," Eve continues, as Mother returns with the sugar bowl, "and come up with a plan, and then go back to the Lakeforth and execute that plan."

"What are you two girls nattering on about now?" Mother asks innocently, having clearly not overheard a word of our conversation from the kitchen.

"Nothing," Eve and I say simultaneously, before glancing at one another.

My sister smiles, but I feel a ripple of dread in my chest as I realize that she is right. I should try to have a good time here at home, but it can't last forever. Once the weekend is over, I really *will* have to go back to the Lakeforth and confront whatever's waiting there. I fear that even if I spend all my time praying on my knees, asking God for mercy, I am doomed to see that face again.

***

"Mrs. Nash?" a voice calls out as I make my way across the busy road. "Mrs. Nash, might I bother you for a word?"

Reaching the road's other side, I turn and see that an elderly gentleman is hurrying after me. I can't even begin to imagine who he is or how he knows my name, but he's waving an envelope at me and he seems quite determined to bother me about something. Honestly, I don't think I've ever been so rudely accosted in all my life. Clearly, despite his respectable appearance, this man is a ruffian.

"I'm dreadfully sorry," he continues, sounding a little breathless as he reaches me. "I would never ordinarily call after a lady like that in the street, but I've been waiting quite some time to catch you."

"What do you want?" I ask cautiously. "If it's money -"

"My name is Edward Albraid," he adds, "and I am an agent for the Desermes family. I don't suppose you're familiar with them at all?"

"I can't say that I am."

"That's quite alright. My employers were hoping that they might speak to you about a rather delicate matter. I'm afraid it concerns your husband, Mr. Jobard Nash."

"If you wish to discuss something with my husband," I reply, "you should take the matter up with him directly. He has a telephone, you know."

"My employers are not at the stage yet where they wish to speak to him. Instead, they're trying to gain a better understanding of the establishment that he runs. That's why I was sent to speak to you, actually. My employers would very much like to ask you a few discreet questions about the Lakeforth, and in particular about the hotel's current arrangements. If you'd be so kind as to accept a dinner invitation, I -"

"That's out of the question," I tell him. "I simply cannot go to dinner without my husband, and I'm afraid he's not in town at present. You really shouldn't even suggest such a thing."

"I'm afraid the situation is quite extreme," he replies. "Mrs. Nash, the Desermes family has taken an interest in your husband and his hotel for a very specific reason. I'm not at liberty to go into the matter right now, but I hope you'll give my employers the chance to explain in person why they desperately need your help."

Reaching into his pocket, he takes out an envelope, from which he produces a set of photographs.

"Mr. Albraid," I say, hoping to extricate myself from the conversation, "I'm not sure why -"

Before I can finish, I spot a familiar face among

the images. I step closer, but Mr. Albraid has already shuffled that particular picture under the others, and a moment later he holds up a photograph that depicts the lakeshore near the hotel.

"These photographs were taken a little over a decade ago," he explains. "By pure chance, some relatives of the Maywhistle family visited a house next to the hotel, and they had a camera with them. The odds are extraordinary, but we're very lucky to have proof that this family existed at all. Have you heard of the Maywhistles, M'am? Does their name mean anything at all to you?"

He flips between different photographs, and I can't help watching in case the familiar face appears again. Sure enough, a moment later, I see the little girl's features.

"Stop!" I snap, reaching out and taking the picture from him.

Staring at the photograph, I try to tell myself that there must be some mistake, but the faded image quite clearly shows the same little girl I have encountered on several occasions at the Lakeforth. Turning the photograph over, I see that somebody has handwritten the year 1934, which means the picture is eleven years old.

"Her name was Ruth Maywhistle," Mr. Albraid explains. "One of two girls, the other being -"

"Mary," I whisper.

"How do you know? Does Mr. Nash talk about them?"

Thinking back to my first encounter with the

girl, back in the basement, I remember how she asked several times about somebody named Mary.

"Where is she?" I ask, trying to affect a tone of calm, detached interest. "I mean, where is this little girl now?"

"Dead, I'm afraid."

I glance at him.

"We're still piecing together the exact circumstances," he continues. "Unfortunately, the legal system prevents us from dealing with Mr. Nash directly, at least until we can gather some more information. The police have been of no help whatsoever, and that is why I have taken the extraordinary step of contacting you directly. Mrs. Nash, I know Jobard is your husband, but he has blood on his hands and -"

"No!" I say firmly, shaking my head. "Absolutely not! My husband is a fine man!"

"You don't know the entire -"

"I know my husband!" I tell him, staring at the photograph for a moment longer before handing it back to him. "I shall inform him of your approach, Mr. Albraid, and of the Desermes family and their apparent determination to meddle in his affairs. I cannot imagine how he'll react, but I would strongly advise you to leave the matter alone. My husband is a powerful man with many connections in this country, and he's not above using those connections if he needs to bring pressure to bear on those who would thwart his interests."

"Are you saying that the names Ruth and Mary Maywhistle mean nothing to you?" he asks.

"Of course they mean nothing to me," I reply,

taking a step back. "I'm sorry I can't help you, but please, let this be the end of your interest."

With that, I turn and walk away, hurrying along the street and hoping that the gentleman will not come after me. When I reach the next corner, I step out of view and then I lean back against the wall, taking a moment to catch my breath. I can't help thinking about the photograph of the little girl, and there is no doubt whatsoever in my mind that she is the same girl I have seen at the hotel. Perhaps, now that I know her name, I shall be better equipped to rid the hotel of her presence and restore my life to some semblance of normality.

"Maywhistle," I whisper, feeling a shudder pass through my chest. "Ruth Maywhistle..."

***

"Ellen!" Eve calls out. "Ellen, wait! Before you go, I want you to take this!"

Stopping in the doorway, I turn just as my sister comes clattering down the stairs. She barely manages to stop in time, and then she breathlessly thrusts something into my hands. Looking down, I'm surprised to see a wooden crucifix.

"You should keep this on your person," she explains. "At all times, when you're in that hotel."

"Eve..."

"Or do you already have one?"

I open my mouth to tell her that she's being foolish, but somehow I cannot quite get the words out of my mouth. In truth, I am dreading going back to the hotel, and I would very much like to have a little piece of home with me.

"Thank you," I say finally. "I'm sure it's not necessary, but I shall take it with me regardless."

"And don't doubt yourself," she continues earnestly. "Not for one second. If you think you hear something, or that you see something, then you must assume that it's real. Whatever you do, don't let others persuade you that you're wrong. *That* is the surest path to madness."

"I shall remember your advice," I tell her, forcing a smile. "Please try not to worry, Eve. I feel much more prepared for this, now that I have had a few days here in the city. I shall go back to the hotel and ensure that everything runs smoothly."

She pauses, before leaning forward and kissing me on the cheek.

"God speed," she tells me, as she takes a step back. "Remember that Jobard Nash is just one man, Ellen. He might like the sound of his own voice, but that doesn't mean he's right about everything. Or about anything at all."

"I shall write soon," I reply, before picking up my suitcase and turning to walk away. Right now, on this suburban street, the great Lakeforth hotel feels so very far away. So far, in fact, that it might almost be another world. But I shall wrestle it into submission, and I shall make it part of this world again. And if there are ghosts there, I shall cast them out.

CHAPTER TWENTY

DEAR EVE,

Life is much better here now. Since my return a couple of months ago, Jobard has been both more attentive and more caring, and we have spent a great deal of time together. It is my honest opinion that all the disagreeable matters from before have been dealt with, and that everything should be plain sailing from now on.

As for the supposed ghosts, I have seen and heard nothing more, and I feel rather silly. Please, do not tell Mother or Father or anyone else about the things I told you. I see now that I was in the grip of some mania, and I am thankful that I have somehow managed to pull through. The Lakeforth is a beautiful and calm hotel, and I am so lucky to call this place my home. I fully intend to make my life here work.

I have kept the crucifix, however, and it rests close to the bed. Not so close that Jobard might remark upon its presence, but close enough I hope that it might offer some degree of protection. Not that protection is needed, but one can never be too careful, can one? Next time I write, I hope very much to have some good news about our family plans. Although I suppose I should not get too far ahead of myself. One thing at a time, and all that.

Your loving sister,

Ellen
November 30ᵗʰ, 1945

***

I have never seen the Lakeforth so busy.

There must be close to one hundred guests on the patio tonight, all enjoying drinks and music now that dinner is over. The lights of the hotel sparkle against the vast, faraway darkness of the lake and the hills, and everywhere I turn there is plenty of laughter and conversation. In fact, as I take my drink and slip through the crowd, I cannot help but notice that tonight – for the first time since I came to the Lakeforth – the hotel feels genuinely, effortlessly busy.

This is what Jobard was trying to build the whole time.

He succeeded.

And what's more, he's down here tonight to enjoy the experience.

Glancing over my shoulder, it takes a moment before I'm able to spot him. I might have had to coax him from his office, but now my darling husband is mingling with a group of visiting bankers, and he's doing a splendid job of entertaining them with his witty stories. Deep down, I always knew that he would be able to rise to the occasion and emerge from his shell, but it is still heartening to see for myself that he is succeeding. I am so proud of him.

Just inside the doorway, our portrait is hanging on the wall. I remember the fear I felt when that photograph was taken, but I think I actually look rather happy in the picture. I see no fear in my eyes whatsoever.

And as I turn and look around at the rest of the guests, I cannot help reflecting upon the fact that I have been back for around three months now, and I have not seen the little girl once. Perhaps her spirit has finally faded away. In fact, I am *sure* she is gone. Thank God, that chapter is finally over.

***

"Did you hear that?"

Sitting up suddenly in bed, I stare across the dark bedroom and watch the door. Nothing moves, and there is no sound now to break the silence, although I am certain that some distant noise *did* wake me. Footsteps, perhaps, outside in the corridor.

Turning, I see that Jobard is fast asleep. For a moment, I consider stirring him, but I suppose he would only be annoyed. I watch him for a moment longer, before realizing that I absolutely cannot sleep while my heart beats so fast and so hard.

Finally, climbing out of bed, I resolve to go to the kitchenette along the hallway and fetch a glass of water. I shuffle across the room, slipping into my gown along the way, before stopping and looking back to where Eve's crucifix rests near the bed. I hesitate, wondering whether perhaps I can finally dare venture out of the room without any means of defense, but my resolve quickly falters. Stepping back over to the table next to the bed, I take the crucifix and slip it into my pocket before heading to the door.

Once I'm out in the corridor, I pause for a few seconds to listen to the silence. The time must be well after midnight, and the hotel's guests are all safely tucked into their beds. There are almost one hundred people staying at the moment, which makes it difficult to believe that the hotel could be so quiet, but I suppose people do not make much noise when they are sleeping. Barely more than if they were dead.

Although I suppose that's a rather morbid thought.

Heading along the corridor, I quickly reach the kitchenette and pour myself some water. As I drink, I look out the window, watching the patio area where electric lights cast bright pools to ward of the encroaching darkness of the forest. The scene is utterly beautiful and tranquil, enough to calm all my fears, and for several minutes my gaze is drawn to the sight of the lake's surface glittering in the distance. We live in such a beautiful location, for which I am eternally grateful.

A few minutes later, having returned to bed, I set the crucifix back in its spot and settle next to Jobard again. Closing my eyes, I try to think of the lake's calm, beautiful surface, and I find that I am even able to imagine a cool breeze on my face. Sleep does not come, not quite, but I doze peacefully for a short while, thinking of the wonderful natural world all around us. At one point, I hear a very faint scratching sound nearby, but I do not even consider opening my eyes. I am so relaxed at this moment, I honestly feel that nothing could ever upset me.

And then, suddenly, I open my eyes and let out a gasp, and I stumble forward before dropping to my knees on the hard pebbles that line the lakeshore.

A breeze blows past, chilling my flesh, and I look down to see that I am wearing only my nightgown.

Turning, I glance both ways and see that somehow I am at the edge of the lake. A moment ago I was in bed with my husband, but now I turn and see the hotel high up on the hill. I have no idea how I ended up down here, but I can only suppose that I must have somehow walked in my sleep. I have heard of such things happening to other people, although I never expected that I might one day become a victim. Still, shivering here all alone in the moonlight, I cannot pretend that this is a dream.

Getting to my feet, I instinctively reach down to take the crucifix from my gown pocket, before realizing that in my daze I must have left it next to the bed. Feeling a flutter of panic in my chest, I look around, hoping against hope that I might simply have dropped the crucifix, but it is nowhere to be seen. I look out across the lake, then along the shore, and finally I realize that I simply must get back to the hotel immediately. After all, this is the first time I have been without the crucifix since I returned, and I feel utterly exposed.

I turn to head back to the path that runs through the forest, but then I freeze as soon as I see the silhouette of the little girl standing about twenty feet away.

"No!" I stammer immediately, taking a step back. "No, you're not real! You were never real!"

I wait, but the silhouette remains in place, and I am certain I can feel her eyes staring at me.

"You're not real!" I shout again, my voice trembling with fear. "Go away! Get out of my sight! I know you're not real, so leave me alone!"

Squeezing my eyes tight shut, I place my hands on either side of my head and focus on forcing this awful apparition from my mind.

"Be gone!" I hiss. "I refuse to imagine you! You don't exist!"

I hesitate for a moment longer, and then I open my eyes again.

She's still there.

Still staring at me.

There are already tears in my eyes, and I daren't go anywhere near the girl. As another gust of cold air blows past me, ruffling my nightgown, I take a step back. I'm shivering, and I keep instinctively reaching for the crucifix, only to be reminded again and again that I don't have it with me.

"What do you want from me?" I ask. "What -"

Suddenly she takes a couple of steps forward, until I can just about make out her face in the darkness.

"I know who you are!" I gasp. "I know your name! You're Ruth Maywhistle, aren't you? I've seen your photograph! I know who you are and..."

My voice trails off, as I wait for her to say something. She's still coming toward me, walking calmly across the pebbles.

"Tell me what you want?" I add finally, my voice trembling with fear. "Please, just tell me what you want me to do for you, and I'll do it if I can. Anything! Just tell me!"

Again, I wait for her to speak.

Again, the only sound is the wind blowing through the nearby trees.

"Mary," she says suddenly, her voice sounding so weak and frail as she edges closer.

"Is that your sister?" I ask, stumbling back. "I know you had a sister. Is Mary her name? Do you want me to find her for you?"

"I know where she is," she replies. "She's behind you."

I open my mouth to ask what she means, before suddenly spinning around. All I see, however, is the wooden jetty and the lake. After a moment, I turn back to the silhouette of Ruth Maywhistle and find that she has taken a few more steps toward me.

"Keep back!" I gasp, stepping away from her again, almost tripping over the uneven ground beneath my bare feet. "I don't understand what you want from me!"

"Mary," she whispers. "She's behind you. She's in the water. I come to her night after night, but she stays down there. I don't understand why."

"You're dead!" I tell her. "You're both dead! There's nothing I can do for you!"

"Dead?" She sounds concerned now, perhaps a little confused. "Mary's dead," she continues finally. "I know that. *I'm* not dead, though. I can't be, I'm still here, I..."

Her voice trails off.

"Sometimes it's difficult to remember how long I've been at the hotel," she adds. "I try to keep track, but my thoughts fade away and don't always come back until..."

Again, her voice trails off, and this time she stays silent as she continues to walk toward me.

"Your name is Ruth Maywhistle," I say finally, still backing away from her, "and you're dead. You died ten years ago. I don't know how, I can try to find out if you want, but all I know right now is that you died. I don't know what you want, but if you can't find your sister's ghost, maybe she's moved on. Maybe she went to a better place, and you should follow her."

"Follow her?" she replies. "How?"

"I don't know," I continue, "but I'm sure you can find a way. Mary probably misses you very much, Ruth. I'm sure she'd be very happy if you went to her. And then the people here at the hotel wouldn't have to worry about seeing you around, and things could go back to how they're supposed to be. Wouldn't you like that? I'm sure your spirit isn't supposed to spend the rest of eternity haunting this hotel. You should move on, Ruth. Find your sister."

I wait for her to reply, for her to admit that I'm right, but still she simply comes closer and closer.

As I continue to back away, I stumble against the entrance to the wooden jetty. Stepping a little further back, I watch as the girl comes closer, and I realize that she seems to be forcing me toward the jetty's farthest end.

"What do you want from me?" I shout, with tears streaming down my face. I don't want to go where she wants, but as she gets closer I have no choice but to step back a little further until I'm halfway along the jetty.

Ruth is at the start of the jetty now, blocking my only way back onto the shore.

"What do you want?" I scream, as I start breaking down into a series of convulsive sobs. "What do you want from me?"

"I want my sister back," she says calmly. "I want Mary to come back up from the water."

"I can't do that for you?" I shout, before looking toward the darkened hotel. "Help!" I scream, as loud as I can possibly manage. "Somebody help me!"

I wait, and a moment later I see a couple of lights flicker to life in different rooms.

"Help!" I shout again. "I'm down by the lake!"

"Bring her back to me!" the girl hisses, stepping toward me again.

"Don't come any closer!" I screech, holding out a hand and imagining that I have the crucifix with me.

Perhaps faith alone will be enough to ward her off. "Please, I'm begging you," I sob. "I have never, in all my life, done anything to hurt you. I'm a good person, I promise, yet you have tormented me endlessly. I don't deserve this! All I want is to be a good wife to Jobard Nash, and to -"

"Jobard Nash did this to me," she replies, stepping closer

"No!" I scream, moving back until I'm at the very end of the jetty.

There are more lights on at the hotel now, but even at full pelt it will take several minutes before help arrives.

"I'm at the lake!" I shout. "Somebody save me from this girl!"

"I want my sister back," she says again. "I don't understand why she hasn't come to me yet, but I can't wait forever. I need somebody to bring her up for me."

"I can't help you!" I whimper, dropping to my knees and putting my face in my hands. "I don't know anything about this! I'm just an ordinary woman, and I don't want anything to do with ghosts! Can't you leave me alone? Can't you have pity on me and end this constant torment?"

My whole body is shaking now, and I feel certain that I shall never be set free from this madness. Perhaps it is my fate to have this child plaguing me for the rest of my life. I do not deserve such horrors. Truly, I have always done my best to be a decent and kind person, yet evidently I am to be granted no peace. For a moment, the only sound I hear is my own breathless, gasping sobs, but finally I slip my hands down and look back toward the girl.

She's gone.

I'm all alone on the jetty.

I look around, unable to believe my luck, but there's truly no sign of her. A moment later, I realize I can hear voices shouting in the distance, and I spot figures running this way from the hotel. I feel a rush of relief in my chest as I realize that I am saved. Tears of relief now flow down my face, but I am far too weak to stand, so I remain on my knees as I listen to the sound of men shouting as they get closer and closer.

"Thank God," I whisper, shivering as a cold wind blows down from the hills. "Thank you, thank you, thank -"

Suddenly a hand grabs my left ankle from behind, and I'm quickly dragged off the end of the jetty and down into the depths of the ice-cold lake. By the time I'm able to scream, I'm already underwater.

CHAPTER TWENTY-ONE

TO MR. ALVIN CARPENTER,

My client, Mr. Jobard Nash esq, has asked me to write to you, in order that I might convey some information concerning your daughter, Mrs. Ellen Nash, nee Carpenter.

Mr. Nash had cause, on December 1ˢᵗ of this year, to commit Ellen to the Mornington Psychiatric Institute in Wimbledon, London. The details of the case are not a matter for discussion here, but suffice it to say that Ellen suffered an incident in which she almost drowned, after which she was quite insensible. Acting on medical advice, Mr. Nash had her committed in the hope that a short stay would clear her head and bring her back to her senses.

Sadly, this has not happened and the doctors have

decided to keep Ellen at the Mornington indefinitely. For this reason, my client has had no option but to institute divorce proceedings, which should be complete early in the new year. He very much regrets this course of action, but it must be emphasized that a man of his considerable standing requires a wife who can play her part in the development of Mr. Nash's business. He trusts that you will understand his predicament in this matter.

A generous sum has been paid to the Mornington, to cover Ellen's expenses, and further treatment will be subsidized provided all concerned have the good sense to keep this sorry tale out of the newspapers. Should news become public, however, Mr. Nash will have no choice but to end his payments.

You will find Ellen on the acute ward of the Mornington Psychiatric Institute, under the care of Dr. Philip Squire. Please do not contact Mr. Nash about this matter. If there are any matters you really must discuss, they should be directed to my office.

Yours faithfully,

Mr. Clement Ballantyne,
Ballantyne and Sourby Solicitors, London,

Acting on behalf of Mr. Jobard Nash esq

December 23rd, 1945

PART SIX

JOBARD NASH
1950

CHAPTER TWENTY-TWO

"AND WHY WOULD I want to go to the funeral?" I ask, watching from my window as the workers finish putting the final touches to the new swimming pool. "I paid for Ellen's treatment at that infernal hospital over the past five years. If she has finally hung herself in one of their rooms, I am sorry, but..."

My voice trails off for a moment, as I watch one of the workmen carrying a slab from a barrow. I have been planning the installation of this new pool for so long, and I cannot help but feel irritated now that Ellen has seen fit to interrupt my work. She probably put the noose around her neck with the express intention of causing me trouble, and to some extent she has succeeded. Even from hundreds of miles away, that woman has found a way to cause me trouble. I should never have married her in the first place.

Turning, I see that Silas is still waiting on the other side of my desk.

"Tell Mr. Ballantyne that I am done with the matter," I mutter. "I am paying not one more penny to that family. Have him write a letter, informing him that I shall sue if any mention of Ellen's illness is made public. That should shut them up. I am willing to pay for a burial plot, and for a modest headstone of the cheaper variety. But if I extend these further generosities, it is on the condition that I never want to hear the name of those parasites mentioned again. Is that clear?"

"Of course," he replies, before hesitating for a moment. "There is one other matter, Sir, that I feel I should bring to your attention."

Sighing, I realize that I am not to be left in peace and quiet just yet.

"What is it, man?" I mutter, unable to hide my displeasure. "Can't you see that I'm too busy to deal with all these trifling problems? I'm trying to focus on the bigger picture!"

***

"It was quite horrid," the wretched woman whimpers, dabbing at her eyes with tissue paper as she looks along the corridor that leads from her room on the upper floor. "I just stepped out and there she was, up at the far end, watching me and..."

Her voice trails off for a moment, before she collapses in a shuddering mess.

"It's okay, Lizzie," her husband says, placing a hand on her shoulder. "I'm sure it was all in your head. I hardly think Mr. Nash is in the business of letting strange little girls wander the corridors of his hotel." He turns to me. "Are you, Mr. Nash?"

"Of course not," I mutter through gritted teeth, unable to stop watching the pathetic woman as she sobs and wails. I want to march over to her, lift her face so that she's looking at me, and beat some sense into her head. While I'm at it, I'd also like to give her foolish husband a good talking to, since he sees fit to let his wife act in such an unrestrained manner. A man who does not control his wife should not, in my opinion, bring her out in public.

Still, I know I must stay calm.

"It's likely just a trick of the light," the husband continues, crouching next to his wife and handing her another tissue, as if he means to encourage this silliness. "There was no -"

"I saw her!" she hisses, staring at him with anger before turning to me. Evidently she thinks it's quite acceptable to talk to a man in such a dreadful tone. Her own husband, no less. "There was a little girl at the end of that corridor, and she was staring at me with the most awful look in her eyes, and I could tell even from this distance that something was horribly wrong with her! And then she asked me to help her! She said she was looking for somebody named Mary!"

I flinch as soon as I hear that name. Glancing over my shoulder, I briefly make eye contact with Silas, and I can see that he too recognizes the coincidence.

But that is all it is.

A coincidence.

"She said it over and over," the woman

continues as I turn back to her. "Where's Mary? Can you held me find Mary? And her voice was getting more garbled each time, as if her mouth was filling with water. And then she started coming this way, walking along the corridor, so I stepped back into the room and locked the door, and she..."

Again, her voice trails off, as if she's lost in whatever fantasy fills her head.

"And then what, Lizzie?" her husband asks. "What did the -"

"Don't encourage her!" I spit.

Ignoring me, the husband hands her yet another tissue. It's almost as if he *wants* her to make a show of herself.

"What happened after you shut the door?" he continues. "Did that end it? Did that make the girl go away?"

"I heard her coming up on the other side," she replies, her eyes widening with horror as she continues to stare along the corridor. "Slow footsteps, and then they stopped as if she meant to come into the room. And that's when I heard her voice again, asking me about someone named Mary. She said she'd been looking for her, but that she couldn't find her anywhere. I made sure the door was locked, and then I retreated to the other side of the bed. Then I turned to the telephone, but suddenly I saw a flash of movement in the corner of my eye. I turned back and somehow she was in the room with me!"

She breaks down sobbing again, her whole body shuddering violently.

"That's when I came back up," her husband says, turning to me. "I stepped out of the elevator and immediately heard poor Lizzie shouting at somebody to stay back. Of course, I hurried to the room, but the door was locked and the key was in the hole from the other side, so I had to bang and bang until finally Lizzie managed to get it open." He pauses for a moment. "There was nobody in here with her. I checked thoroughly. She insists there was a little girl, but evidently this apparition had vanished by the time I got here."

He stares at me, as his wife continues to sob on the chair.

"Does that name mean anything to you, Mr. Nash?" he adds.

"What name?"

"Mary."

He continues to stare at me, as if he expects me to add fuel to this ridiculous fire.

"Nothing at all," I tell him sternly. "Of course not."

"Are you sure?"

"I am not in the habit of being unsure about anything!"

"Where's Mary?" the woman whimpers. "That's what she kept saying. Over and over again! The more she said it, the more she sounded... I don't know, less like a scared little girl, and more like someone rather angry."

She looks up at me, and now I have the pair of them staring at me as if they expect me to tell them that I

231

believe their story.

"Well," I say finally, turning to the husband, "I can't imagine what you want *me* to do about the matter. If your wife is prone to delusions, that is very much your problem."

"Delusions?" she sobs. "How dare you!"

"And how dare *you*?" I reply, deeply unimpressed by the way she addresses me. "You have entered my establishment and seen fit to cause tremendous trouble. Why, I can't imagine what you expect to get out of it. I can only assume that you are of weak character, and that you will apologize when you come to your senses. Either that, or your husband tolerates such excesses and will turn a blind eye to this idiocy."

"Weak character?"

She gets to her feet, her eyes filled with anger, and her husband quickly puts a hand on her arm as if to calm her down.

"I'm sure Mr. Nash didn't mean it that way," he whispers to her.

"That girl was real!" she hisses at me. "She was right in front of me, as surely as you all are now! You're the one who should apologize, for letting people stay here when you clearly have some form of spirit haunting the hotel! Surely my wife is not the first person to encounter such a presence?"

"Nonsense!" I spit.

"I saw her!" she shouts. "And if I saw her, then other people must have seen her! Or they will soon, at least! You can't keep something like this hidden, Mr.

Nash! You can't just sweep a ghost under the carpet!"

"A charming image," I mutter.

"The truth will come out!" she sneers, stepping closer to me before her husband takes her arm and starts guiding her into their room. "People will find out what you did! You think you're the king of this place! You think that out here, you can do anything you want and get away with it! But the ghosts won't just fade away! They're going to make sure you pay for all the pain you've caused! They'll haunt you until the day you die, and you couldn't run from them even if you tried!"

"That's enough!" her husband hisses, finally getting her into the room. After a moment, he turns back to me. "Are you sure the name Mary means nothing to you, Mr. Nash? Or the idea of a strange young girl haunting the hotel?"

"Don't be absurd!" I snap.

He stares at me for a moment longer, almost as if he's studying my features.

"Interesting," he mutters finally. "Well, thank you for your time, Mr. Nash. It has been most illuminating."

With that, he swings the door shut, and a few seconds later I hear hushed tones coming from the other side. I pause, trying to make out what they're saying, but I suppose there's no point wasting my time.

"Well," I say finally, forcing a smile as I turn to Silas, "she certainly seems to be a rather angry young lady, does she not? Spouting nonsense like that. Honestly, I don't know what the world is coming to."

I wait for Silas to reply, but he seems barely

about to meet my gaze.

"I hardly see that you needed to bring me down here for that," I continue, turning to head back to the elevator. "The woman is an utter -"

"That's not all of it," he says suddenly, interrupting me.

I turn to him.

"I've been watching them since they arrived a couple of days ago," he continues, finally looking me in the eye. "I could tell something wasn't right from the moment they checked in. I've got a good nose for that sort of thing, and it turned out I was right. Sir, have you ever heard of the Desermes family?"

"Never in my life. Why?"

"Because Robert and Elizabeth Desermes are here with two friends. His brother, and his brother's wife. And with all due respect, Mr. Nash, I don't think they're here merely for a holiday. I think they've got some business here, something they're trying to cover up. And I think that little scene just now was mostly for your benefit. As a kind of test."

"What are they here for, then?" I ask, feeling a flicker of concern in my chest.

"I caught them doing something last night," he continues. "Down in the dining room. Something that maybe they shouldn't have been doing. Something that suggests they know more about Mary and Ruth Maywhistle than they're letting on. Sir, either way... I think this should be a matter of concern for you."

CHAPTER TWENTY-THREE

"SIR EDWARD, I AM truly honored that you saw fit to grace us with your company this evening. I hope you are enjoying the luxuries of our humble Lakeforth Hotel?"

"Luxuries?" the old man replies, turning to me and staring at me through his monocle.

"We try out best," I continue, as the serving staff remove our plates. "And did you enjoy dinner? I employ a wonderful chef. He's from all the way up in Edinburgh."

"Exotic, eh?" Sir Edward replies with a chuckle. "It was fine, Mr. Nash. Very fine."

"Only fine?"

I feel a flicker of concern as I realize that Sir Edward Barringham seems only moderately satisfied with his stay so far. He's the first member of the gentry to visit the hotel during my time here, and I need him to be impressed so that he'll spread the word when he gets back to London. Still, I tell myself not to panic, and that there'll be plenty of over the next few days to ensure that he recognizes the proper qualities of the hotel.

Spotting movement nearby, I turn and see Robert Desermes and his wretched wife heading out of the room, along with two others. I'm tempted to ask them to leave the hotel altogether, but I suppose I should hold fire. I briefly make eye contact with Silas, who is in his usual spot by the door, greeting new arrivals. I am sure he can deal with any problems that arise during the evening.

"Dessert will be here shortly," I explain, turning back to Sir Edward with a smile. "The fork on the left should be used."

He furrows his brow.

"Well, I know *that*!" he mutters grumpily. "I'm not a savage, you know!"

"Of course not," I stammer, "I merely -"

"Maybe you people out here don't know which fork to use when," he continues, "but in London we have a little more class. You shouldn't assume that the rest of us are fools, Mr. Nash. You shouldn't warn a man about his table manners in advance. It's rather rude."

"I'm terribly sorry," I reply, feeling utterly humiliated as I look down at my cutlery. I want to apologize again, but I tell myself to stay quiet, even though I feel I am blushing terribly. I have made a dreadful faux pas, and I'm sure Sir Edward will spread the news when he gets back to London. I shall simply have to find some way to make it up to him. Some other effort is required.

"You know, you have a growing reputation in

London, Mr. Nash," he says finally.

"I do?"

He nods. "People are talking about you."

I feel a flicker of excitement in my chest. Perhaps finally I am to be given the esteem I deserve, and the rancid upper classes of London are going to recognize my achievements.

"They say," he continues, "that you're the kind of man who could strike a deal with the devil. I suppose that's a compliment."

"I suppose it is," I reply, although I'm a little uncertain. After a moment, however, I realize that it *must* be good to have such a reputation. "Everything in life boils down to deals, in the end," I add, forcing a smile. "Contracts. Give and take. Perhaps I'm just a little more honest about that fact. I can't say I'm entirely surprised to learn that this approach has afforded me a glowing reputation in our fair capital."

"I didn't say it was glowing," he mutters, as the waiter approaches the table. "Just that you have a reputation."

***

The room is quiet. Absolutely quiet. In fact, as I sit on the end of my bed and listen to the silence, I cannot help but marvel that the entire hotel seems to have fallen into a lull. I could honestly believe, at this moment in time, that I am the last man left in the world.

Finally, the silence is broken by the sound of footsteps out in the corridor, and I get to my feet just as I hear a knock at the door.

"Are they doing it again?" I ask, as I pull the door open and find Silas standing outside. "What time is it, man?"

He checks his watch. "A little after 2am."

"And they're down there?"

He nods. "Robert, Elizabeth, Tobias and Emily Desermes. Sir, they're in the drawing room, and they're doing that..."

He pauses, with a hint of disgust in his features.

"That *thing*," he manages to spit out finally. "That awful, irreligious thing. They're messing with elements they don't understand. Sir, I don't understand why you didn't just throw them out when I told you earlier. Why did you wait? Why do you have to see it for yourself?"

"I am a curious man," I reply, stepping out into the corridor and pulling my door shut. "Do I detect fear in your voice, Silas? I never had you down as superstitious."

"It's not that, it's just..."

Again, his voice trails off.

"You needn't accompany me," I tell him. "If you would prefer to retire to your quarters for the night, I understand. Perhaps you find it difficult to deal with such events. So long as Sir Edward is safely in his room and cannot witness what occurs, I shall be content."

"I just think they're stirring up trouble. Sir, if -"

"So be it," I reply, cutting him off. "I shall go down alone. Don't worry, Silas, I doubt the situation will call for a man of your physical talents. I shall simply observe these Desermes trouble-makers and see if they find what they're looking for. Perhaps they'll make contact with their target."

Silas immediately makes the sign of the cross on his chest.

"Go to bed," I mutter, turning and walking toward the elevator. "Oh, and in the morning, remove that portrait of my wife and I from the lobby. I don't care where you put it, but hang it somewhere so that I won't ever have to see it again. The sight of her face, even in reproduction, makes me nauseous. I do not wish to be reminded of her emotional weakness."

***

"Ruth Maywhistle, are you here? We want to speak to the spirit of Ruth Maywhistle. Ruth, if you're here, can you give us a sign?"

Standing in the doorway, staying in the cover of shadows, I watch as these four interlopers sit at the far end of the dining room and conduct their unholy little ceremony. Robert and Tobias Desermes, and their wives Elizabeth and Emily, are seated at a table by the window, and they each have a hand on a small wooden device that they have placed on some kind of board. Silas informed me that this device is a Ouija board, something that cretins believe will allow them to contact the dead. Evidently, these four members of the Desermes family have come to the Lakeforth because they wish to speak to a ghost.

And that whole scene earlier, when Robert

pretended to comfort his crying wife, was clearly staged. They wanted to see how I'd react. Well, I shall show them a reaction, alright. Just as soon as I have seen exactly what they're up to.

"Ruth Maywhistle," Robert continues, his voice tense with anticipation. "It's very important that we speak to you. We have a message for you, a message from your sister Mary."

Now I *know* that these people are idiots. Ruth Maywhistle died a decade ago, when I shot her in the head during one of my drunken adventures. I was trying to shoot a paperweight from her hand, and I'm afraid the whiskey caused me to miss. I had Silas dispose of the body, which I believe he weighed down and threw over the end of the jetty. Meanwhile, her sister Mary was a crippled little thing who I had killed and tossed out at the same time. Silas disposed of that body, too, so I'm sure the dead girls have no need of any intermediary. Their ghosts can simply speak to one another directly, and leave the rest of us well alone.

Not that ghosts exist at all, of course. Of that, I am certain. I have been certain since the day my father sealed me inside my grandmother's coffin.

"Ruth Maywhistle," Robert Desermes says again, sounding a little more desperate this time. "Please, we have a message for you from Mary. Are you here? Can you -"

Suddenly he falls silent as something moves on the board.

"Is it her?" Elizabeth asks.

"Is it you, Ruth?" Robert continues. "Please -"

Before he can finish, the item on the board moves again, dragging their fingers to one of the corners.

"Yes!" the other woman says excitedly. "We've done it! We've made contact!"

"Ruth," Robert stammers, as if he can barely wait to get the words out, "my name is Robert Desermes, and I came here tonight specifically so that we could talk to you and deliver a message. We believe we have uncovered the truth about your death. We've been working with your sister Mary, we've been talking to her, and now we just need to hear your side. Can you appear to us, Ruth? Are you able to physically manifest?"

Silence falls, and the four idiots wait.

"Talk to us," he adds, sounding a little desperate now. "Please."

"Please, Ruth," the other gentleman says. "Don't be shy now."

Again, they wait.

Again, there is only silence.

"Does that mean she can't," Elizabeth asks finally, "or that she refuses?"

"I don't know," Robert continues, "but -"

Suddenly he looks this way. I step back, further into the shadows, and after a moment he turns to the others again. I find it absurd that I must sneak about in my own hotel, but I wish to observe these idiots for a while longer.

"What is it?" one of the women asks.

"Nothing."

"Did you hear something?"

"Just a bump. I don't think it was her." He pauses, staring back down at the board. "Ruth Maywhistle," he continues finally, "we know you were murdered. We know your death was unjust, and that you seek retribution. That's why we're here. We want to help you, but first we need to understand more about what happened. Mary could only help us with so much, but she couldn't tell us enough."

They all sit in silence for a moment.

"Something's wrong," he adds, clearly frustrated. "She's here, but at the same time she's holding back. It's almost as if there's some kind of force that's making her scared to appear."

"Maybe it's that awful Nash man," Elizabeth mutters. "You saw him earlier, Robert. The man has a ghastly countenance, he almost seems to chill the air when he walks into a room."

Charming.

"The ghost of Ruth Maywhistle is certainly fearful of something," Robert replies. "Ruth, whatever worries you, you must not let it stop you. For your sister's sake, if not for your own, please come to us. We can help you, I promise!"

As he babbles on some more, I am tempted to step forward at once and end this whole charade. Why, I could toss these four idiots out of my hotel in the middle of the night, and I would certainly have every justification for doing so. There is something amusing about them, however, and I remain in the shadows for a few minutes longer as I observe their pathetic attempts to contact the spirit of little Ruth. Just as I am contemplating an interruption, however, I realize I can see a very faint shape in the darkness over by the table, almost as if some figure is edging toward them.

It's her.

I feel a flutter of fear in my chest as I realize that I can see the form of a little girl. Her features are not particularly clear, and she seems to possess an ethereal glow that marks her as distinct from the world around her. I tell myself that this is a form of show, that they have dressed some other child up in an act of theatrical showmanship, but deep down I know that the girl's features seem awfully familiar.

It cannot be her, though.

She's dead.

"Please Ruth," Robert Desermes continues, patently unaware of the flickering vision that stands just a few feet from his side, "give us a sign."

Unable to help myself, I take a cautious step forward, marveling at the sight of the girl as she approaches the table. I can see her face a little more clearly now, and her dark, intense stare. She's watching the board, almost as if she means to communicate with the four idiots. The more I watch her, the more I feel my disbelief starting to crumble, and the more I find myself contemplating the possibility that her ghost really *has* been summoned.

Is it possible?

Was I wrong, all this time?

"Ruth, talk to us!" Robert says firmly.

I take another step forward, out of the shadows.

Suddenly the little girl turns and looks straight at me, and immediately she opens her mouth and emits an ear-piercing scream. Her face distorts into a rictus of anger, and her flickering form briefly becomes more clear. Startled, I take a step back, bumping against the wall, and in an instant the sight of the girl is completely gone, even as her scream rings in the air for a few more seconds.

"What was that?" Elizabeth Desermes stammers, getting to her feet and looking around before spotting me.

"It's him!" Robert adds, standing and making his way around the table. "That's why she couldn't bring herself to talk to us! He was scaring her away!"

I open my mouth to tell him he's a damn fool, but I can only stare at the spot where the spectral figure was standing. I feel a prickling sweat on the back of my neck, and for the first time in my life I'm contemplating the possibility that ghosts might be real.

"I heard something else," Elizabeth continues, still looking around the room. "Didn't the rest of you? It was as if somebody was crying out..."

"We know about you!" Robert sneers, ignoring his wife and marching toward me until finally he stops in the middle of the dining room. "We know what you are, Jobard Nash! You're a monster! You're a killer!"

"Is that a fact?" I reply, struggling to compose myself as I see the girl's screaming face once more in my mind's eye. "You seem very sure of yourself, considering you are in possession of no facts whatsoever."

"You're a murderer!" he hisses.

"I have never laid hands on another soul," I tell him. "Not once."

"Only because you get others to do your dirty work!"

Forcing a smile, I step toward him. I am perfectly willing to lie to this wretched man. After all, certain types of people are not to be trusted with the truth.

"Might I remind you," I continue, "that you are on my property, and that while you are here, you are my guests. Now, I know that you are paying for the privilege, but I rather feel you could be a little more polite. The deaths of Ruth and Mary Maywhistle were a tragedy, but -"

"Mary Maywhistle isn't dead."

I open my mouth to reply, although the words catch in my throat.

"That made you take notice, huh?" he continues, with a sickening grin. "I know you *wanted* her dead, but that little girl was made of stronger stuff. She literally dragged her burned, battered body from the spot in the forest where she was dumped, and she made her way to the road."

"I..."

Hesitating, I feel certain that this is part of some trick.

"For the past ten years," he explains, "she's been receiving care at a home in London. She was taken in by my father, who happened to be the one who found her. Mary can barely speak, but she told us enough and we quickly realized where she'd come from. The police might not have been much use, but that doesn't mean we're going to let you get away with what you did. As soon as we've gathered a little more evidence, the Desermes family will ensure that -"

"What evidence?" I spit. "The words of a ghost?"

"You're scared," he replies, as his smile grows. "I can see it in your eyes, man. You're almost panicked!"

"Rot!"

"So you're not bothered by the fact that Mary is alive?"

"I don't even believe you," I mutter. "You're a gullible fool, and you think others are gullible too. I don't know your true purpose in coming here, but -"

"Justice!" he shouts, stepping closer. "Justice for Mary Maywhistle, and justice for her dead sister Ruth!"

"There's no such thing as justice," I tell him. "Justice is whatever rich men, *powerful* men, wish it to be. And I assure you, there is nobody in this land who cares one jot about two scrappy little girls who died a decade ago."

"Keep telling yourself that, if it makes you feel any better. But Mary is alive. She's in London, and one day she'll be well enough to tell us more. One day, Jobard Nash, you will pay for every foul deed that you've committed, and for every deed that you've commissioned from others, and the world will know that you are a monster!"

Hesitating, I cannot help but find his righteous indignation rather amusing. A faint smile crosses my lips, and I rather think this young gentleman is on the verge of losing his temper entirely and striking me. I wait a moment longer, hoping that he *will* make a move, so that I can have him carted off by the police, but unfortunately he is just about able to hold his resolve. And the more he does so, the more I feel my own weakening.

He's lying.

He has to be.

Mary Maywhistle has been dead these past fifteen years. Of that, I am certain.

"Come on," he says finally to the others, "we're done here. We'll never make contact with Ruth while this monster is in the building. We'll come back and speak to her once he's rotting in a jail cell somewhere."

"I hardly think that is going to happen," I mutter, as the four of them make their way past me and head out of the dining room. "You would require far more evidence that the witterings of a dead young girl, made during a seance." Turning, I watch as they head across the lobby. "You will leave my business alone!" I call after them. "Do you hear me? I will not tolerate this interference in the running of my hotel!"

They have the temerity to go up the stairs without even turning to acknowledge me, but I am quite certain that they heard every word. My initial instinct is to go after them, but instead I turn and look over at the table next to the window. The fools have left their childish board behind, and I wander over, so that I might inspect the damnable thing a little more clearly.

There are letters on the board, as well as a small

wooden block with some form of lens at its center.

"Is this it?" I mutter, finding their efforts to be rather pitiful. "Is this how one attempts to contact a spirit?"

Picking the board up, I examine it for a moment longer, before taking holds of the side and breaking the childish toy against my knee.

"There," I continue, "let us see how -"

Suddenly feeling something brush against my elbow, I turn and see that there is nobody behind me. My heart is racing, however, and I am quite certain that some force briefly moved against me. Perhaps in their foolishness, the four idiots nevertheless managed to stumble upon something real. If the ghost of Ruth Maywhistle *is* at the hotel, then perhaps my former wife's rambling claims five years ago were rooted in truth after all. In the circumstances, I might have been a little hasty in having her hauled off to an asylum, and -

No.

No, I am not that weak.

I refuse to let a few cheap parlor tricks rob me of my sense.

I know two things, among many others, to be true. One is that Mary Maywhistle is long dead. And the other is that what I saw tonight was not the ghost of her sister Ruth. At most, I saw a stir of vapors, some concoction or trick. I shall not allow myself to be tricked.

And there is one very easy way to make certain that Mary is, indeed, long dead.

***

"I am sorry," Silas says quietly, bowing his head in shame. "I have carried out every order you have ever given me, except... I could not bring myself to kill Mary Maywhistle."

"Yet you had no trouble disposing of Ruth's body?" I ask, struggling to understand how this strong, dependable employee can suddenly appear so weak. I should strike him for his foolishness.

"She was already dead," he replies. "It was different, dropping her corpse into the lake. But Mary was still just about alive. I did everything else you wanted. I took her out into the forest, I even held a rock in my hand, ready to crush her skull, but I just couldn't do it. I thought if I left her there, she'd die of exposure. I just couldn't murder a child."

"So you left her to freeze?"

He nods.

"And somehow," I continue, "that seemed *less* cruel to you? Even though it would doubtless have taken so much longer for her to perish?"

"I just couldn't do it. I tried. She was sobbing and begging me to end her pain, but I failed."

Pausing for a moment, I realize that I can no longer deny the truth that has been presented so plainly to me. I might not believe in ghostly young girl, but live ones are another matter.

"And now that Mary Maywhistle has turned up alive in London," I tell him, "do you have any idea how gravely you have let me down?"

"Am I to be dismissed?"

Staring at him for a moment, I know in my heart that I cannot possibly trust him ever again. At the same time, I am not entirely certain that I would feel comfortable cutting him loose. He is still a useful man, and it would be foolish to dispense with his services entirely.

"I must ready myself for a journey," I tell him finally. "In the meantime, those four idiots are going to check out of the hotel very soon. There is one thing you can do for me, Silas, that will demonstrate that I might still rely upon your services."

"I'll do anything," he replies, with a hint of desperation in his voice. "Well, except..."

"Except kill a child," I continue, rolling my eyes. "Yes, I understand now that you have this unfortunate limitation. Fortunately Robert Desermes, his brother, and their wives might be childish and immature, but they are most certainly not children. So I doubt you'll have the same problem again."

CHAPTER TWENTY-FOUR

"HAVE YOU BEEN TO the palace, dear boy?" Sir Edward asks, peering at me once again through his monocle as we sit at dinner the following evening.

"Which palace would that be?" I reply, trying to affect a casual air. "I have walked past Kensington Palace several times, during my trips to London."

"Kensington?" His monocle falls out, as if he's genuinely shocked, and he takes a moment to put it back in place. "I mean Buckingham Palace, of course. When were you last there?"

"Well, I..."

My voice trails off as I realize that most likely the game is already up. Sir Edward Barringham, like all the rest of London high society, was born with a silver spoon in his mouth. To him, a visit to Buckingham Palace is nothing, whereas to me such an honor remains out of reach. Perhaps I shall never persuade him, or any of his moneyed friends, to accept me as one of their own. The stench of my meager upbringing will always linger.

"Never mind," he mutters, taking a sip of wine. "You're doing alright for yourself out here in the provinces. Not everybody is cut out for London."

"Well, I -"

Before I can finish, I hear the most dreadful noise coming from the lobby, as if somebody is yelling in a most uncouth manner. I turn to Sir Edward and see that he, too, has noticed the commotion.

"You must excuse me a moment," I say, as I get to my feet. "I'm sure it's nothing. I shall be right back."

***

"What are they still doing here?" I snap, standing in the lobby and watching as Robert Desermes leads his reprehensible relatives through to the library. "I expected them to be gone by now!"

"I didn't realize they were going to come back like this," Silas explains. "I'm sorry, I tried to make them leave, but they threatened to call the police and I wasn't sure if that was a good idea. I decided that maybe I should wait until you returned."

Hearing raised voices in the distance, I'm shocked to see two other guests quickly hurrying out of the library and making for the stairs. It's as if wild, common beasts have been let loose in my fabulous hotel.

"We've had rather a lot of early departures," Silas continues. "I'm afraid Mr. Desermes and his associates have been upsetting the guests with all their talk of ghosts and spectral figures. The whole thing seems almost contagious. Already, we've had eight further reports of a little girl being spotted in the corridors and rooms upstairs. Sometimes, she's even been seen in two places at once. I don't know much about this sort of thing, but I'm starting to think that people are rather easily influenced."

"Easily influenced?" I sneer, feeling a rising sense of fury as I realize that these fools seem determined to destroy my hotel. "They're idiots, through and through! There's no other word to describe it!"

A moment later, a man and a woman come rushing down the stairs, carrying suitcases to the reception desk.

"We're checking out!" the man stammers, tossing his key to the woman on the desk's other side. "We can't stay one more night in this wretched place!"

"And why is that?" I ask, stepping toward them.

"My wife saw a ghost in our room!" he explains, almost tripping over his own tongue as he struggles to get the words out. "A horrible little girl!"

"And what did this little girl look like?"

"I didn't see her face," the woman sobs. "She had a sheet over her head, just like the ghosts you see in storybooks!"

"No doubt," I mutter, rolling my eyes. "And tell me, did you witness this sight shortly after you heard some of the other guests discussing such things?"

"Well, I..." She hesitates, as if she's reluctant to even consider the possibility that she was influenced by such talk. "There was a discussion, yes. I overheard it in the dining room. I didn't feel up to much straight after, so I went to bed for a rest, and that's when I saw that... *thing*!"

"You saw no ghost," I continue. "Like most of the other fools here, you simply allowed your imagination to run riot and now you're running away like a frightened child! Well, good riddance!"

"That's no way to speak to my wife!" the man protests.

"I'll speak to her however I wish!" I say firmly. "This is my hotel, and if your wife chooses to play the fool here, I will most certainly let her know what I think! And right now, she is acting like some kind of lunatic!"

"I've never been so insulted in all my life!" he replies. "And neither has my wife!"

"Get out of my hotel!" I snap, grabbing their suitcases and carrying them to the door myself. These fools aren't worthy of staying at the Lakeforth, and I am most certainly not going to tolerate their presence here. Tossing their bags down the steps, I turn and see the man and woman staring at me with shocked expressions. "If you act like idiots," I continue, "you must expect to be *treated* like idiots! Please, consider yourselves barred, and do not ever sully my establishment with your petty presence again. And since idiocy loves company, I'm sure all your friends, family and acquaintances back home are fools too, so kindly inform them that they are not welcome either!"

As the morons grumble about my supposed rudeness and head outside, I make my way back through the door and stop as I see that another couple has arrived to check out.

"Is this all the work of those four Desermes idiots?" I mutter darkly.

"I believe so," Silas replies. "As I said, they've really been upsetting the other guests. They keep trying to contact the dead, and I'm afraid their efforts have rather eroded the hotel's atmosphere. They've divided into distinct groups, each of them attempting to get in touch with Ruth from a different room. I'm sorry, I know you wanted me to get rid of them, but they haven't made it easy."

"Deal with the other three," I reply, as I spot Robert Desermes hurrying up the stairs again. "I'll speak to the ringleader myself."

At that moment, I spot Sir Edward at the door to the dining room, watching the scene with an expression of utter bemusement.

"Nothing to worry about," I tell him, forcing a smile. "Please, return to the table and enjoy your dessert."

***

"Ruth, can you hear me? Ruth, I know you're scared, but I'm going to have to ask you to be very brave. Can you do that for me, Ruth? We need -"

Robert turns suddenly, evidently having heard me reach the doorway. As soon as we make eye contract, I see his resolve strengthen, and it's obvious that the mere sight of me is enough to drive pure disgust through his body. I remain calm, of course, but deep down the feeling is entirely mutual.

"She won't come while you're here," he tells me. "She's terrified of you."

"I can't imagine why."

"She's told us about you, you know," he continues, as I step into the library. "As soon as you left yesterday, we began to have better luck contacting her. She's already talked to us about the things you did. About how you burned her family's home to the ground so you could take their land. About how you had Mary dumped in the basement for a few days. About how you care nothing for the sanctity of human life. About how you couldn't even find it in your heart to give her a decent Christian burial."

"I find it rather interesting," I reply, "that this supposed ghost apparently doesn't even know where her own body has been laid to rest."

"That's one of the things we're going to do for her," he sneers. "We're going to help her, so she can have a little peace."

"She's in the lake," I continue. "Honestly, little Ruth's ghost sounds awfully confused if she can't keep these facts straight in her head."

"She didn't even realize she was dead," he tells me. "At first, she insisted she was alive, that she was searching for the ghost of her dead sister. We had to tell her over and over again, we had to make her understand that Mary had escaped, that she's alive and in London as we speak."

"And where in London might she be?"

"As if I'd tell you that!"

"You're testing my patience, Mr. Desermes. That is not a very wise move."

"Ruth understands now," he continues. "She knows that she's dead. The newly departed sometimes struggle with this realization. They can't, or they won't, accept that their lives are over, but Ruth is past that stage now. And she's angry, Mr. Nash. She's furious. She wants us to recover her body and give her a proper funeral, and she wants her sister Mary to visit her grave. Then, maybe, she can find the peace you would so cruelly deny her."

At this, I can't help laughing. The poor man is so utterly deluded, it's difficult to believe that he doesn't deserve a place in one of the country's growing number of asylums.

"Laugh all you want," he continues, stepping past me and heading out of the room. "It won't change anything. Ruth even told us about the night she was with your wife on the jetty. She told us things that nobody else could possibly know. She reached through to us from the world beyond death, and she helped us to understand what kind of monster we're dealing with."

"My wife was a weak and feeble woman," I reply, turning to him.

"But she saw Ruth that night, Mr. Nash. She saw her as clearly as you and I see one another now. Once we obtain some more information from Ruth's ghost, we should have enough to uncover all your dirty little secrets. And then we can ensure that your pathetic little empire comes crashing to the ground."

I watch as he walks away, and I can't help

feeling that this awful man deserves a taste of his own medicine. At the same time, it's clear that he won't be happy until the Lakeforth has been completely ruined, which means I must deal with him as quickly as possible.

With that thought in mind, I set off after him. He's heading toward the library's exit, and then he'll be in the corridor that leads to the lobby. I cannot let him get that far, not with Sir Edward still somewhere nearby, so I hurry up behind him and take the knife from my belt.

CHAPTER TWENTY-FIVE

"I GAVE THE WORKMEN some time off," Silas explains breathlessly as he drags another of the large bags over to the hole that has been dug at the patio's edge. "They didn't complain too much."

Clearly struggling a little with all the effort, he hauls the bag past me and throws it down into the still-wet cement that has been laid at the bottom of the hole. I am finally having a proper swimming pool built, one that I feel certain will draw even more guests from far and wide, and work can begin properly tomorrow once the concrete foundation is set properly. Staring down now into the hole, I cannot help but marvel at the four large bags that Silas has tossed down into the cement, and I rather like the idea that the pool will be built directly on top of them.

"I trust Robert Desermes and his family checked out properly first?" I ask.

"Of course."

"And has anybody been in touch yet, to ask whether they left?"

"A solicitor from London called," he replies. "A Mr. Albraid, I believe. I simply told him that the four guests had left as scheduled, and that as far as I knew they should be back in London by now. He sounded a little worried, but as I pointed out, there was nothing I could tell him about the guests' exploits once they'd checked out. I mean, the guests are no longer our responsibility once they've turned their keys back in, are they?"

"Absolutely not," I mutter, still watching the four bags as they rest in the cement. "Perhaps now things can get back to normal."

Turning, I look back toward the hotel. The events of the past few twenty-four hours have emptied the place, with all the guests having departed. Even Sir Edward left a day early. Word has apparently spread to London that there were certain unusual occurrences here, and I'm resigned to the fact that it will likely take quite some time before the damage has been undone. But it *shall* be undone, because I refuse to accept any other eventuality. This fuss is a setback, but one that shall prove only temporary.

"I'll get this filled in," Silas explains, heading over to the cement barrow. "Once the bodies are covered, the workmen can get on with building the pool."

"Oh, I wouldn't worry too much," I reply, going over to join him and taking a knife from one of the trestle tables. "I can manage from now on, Silas. You've served me well, but I'm not sure I can rely on you any longer. Not after your failure with regards to Mary Maywhistle."

He turns to me. "What -"

Before he can get another word out, I drive the knife into his chest, quickly twisting the handle and forcing the blade to slice through his heart. He lets out a pained gasp, but then he seems almost to freeze, and it's no trouble at all to push him back and send him crashing down to join the bagged bodies in the cement. He struggles a little once he's landed, and I see some blood running from his mouth as he makes a deep choking sound, but all things considered I'm surprised by just how quickly and easily he slumps down into the gray sludge.

Turning, I look over at the shovels resting against a nearby wall. Fortunately, I've become rather accustomed of late to the idea of performing important tasks myself. I have relied upon Silas for many years, but everybody has their expiry date. If I am to complete my work at this hotel, I can only truly trust my own efforts.

***

"Where are you?" I shout, stumbling against the shoeshine machine but quickly steadying myself against the wall as I take another sip of whiskey. "Do you hear me, girl? Show yourself!"

I wait, but all I hear is silence. The entire hotel has fallen still, ever since the last of the guests departed in the wake of the Desermes debacle, and it seems I am unable to summon the ghost of Ruth Maywhistle. Evidently she is happy to come when she is summoned by a group of idiots and their foolish toys, but she hides in the shadows when her presence is demanded by a man of substance.

The ghost is scared of me.

Good.

That is how it should be.

Then again, perhaps she does not even exist.

"I wonder if you are real," I mutter, stumbling along the corridor, bumping a little into the wall on the left and then a little into the wall on the right. "Do you hear that, child? I find myself wondering whether ghost sightings are, in fact, more than just the preserve of madmen and foolish women. I wonder whether your spirit is knocking about here somewhere, but I'm afraid I have news for you. If you think you're going to be allowed to haunt my hotel, you've got another thing coming. If you *are* real, we shall have to put a stop to that at once."

Stopping at the top of the stairs, I look down toward the lobby. With all the guests having departed, and no more booked in for the next week, I sent the staff home, so I am the only soul left at the hotel. Well, the only *living* soul. I have spent several years building this place up, turning the Lakeforth into the epitome of style and class, and it has all been sent crashing down around me. A lesser man would give up and accept his failure, but fortunately I am made of sterner stuff. I count this experience as a lesson, and I shall learn from that lesson.

And the Lakeforth is going to rise from the ashes. The likes of Robert Desermes will not win.

"This place will be teeming again!" I announce proudly, for the benefit of Ruth Maywhistle and any other ghosts who might be listening. "You'll see. I'll show them all. I'll make them all marvel at my efforts. And then Sir Edward Barringham and his blue-blooded friends will see that they were wrong about me!"

I stumble forward, only to trip on the top step. Tumbling down the stairs, I land hard at the bottom, dropping my bottle and sending it skidding across the marble floor until it slams into the wall. As for myself, I feel stiffness and pains in a few joints as I sit up, but I am otherwise unharmed. Perhaps it is true that, when inebriated, one tends to fall more softly.

Of course, I pinch myself on the arm, just to make sure that I have not joined the ranks of the ghosts.

"Are you laughing at me?" I ask, getting to my feet and heading over to retrieve the bottle. Some of the whiskey has spilled out, leaving just a dribble, but I have plenty more in the library. I stare down at the bottle for a moment, feeling a rush of anger in my chest, and finally I turn and throw the cursed thing at the far wall.

The bottle smashes, and shards of glass fall to the floor.

"I will not be denied!" I scream, so that every possible ghost will hear me, even those who might cower in the basement. "I am a great man and it is my destiny to make this the greatest hotel in England! And I -"

Stopping suddenly, I realize that there is a figure

standing at the top of the stairs, watching me. Even before I have looked up into her eyes, I know that it is Ruth Maywhistle. A faint smile crosses my lips.

So she *is* real, after all. In which case, perhaps I really *did* see my grandmother's dead body move all those years ago. If ghosts are real, then I must be particularly cursed when it comes to seeing them.

"Look at me," I say, holding my hands out to my sides. "Marvel at me, child. No matter how the bastards try to bring me down, I always get back up."

I wait, in case she might say something, but she merely continues to stare at me.

"I was not born into wealth," I continue, feeling a hint of tears in my eyes. "I worked for it. I used my brain. Every man born into this world has the chances that I had, but how many take those chances? Almost none. Yet I, Jobard Nash, fought my way up from nothing. I always knew I would need a grand project, something to make those snobs in London pay attention, and that is when I conceived of this hotel. It began as a stepping stone, if you like, to greater riches, but now I believe it has become something more important. It has become the great foundation of my life."

Again I wait, and again she says nothing.

"I shall not let ghosts stop me," I mutter, turning and limping toward the double doors that lead into the library. "You'll fade, child. And if you do not, you'll be able to watch as I rebuild this place. The Desermes family tried to meddle, and I dealt with them. I have been quite methodical in my approach, and I have made certain that every enemy in my path has been brushed aside. I am unstoppable."

Reaching the doorway, I stop for a moment before turning. To my surprise, I find that the ghostly figure of Ruth Maywhistle has silently made her way down the stairs and is only a few feet behind me, watching me with those dark, rotten little eyes.

I cannot help but chuckle at the sight of her.

"Do you doubt me?" I ask. "Do you think I shall fail? Do you think you, and perhaps some other ghosts, can drag this hotel down into the mire?"

I wait.

She does not reply.

"What's wrong?" I ask. "Cat got your tongue?"

Again, her lips do not move.

"For a ghost," I mutter, "you're not very lively, are you?"

Smiling, I look into her eyes and see a flickering sense of hatred. No doubt she blames me for everything that happened to her, but it is simply the way of the world that the strong should sweep aside the weak. Should I have done nothing when she and her family stood in my way? Perhaps I shall even enjoy her efforts to haunt me. They will provide amusement while I -

Suddenly she steps forward and screams, and her ear-piercing cry fills the air as her face fills with the plump, pus-filled tones of rotten flesh. The scream continues for several more seconds, its intensity increasing, until finally the poor child seems to understand that I am unmoved. She falls silent again, although still she stares at me with eyes that seem yellowish and slightly swollen.

In fact, I can't help but feel fascinated by the fact that her entire face appears rather rotten. I suspect that as the years go past, her spectral appearance is beginning to take on more and more of the features that mark her rotting physical body. The overall effect is quite fascinating, even if the sight of protruding bones poking out from beneath patches of gelatinous skin is a little discomforting.

If she could truly hurt me, however, I am sure she would have done so by now.

"Do your worst," I tell her, taking hold of the handles at either side of the double doorway. "See if I care. I shall be too busy rebuilding my hotel to care. And when this place is full and busy again, nobody will pay any attention to the faded ghost of a sad little girl who lurks in the shadows."

I give her a chance to scream again, but she merely stares at me.

"Do you doubt me?" I ask with a faint smile. "If you doubt me, then evidently you don't know me. And if you don't know me, then you can't haunt me."

With that, I slide the doors shut, before turning and making my way over to the liquor cabinet. I need to plan my journey tomorrow, since there is one final obstacle that I must clear from my path.

CHAPTER TWENTY-SIX

THE VAST ROAR OF London – the stinking mass of noise that erupts from the streets at every moment – remains one of the most dispiriting experiences any decent man can ever encounter. Even now, as I step down from the train carriage and wait for the porter to fetch my bags, I cannot help looking around at the vast station and feeling a shudder pass through my chest.

There is a reason I left London long ago, and that reason is the noise. I cannot imagine how any man can live in this place and not lose his mind, such is the violence of the shouting voices that assault one's person from every direction. Even now, on the concourse at Paddington Station, I feel as if I must brace myself for my journey through the city. As the porter finally gets my bags onto a trolley and beckons me to follow him, I feel a stir of nausea deep in my gut. I had hoped to never visit London again, not in all my life.

Now that I am here, however, I must simply get

my work done as swiftly as possible, so that I might leave again.

***

"This is most generous," the director stammers, his eyes almost popping from their sockets as he stares at the money order. "Mr. Nash, considering the size of this donation, I feel that perhaps we must rename one wing of the hospital in your honor."

"I require no such aggrandizement," I tell him. "I merely heard that the hospital was short of funds, and I felt that I could not visit without bringing a gift. The money is really no great loss for me, and I only hope that it helps you to continue your wonderful work here."

I wait for a reply, but the bald, hunched little man seems too stunned to speak.

"Personally," I continue, "I believe that it is the moral duty of great men to make a difference in the world. Anybody can accrue riches, but it takes a man of true character to use those riches in order to bring benefits where they are most needed. I'm sure that when news of my donation spreads through the higher echelons of London society, some heads will be turned. Especially after the hospital is named after me."

"Well, a wing might -"

"The hospital, I feel. That would be more appropriate."

"I don't mind admitting, Mr. Nash," he stammers, "that this money will make the difference between a thriving hospital, and one that was going to have to close at the end of the year. You have saved us!"

"Wonderful news," I reply with a faint smile. "But please, I'm afraid this charitable donation was not my sole reason for coming to visit this afternoon. I wish to visit a patient who I believe resides in one of your beds. She has been under the care of the Desermes family for some time. Her name is Mary Maywhistle, and I should very much like a moment or two alone with her."

"I..."

He hesitates, and clearly he's a little uncertain.

"I hope this won't be a problem," I continue. "I would have thought that, since I am now a benefactor, any rules concerning such visits might be stretched just a little. I have traveled up to London especially for this visit, and I should not like to leave before I have seen her."

He looks down at the money order for a moment, as if lost in thought, and then he smiles at me again.

"Of course," he stammers finally. "Why not, eh? It's not as if she's exactly swamped by visitors."

***

Now that I am here in the girl's room, with the door shut and the orderly having left to get on with other work, I am finally free of the city's overwhelming noise. Standing in silence, I take a deep breath and try to compose my thoughts, and I am starting to feel a little more like myself again. In all honesty, I believe I am becoming less tolerant of excess noise as I get older.

A moment later, there's a faint rustling sound as the figure on the bed moves, disturbing its sheets slightly. Still, she hasn't looked at me. Not yet. Perhaps she doesn't even quite realize she has a visitor. Perhaps she is dull of mind.

"Mary?" I say finally. "Mary Maywhistle? Is that really you?"

I wait, and she shifts again, but still I cannot see her face.

"I had thought for so long that you were dead," I continue, stepping over to the bed and wiping some dust from a wooden chair, before taking a seat. "Imagine my surprise when Mr. Robert Desermes informed me recently that you had crawled your way to safety, and that -"

Suddenly she rolls over and turns to look at me, and I'm startled to see her wretchedly scarred face. I remember how bloodied and raw she appeared while I had her in my basement, and she appears scarcely much better now. She is older, of course, and is now around her early twenties. The flesh on her face has knotted and healed to some extent, but the scars are thick and the skin around her left eye is particularly mottled. In fact, as I look at her features, I see that her left eye is malformed, as if the fire caused it to develop several bumps. Her right eye, however, is staring directly at me, and a moment later a faint whimpering sound emerges from her lips. Nothing too loud. Just a brief, almost animal-like gasp.

"Come now, Mary," I say with a smile. "I mean you no harm. It has been a long time, has it not, since we last saw one another? Since I had my men save you from the fire that killed your parents."

Her lips move slightly, but I cannot quite make out what she's trying to say.

"I cannot imagine the ordeal you went through," I continue. "Dragging your burned body through the forest, and then along the road, you must have been in agony. And then, by some miracle, you were discovered. My understanding is that you have never managed to give a sensible account of your suffering, that your mind is considered too badly damaged, but that you can slip out the occasional word now and again. That is very commendable, Mary."

She stammers something, and I think one of the words might be the name of her sister.

"Ruth?" I ask. "You want to know about Ruth? She is long dead, I am afraid. Did the Desermes family not inform you of that fact?"

She lets out a slow, whimpered groan, and her remaining good eye blinks furiously.

"It is said that her ghost still haunts my hotel," I explain. "Whether you believe in such things or not, I have no idea. I myself have seen some kind of apparition, and I am sufficiently open-minded to accept that such spirits might exist. Not that it matters much either way, of course."

I wait, but now Mary is simply staring at me, as if she still can't quite believe that I'm really here.

"I would have come sooner," I tell her, "had I known that you were here. Unfortunately, the members of the Desermes family saw fit to hide your survival from me. They seem to have come up with some strange theory about what happened to you before they found you on the side of the road. You know what some people are like, Mary. They love a chance to make themselves feel pious. I'm sure they greatly enjoyed looking after you. Perhaps they felt that God put you on that road and ensure that by pure chance, a member of their family happened to find you. Perhaps the whole thing made them feel more important."

She tries to say something, but the flesh around her mouth seems too tight and damaged, and she sounds rather foolish. She certainly can't form proper words, although her efforts are rather amusing. A moment later, she reaches toward me with a clawed hand that is missing several fingers. I remember that same hand, back when I first met her. Evidently the doctors here have not been able to do too much to improve her condition.

"Are you in pain?" I ask.

She lets out a faint groan.

"What's that supposed to mean?" I continue. "Yes? No? Maybe?"

I can't help chuckling as she turns and looks toward the door. She starts moaning, and after a moment I realize that she seems to be trying to summon help. Her whole body is shuddering slightly, and it would appear that she fears being left alone with me.

"Nobody is going to come, you know," I tell her. "I wouldn't expect much from the Desermes family, either. Quite soon, they're going to have a great deal of trouble on their hands, and I imagine they'll forget all about you. Sir Roderick Desermes will learn that his two sons, and their wives, never returned from Lakeforth Hotel. I'm sure he'll wish to determine what happened to them, but I'm afraid I've arranged for some unfortunate items to be discovered in one of his warehouses. He'll be far too busy dealing with the police. Perhaps he'll learn, too, that new money can fight as dirty as old."

Another choked cry emerges from her lips, as tears rolls down her cheeks.

"You were exceedingly lucky to be found on that road all those years ago," I explain, "but everybody's luck runs out eventually. Besides, you have no life left to live. I understand that you spend all your time here in this room, barely even able to communicate with the poor souls who come to slide a bed-pan under you thrice a day. Wouldn't you much rather slip away into the peace of death?"

She lets out another groaning sound, and now she's clearly becoming very agitated. If she carries on like this, she might even end up throwing her scarred, battered body off the bed.

"Let me help you," I mutter, reaching over and slipping one of the pillows from under her head, before placing a hand on her chest and gently pushing her back down against the bed.

She tries to push me away, but of course she's powerless.

"Did you think you'd come back to the hotel one day and mete out justice?" I ask. "Was that the plan? Real life doesn't work that way, my dear. As I have told many people in the past, there is no such thing as justice.

Perhaps you enjoyed your revenge fantasies as you lay on this wretched little bed, but that's all they were. Fantasies. You should have died back at the hotel, once I realized I had no further use for you. If it's any consolation, I hope you understand that I am going to make very good use of the land I acquired from your father. My name..."

I hesitate, struck by the sudden realization that I can tell this girl anything.

"I was born under the name Maurice Mecklethorpe," I continue finally, saying that wretched name out loud for the first time in many years. "I had a horrible common accent, utterly lower class and foul. I changed my name to something that sounded more robust and respectable. I became Jobard Nash. And I forced that wretched accent away, until I sounded as if I belonged in the upper classes. I have told nobody about this, but I believe I can tell *you*. After all, it's not as if you'll get a chance to relay the information to anyone else. But I, the great Jobard Nash, was born Maurice Mecklethorpe, and I single-handedly dragged myself up from poverty."

She stares up at me, her eyes widening with horror, and slowly she lets out a pained groan.

"You should thank me for this," I tell her.

"You killed her," she whimpers, finally managing to get some actual words out of her twisted, burned mouth. "You killed Ruth and -"

Forcing the pillow against her face, I get to my feet and press down hard. She immediately starts struggling, and her pathetic, three-fingered hand claws futilely at my wrist. There's nothing she can do, of course, but that doesn't stop her putting up something of a fight, and I'm surprised by just how long it takes to snuff out her life. She even tries to scratch my flesh with her remaining fingers, and I must admit to a mild sense of amusement as I watch her desperate attempt to make me stop. Finally her body falls still, but I don't ease the pressure just yet. This wretched girl has slipped away from certain death once already, and I do not intend to give her another chance.

After a few more minutes, however, I see fit to move the pillow aside, and I immediately see that she's dead. Her eyes are filled with fear and her mouth is wide open, and when I check the side of her neck I find that there is no pulse whatsoever. Still, preferring to be absolutely sure, I take a box of matches from my pocket and light a small flame, which I then hold against the white of her good eye.

She doesn't react at all, not even as the flame starts to darken her eyeball.

"Rest in peace," I whisper, extinguishing the match and setting it on the bedside table, before lifting the girl's head and slipping the pillow back under. "Perhaps in death, you can find your sister and lead her away from my hotel. Although, so long as you can no longer interfere in my business, I can't honestly say that I care much either way."

With that, I sit for a few minutes in silent contemplation. Was it a moment of weakness, when I told young Mary my real name? Perhaps, but it matters not. In a strange way, she was closer to me at the moment of her death than anyone has ever been. Closer than Ellen, certainly. So I reach out and stroke her head for a few seconds, and I cannot help but smile.

***

"Mr. Nash!" a voice calls out a short while later as I walk away from the hospital's main door, and as a light drizzle falls from the gray sky above. "Mr. Nash! Wait!"

Turning, I see that the hospital director is running after me. When he stops just a few feet away, I can immediately tell from the look in his eyes that Mary's corpse has been discovered.

"She was looking rather peaky when I left," I tell him. "Pale, even. I do hope her ill health hasn't finally caught up to her after all these years. She seemed like such a fighter."

"She..."

He stares at me, and the poor fool seems utterly lost for words.

"I also hope," I continue, "that you will make good use of my generous donation. Although if for some reason you do not feel that you can accept my money, I will of course understand."

"We..."

Again, his voice trails off.

"Then it's settled," I add, forcing a smile. "I'm not a vain man, but I like the idea of this hospital bearing my name. I'm afraid I probably won't come to the ceremony, but it will be nice nevertheless to know that my generosity to this institute has been recognized. I hope very much that you can continue your good work."

With that, I turn and walk away, leaving the blathering old idiot far behind. Checking my watch, I see that it's almost 5pm. I had expected that I would need to stay the night in London, but now I'm wondering whether I could make the last train home after all. There is so much work to be done at the hotel, and I really can't afford to waste any more time here in the city.

I belong at the hotel. And this time, once I get back, I think I shall never leave. There is just one other place I must see before I leave.

***

The Moorchester still stands, after all these years. Still brightly lit and dazzling, still a monument to class and elegance. On the way here, the carriage passed my father's old workshop, which lay in darkness. I have no idea whether the man is still alive, and I do not care to check. Instead, I climb from the carriage and instruct the driver to wait, and then I make my way toward the grand entrance of the Moorchester.

"Good afternoon," the doorman says, as he pulls the door open for me.

"Good evening," I reply, affecting a casual tone even though I have long dreamed of this moment.

The Moorchester's lobby is utterly stunning, with a vast chandelier hanging high above. I always thought that the Lakeforth was the perfect hotel, but now I see that I set my ambitions too low. The Moorchester is the standard that all must try to match, and for a moment I am transfixed by the opulence of the place. I still remember, as a young boy, staring in through the window. Ever since that moment, I have longed not only to build my own hotel, but also to one day come here and find myself welcomed by the upper classes. Now, as I step over toward the door that leads into the dining room, I realize that I feel completely at home.

I have made it.

A moment later, just as I am about to turn and leave, I hear a familiar voice holding forth at one of the tables. Peering into the dining room, I'm astonished to spot Sir Edward Barringham speaking to several other men, and I allow myself a faint smile as I realize that I should go and introduce myself. There is a part of me, deep down, that still feel I do not belong in such a grand place, but I suppose that is simply the voice of young Maurice Mecklethorpe speaking. I am Jobard Nash now, and I am a part of high society. Maurice Mecklethorpe might as well be dead.

"You should have seen the place," Sir Edward is saying as I head over to the table. "No taste at all. Garish and obscene, if you ask me."

I stop next to him, but he seems not to have noticed me.

"The man wouldn't know refinement if it bit him on the behind," he continues, causing the others to start chuckling. "I assure you, there's no need to trek out into the wilderness and visit the Lakeforth. The place is an abomination. I mean, even the name is so trite and -"

I feel a shudder pass through my chest, at just the moment that Sir Edward looks up at me.

"Nash?" he says, clearly shocked. "Is that you?"

"Just passing through," I reply, taking a step back. I feel as if I am sweating profusely, and I am certain I must leave at once. "I thought I heard a familiar voice, and I merely wished to big you good afternoon."

"Good afternoon," he mutters. "As you can see, I'm afraid I'm rather busy."

"Of course," I stammer, "I didn't mean to interrupt you or -"

Catching myself just in time, I realize that I have slipped into my old, common accent. Sir Edward and his associates are staring at me as if I'm the strangest thing they have ever seen, and my heart is pounding as I realize that I must get out of here as quickly as possible. Muttering some terribly poor excuse, I turn and hurry out of the room, ignoring the sound of muffled laughter over my shoulder. I thought I belonged here, I thought I had finally proven my worth, yet now I find that I am an object of ridicule.

Hurrying out of the hotel's front door, I quickly make my way across the street. I don't even know where I'm going, although after a moment I remember that I have a carriage waiting for me. I turn to go back, but at that instant I trip on a broken cobblestone. Falling, I land hard on the pavement, letting out a gasp of pain.

Just as I am about to haul myself up, I realize that I have been in this exact location once before. Many years ago, this is where I fell while I was carrying a bag of coal. And now, staring at the bright lights of the Moorchester Hotel, I cannot help but think that I have not traveled as far from this very spot as I had hoped.

PART SEVEN

STEVE CULSHAW
2006

CHAPTER TWENTY-SEVEN

"STEVEN, STOP!"

Putting out a hand, Mum grabs my collar as I run past the dining table. I instantly try to twist free, but as usual she's holding me way too tight.

"Listen to me," she continues, putting on that tone of voice she always uses when she wants to sound strict. "Steven, will you listen to me for a moment?"

Sighing, I turn to her. At the far end of the room, an Elton John impersonator is crooning at the piano, keeping all the pensioners happy.

"You mustn't be so noisy, okay? People are trying to eat, and they want to hear the music."

"But -"

"Your great uncle's hotel isn't a playground," she continues, before leaning closer and lowering her voice to a conspiratorial whisper. "Half the people here are in their seventies. The place is basically a retirement home by any other name, and I don't want you barging into some old dear and breaking her hip. If you really can't sit still and behave, go play in the lobby, or out by the pool, or anywhere else. Just don't bug people!"

"Fine," I mutter.

"Have you finished eating?"

I sigh again. "Yes!"

"You're eleven years old," she adds. "I'm sorry there are no other kids here, but you're just going to have to make the best of it. Grow up just a tad, okay?"

"Can I go swimming?"

"It's almost seven in the evening."

"So can I go swimming?"

"No, you can't!"

"But -"

"They put special chemicals in the pool in the evenings, Steven. If you went in there at night, your hair'd go green."

"Brilliant!"

"You can swim tomorrow, and not before." She pauses, before sighing as she lets go of my collar. "Don't do anything to embarrass me, okay? I've had enough of that from your father this evening. And don't go too far."

"I won't!" I tell her, turning and hurrying out through the door and into the lobby, where I see two elderly women dozing on the sofa. I swear, the Lakeforth is more like a retirement village than an actual hotel.

The woman behind the reception desk is talking to somebody on the phone, while an old man is making his way carefully down the stairs. Mum and Dad have been bringing me to the Lakeforth for years now, and

I'm totally used to the fact that everybody else here is basically ancient. I mean, sure, I'd like to go to somewhere like Alton Towers or Disneyland, but I don't actually *hate* coming to the Lakeforth. There's always something to do, and some new place to explore, although I wouldn't mind if someone my own age showed up eventually.

And that receptionist is *really* pretty.

Heading across the lobby, I make my way to the arched door at the rear, and then I step out onto the patio and find that several elderly guests have come out here to sleep off their dinners. One of them is actually snoring. Picking my way between the chairs, I wander over to the swimming pool and look down into the greeny-blue water, and for a moment I actually consider jumping in. It'd be so cool to have green hair, although I know Mum'd freak and I guess I don't want to make her angry at me, not when we've still got several more days here before we can go home.

I can save green hair for the last night. That way, I might still have it when I get home. Everyone at school will think I'm so cool.

Turning, I look up at the side of the main building, and I quickly spot a shadow in the highest window. That'll be my great uncle, Jobard Nash, working at his desk. I've barely ever met him, and they say he works all the time, only sleeping for two hours each night. If you ask me, there's something slightly creepy about him, although in a way I find all really old people creepy. I definitely don't want to ever turn into some wrinkly, stooped old thing.

"Are you having fun there?" a cracked voice asks suddenly.

Glancing over my shoulder, I see that an old lady is smiling at me as she sips from her cocktail glass.

"Yes, thank you," I reply, before turning and making my way along the side of the pool, hoping to get away from the other guests. To be honest, I don't really like old people very much.

Ahead, the dark forest spreads from the edge of the patio, and I know from previous visits that it runs all the way to the shore of the lake. Mum told me to stay close, but I figure the lake isn't *that* far, so I start making my way through the long grass and finally I reach the forest. I can barely see a thing, so I hold my hands out to make sure I don't bump face-first into any of the trees. The ground beneath my feet is a little soft and uneven, and every step I take causes a crunching sound, but I quite like being out here on my own.

Looking back, I can just about make out the lights of the hotel between the trees, and I can hear the distant piano music drifting out through the night air. I guess old people like that kind of thing, but I want to explore. A moment later, I spot a faint flash of light coming from one of the hotel's upstairs windows.

From the darker part of the building. The part that's off-limits to everyone except Mr. Nash.

It takes about twenty minutes for me to find my way through the forest. There's not a lot of moonlight tonight, but after a while I can just about see the water of the lake glittering in the distance, and eventually I stumble out past the tree-line and find myself at the shore. With the hotel far behind me and the music not reaching all this way, I stop and listen to the sound of water gently lapping at the legs of the nearby jetty, and I take a deep, deep breath. I'm all alone down here, and there's nobody about for miles, and I feel as if I've finally managed to get far enough away from that stupid hotel. It's like I've reached another world.

Trampling across the pebbly shore, I make my way toward the jetty and then I stomp along the wooden boards. I'm a little cold, but that doesn't matter. For a moment, all I can think about is how cool it'd be if I had a girlfriend, and how I'd love to come swimming with her. When I reach the end of the jetty and look down into the pitch-black water, I imagine my girlfriend jumping down and pulling me in with her. We'd be laughing and splashing about, and she'd be so pretty that everyone else in the whole world would be jealous.

I'll get a girlfriend like that one day. And when I do, she'll be really pretty and really fun, and we'll be happy forever.

For the next few minutes, I stand at the end of the jetty and simply stare down into the water, thinking about what it'll be like when my girlfriend and I are having fun. The only real sounds I hear are the water against the jetty's wooden legs and an occasional creaking sound on the boards behind me, but in my head I can hear my future girlfriend laughing and giggling, and my own voice calling out to her. In my mind, we're here with some friends and it's a warm sunny day, and we're doing lots of cool stuff like sailing and paragliding and going on jet-ski rides. There are other girls here, but *my* girlfriend is the prettiest and -

Suddenly I hear a much louder creaking sound, and I turn to see that there's a figure standing halfway along the jetty, silhouetted against the dark, pebbly beach.

She's staring at me.

"Who are you?" I ask, squinting in an attempt to see her face. I can't make out any of her features, but she looks a little shorter than me, so I don't think she's very old. Definitely not the kind of girl I'd want for a girlfriend. She's probably not even pretty.

I wait, but she doesn't say a word. I guess maybe she followed me down from the hotel, although I don't remember seeing any other kids up there.

"Are you stalking me?" I ask.

Silence.

"I don't know what you want," I continue, "but it's pretty rude to just stand there like that. You should say what you want or go away. I was here first, so you have to go find somewhere else to be. I never -"

Stopping suddenly, I realize the girl seems to be whispering something under her breath. I can't make out a word of what she's saying, so I take a step closer. I don't know what's wrong with her, but I'm starting to think she might be totally brain-dead.

"I can't hear you, dumb-ass," I tell her. "Are you stupid? If you want me to hear you, you need to talk properly."

She doesn't raise her voice at all. Instead, she continues to whisper, and there's something creepy about hearing those hushed words coming from a face that's bathed in darkness. I can just about make out the shape of her silhouette, and I can tell that she has long hair and that she's wearing some kind of long dress, but as I step closer I find that I still can't quite see her face properly.

"What do you *want*?" I ask finally. "Are you chanting or something? What -"

Suddenly I let out a gasp as the girl vanishes right in front of me. It's like she was right there, and then a fraction of a second later she disappeared. I didn't even blink, I swear, but as I look around at the dark jetty I find that I'm completely alone.

"Hello?" I shout, trying not to let myself sound too scared. "Where are you? How did you do that?"

I turn and look over my shoulder, and then back toward the shore, but still there's no sign of her.

And then I hear the scratching sound.

Turning slowly, I look toward the jetty's dark, farthest end, and I realize that I can hear something scratching down at the water's edge. I immediately think of the jetty's wooden legs, and I feel a tightening sense of fear in my chest as I listen to the scratching sound slowly making its way up from the water, as if something is dragging itself with great effort from the depths and is going to appear at any moment.

Frozen in place, not daring to move, I watch the jetty's end and wait for some sign of movement. The scratching sound seems different now, more labored and twisted, as if rotten old branches are being dragged against the wooden legs that support the jetty. There's a faint gasping noise, too, and I'm convinced that at any moment I'll see a hand reach up from beneath the jetty and grab the wooden boards, hauling itself out of the lake.

Instead, the sound finally stops, leaving me standing alone in silence.

I try to open my mouth, to call out, but my throat is too dry.

"Hello?" I manage to whisper finally, before realizing that I must have imagined the whole thing.

I turn and look over my shoulder, just to make sure that I'm alone, and then I look back toward the end of the jetty.

It can't have been real.

The girl. The scratching sound. All of it was just in my head. I force a smile, trying to make myself relax, and I tell myself that I should head back to the hotel. Still, instead of turning to leave, I find that I can't stop staring at the end of the jetty, and I realize after a moment that I have to go and take a look. If I simply walk away, I'll know deep down that I'm a coward, and that I wasn't brave when it mattered. Instead, I have to march right over there and look down past the jetty's end, into the water below, and prove to myself that all I heard – at the very most – was a few gusts of wind.

Still; it takes a moment before I can force my legs to move. Even then, I only take a very cautious step forward, and I'm poised to run in case I see or hear anything in the darkness.

"She wasn't real," I whisper. "She looked real, but she wasn't."

Those words don't help much, however, and I can feel my heart beating faster and faster as I approach the end of the jetty. With each and every step, I feel an overwhelming urge to turn and run, but somehow I manage to keep going until finally I reach the final set of boards, and I force myself to look down into the dark water.

There's nothing there.

I breathe a huge sigh of relief. All I see is water gently rippling in the breeze as it rises and falls around the jetty's old wooden legs. I guess I should be feeling pretty stupid right now. After all, I -

"Help me!" the girl screams suddenly, lunging up from the depths and grabbing my ankle with a rotten hand.

I pull back, but her grip is too tight and I quickly crash down against the boards. As she squeezes tight, I feel her gummy flesh pressing against me, and then the bones of her fingers seem to cut through her own skin and slice into mine.

"Help me up!" she gasps, pulling harder and harder. "You have to be -"

Kicking her in the face, I almost manage to push her off. She lets out a groan and tries to grab my other leg, so I kick her again and this time the heel of my shoe tears a patch of flesh from her cheek, exposing the bony socket of her eye and several thread-like muscles on the side of her jaw. Too horrified to think straight, I kick her again and again, and finally she lets go of my ankle and falls back, splashing down into the water.

Not daring to stop and make sure she's truly gone, I scramble to my feet and limp back along the jetty, screaming for Mum to come and help me.

CHAPTER TWENTY-EIGHT

"STEVEN -"

"I know what I saw!" I gasp, trying once again to sit up in bed, only for Mum to place a hand on my chest and gently force me back down.

"I should never have let you stay up so late," she mutters. "Steven, you didn't sneak some alcohol from one of the other tables, did you? You're not -"

"I told you!" I hiss, almost shaking with fear as I see the disbelieving look in her eyes. "I was on the jetty and I saw a little girl! And then she tried to drag herself out of the water and I had to kick her back in!"

She sighs.

"It happened!" I shout, pushing her hand away when she tries to pat my shoulder. "Don't call me a liar! I'm not a liar! She was really there! If you go down and take a look, you'll see her in the water!"

"Steven -"

"Wait, don't go and look!" I add, lunging at her

and grabbing her arm. "Mum, you can't! It's a miracle I managed to get away! She'd probably drag you down into the water and eat your brains!"

"Drag me *down*?" She raises a skeptical eyebrow. "A moment ago, you said she was trying to climb *up*."

"I don't know what she wants!" I continue breathlessly. "All I know is that she's real, and that she wanted me to help her! I didn't give her a chance to explain what she needed help with, but it can't be something good!" I hesitate for a moment, before pulling her arm even tighter. "Please don't leave me alone tonight!" I sob. "I'm scared! If you leave me alone, she might come back!"

"Your father -"

"Dad can sleep alone! She won't try to hurt him! It's me she wants!"

She stares at me, not saying anything for a moment and seeming completely lost in thought.

"You're eleven years old," she says finally. "Don't you think that's a little old to be making up scary stories and -"

"I'm not making it up!"

"Whatever you're doing, then. Aren't you a little old? The way you came running and yelling back up to the hotel earlier, I was terrified. I thought something bad had happened!"

"There's a ghostly little girl down on the jetty," I stammer, "and she wants something from me! Please, if you love me, you have to look after me and not leave the room, not even for a second! If you do, she'll come and drag me down to the jetty and drown me, and I'll be gone forever!"

"Steven -"

"I saw it in her eyes!" I hiss, feeling a tight grip of fear in my chest. "She's hungry! And angry! She obviously wants revenge for something, and she won't stop until she gets it! You have to promise to stay with me all night, and then you have to promise that we'll leave first thing in the morning. If we stay any longer than that, she'll kill me! She'll drag me into the water and rip my heart out and then you'll find my body on the shore in the morning! And then you'll feel sorry, because I'll be dead and you'll know it's all your fault!"

Leaning toward her, I wrap my arms around her waist and hug her tight, while sobbing gently. After a moment, she reaches up and starts stroking the side of my head.

"I'll stay in here with you tonight, Steven," she says with a sigh, as if she still doesn't quite believe me. "But after that, you're going to have to be a brave boy for the rest of our holiday."

"You saw the scratches on my ankle!" I sob. "She did that!"

"Of course she did, sweetheart," she replies, stroking the top of my head. "Of course she did."

***

The following morning, as we enter the dining room for breakfast, I can't help glancing around and checking to make sure the strange little girl isn't here. I'm trembling slightly, even though I really don't want anyone to see that I'm afraid.

"We'll take our usual table," Dad says, leading Mum over to the buffet.

Holding back, I look at each and every person in the room, just to check who they are. All I see is a row of elderly faces, and I feel a faint flicker of relief as I realize that perhaps the girl really isn't going to come up to the hotel. After all, I only saw her on the jetty, so I suppose it's more than possible that she's somehow stuck down there. So long as I stay away from the jetty, I might be safe.

"Steven?" a female voice says suddenly, as I feel somebody tap my shoulder from behind.

Gasping, I spin around, only to find that the pretty receptionist is smiling at me. She's gorgeous, and I wouldn't mind a girlfriend like her when I'm older. Taking a deep breath, I force myself to stop shaking.

"You're Steven Culshaw, aren't you?" she continues. "Mr. Nash's nephew?"

"That's right," I stammer. "Why?"

"There's nothing to worry about," she says, as her grin widens. "Mr. Nash simply left a note at the front desk this morning. He wondered whether, after breakfast, you might be able to go up to his room and speak with him for a moment. So long as your parents don't mind."

"Mr. Nash wants to see *me*?"

She nods. "He said it's very important."

***

"Go on!" Mum whispers behind me, and I turn to see her and Dad peering around the corner as if they're scared to come any further. "Knock on the door!"

"Can't you come with me?" I ask.

"Of course not!" Dad hisses. "He didn't ask to see all three of us, did he? Just you. I know enough about Jobard Nash to realize that he's always very specific about these things. If he sent for you, Steven, there must be a reason!"

"Have you ever met him?" I stammer.

Mum and Dad glance at one another, before turning back to me.

"He's a recluse," Dad explains. "There are probably only two or three people who've seen him in the past thirty years. He spends all his time in his office, directing the hotel's operations by phone and leaving notes downstairs. According to the receptionist, you're the first person he's actually asked to see in person since... Well, since she started working here. This could be a big deal!"

"Just go in there and be as polite as you can," Mum continues. "Remember, first impressions are everything! You want Mr. Nash to like you, don't you?"

"Nash isn't even his real name, is it?" Dad mutters. "It's Maurice Mecklethorpe. What kind of ponce changes his name like that?"

"Go on, Steven!" Mum hisses. "Don't keep him waiting!"

Although I really don't want to do this, I guess it's better than spending time downstairs. After all, I'm still worried about the little girl showing up again, so I turn and make my way toward the door at the far end of the corridor. This entire hotel is starting to feel incredibly freaky, and when I get to the door I turn and look over my shoulder. Sure enough, Mum and Dad are still watching my every move.

"Just leave me alone," I mutter under my breath, before turning to face the door.

I take a deep breath.

This is ridiculous.

Reaching out, I knock.

From inside the office, there's a faint creaking sound.

"You may enter!" an elderly voice croaks finally.

I hesitate for a moment, wondering exactly what I'm going to find, and then finally I reach out and turn the handle. Pushing the door open, I look through and see a large, open room with large sunny windows. At the far end of the room, there's an old man sitting at a desk, and he continues to write in some kind of large book as I step inside.

"Close the door," he continues, not even looking up at me. "There's a good boy."

I push the door shut, before making my way cautiously across the room.

"I must warn you," he continues, "that I am not accustomed to speaking to children. In fact, I have never spoken to one before, not in all my life. I shall speak to you as if you are an adult, and you must simply try to raise yourself to my level. If you cannot do that, our business will be brief."

I wait, wondering whether he wants me to speak yet.

"So you're my brother's grandson, I believe," he mutters, not sounding particularly impressed as he finally sets his pen down and looks at me. "The heir to the throne, so to speak. I've been told that you and your parents have visited the hotel on several occasions over the years. I never came down to greet you, of course, because I simply had too much to get done up here. I never paid much attention to matters concerning my extended family, or -"

He stops suddenly, although his jaw is still moving, as if he's chewing something. He's so old, I guess maybe he's dying. I want to turn and leave.

"They're always telling me I should get out of this room," he continues, sounding a little breathless now. "I have a private doctor who insists on coming to visit me, once every month. He goes on and on about the need for a little fresh air, and he seems to be of the opinion that I'd benefit from going downstairs and mingling with the guests. What he doesn't understand, of course, is that this hotel will not run itself. Without me, the place would surely go to ruin. I am this hotel, and this hotel is me. Can you understand that, boy?"

He pauses, still watching me.

"Well?" he adds finally. "What's wrong with you, child? Cat got your tongue?"

"No," I reply, "I just... I don't know what to say."

"Well, at least you're honest, I'll give you that. At least you're not one of those blatherers, rumbling on and on, even when their heads are empty. It's a wise man who knows when to shut up. You remind me a little of myself at your age. That's a very..."

He pauses, as if he's struggling to get his breath back.

"A very good thing..."

Reaching down, he slowly turns and wheels himself past the side of the desk. I hadn't realized he was in a wheelchair, but now he's slowly coming closer and I have to fight the urge to step back. In all my life, I don't think I've ever seen somebody who looks so old, and there must be a million wrinkles running this way and that all over his face. As he reaches me, I realize that he must be close to a hundred years old. Maybe even more. In fact, I think I might have overheard Mum and Dad saying that he's something like 105.

"I sit and look out the window every night," he says, parking himself directly in front of me. "I watch the patio, and the area around the swimming pool. It's my way of keeping up with the world, and I can see more than is strictly necessary. Last night, for instance, I saw a young boy making his way into the darkness of the forest. It's not often that somebody goes out there late at night, so I took my binoculars and I trained them on the distant lake. I could just about make out the jetty, and what do you think I saw there, hmm?"

I swallow hard. "I don't know. Sir."

"I saw *you*," he continues. "You walked all the way to the jetty's far end. Not so unusual, I suppose. But then you turned around, didn't you? Because you saw something."

"I don't know."

"You don't know whether you saw something?"

"I mean..."

My voice trails off.

"You saw *her*, didn't you?" he adds, leaning toward me slightly as his voice fills with anticipation. "You saw the ghost of Ruth Maywhistle."

I feel a flutter of fear in my chest. "I saw *someone*," I tell him. "A little girl. But no-one believes me."

"I believe you, Steven."

"She scratched my ankle."

"Let me see."

I pause for a moment, before reaching down and pulling my trouser leg up, and then I turn so that the old man can see the set of scratches that run through my flesh.

"I wanted to get it checked by a doctor," I explain, "but Mum said it wasn't too deep. She's like that."

"And you saw her?" he continues, sounding breathless once more. "You really saw her?"

"I saw her silhouette. It was a little girl."

Dropping my trouser leg, I look at the old man's face and see that he seems lost in thought.

"It's been a long time since she was spotted in the hotel," he says finally. "A long time since she was spotted anywhere. Until I heard you crying out last night, I rather hoped she might have faded away entirely, but now I see I was gravely wrong. If she is confining herself to the area around the jetty, she must have a reason. It is my belief that she is trying to reconcile her spectral and physical forms. Do you know what I mean by that, child?"

I shake my head.

"It means she wants to raise her body from the water."

Again, I swallow hard.

"If she manages it," he continues, "she'll walk back up here and she'll come for me. She knows she needs a physical form if she's going to get close, because she knows I'll simply ignore her spirit. She's resourceful and sly, and I dare say that she has come up with a rather good idea. I suppose the lust for vengeance can do that to a person. She was just a dumb, idiotic child when she died. She has changed since then, and I doubt she can ever change back."

"I don't know what you're talking about," I stammer. "I just -"

"Of course you know," he snaps, interrupting me. "Don't try to play me for a fool. Now, I called you up here today because I want to make a deal with you. I'm a businessman at heart, and making deals is the only way I know of dealing with any problem. I have something to offer you, something very valuable, and it's yours provided you'll perform an act of kindness for me."

"I don't know what you mean."

"Don't play the fool. I'm offering you the hotel, boy. I'm offering you all I have left."

"The..."

I pause for a moment. My heart is racing, but I'm

still worried that I might be misunderstanding what he's saying.

"The hotel?" I ask finally.

He nods. "Would you like it? Upon my death, of course. Not before."

"Well, I..."

Again, my voice trails off.

"I have no children of my own, you see," he continues. "I only married once, and that was a brief, unsuccessful arrangement. I never thought I'd need to sire offspring, but now I'm getting old and I don't have much time left. Somebody must continue my legacy, such as it is. I propose to give you the hotel, and in return you only need do one thing for me. One thing for *us*."

Reaching out, he places a hand on the side of my arm, although I can't help noticing that he's trembling severely.

"Tell her I want to end this," he explains. "Tell her I've had long enough to think about it now, and I want to make amends. I'll have divers go into the lake and recover her body. I'll have her brought to the surface and given a proper Christian burial. She'll be interred alongside her sister, whose body I'll have brought down here so that they can rest side-by-side in the churchyard at Gilham, a few miles away. Tell her that all she has to do in return is leave this hotel alone."

Swallowing hard, I wait for him to continue. There are tears in his eyes, and he seems like a pretty cool old guy, but I honestly don't understand all this talk of crimes and forgiveness.

"So you..."

I hesitate for a moment.

"So you think she's real?" I manage to ask finally. "The ghost? The girl on the jetty?"

"Oh, I know she's real. Absolutely, without any doubt whatsoever."

"You've seen her?"

"Tell her this is the only deal I am willing to offer. The hotel is going to be my legacy, and I cannot leave it haunted by the spirit of some wretched child. I'm getting old, Steven, and I have to tidy up the loose ends of my life. I have to offer her some kind of truce. For the sake of the -"

Suddenly he breaks into a coughing fit, one that makes his whole body shudder as he leans forward and puts a hand to his mouth. The coughing doesn't stop, and I actually start wondering whether he's going to die. Finally, figuring that I should just get out of here, I take a couple of steps back.

"Wait!" he splutters, still coughing. "I'm not finished with you!"

"I have to go..."

"Wait!"

He reaches toward me, but I slip away from his hand and hurry to the door.

"I have to go!" I stammer, turning the handle but finding that it appears to be locked. I try again, before banging my fists against the panel. "Mum!" I call out. "Dad! I need to come out now!"

"I had them escorted downstairs," Mr. Nash explains as his coughing fit starts to subside. "I feared you might overreact, but I'm certain I can change your mind. Steven, I am an old man, and -"

"Let me out!" I yell, battering my fists against the door now as I feel tears welling in my eyes. "Please! Somebody help!"

"Try to contain yourself," he continues, as I hear him wheeling himself closer. "You're letting emotion guide you, Steven, when you should be more logical. I'm disappointed by your reaction, but I believe I can make you come around to my way of thinking. You've spoken to little Ruth once, so you should be able to do it again. And I need you to deliver a message to her on the jetty."

Still pulling on the door, I suddenly feel the old man's hand on my shoulder. I immediately spin around, terrified that he might hurt me, and I find that he has begun to rise from the wheelchair, leaning heavily on a walking stick.

"The hotel will be yours in return," he stammers. "You can become a rich man! You can achieve the kind of success that I never managed! The world will be your oyster!"

I shake my head.

"You can have it all!" he hisses.

"I don't -"

Suddenly he smacks the walking stick against my face, hitting me so hard that I fall to the floor. Clutching my cheek, I'm shocked to feel a sliver of blood, and I look up just in time to see Mr. Nash sinking back down into his chair. I want to get up and scream for someone to come and help me, but I'm too scared to move, even as the old man wheels his chair back a little.

"Get up," he mutters finally. "You look pathetic down there."

I freeze, still too scared to move.

"Get up!" he roars.

Stumbling to my feet, I watch as he takes a handkerchief from his pocket and holds it out to me.

"Clean that mess," he says darkly.

Taking the handkerchief, I hold it against the cut on my cheek.

"You should not have angered me like that," he continues. "You are only reminding me, so far, why I despise children. But you have potential, Steven, and I want to give you a chance to meet that potential head-on. Do you know what will become of you, if you turn down my offer and walk away?" He pauses. "You'll live a dull, unremarkable life. Forgettable. Insignificant. At most, the very best you can hope for is that you'll find a dour, moderately attractive woman who sours with age and becomes a foul creature. Perhaps you will have some screaming children, perhaps not. You will get old, and you will die, and you will be forgotten."

I want to tell him that he's wrong, but I'm scared he might hit me again. Why did Mum and Dad let me come up here?

"Or you can take my offer," he adds. "You can become, in time, the owner of this hotel. You will have a chance for greatness. I have struggled all my life to make the Lakeforth a marvel of the world. I have achieved much, but for a long time I have felt that I am falling short. Now I realize that I must pass the hotel on to somebody who can finish the job for me. That person can be you, Steven. You are like me. I see it in your eyes. I have observed you through the cameras that are positioned around the hotel. I have seen how much you despise your own parents. I despised my parents when I was your age, too. And I chose to do something about that fact, rather than letting them drag me down. Your parents are worthless, pathetic scraps of humanity. Do you want to be the same, or do you want to amount to something worthwhile in this life?"

Swallowing hard, I realize that he might be right. About Mum and Dad, at least. And then, slowly, another idea forms in the back of my mind. I hesitate for a moment, watching the old man's eyes, as I start to realize just how much I might gain if I inherit this place.

"I could get a girlfriend," I whisper.

"I beg your pardon?"

"Girls like rich men, don't they?"

He furrows his brow. "Well -"

"I wouldn't have to end up like you. All alone, spending my time here in one room. I could have lots of girlfriends. They'd love me because of the money."

"Is that what appeals to you?"

I pause, before nodding. I can't help smiling, and in my mind's eye I can already see myself turning this place into a big casino with lots of pretty girls at every table. I'd be the most popular guy in the whole world, and all those stupid bullies at school would be begging to get through the front door. I wouldn't let them in, though, because I'd be too busy hanging out with my rich, famous friends and my gorgeous supermodel girlfriends. I wouldn't even let Mum and Dad into the hotel. I'd be the greatest man alive.

"Steven?" Mr. Nash continues. "Are you finally seeing this the correct way? Are you finally coming around to my way of thinking?"

Staring at the crazy old man, I realize that he's serious. My gut tells me to turn him down, of course, and I'm terrified by the thought of ever seeing that little girl again. Then again, if I actually know what's happening this time, I suppose there's no real reason to be scared.

"She can't actually hurt me, can she?" I ask cautiously. "Right?"

"Of course not," he replies, as a faint smile grows across his lips. "All you have to do is take me down there. You're the only one I can trust, Steven, because you're the only one who can possibly understand." He hesitates, before reaching past me and slipping a key into the lock. "There," he adds, turning the key. "The door is unlocked. If you can find the bravery within your heart, be ready at 8pm tonight. I believe in you, Steven. You can rise to this request."

I stare at him for a moment, before muttering something about thinking about it. Turning, I hurry out the door and make my way along the corridor.

I don't look back.

I can't.

That little girl was so creepy on the jetty last night. There's no way I can ever go back down there.

CHAPTER TWENTY-NINE

"NO, I'M WORKING ALL evening. No, Roger, I can't. Because I'm working, that's why. You'll just have to be a patient man, won't you?"

Standing near the stairs, I watch as the receptionist giggles. She's at her desk near the door, laughing as she talks to some guy on the phone. Whoever he is, he's clearly good at making her smile, and she's been keeping her voice low so that none of the guests overhear. Fortunately, she hasn't noticed me edging closer, so I'm able to hear every word.

"I can't talk about that right now," she continues, as she starts blushing. "I'm at work, Roger."

She glances around, and I step behind a pillar so she won't see me.

"I'll be all yours tomorrow night," she says after a moment. "Yes, Roger, I'll be wearing the little black dress you like so much. And you can slip it off me as soon as we get back to your flat from dinner."

She pauses, and then she giggles again.

"Well, that's just dirty," she adds. "Listen, I should get going. Some old bag'll be along soon to complain about something."

Again, she pauses, and I can just about hear a faint tinny sound coming from the phone as this Roger guy continues to talk.

"I'm going to get off the phone now," she tells him. "You don't have to worry about me meeting someone else at the hotel, Roger. Who else could I possibly meet? You're the only big, strong man in my life. And I'll see you tomorrow, so you can remind me of those muscly arms!"

Laughing once more, she sets the phone down. A moment later, I hear her dialing another number.

"Hey sweetie," she says as soon as someone answers on the other end of the line. "It's me. Listen, I'm gonna have to cancel tomorrow night, I've got to work."

I hear a tinny voice replying.

"But I'm free the night after," she continues. "How about then? Don't make me feel bad, Todd. But the night after tomorrow, you've got me all to yourself at your flat. I guess that gives you a little longer to figure out what you're going to do with me, huh?"

She pauses, and then she bursts out laughing.

"I can't talk now," she adds. "But don't beg, sweetie. It's not exactly attractive. I like my guys tough and confident and brave, so try to remember that. And I'll see you the night after tomorrow. Okay?"

With that, she puts the phone down, just as an elderly lady shuffles toward the desk and starts complaining about the temperature in her room.

Still standing behind the pillar, I find myself lost in thought for a moment. I know the receptionist is too old for me, but she's exactly the kind of girl I want to date one day. If I'm going to do that, however, I need to make sure I'm really impressive and attractive. Maybe I need to change a little. Maybe I need to be brave after all.

***

Mum and Dad are arguing again.

Every time we come on holiday, they have one huge argument. Just one. I always know it's coming, I always sense the needling little comments that serve as build-up, and I always hate when it finally explodes into all this shouting and storming about. Even now, they're in the bathroom getting ready for dinner, and I think they actually don't realize that I can hear them. They don't seem very aware of the world around them.

Sitting on the end of the bed, I try to ignore every word they're saying, and I focus instead on what Mr. Nash asked me to do tonight. It's almost 5pm, and we're going to dinner soon. That means I have three hours before I decide whether or not to help Mr. Nash.

"She's just a ghost," I whisper, trying to find some way to give myself a little extra courage. "Ghosts can't hurt you. There's no reason to be scared."

When I left Mr. Nash's room earlier, I was certain that I'd never, ever go back to the jetty with him. As the day has worn on, however, I've found myself thinking more and more about his proposition, almost as if some hidden voice in the back of my head is trying to persuade my conscious mind. I can't help fantasizing about what it'd be like if I was brave, and if Mr. Nash gave me the hotel in return. I'm still scared of seeing that little girl again, and of feeling her hand grabbing me, but finally I lift my leg up and take a look at my ankle.

The scratches aren't *that* deep.

They're nothing, really.

It wouldn't be so scary a second time, not if I knew to keep away from the end of the jetty. Plus, Mr. Nash told me a bit about the girl, which makes it easier to push my fears aside. I know it's Mr. Nash she's really angry with, and she'll basically ignore me if he's also on the jetty. If push comes to shove, I can just abandon him there and run back to the hotel. The ghost will be too busy with him, she won't chase after me. All I have to do is be brave tonight, and my life will change forever.

"Go to hell!" Mum shouts suddenly, storming out of the bathroom and hurrying to her suitcase on the dresser. As she pulls the suitcase open, she glances at me. "Do you know what I'm going to do when we get home, Steven?" she snaps. "I'm going to divorce your lousy, no-good, rotten stupid father! And I'm going to take him for every penny he has!"

I swallow hard. She's said things like this before, and she's never gone through with them. Besides, I'm not scared of her anymore, or of him. I'm going to inherit this hotel, which means I'll be rich and popular. Once the Lakeforth is mine, I won't even *need* parents anymore. I might be scared of going to the jetty, but I'm *more* scared of ending up like Mum and Dad.

***

"You'll be pleased to know, young man," Mr. Nash continues as I push his wheelchair through the dark forest, "that I telephoned my solicitor earlier this evening. The wheels are already in motion for the hotel to be left in your name after I am gone. How does that make you feel?"

"Thank you," I reply, although at the same time I can't help but grin. All through dinner, I was fantasizing about the grand parties I'll be able to hold, and about all the pretty girls who'll want to be with me. I won't have to go to university or anything like that. I can just move here to the hotel as soon as I'm sixteen, and every part of my life will be perfect. I'll never have to worry about Mum and Dad again.

"I shall give you some lessons, of course," he mutters. "Running this hotel is a full-time job, young man, and you'll need to learn a thing or two. About how to deal with people, and how to be tough with them. You'll have to do things that other men might consider beyond the pale, but that doesn't matter. Men such as myself, we do what is necessary, regardless of society's expectations. That's how you must come to see the world, too. When I -"

He pauses for a moment.

"Stop!"

"What do you mean?" I ask.

"Stop!" He sounds panicked suddenly. "Stop at

once!"

Bringing the wheelchair to a halt, I stare ahead and see moonlight glittering on the distant lake. There's something strangely serene about this place, and I feel almost as if I'd be wrong to make a noise.

"I haven't been down here in many, many years," Mr. Nash continues finally. "Tell me, boy, have you happened upon the ruins of an old house near the shore of the lake?"

"I don't think so."

"It's there somewhere. Once I had ownership of the Maywhistle land, I allowed myself to become distracted. Owning the land was enough, I suppose. The Maywhistle man was a wretched, pathetic fool. He didn't know a good deal when one was thrust before him. I gave him what he deserved in the end. When you take charge of the hotel, Steven, you must find the ruins of that little house and have then wrenched from the ground. Do you hear me? Wipe away all trace of that house."

"Okay," I reply, not really understanding what he means. I wait for him to continue, but now he seems lost in thought. "Should I carry on?" I ask finally.

He doesn't reply straight away. Instead, he seems completely transfixed by the sight of the water.

"This ghost has been holding my hotel back for years," he says suddenly. "No matter what I did, her spirit cast a pall over the place. It took a long, long time before I was able to recognize that fact. Perhaps I was stubborn."

"But she's..."

My voice trails off.

"Just a ghost?" he adds. "Is that what you were going to say?"

"Well. Kind of."

"People have always seemed to feel uneasy at the Lakeforth, Steven. I believe Ruth Maywhistle is the reason. A grand hotel on the shore of a beautiful lake... This place should have been so popular. Yet something lingered, something that gave people pause. If I am to complete my legacy and have the hotel reach its potential before I die, I must get rid of the ghost. And to do that, I must give her what she wants."

I swallow hard, still watching the moonlit lake for any hint of the girl.

"But she might not appear, right?" I stammer finally. "She might not be real."

"Take me to the shore."

"But -"

"Do it, boy. I want to get this over with."

I wheel him onward, bumping his chair between the trees, until finally we reach the edge of the pebbly lake-shore. I automatically take him toward the jetty, and I can't help looking all around, just in case the little girl is already here. I keep telling myself not to be scared, but after a moment I notice that Mr. Nash seems to be trembling more than ever, as if pure fear is starting to take over his body. He's clearly terrified, but I'm surprised he lets it show. I thought he was better than that.

"Stop a moment!" he gasps finally, once we're at the start of the jetty. "Have you seen her yet?"

I look around again, but there's still no sign of the girl.

"She'll be along shortly," he continues. "It's cold here. Are you cold, Steven? I'm terribly cold."

"It's a bit cold," I mutter.

"I'm freezing. Perhaps that's her. Perhaps she means to give me pneumonia." He sounds agitated now, as he turns and looks around. "Are you sure you don't see her? She must be here, she simply must!"

Again, I glance all around, but all I see is the bare, pebbly beach stretching in both directions away from the jetty.

"May the Lord have mercy on my soul," Mr. Nash continues, shaking so much now that his voice is starting to tremble. "I suspect I know the cause of her reluctance. You must leave me now, boy. Come back in an hour, but go all the way to the hotel first. I imagine the child wants to be alone with me."

"Are you sure?"

"Quite. I must negotiate with her alone."

I pause for a moment.

"But... The hotel will still be mine, won't it?" I ask. "Even if I don't stay?"

"Absolutely. You have done what I asked of you. A deal is a deal, and Jobard Nash does not go back on his word." He pauses. "I am sure the ghost of Ruth Maywhistle can be reasoned with. I shall present her with an offer she cannot refuse. Even ghosts must have a sense of reason."

"But you can't be sure that -"

"Are you questioning my judgment?" he snaps.

315

"No! Of course not!"

"Then leave! She must be close, but she will only show herself when you are gone. I see no need to delay."

I look around one more time, before realizing that the old guy is probably right. If the ghost is truly angry with him, then she probably wants me to go away so she can come and really haunt him. Letting go of the wheelchair, I take a couple of steps back, and then I watch as Mr. Nash reaches down and starts slowly wheeling himself toward the jetty's far end. He looks so lonely and frail as the wheels of his chair squeak in the night air, and I can't help expecting to see the creepy little girl appear at any moment.

"So you want me to come back in an hour?" I call out to him.

He doesn't reply. I guess he's focused on the task at hand.

"I'll come back in an hour," I stammer, before turning and hurrying back through the forest. I look back a couple of times, but still all I see is the old man in his chair, silhouetted against the glittering lake. Clambering up a steep incline, I can see the lights of the hotel far ahead now, but I look back one more time.

And I see her.

The old man is still on the jetty, looking out toward the water. But I can see the silhouette of the girl, too, stepping up behind him.

My heart is pounding as I watch, but I can't tear myself away. The girl is getting closer and closer to him, and he must know by now that she's there. Maybe she's talking to him, maybe he's begging her for mercy, or maybe -

Suddenly she's gone again.

I peer between the trees, but now in the distance all I see is the old man alone once again on the jetty.

I take a step forward.

"Leave us!" the girl screams, lunging at me through the darkness and sending me stumbling back until I fall to the ground.

She's already gone, but now my heart is thudding in my chest. As I scramble to my feet, I see that she's already back down at the jetty, although this time I don't dare stop and watch any longer. Instead, I turn and race between the trees, almost slamming into several in the darkness, before finally I spill out at the edge of the hotel's patio and almost run straight into the swimming pool. I manage to stop myself just in time, however, and I end up staring at the hotel's guests as they sit chattering to one another and drinking wine. The pianist is still playing, and everybody here seems to think that this is just another ordinary evening.

***

"Do you know what your father is?" Mum asks, in-between sips from her latest cocktail. "He's an arse, that's what. Did you know that, Steven? Your father is a grade-one arse. You need to make sure you don't grow up to be like him. The last thing you want is to end up being one of those men who everyone agrees is a total arse. Because everyone does, you know. Back home, I mean. Everyone knows your father is an arse! They all wonder why someone like me is with someone like him."

Ignoring her, I look toward the forest and try to imagine what might be happening down at the jetty. It's only half an hour since I left Mr. Nash down there, so it's too early to go back. Besides, the girl seemed to want him alone, and I'm worried that she might not like it if I return. Even though I promised to go back after an hour, I might leave it just a little longer, so that they have time to do whatever needs doing. Maybe the old man has cut a deal with the ghost by now, and everything's fine.

"What are you sitting like that for?" Mum mutters suddenly.

Turning to her, I see that she's frowning at me.

"You look completely stupid," she continues. "You're sitting all rigid. What's wrong? Aren't you having fun?"

Looking down, I see that I'm gripping the edges of the seat with my hands.

"Stop it!" she hisses, slapping me on the shoulder. "Relax, Steven!"

I lean back in the chair and lay my hands on the arms, and that seems to calm her down for a moment. Besides, she's quickly distracted when Dad wanders over and starts gathering her empty glasses.

"Don't you think you've had enough, dear?" he asks. "Too many more of these, and you'll be in danger of turning into a shrill bitch again. Or are we already past the point of no return for tonight?"

"Go screw yourself," she grumbles.

"Well no-one else is going to screw me tonight."

"Ha-bloody-ha. Why would anybody want to go near you? And I'll drink whatever I bloody well want, thank you very much."

She snaps her fingers at a passing waiter.

"Another!"

"Are you sure that's wise?" Dad asks her, as the waiter heads back inside.

"Oh, I've done a lot of unwise things already in my life," she replies. "Like marrying you."

Sighing, Dad turns to walk away, before glancing at me.

"Steven, don't sit like that!" he snaps. "You look bloody stupid!"

Realizing that I've been gripping the chair's arms again, I sit up straight. Dad's looking at me with a hint of disappointment in his eyes.

"Leave the boy alone," Mum tells him. "If he wants to sit slumped all evening, then let him. It's not like -"

Suddenly an agonized screams rings out, and everybody turns to look toward the forest. Getting to my feet, I immediately realize where the scream is coming from, and the horrific sound continues for several more seconds, twisting and rising through the night air before cutting short as suddenly as it began.

"What the hell was that?" Dad asks, as he and a couple of other men hurry past the pool, as if they're going to run into the forest and investigate.

"Mr. Nash," I whisper.

"What did you say?" Mum asks, staring at me.

"Steven, why would that be Mr. Nash? Mr. Nash always spends his evenings in his office, he never leaves the -"

Before she can finish, the cry rings out again, sounding a little choked this time. Whatever's happening down there, he sounds like he's in absolute agony, and already some of the men are hurrying into the forest. I know I should probably go with them, so that maybe I can explain what's happening, but I'm too scared to move so instead I simply sit in my chair and wait as the scream dies down. All my bravery from earlier has slipped away.

"I wouldn't like to be that poor bugger," Mum mutters, taking another sip from her cocktail. "Whoever he is."

CHAPTER THIRTY

"IS HE DEAD?"

The doctor hurries across the lobby, speaking into a mobile phone. Running after him, I try to hear what he's saying, but he's talking about drugs and all these medical terms that I don't understand. Even by the time we get to the hotel's main door, I haven't figured out whether Mr. Nash has been saved.

"Is he dead?" I ask again, stopping at the top of the steps and watching as the doctor heads to his car. "Do I get the hotel now?"

I know he's not going to answer. To him, I'm just a stupid kid. The hotel is bustling this morning, and everyone wants to know what happened last night. Several men ran down to the jetty, and there are rumors that they found Mr. Nash out of his wheelchair, screaming on the jetty's wooden boards and crying out. Those of us by the pool certainly heard plenty more screams until the old man was finally carried back through the forest, and I caught a glimpse of him as he was taken inside. Since then, he's been up in his office and there have been no more cries, although all the hotel's guests seem very worried.

The doctor takes something from the boot of his car, before coming back toward the hotel.

"Is he dead?" I ask, staying in the doorway, hoping to keep him from coming through before he's answered. "Please, I just -"

"Out of the way," he mutters, putting a hand on my shoulder and pushing me aside.

"I just want to know!" I continue, rushing after him.

"Steven!" Mum calls out from the door to the dining room. "Come here at once!"

"Not now!" I hiss, still walking after the doctor. "This is important, I just need to -"

"Steven!"

Feeling a hand on my shoulder, I turn and find Mum standing behind me. She looks hungover, as usual, although hangovers tend to leave her confined to bed. This time she's up and about, and she looks awful. There are bags under her eyes, she's pale, and her hair is a mess. She stares at me for a moment, as if she's worried about something, and then she crouches down in front of me as if she wants to look more carefully into my eyes.

"What?" I ask, worried that she knows something about last night. "Is Mr. Nash dead?"

"I don't think so," she replies, "not yet, but..."

Her voice trails off.

"People are wondering how he got all the way

down there," she continues finally. "He was in a wheelchair, so it's hardly likely that he could have made it through the forest all by himself. And I can't help noticing that you weren't around for a while during the evening." She pauses again. "What did he talk to you about yesterday morning? When he called you to his room, I mean. You never *really* explained."

I swallow hard. "Nothing."

"Don't lie to me, Steven. This is important."

"You smell bad," I tell her.

"I beg your -"

"You smell of alcohol and sweat," I continue, taking a step back. "And vomit. You look rough as a dog."

Her eyes widen with shock.

"What I talked to Mr. Nash about," I add, "is none of your business. It's between me and him. If he'd wanted you to know, he'd have told you. In fact, he specifically told me not to tell anyone else. He said nobody would believe us, and I think he was right. He also said that a good businessman never divulges the terms of a deal to outsiders. So you see, I can't tell you!"

"Steven..."

"So why don't you just go and argue with Dad some more? That's what people like you always do when we're on holiday, isn't it?"

"People like..."

Her voice trails off, but there are tears in her eyes and I can tell I've upset her. Good. That's what I wanted. She and Dad are always so mean to me, and I'm sick of it.

"Steven Culshaw?"

Turning, I see that the pretty receptionist is coming down the stairs.

"Steven," she says cautiously, as if she's a little shocked by something, "I need you to come with me. Mr. Nash has asked to see you again."

"Why?" Mum asks, getting to her feet.

"I'm sorry," she continues, "but I'm not at liberty to say. Mr. Nash simply said that he wishes to speak with Steven alone, and that nobody else is permitted to go into the room with him. Honestly, that's more or less all I know."

Turning to Mum, I can see the confusion in her eyes.

"It's nothing to do with you," I tell her, feeling a flutter of excitement in my chest. "Go and argue with Dad. Or if you can't find him, have another drink. Those are the two things you do best."

***

"She came to me," Mr. Nash groans, barely able to get the words out at all since one side of his face was frozen by the stroke. "I saw her, for the first time in..."

His voice trails off, and for a moment he seems impossibly breathless.

"I'll be right outside," the doctor says, and I can tell he's reluctant to leave at all. "Mr. Nash, if you -"

"Leave us," the old man gurgles, his body briefly shuddering on the bed. "Go, man! Go!"

We sit in silence for a moment as the doctor

heads out of the room. I honestly don't know what I'm supposed to say, and for now I'm just horrified by the change in Mr. Nash's appearance. The left side of his face seems so saggy and dead, and the eye is closed. His right side is able to move a little, but not much, and he seems to be struggling just to draw breath.

"I underestimated her anger," he continues finally. "She was an ordinary, unremarkable girl when she was alive. I suppose I thought that she'd still be the same now, underneath it all."

"Wasn't she?" I ask.

"I changed her. I suppose it was me, anyway. The manner of her death, and the death of her sister, must have driven her insane. I cannot pretend to understand it all, but I saw the fury in her eyes. I tried to explain the deal, but she wouldn't listen. She was trying desperately to bring her rotten body up from the water. She tried over and over to climb the jetty's wooden legs, but each time she fell back. I fear that she needed her body, in order to do to me the things she feels I deserve."

"And she didn't manage it?"

"I cried out. I'm sure you heard me. In-between her attempts to raise her body, I believe she was trying to drive me out of my mind. She knows everything about what I did. She didn't before, but now she understands. About how she died, about what really happened to her sister... I suppose she learned long ago, from those wretched Desermes people. I tried to offer her a deal, but she was too emotional. Emotions have no place in business, Steven. One must be rational and calm. She should learn that."

I sit and wait for him to continue. Honestly, I'm not quite sure what I'm supposed to say, and I'm still thinking that maybe this old man is partly out of his mind. I mean, I know the girl is real, but Mr. Nash seems totally nuts. I wonder whether, once I get away from the madness a little, I'll start to think that none of this really happened.

"How did Ruth Maywhistle die?" I ask finally.

I wait but he doesn't reply.

"How did Ruth Maywhistle die?" I ask again. "Why is she haunting the hotel? Did you..."

My voice trails off.

"Did you kill her?" I whisper.

"I did what was necessary."

Feeling a shudder pass through my chest, I realize that I'm right. I don't suppose I need to know the details, not really, but it's obvious that Mr. Nash killed the little girl many years ago.

"And what happened to her sister?" I ask.

Again, he doesn't reply.

"You said the sister's name was Mary," I continue. "How did she die?"

"Smothered," he says after a moment. "There was nothing left for her. She was a pointless thing, just a burden on others. I put her out of her misery."

"You..."

I pause, realizing what he means.

"You killed her too?"

"I performed an act of kindness," he replies. "Emotion clouds decisions, Steven. You must remember that, you must..."

He pauses, and I watch as a single tear runs from his left eye. His mouth is trembling, as if he's on the verge of speaking but can't quite get the words out.

"It's all too late," he stammers finally. "She won't leave me alone. She'll come back, she'll come to the hotel eventually, to finish me off!"

I watch as he tries to get up. His body is wrecked, and he quickly slumps back down against the bed. Struggling to draw breath, he seems to be panicking, and finally he looks over toward the door.

"Have you seen her here?" he gasps. "This morning, I mean. Has she come up here yet?"

"I -"

"I can't see her again! Not after last night! I can't, I just can't! I have to make her stay away!"

"You said not to be emotional," I reply. "Aren't you -"

"I have to destroy this place," he stammers suddenly, starting to sound more agitated than ever. "The hotel cannot be allowed to remain. As long as the hotel stands, she'll keep coming after me! I have to destroy it, and then I have to get as far away from here as possible!"

"What do you mean?"

"It's over," he continues, trying but failing to lift himself from the bed. Letting out another pained gasp, he collapses back down. "You must help me, boy! You must help me get out of here as quickly as possible! And then I shall arrange for the Lakeforth to be utterly destroyed! This cursed place must be torn down, or burned, or otherwise leveled so that nothing remains here but flat, salted land! I was a fool to think that I could ever turn this place into something special. I am still the same common runt that I was all those years ago. My whole miserable life has been a lie! If we..."

He hesitates, as if some deep thought has suddenly struck him dumb.

"If we are born in the mud," he whispers finally, "we can never entirely rinse ourselves clean. I have tried to be something I am not. I am a fool. This hotel... I must have it torn down."

"The hotel is mine!" I remind him, trying not to panic. He seems to be completely out of his mind, as if fear has turned him into a total psycho.

"Perhaps if I let her ghost have the ruins of this place," he gasps, "she won't come after me! Not if I go far enough away!"

"So are you going to sell it?" I ask. "Will I get the money?"

"The land must be held in trust," he stammers, "so that there is no danger of it ever being used again. I don't care about anything else, not now! All I care about is making sure that she never comes after me! I thought I could make a deal with her, but I was wrong! She's too angry, too full of fury! Please, pass the telephone, so that I can call my solicitor in London and tell him of my new instructions."

"But you promised," I reply. "You said I'd get the hotel."

"This is not the time for recriminations. Pass me the telephone."

"You promised!"

"Child -"

"You promised!" I hiss, feeling a sudden burst of anger in my chest. "You told me I'd get it! You can't break your promise! You said we had a deal, and you said you never go back on a deal!"

"There's no time!" he hisses. "She might appear at any moment! Get me the telephone, you wretched boy! Hurry!"

"I want to get away from them," I mutter, feeling a sense of shock at the idea that I might have to stay with Mum and Dad. It's less than twenty-four hours since I was promised the hotel, but already the idea of its riches has taken root in my mind. I can't imagine going back to how things were before. "I want to be a successful businessman."

"Steven..."

"You promised," I continue, staring at him as I feel my anger growing. "You can't take it back. Not ever."

"Don't argue with me!"

"Why did they never catch you?"

"What are you talking about now?"

"If you smothered that little girl Mary," I continue, "how did you get away with it?"

"Call my doctor back in!" he gasps. "I have much to do before I..."

His voice trails off.

He's almost dead already.

I watch for a moment as he struggles to breathe, and deep down I already have an idea. I hesitate a little longer, and then I glance toward the door.

There's no sign of anybody coming back into the room.

"Please," Mr. Nash groans, filled with panic, "you must call my doctor."

Slowly, I get to my feet.

"You'll understand one day," he continues, staring up at me with scared, tear-filled eyes. "You're just a child, Steven. It's beyond your comprehension, but I assure you that one day you *will* see the sense in what I am doing today. I cannot see that girl again! I have to get out of here!"

He starts sobbing. Not just weeping, but really sobbing. I thought he was a great man, a man of resolve and brilliance, but now fear is turning him into a sobbing, spluttering wreck. The great Jobard Nash is letting a little girl tear him apart. I'm sure he must be losing his mind, and that deep down he'd never want to be like this. What he needs, I suppose, is an act of kindness.

I stare at him for a moment, before reaching past the bed and taking one of the spare pillows from a nearby table.

"Please," he gasps, "send for my doctor."

I hold the pillow carefully, trying to decide the best way to do this. I know I need to be quick, and I'm surprised to find that I'm not scared at all. I just want to make absolutely certain that I get the hotel, and to spare Mr. Nash the humiliation of letting other people see him like this.

"I recognize a lot of myself in you, Steven," he splutters. "You're a bright boy. Perhaps Ellen was right all those years ago, perhaps I can never escape who I really am. Please, help me! I'm begging you, I need -"

Suddenly I place the pillow over his face and push down, telling myself that I have to act fast. As the old man shudders and tries to fight back, I press my hands hard against the top of the pillow, and I can just about feel his face beneath. He's trying desperately to push me away, and after a minute or so I realize that he still doesn't seem to be any closer to dying, so I switch my angle and press my shoulder hard against the pillow, pushing as firmly as I can manage. At the same time, I start trying to think of other ways I might do this if suffocation doesn't work, although after a moment I realize that the old man is struggling less and less.

"Just die!" I whisper. "Please!"

Finally he falls still, but I don't dare let go yet. He might be bluffing, or he might still recover, so I keep my shoulder pushed against the pillow for several more minutes before figuring that it's probably safe to stop.

I pull the pillow away, and immediately a shudder passes through my chest as I see his wide-open mouth and his terrified expression.

After setting the pillow back where I found it, I check to make sure that Mr. Nash no longer has a pulse, and then I gently close his mouth. I don't really like touching a dead guy, but I figure it might look a little less suspicious if the mouth is closed. Mr. Nash probably did the same thing to Mary Maywhistle all those years ago, and I feel pretty pleased with myself for being so smart.

"I'm sorry," I whisper. "I just really, really

wanted the hotel after you promised it to me. It was the only way I could be kind to you."

With that, I turn and head over to the door. Once I'm out in the next room, I see that the doctor is speaking in hushed tones to the receptionist. They're obviously very worried, and it's already clear that they expect Mr. Nash to die soon. When they see me, they seem to wind up their conversation pretty quickly, and the doctor comes over to pat me on the shoulder.

"All done in there?" he asks.

I nod.

"You mustn't be too upset," he continues. "Jobard Nash is an old man, and he's had what we call a good innings. I'll make sure he's well looked after during the time he has left. I'll ensure that he's comfortable."

"He seemed pretty sick just now when I left the room," I tell him. "Gasping for breath, that sort of thing. He said he wanted you to go in and see him."

"And I'll do just that," he says, turning and opening the door. "Ms. Lucas will take you back to your parents."

As I head back over to the receptionist, I hear the sound of the door swinging shut behind me. Any moment now, the doctor will discover Mr. Nash's body, but I'm pretty sure he'll just assume that he must have died from the stroke he suffered last night.

"You're a sweet little boy," the receptionist says with a smile, putting a hand on my shoulder as she leads me toward the elevator. "It's very nice of you to spend time with Mr. Nash. I'm sure he appreciated it a lot."

"Thank you," I reply, even though deep down

I'm terrified in case the doctor realizes the truth. "He's really a very great man."

CHAPTER THIRTY-ONE

"I just don't understand," Dad says, staring in shock at the pile of papers on the solicitor's desk. "Steven only met Jobard Nash a couple of times. Why would the old man leave him his entire estate?"

"Mr. Nash had no children of his own," the solicitor replies, his voice all plummy and aristocratic. "If he wanted to keep the hotel within the family, I imagine young Steven would have been one of the more obvious candidates."

"But still..."

Dad's voice trails off, and it's clear that he's completely shocked. When I turn to Mum, I see that she looks even more confused, and I can't help smiling as I realize that they're both amazed by my good fortune. They've probably realized that I won't need them anymore, that at the grand age of eleven I'm going to be set for life. I imagine they're running through all the times they've been mean to me, and wondering whether

334

there's time for them to suck up and make me like them again.

Fat chance.

"Steven," Mum says finally, placing a hand on my knee, "I know you probably don't appreciate the magnitude of this news, but -"

"I appreciate it," I reply, interrupting her. "I'm not stupid. I understand. I'm inheriting Mr. Nash's hotel."

"Yes, and -"

"So it's going to be mine," I continue, "and nobody else can tell me what to do with it. Not ever."

I pause, watching the growing sense of shock on her face, and then I turn and see that Dad looks just as dumb.

"I was the last person to see him alive, wasn't I?" I add, before glancing at the solicitor. "I guess that means I meant something to him. At the end, anyway. He seemed like he was falling into a peaceful sleep just before I left the room. The doctor said his death was caused by the stroke." I pause, allowing my smile to grow. "I wanted to go to the cremation ceremony, but Mum and Dad wouldn't let me. They said it was too far to travel."

"That's not entirely right," Mum stammers, clearly embarrassed. "We just didn't want to take Steven out of school for those days. We thought it'd be too disruptive."

"So when do I get the keys?" I ask.

The solicitor raises a skeptical eyebrow. "The keys?"

"To the hotel. I need to start thinking about what changes I want to make to the place."

He stares at me for a moment. "Mr. Culshaw," he says finally, "I must point out at this juncture that you are only eleven years old."

"So?"

"So while the hotel *has* been bequeathed to you, it has been done so in trust."

I feel a faint stir of concern in my chest. "What does that mean?"

"It means that Mr. Nash required the formation of a trust that will manage the hotel on your behalf and protect the estate until you reach the age of twenty-one. Then, and only then, will you take control of your inheritance."

"That's ten years away!" I hiss.

"The trust shall be comprised of myself," he continues, "your parents, and most likely one of my colleagues from this law office. Together, we shall ensure that the value of Mr. Nash's estate will be protected. I can assure you that we will do a sterling job, and upon your twenty-first birthday you will of course take complete control yourself."

Staring at him, I realize that he's absolutely serious. This madman expects me to wait an entire decade before I take over the hotel, and when I turn to Mum and Dad I see that they're not surprised at all. Mr. Nash left the hotel to *me*, not to these idiots, but they're conspiring to push me out of the way and run the place themselves.

"I won't let you do this," I stammer. "I want the

hotel right now!"

"The legal situation is quite clear, Mr. Culshaw."

"It's mine!" I shout. "I want it!"

"Steven, please!" Mum hisses, nudging my arm. "Remember your manners!"

"I don't care about manners!" I yell, pulling away from her as I get to my feet. "I'm old enough to have the hotel now! That's what Mr. Nash wanted!"

"His instructions were quite clear," the solicitor replies. "Ten years isn't such a long time, young man, and I'm sure that in the end you'll be very thankful that people were around to look after your best interests. The running of a hotel is not a trifling matter and -"

"I hate you!" I shout, turning to Mum and then to Dad. "I hate all of you! You're trying to take it away from me, but it's mine! Mr. Nash gave it to me!"

With that, I turn and run out of the room, then along the corridor and finally out onto the street. There are several people wandering past, but I quickly rush across the road and over to the village green. Sitting on one of the benches, I put my head in my hands and try to get used to the idea that I'm going to have to wait ten whole years before I'm able to get the key to the hotel.

Ten years.

That's forever.

Ten years before I can become rich and successful. Ten years before I can get a proper girlfriend. Ten years before I can be like Mr. Nash.

Letting out a gasp of anger, I lean forward and try to make sense of the thoughts that are rushing through my head. I want to scream, but I also know that people will only start staring.

Taking a series of deep breaths, I finally realize that my only option is to turn this setback into an opportunity. Over the next ten years, I can make a lot of plans, and I can figure out *exactly* what I'm going to do with the hotel. And when I'm twenty-one years old, I'll go back there and make sure that the Lakeforth becomes the greatest hotel in the world. I even think I can sense Jobard Nash's voice deep in my mind, as if he's guiding me from beyond the grave.

I won't end up like Mr. Nash, though. I won't let some stupid little ghost break me. I'll be strong. And if the ghost of Ruth Maywhistle tries to stop me, I'll make her pay. After all, I've got ten years to figure it all out and come up with a better plan.

One day, I'm going to be the coolest, richest person on the planet. The world's going to bow down before the great Steve Culshaw.

PART EIGHT

STEVE CULSHAW
TODAY

AMY CROSS

CHAPTER THIRTY-TWO

"I'M SORRY, BETH," I say firmly, as I force the knife deeper into her back, "but I really need you to stay."

She slumps toward me, and I barely manage to catch her in time. Gasping and struggling futilely to push me away, she seems unable to stand properly, as if her legs have buckled. Hell, I figured she'd at least *try* to put up more of a fight, but instead she's folding so fast. I twist the knife slightly, causing her to let out an agonized cry, and then I carefully lower her down onto the cold, damp patio. That was so, *so* much easier than I ever expected.

"There's nothing you can do now," I tell her. "Just try to stay calm. You're gonna lose a lot of blood."

Suddenly her whole body starts shuddering, as if the knife's blade flicked a switch deep inside, and a trickle of blood erupts from her mouth. Her trembling hands reach toward the blade that's jutting out from her chest, and her eyes are wide with shock. I think she's still in the denial stage, still hoping that somehow this isn't really happening. I watch as her fingertips brush against the blade, smearing her own blood across the metal.

"There's nothing, Beth," I continue. "Don't fight it. Hush now. I've got you."

She grunts and tries to twist away, but I hold her down so that she can't get anywhere.

"It's not fatal," I add. "Hopefully not, anyway. I was very careful about where I stabbed you. I want you to see what I built here, Beth. I couldn't tell you before, I knew you wouldn't understand, but this hotel belongs to me now. I've spent ten years waiting to get my hands on it, ten years coming up with so many ideas, and now I'm finally twenty-one so it's all mine. The trust shuttered the place, they said it couldn't turn a profit, but they were just short-sighted. They didn't see the potential that I see. They weren't great minds."

"Help!" she gasps, as more blood runs from her mouth. "Somebody..."

"Hush," I whisper, kissing the top of her head. "I know how to patch you up. I've got great plans for us, Beth. Great, wonderful plans. You're in shock now, but you'll understand soon enough, and then you'll realize that I'm doing something really brilliant. You're gonna have so much respect for me."

I kiss her again, this time taking a moment to enjoy the smell of her hair.

"They're all going to see what I can do with this place," I add. "All those lousy, stinking assholes who doubted me. I've had Jobard Nash's ghost guiding me, pushing me along. I can do this!"

"Help!" she groans, reaching out with her trembling right hand. "Please, Annie..."

It takes a moment before I realize that she's talking to the vision of her sister. Looking up, I see Annie's form shimmering in the night air. She can't actually *do* anything to help, of course, since her physical body is still down in the swimming pool. All that's up here right now is a whisper of her former self, and like all new ghosts she's barely even aware of who she is or how she got here. I've studied ghosts over the past ten years, and I've begun to understand more and more about how they work. Perhaps Annie will gain a stronger sense of herself over time, perhaps she'll get some of her old personality back and she'll start causing trouble. Or, perhaps more likely, she'll simply fade away to nothing.

"I have to get moving," I mutter, reaching under Beth's arms and hauling her up. "Come on, babe. We can't stay out here all night. It's too cold, and I have a delivery coming soon."

She lets out a grunt of pain, but that's only to be expected. After all, she's got a great big knife skewered straight through her chest on the right side, just at the top of the breast.

"I know it hurts," I tell her, "but don't worry, this is all part of the plan I've been working on for the past few years. I always knew I needed a girlfriend here with me, somebody to share the journey. You're going to have such fun!"

I start pulling her back toward the doors that lead into the dining room, but after a moment I stop and look over at Annie's ghostly form. Even though I've studied ghosts and come to understand a great deal about them, I still find myself transfixed by their beauty. Plus, Annie was hot and I always kind of hoped she might come around to my way of seeing things. Oh well. Too late now.

"And as for you," I tell her with a faint smile, "you don't really matter at all. Do what you want. I'm not scared of you. You're nothing I haven't seen before. This hotel is already full of ghosts, but I guess one more can't hurt."

PART NINE

BETH HAYES
ONE DAY LATER

CHAPTER THIRTY-THREE

"HEY, DO YOU WANNA come with me and check out this weird-ass hotel?"

Squinting slightly, I try to check the time on my phone, only to find that the numbers are swimming slightly. I focus, but still the numbers wriggle and squirm, refusing to take any kind of form that I recognize.

"Beth?"

"Wait," I whisper, still watching the phone. "I can't -"

"Ignore that."

Grabbing the phone from my hand, Steve sets it face-down on the table and grabs my shoulder, forcing me to turn to him. He's on the other side of the bed, with morning light streaming through the blinds and catching the side of his face. Outside the window, London sounds so noisy and busy.

"Do you wanna come with me and check out this

hotel?" he asks again. "It's about a day's drive from here. It's where my parents used to take me as a kid."

"Uh-huh." I wait for him to explain, but he's just staring at me. "Why exactly do you want to go back there?"

"I just think it'd be cool. We could swing by on our way to Brighton."

"I only have a week off," I tell him. "Plus, my dumb-ass sister is -"

"She can come too."

I open my mouth to reply, but I feel strangely dizzy. "What time is it?" I manage to stammer finally, as I realize I can hear music in the distance. A waltz.

"I'll book us rooms," he continues, with a faint smile, as if he's not quite telling me everything. "The place used to be full of old people. I wanna go and see if it still is."

"I'm not sure I can afford a -"

"I'll pay."

Sighing, I realize that he's serious. "Okay. Whatever, I just -"

Before I can finish, I realize that the sound of the city has suddenly vanished. Turning, I look over at the window and see nothing outside except darkness. Suddenly night has fallen. I've had dreams like this, but I'm not dreaming *now*. I can't be. At the same time, placing a hand on my chest, I can't help noticing a sudden throbbing pain that seems to be slicing straight through.

"Don't worry," Steve continues, his voice starting to twist and warp in the air around me. "It won't be creepy. It'll be just us, in that big old empty hotel."

"I thought you wanted to see the other guests," I reply, turning to him.

"Oh, right. Sure. Yeah, totally." He forces a big grin. "It'll be fun, Beth, I promise. And we're so close to the Lakeforth already. All you have to do, really, is open your eyes."

"Do what?"

"Open your eyes."

"They are open."

He shakes his head, still smiling.

"They are open," I stammer again, although I'm starting to doubt myself. I can feel my mind rising through the air, through a cloud of darkness, and the distant waltz music is getting closer. At the same time, there's a beeping sound, accompanied by flashing lights.

"Open your eyes, Beth," Steve says yet again, staring at me with fresh intensity. "You can't stay knocked out forever. You have to open your eyes."

***

Opening my eyes, I find myself in darkness. I quickly realize I can hear music in the distance. Beautiful music, maybe a waltz. For a moment, I have no idea where I am, but then the memory of the hotel settles in my head again. The music must be coming from the ballroom downstairs. It has to be. But then, why would I be up here all alone in the dark, in a cold room?

I bet the dancing is really something.

But it's not real.

It can't be real.

And that's when I remember the moment when Steve stabbed me from behind. I let out a gasp and try to sit up, but the pain catches my chest tight and holds me down against the bed. I grab the sheets, squeezing as hard as I can manage while I wait for the worst of the agony to pass.

Suddenly the music stops, and I realize that I was in another daze. The pain in my chest is intense and tight, and I'm starting to worry that I'm developing a serious infection. I remember what happened now, after I was dragged back into the hotel. Steve claimed that he knew how to clean the wound after he pulled the knife out, but I don't think he *really* had a clue what he was doing. I feel hot and sweaty, and I'm struggling to stay awake for more than a few minutes at a time.

I think I might have lost a lot of blood.

A moment later, I realize there are bright lights flashing in the darkness outside one of the windows. I turn just in time to see the lights swing away, accompanied by what sounds like a large truck driving past the hotel.

Tilting my head back, I try to cry out, but there's a tight gag over my mouth. All I can manage is a very faint, very muffled groan, although deep down I know that there's nobody else for miles around. I start struggling with the ropes around my wrists, but they're far too tight. I can feel the rough fibers rubbing against my flesh, cutting through my wrists, but I still can't make myself stop pulling. I continue to wriggle for several more minutes, trying to find some way that I might get free, and then finally I fall still for a moment.

The sound of the truck has faded into the distance, and the lights are gone too.

Tears are rolling down my cheeks.

"You should see the place," Steve told me earlier, while he was settling me onto the bed. "It's so beautiful, Beth. I can't wait until it's all finished and you're well enough to enjoy one of these nights with me. I have a dress all picked out for you, but I'm afraid I can't trust you, not yet. You see, I didn't get to where I am today by trusting the wrong people. I'm a great judge of character, Beth, and you... Well, you're just not ready yet. It's going to take a while before you see things from my point of view. But you will. I promise."

And then he stroked my hair tenderly for a moment, even though I was struggling and desperately trying to slip the gag so I could cry out.

Suddenly, hearing footsteps coming toward the door, I turn and look across the pitch-black room. A moment later, a light flicks on in the corridor, creating a faint outline of the door, which finally opens to reveal a familiar figure bringing a tray of food for me. I immediately flinch as I watch him coming closer, and then I wait as he sets the tray down and flicks a switch on the wall.

The lamp comes to life next to the bed, and I find myself staring up at Steve's smiling face.

"Hey, how -"

I immediately try to scream, but the gag is still too tight.

"Hey there," he continues, as he starts busying

himself with the contents of the tray. "Let me tell you, I'm really coming up with a lot of ideas tonight. I mean, I came up with ideas before, when I was planning all of this, but it was hard to really visualize the place. Now that I'm here again after all these years, I've got so many ideas flooding into my mind, I almost kinda wish I could slow them down a little. That's crazy, huh?"

I struggle to pull my hands free from the leather restraints, but Steve has tied them far too tight.

"Don't worry about all that," he says, fiddling with something on the tray for a moment before moving a spoonful of mashed food to my lips. "Now, you need to keep your strength up, don't you? I know you've been resting, and that's good, but you still need your vitamins and minerals. I wouldn't want to see you looking sick. I worry about you a lot, you know. You're not going to spend forever here on this bed. This is just a temporary measure while I wait for you to come around to my way of thinking."

I try to tell him to go to hell, but I can't get any of the words out. Struggling for breath, I pause for a moment, trying to figure out how else I can get out of here, and then suddenly Steve reaches over and pulls the gag clear.

"Help!" I scream, as loud as I can manage. "Somebody help me!"

"Who do you think's going to hear that?"

"Help me!"

"There's nobody for miles, Beth. You saw how far this place is from civilization. Or are you thinking that maybe your sister's ghost might come and untie you? Well, that's not how it works. In fact, I haven't seen Annie since yesterday morning. I'm afraid I think she's faded away. That happens with some ghosts, you know. I think it's 'cause they just don't have that pure force of personality, you know? They're not angry enough to stick around. Annie was loud when she was alive, but in the end there wasn't really very much to her."

"You're insane!" I sob, as my whole body convulses and I feel a shuddering pain in my chest. "How the hell did I not see that before?"

"Because I didn't want you to," he replies. "Anyway, I'm not insane. That's a really mean word, Beth. God, I feel so -"

"Go to hell!" I scream. "You're a psychopath, you -"

Suddenly he slaps me hard, forcing me to turn away as I feel a harsh stinging sensation on the side of my face.

"I'm sorry," he stammers, leaning closer and kissing me on the cheek.

Turning, I spit at him, and he immediately pulls back. He looks utterly startled.

"I didn't mean to hit you," he continues. "Honestly, that was a mistake. You just provoked me, that's all. It won't happen again, though. I don't hit women. I just need you to start seeing all of this from my point of view. The hotel can be a wonderful place again, and I need someone to share it with. Someone to be by my side. I want that someone to be you, Beth."

"Have you always been like this?" I ask, as tears stream down my face. "Have you always been crazy?"

"You're funny. Did anyone ever tell you that?"

"Was any of it true?" I stammer. "About you coming here with your parents? About this place meaning something to you?"

"Of course. All of that was true. I just left out the past where old Mr. Nash left the hotel to me in his will. He was the guy in that photo I showed you. He was nice, he taught me everything I know. And then I added some ideas of my own, naturally."

"Where's Annie?"

"Beth -"

"Where's Annie?" I scream.

He sighs.

"Where's my goddamn sister, you -"

"Time to eat," he says firmly, pushing the spoon into my mouth and forcing it deep down my throat. I start gagging as I feel the spoon's plastic tip scraping against the back of my tongue, and as Steve turns the spoon and wipes the mash loose. Some of the food falls down my throat, and some remains stuck on my tongue as he pulls the spoon out.

Almost choking, I struggle with my gag reflex until finally I manage to swallow the whole spoonful.

"That wasn't so bad, was it?" Steve continues, as he loads up some more food. "I'm sorry I left you up here all day today, but I've been out exploring the site. Can you believe, this whole place is mine? My parents thought they could get their grubby hands on it, they wanted me to sell it. They probably thought I'd pay off their mortgage, something like that. Well, that didn't work out too well for them."

He pauses, clearly simmering with anger.

"Nobody'll find them now, anyway," he mutters. "I sorted them both out before I picked you up to drive here."

"What do you mean?" I ask, trembling with fear.

I wait, but he doesn't reply. Instead, a faint smile crosses his lips, and he seems to be lost in his own thoughts.

"What did you do to them, Steve?" I continue, trying to stay calm. "Are your parents okay?"

"They were idiots. They deserved it."

"Steve -"

"Don't ask about them!" he snaps, reaching the spoon toward my lips again. "Come on, I need to feed you before I go back downstairs. I have so much more work to get done tonight."

He starts slipping the spoon between my lips, but I quickly spit the mash back at him.

"Stop that!" he yells, smashing the back of his hand against my cheek.

Wincing, I turn away.

"You did it again!" he hisses, wiping the mash from his shoulder before spooning some more from the bowl. "I don't hit women, Beth, so stop making me do it! You're gonna be my princess here at the hotel. You're gonna have the most perfect, luxurious life. No more scrimping and saving, no more pulling double shifts to put yourself through some pathetic, pointless college course. All you've got to do is accept everything I'm offering you. And you will. I know it."

"I won't ever take anything from you," I

stammer. "People are going to notice that I'm missing, Steve. I told people I was coming here with you!"

"Uh, no, you didn't." He smiles. "Not anyone that can help you, anyway. It was all quite last-minute, remember? Annie knew, but she's dead. And my parents knew, but they're dead too. Is there anyone else you told, Beth? Be honest now."

I open my mouth to lie and tell him there were others, but I can already tell that he's got me sussed.

"By the time anyone else comes here," he continues, "the Lakeforth is going to have been reborn. I have so many plans, and you're gonna be amazed. Just wait, Beth, and have a little faith. Maybe my methods are kinda rough, I'll admit that, but you're gonna be proud of me eventually. I'm gonna do everything Jobard Nash couldn't, and I'm gonna start by taking the problems he faced and turning them into solutions. That's what makes me a real businessman. I'm gonna succeed where he failed."

Before I can tell him again that he's insane, he forces the spoon back into my mouth, and this time he plunges the tip deeper than ever into my throat. I start gagging desperately, but he's scraping the plastic tip hard and wiping more of the food against the back of my tongue. Barely able to breath, I shake violently as I try to get free, and as the spoon's tip slips deeper and deeper down my throat.

"I've got such big plans!" Steve adds with a grin. "And you're gonna stay right here to watch!"

CHAPTER THIRTY-FOUR

LETTING OUT A GASP of pain, I feel a bead of liquid start running down from my wrist and onto the palm of my hand.

Blood.

I must have worn through the flesh of my right wrist, after spending the past few hours desperately trying to break free of these leather restraints. I know I have to get off the bed, but I'm all out of ideas and my only option is to somehow force my wrists free. I've considered breaking my thumb, the way I've seen people get loose in films, but I think even that might not help. Besides, as I work in the pitch-black room, I can't help thinking that there has to be another option.

There has to be a way to get free before Steve comes back up.

I just have to be smart enough to figure it out.

Steve's been gone for hours now. After feeding me, he ranted on for a little while longer about Jobard

Nash and about the history of the hotel, and about all the ways this Nash guy failed. Steve keeps talking about having some great master-plan up his sleeve, and I think he genuinely believes that eventually he'll not only turn the Lakeforth into the most successful hotel in the world, but he'll also persuade me to see things from his point of view so that I'll become his wife. I wasn't planning to marry the guy *before* I found out he was a murderous psychopath, and nothing over the past twenty-four hours has changed my mind.

"You can do this," I tell myself, twisting my right hand a little and focusing on the fact that I'm going to have to push through the pain barrier. Even if I lose half the skin around my wrist, I have to get off this bed.

I pause for a moment, before starting to pull as hard as I can manage. As the pain builds, I start letting out a muffled groan, straining against the gag as I feel sweat starting to roll down my face. I know I can't stop, and I can feel my flesh slowly tearing beneath the restraints, but I think that maybe – just maybe – I might be able to do this. I pull and pull, tensing every muscle in my body, telling myself that somehow I'm going to get out of here.

And then, just as I think I actually have a chance, I lean too far and the bed collapses beneath me. One of the legs must have broken, and I quickly crash down to the floor with a thud. Letting out a gasp of pain, I'm able to start sliding the restraint away from the bed's wooden board, which finally leaves me still wearing the damn thing but with my right hand no longer attached to anything. I can't see clearly in the darkness, but I maneuver myself around and immediately pull the gag from my mouth, and then I start working on my other wrist, hoping that I can demolish the rest of the bed's frame and somehow get out of here.

A moment later, however, I stop working as I realize I can hear footsteps heading this way along the corridor.

I turn and look toward the door, expecting to see a light in the corridor, but everything remains dark. The footsteps stop on the other side of the door, and for a moment I start worrying that maybe Steve heard my struggles and came to investigate, but if that was the case then I'm sure he would have entered the room by now. My heart is pounding, and I know that this might be my last chance to get away.

"Steve?" I stammer finally, hoping to buy myself some time as I fumble for one of the broken pieces of wood. Finding one with a sharp end, I figure that while I'm still partly attached to the bed's frame, I can at least defend myself. "Steve, is that you?"

I wait, but there's no reply.

It has to be him, though.

There's nobody else here.

"Steve, are you coming in?" I ask, telling myself that I need him to come close if I'm going to use the broken wood against him. At the same time, I'm working furiously to free myself from the last of the restraints. "Come on, you bastard, I dare you! Or are you even more of a coward than I realized?"

Nothing.

Silence.

"Screw you, then," I mutter, turning and struggling in the darkness to break another section of the bed's frame. "I'll be -"

Before I can finish, I hear the door-handle starting to turn. Looking over my shoulder, I'm just about able to see the door swinging open in the darkness, but there's nobody standing on the other side. Just an empty corridor with a patch of moonlight on the far wall.

Swallowing hard, I realize that Steve must be playing some kind of game. He probably wants me to think that there are ghosts here. The little girl I saw earlier was obviously a trick, one that he's trying to pull again.

"What's wrong?" I ask. "Are you scared? What have you got to be scared of? I'm defenseless, right? It's not like I can fight back. Come on, asshole, do your best!"

I'm trembling with fear, but I genuinely want Steve to step into view and come at me. I might be at a disadvantage, but right now I'm certain I can take the bastard down, even if I can only use one arm and my only weapon is a broken piece of wood. Steve's tough and fit, but I'm damn well not going down without a fight.

"Come on!" I yell. "What are you waiting for? Come and get me!"

I wait, but there's still no reply, so finally I shift around to the side of the bed and start kicking furiously at the frame. I can already feel the damn thing starting to come loose, and finally another of the panels splits down the middle, which is just enough to let me twist the other restraint loose. Pulling away, I'm finally free, and I scramble to my feet while still holding the broken piece of wood in my right hand. I take a step across the dark room, heading toward the open doorway, but then I hesitate as I realize that Steve is most likely lurking outside, ready to strike as soon as I get closer.

Adjusting my grip on the piece of wood, I take a step forward, but I immediately feel a burning sensation in my chest. Looking down, I'm finally able to see that there's a thick patch of blood on the front of my torn shirt, and it's clear that some of the fabric has become stuck to the wound. I try to pull the shirt free, but I feel a tearing pain that forces me to stop.

I'll deal with the wound later. Right now, it's a miracle I can move at all, and I intend to make full use of that miracle.

"Okay then, asshole," I mutter, raising the piece of wood as if it's a baseball bat and starting to make my way toward the door. "Let's see what you're made of. You'll only get one chance, though, 'cause I've gotta warn you... I'm gonna fight back, and I'm not gonna stop until one of us is out cold on the floor. Or worse. Do you really think you've got the balls to take me?"

I'm trying to goad him into making the first move, but so far he seems to be holding firm. As I get closer and closer to the door, I find myself wondering whether he's already left, although I know I can't afford to make any assumptions. Finally, once I'm so close that I have no other options, I decide to see if I can trick him into striking out. I turn the piece of wood in my hands, and then I briefly flash it forward through the doorway, hoping that Steve will be tricked into attacking.

Nothing.

Lunging forward, I let out a cry as I swing the wood, but I quickly slam into the opposite wall and then turn to find that Steve is nowhere to be seen.

"Where the hell are you?" I mutter, figuring that he must have backed away after opening the door. I was trying to make him angry when I suggested he was a coward, but now I'm starting to think I might have been right.

Turning, I start making my way along the corridor, heading toward the top of the stairs. If I just -

Suddenly I feel someone bump against me from behind. I turn and swing the piece of wood, but there's no sign of anyone and I simply hit the wall as I take a step back. My heart is racing and I look both ways along the corridor, but I know nobody could have touched me and then run away so quickly. It's impossible.

"Keep your head together!" I mutter as I once again start walking slowly toward the top of the stairs. I listen out for any hint of movement, for anything that suggests Steve might be nearby, but so far the hotel seems completely silent.

I want to call out to Annie, but I don't dare.

She's alive, though.

She has to be.

By the time I get to the far end of the dark corridor and look down the stairs toward the next level, I'm starting to wonder whether Steve might have left. After all, if he thinks I'm safely secured, he might have had enough confidence to go away from the hotel for a few hours. I can't even begin to imagine what he could be doing, but I don't think this is the right time to worry about second-guessing this maniac.

I have to get out of here, reach the road and run. And then I have to not look back until I find help.

For the next few minutes, I make my way cautiously down several sets of stairs, constantly stopping to make sure that Steve can't sneak up on me. The lights are all off in the hotel, so I can barely see where I'm going, and all these zig-zag-carpeted corridors are starting to look the same. At least the place is quiet, though, so I can listen out for even the slightest hint that Steve is getting closer. Whatever he's up to right now, it seems to have been keeping him busy, and hopefully he won't be done for a little while longer.

Reaching the top of the stairs that lead down into the lobby, however, I have to stop for a moment and lean against a wall. I'm starting to feel dizzy, and sweat is running down my forehead. The wound on my chest seems to be getting very warm, and I'm more convinced than ever that I'm running out of time. Sooner or later, the blood-loss alone is going to knock me out.

Stepping forward, I start making my way down the grand staircase, only for my right leg to suddenly buckle when I'm about halfway. Letting out a gasp, I try to steady myself against the banister, but I'm too late and I quickly tumble down the stairs, landing in a crumpled heap at the bottom. For a moment, I feel as if I might not be able to get up again, but somehow I manage to start forcing myself to my feet. My right ankle was hurt in the fall, but I push through the pain and turn toward the main doors.

And that's when I see the set of bones in a glass case.

Horrified, I limp forward, staring at what appears to be a bare human skeleton encased in some kind of resin slab. As I get closer, I realize that the bones are a little small, perhaps belonging to a child, and finally I stop at the front of the case and stare up at the skull. Two empty eye sockets stare back at me, while the jaw bone is hanging down a little in a silent scream. After a moment, I see that one of the girl's hands only has three fingers.

"Mary Maywhistle."

Gasping, I turn and see Steve sitting on the floor at the far side of the room. He immediately gets to his feet, although he takes only a single step forward before stopping again.

"Isn't she beautiful?" he continues, with a hint of awe in his voice. "I had to have her remains disinterred from a cemetery in London. It wasn't quite official, but one can get away with these things in the middle of the night. The poor girl had lain there for more than half a century, rotting in her coffin. Turns out, Mr. Jobard Nash had paid for a full funeral back in the day. Out of guilt, perhaps, or maybe he just wanted to make sure she was safely down in the ground. Whatever. She's here now, where she belongs."

Turning back to look up at the set of bones, I finally take a step back.

"I've been planning ahead," Steve continues. "I had Mary and a few others delivered not long ago. She's part of the hotel's story, after all. I might be wrong, but I think the ghost of Jobard Nash has been reaching out to me over the years, subtly guiding me to make sure that I reach this point."

Hearing footsteps behind me, I turn and watch as he makes his way to a large crate next to the dining room door. Reaching up, he loosens a panel and lets it swing down until it crashes against the marble floor, revealing another set of bones in a case. This time, the bones have a lot of meat left on them, along with a full head of hair, and the corpse seems to be dressed in some kind of dark suit.

"The great Jobard Nash," Steve explains proudly. "Again, raised from a grave. This one was a little more difficult to access, since he'd had himself placed in a kind of mausoleum, but I found some men who got the job done. He rested in peace for ten years, but I think that was quite *enough* peace. I'm sure that he, of all people, would appreciate the need for him to come back to Lakeforth and take his rightful place. He's another very important part of the hotel's history."

He stares at the preserved body for a moment, before turning to me.

"Are you speechless?" he says with a faint smile. "I'll take that as a compliment."

"What the hell is wrong with you?" I stammer.

"Wrong?"

"Are these real?" I ask. "Are these bodies real?"

"Of course. I'm not in the business of exhibiting fakes."

"Where's my sister?"

"Beth, you -"

"Where's Annie?" I scream. "What have you done to her?"

"Try to calm down."

"Where the hell is my sister?" I sneer, limping toward him. "What have you done to her?"

"There seems to be something nasty in the swimming pool," he replies. "That was a surprise, I have to admit. I can only assume that long ago, Jobard Nash had someone buried down there, under the foundations. I need to think carefully about what I do there, because I don't want my live guests getting -"

"Where's my sister?" I shout, with tears in my eyes. "Answer me, you asshole, or I swear to God I'll make you pay!"

"She's dead, obviously," he mutters. "It's okay, I can incorporate her into everything else. I'm very good at thinking on my feet."

Stopping just a few feet from him, I tell myself that he's lying. He has to be. Maybe he *thinks* Annie is dead, but she's way too smart to let some idiot kill her. She'll have found a way to get out of here. She's probably already going for help.

"You look so lost and confused," he says after a moment. "So scared. That's okay, Beth. It's a lot to take in."

I turn and take a step toward the main door, but he quickly moves to block me.

"Wise move," he continues, as I start backing away. "Look around, Beth. Look at this place. Any other man in the whole world would be hell-bent on renovating the Lakeforth, on returning it to its former glory. They'd be planning a whole new marble floor, and a new chandelier, and vast, sumptuous displays of excess. They'd want to cover the cracks of the past and pretend all those awful things never happened. But not me. The way I see it, this hotel is now perfect. The richest, the wealthiest people in the world are going to flock here. Not *despite* the history of the place, but *because* of it."

I watch as he heads over to yet another large crate. He loosens the front and lets it fall down, revealing yet another set of bones. This body has some meat left too, and I can tell from the tattered remains of a dress that it belonged to a woman. There's a rope around its rotten neck, too, like some kind of noose.

"A theatrical touch that I'm still not too sure about," Steve explains. "This is Ellen Nash, nee Carpenter. She was married to Jobard for a while, but eventually she hung herself at a psychiatric hospital in London. I tracked down her nephew and niece, whose mother Eve is said to have told them all about poor Ellen's troubles. It seems that being the wife of Jobard Nash, and living here at the hotel, drove her quite insane. I felt a little bad, bringing her body back, but the exhibition would be incomplete without her."

"Why are you doing this?" I ask, as he starts coming closer.

"Beth -"

Instinctively, I hold up the broken section of wood. I might not be able to hide the fact that my hands are trembling, but I'm pretty sure I can still swing this thing at him.

He smiles. "Beth, really. What do you think that can do to me?"

"It's worth a shot," I mutter darkly.

"This hotel is haunted," he continues. "It's been haunted for years. The ghost of a sweet, kind young girl named Ruth Maywhistle has been seen on several occasions. Except, she's *not* sweet and kind. Not anymore. No, it seems the manner of her death changed her, as did years and years of wandering the hotel and its grounds. Apparently a good person can become a perfectly wretched, evil ghost, so long as the conditions are right. A sweet little girl, if murdered in a certain manner, can become a vengeful, murderous spirit. How much money do you think the wealthiest people will pay, in order to spend even one night in a house that is genuinely proven to be haunted? Provided certain safeguards are in place, of course."

"Stay back!" I yell, holding the piece of wood up higher as he takes another step toward me.

"I'm not going to hurt you," he continues, holding his hands up as if in surrender. "I'm showing you what I'm going to create here. And when we're married, our little zoo of ghosts will -"

"Go to hell!" I shout.

He laughs.

"You're completely out of your mind," I continue, backing away as he steps closer. "Do you really think you can get away with digging up bodies and putting them on display? I'm going to find out what you've really done to my sister and -"

"Oh, I can show you that," he replies, hurrying to the far side of the room, where another crate waits under a sheet. "I was just waiting for the right moment. A spot of showmanship."

"No," I whisper, stepping forward. "Please -"

Before I can finish, he pulls the sheet away, revealing not a crate but a large glass case. Horrified, I see Annie's body suspended in some kind of clear liquid. Dropping the piece of wood, I hurry over to help her, but by the time I reach her I can tell it's too late. Her dead eyes are wide open, staring out from the case, and there are thick scratches all down her neck and chest. Her hair is suspended above her head, caught in whatever viscous liquid was poured into the case, and there are just a few tiny air bubbles clinging to the side of her bloodied jaw. She looks as if she's been suspended in time, and there's a hint of shock in her dead eyes as they stare out at me.

"Preserved in formaldehyde," Steve explains calmly. "Well, formaldehyde and a petroleum reduction, anyway. I came well-prepared. With so many bones on display, I think it'll really liven the place up to have a body with all its meat still attached."

"Annie, please," I stammer, placing a hand on the glass as I stare up into her lifeless eyes. "Please, no..."

I wait, but deep down I know it's too late. This isn't some dummy or mock-up. This is really all that's left of my sister.

"As I said earlier," Steve continues, sounding a little proud of his work, "her ghost seems to have faded away now. Evidently that happens with some people.

For all her noise and commotion when she was alive, it turns out that her spirit was rather weak. I guess her ghost won't be part of the hotel's collection, but that was never part of the original plan anyway. I truly didn't mean to hurt Annie, but you're the one who insisted on inviting her along on our little trip. Now that she's dead, I can't waste her body and just -"

"Go to hell!" I scream, stumbling to my feet and lunging at him.

"Beth, please..."

Grabbing me by the throat, he holds me back as I try to scratch his face.

"You're a murderer!" I shout.

"Beth, calm down. I don't hit women, but -"

"You won't get away with this!"

Throwing my full weight at him, I slam him against the wall, but he manages to keep hold of my throat.

"Beth! Please! I don't hit women! Try to -"

"You're going to rot in jail!" I hiss. "You're -"

Suddenly he punches me, slamming his fist against the side of my face with such force that I stumble back. I immediately try to lunge at him, but he punches me again and this time I fall back, slumping against the marble floor. The pain is so intense, I feel as if my entire jaw is shuddering.

"Are you happy now?" he asks, sounding a little annoyed. "I don't hit women, Beth, but you really need to calm down. This is happening whether you like it or not!"

As he steps past me and makes his way back

across the lobby, I look up again at Annie's suspended body, and I feel tears running down my face as I see her dead features. Crawling over to the case, I stare at her eyes, and I see faint clouds of smoky blood frozen in the formaldehyde. She's been trapped like an insect in amber, and it's all my fault. I should never have let her come on this trip, I should have dragged her from the car when she insisted. I'm older than her. If I'd been firm, she'd still be safe at home.

"I'm sorry," I sob, reaching up and placing my hand on the front of the case, as close to hers as I can manage. "Annie, I'm so sorry. I should never have let you come."

"And this is my main exhibit!" Steve calls out from far behind me, accompanied by the sound of another crate being opened. "The *piece de resistance*, if you like. The crowning glory. All the others are perhaps mostly for show, but this final item is what will set my hotel apart from all the others. This is going to make sure that the place is truly haunted."

Wiping tears from my eyes, I turn and see that this time he's unveiled some kind of large cage, with thick silver bars. There's something inside the cage, something slumped on a plinth. It takes a moment before I realize that it's yet another dead body.

"Well?" Steve asks, as I stumble to my feet. "Aren't you going to come and take a closer look? You're very lucky to be getting a sneak preview, Beth."

Limping toward him, I peer at the cage and see that there's another body on a kind of raised white pedestal. The body is dark and rotten, although after a moment I realize I can just about make out a patch of dark hair at one end, along with the pale, partially-decayed flesh of an arm. A faint, yellowish line of liquid has run down one end of the pedestal, as if something is slowly oozing from the corpse.

"Forgive the smell," Steve continues, stepping back proudly. "The high clay content in the lake's water preserved the body to some degree, but not entirely. I'm going to have her properly fixed soon, so that she won't deteriorate. Then again, perhaps the smell will be part of the fascination. I'm sure people will flock to see her. After all, she's the centerpiece of the entire show, and it's her ghost that haunts the corridors and rooms of the hotel, not to mention the dark forest beyond."

Stunned, I reach the bars and look through, and finally I see the decomposing body of a little girl.

"If one wants a haunted hotel," Steve says after a moment, "one needs to keep one's ghosts hungry. Not dangerous, but hungry. And I think little Ruth Maywhistle is going to be very hungry indeed."

"You can't be serious," I whisper. "This is monstrous."

In the distance, there's a faint bumping sound, coming from far off in the building.

"Did you hear that?" Steve asks suddenly, turning and looking past me. "I think she's close."

Too horrified to even move, I continue to stare at the dead little girl. I can just about see the side of her face, with pale, rotten flesh still clinging in places to the bones. Her mouth is slightly open, revealing a row of stained teeth.

"From what I can tell," Steve explains, "little Ruth has spent several decades haunting the hotel, begging people to raise her body from the lake and reunite her with her sister Mary. Well, I've done both those things for her, although somehow I doubt she'll be happy. Be careful what you wish for, eh?"

In the distance, there's another faint bump, as if someone slammed a door in a corridor somewhere above us.

"That's her," Steve continues. "It has to be. She's been trying to manifest a more solid form, but she's not very good at it. Most of the time, she's just a specter in the air. I'm worried she might fade away entirely if her anger isn't stoked. I need to keep her around, but I need to make sure she can't take her body back. Hence the bars."

"Why are you doing this?" I ask, feeling a cold shudder run through my chest as I continue to stare at the girl's dead, bloated face.

"People will pay millions to spend a night in a haunted hotel, Beth. I'll only allow a very select few to attend. Jobard Nash thought that ridding the hotel of ghosts was the key to its success, but he simply lacked the necessary vision. He didn't understand that human nature is something to be used for profit."

"You're sick!" I shout, turning and hurrying to the main doors, pulling to get them open but finding that they're locked. "Let me out of here!"

"Not a chance," he replies, heading back across the lobby toward the stairs. "I lied when I said I hadn't been here for a long time, Beth. I was here just last week, overseeing some improvements to the security of the place. You won't force your way out, not through steel-reinforced doors with state-of-the-art locks, and certainly not through strengthened windows. Better to accept what's happening and adjust to your new role. You're part of the hotel now."

Still desperately trying to get the doors open, I pull harder and harder on the handle before finally hurrying to the window. I grab a vase from the floor and throw it at the glass, but the vase simply falls back and crashes against the floor, shattering as it lands.

"I'm going to check on Ruth's progress," Steve calls out to me. "Please, Beth. Entertain yourself for a few minutes. We'll talk again once you've tired yourself out."

I turn just in time to see him disappearing up the stairs. Figuring that I need to find a way out of here as quickly as possible, I run across the lobby and through to the dark dining room, although I find that the double patio doors are securely locked. I look around, hoping to find something I can use to smash the glass, but a moment later I realize I can hear a faint sobbing sound nearby.

Turning, I see a woman crumpled on the floor, holding her hands over her face as she weeps.

CHAPTER THIRTY-FIVE

"WHO ARE YOU?" I stammer, taking a step toward the woman. "Are you..."

My voice trails off as I realize that the woman's clothing looks distinctly old-fashioned. There's something strange about her appearance, as if she's almost shimmering slightly in the darkness of the room, and I feel the air getting colder all around as I get closer.

"We have to get out of here," I tell her, and now my chest is tightening with fear. No matter how hard I try to remind myself that this woman can't be a ghost, I'm starting to realize that she looks like the woman from the photograph Steve showed me the other day. "Are you... Are you Ellen Nash?"

She pauses, before slowing lowering her hands to reveal a pale face. Her eyes are bulging from their sockets, and I take a step back as I remember that Ellen Nash was found hanging in her room at a psych hospital.

"Please," she sobs, "don't let her come to me

again. I can't bear to see her awful little face!"

"What are you talking about?" I ask. "I don't know what you've been told, but -"

"I never wanted to come back here!" she blurts out. "I just wanted to stay at the hospital forever! Why am I back here?"

Forcing myself to step closer, I once again feel the air getting colder. By the time I'm standing next to the woman, I'm almost shivering, and I can see now that there's a thick red mark around her neck.

"I don't know who you really are," I continue, "and I don't know if this is some kind of trick, but we have to leave! Right now! Do you know a way out?"

"I'll never get out," she whimpers. "We're all trapped here forever. There's nothing but the misery of this hotel for the rest of time."

She looks up at me, and after a moment I realize her eyes are bulging further and further from her sockets, while the red mark on her neck is tightening as if an invisible noose is squeezing hard. Hearing a faint cracking, splitting sound, I watch in horror as her left eye pops completely out of the socket.

"Wait," I stammer, "you -"

"Help me!" she shouts, stumbling to her feet and reaching for me, grabbing my arm with an icy hand. "Don't make me stay here!"

Suddenly an ear-piercing scream rings out from elsewhere in the house. I turn and look toward the door as I realize that the scream seems to be coming from a child, and a moment later I feel the cold hand leave my arm. Turning, I find that the woman has disappeared, although I can still feel the sensation of her cold fingers against my flesh.

Hurrying to the door, I look through to the darkened lobby as the scream continues, and I swear the noise seems to be getting louder and louder. I put my hands over my ears, trying in vain to force the scream from my head, as I step out into the lobby and -

"Do you hear her?" Steve hisses, grabbing me and pulling me to one side, while placing a knife against my throat. "She's seen what I'm doing. She's seen the wonderful work I've begun, and she's doing exactly what I wanted. Now imagine a handful of the world's richest people here in the hotel, hearing that scream. They'll pay millions for the chance to encounter a real ghost."

"Make it stop," I stammer, as the scream gets even louder. "Please..."

"Ruth Maywhistle is the perfect ghost," he adds excitedly. "Perfect in every way. The others are just window-dressing. They can haunt the place, and that's fine, but Ruth is the showstopper. She can't actually hurt anyone, not while she's just a specter, not while her body is safely caged. You're impressed, Beth, aren't you? You're finally ready to admit that this is a good thing."

"You're insane!" I sob, feeling as if the scream is loud enough make my ears bleed. "You're a monster! You killed my sister!"

"Can you still not get past that?" he asks with a sigh, as he drags the knife's tip down past my throat and onto the front of my shirt. "You're still stuck on that part of it, huh? Well, maybe you're not the girl I thought you were. I promise you, there are others out there, girls who'll appreciate me and realize that I'm a great man. I really, truly hoped that you'd be that girl, Beth, but there comes a time when I have to cut my losses. If all of this doesn't impress you, then maybe you won't make a good wife after all."

I flinch as he leans closer, and suddenly he kisses the side of my neck.

"But you might make a good ghost for the hotel," he whispers.

Before I even have time to cry out, he drives the knife deep into my belly. As the little girl's tortured scream comes to an abrupt halt, I feel Steve pulling the knife clear, and then he pushes me forward until I stumble and trip. Landing hard on my knees, I put my hands over the fresh wound, and I feel hot blood running between my fingers.

"You can't say I didn't give you a chance," he continues, stepping around me. "That's all you can really do for a person. Give them a chance, and then hope they take it. But you've disappointed me, Beth. You've let me down. A great man requires a great wife, and you're not up to the task. Maybe I..."

His voice trails off as I start dragging myself forward. The pain in my belly is extreme, and I can feel smeared blood beneath my body as I haul myself across the lobby.

"Where are you going, Beth? You're not *still* fighting, are you?"

I scream as I feel the knife slicing into my left thigh. He pulls it out quickly, and I hear him stepping over me.

"You need to suffer," he explains, as I once more start pulling myself across the floor. "You're a nice girl. A little boring, a little vanilla, but very nice. Nice ghosts don't interest people, though, so I'm going to have to make sure your death is nasty. That way, you'll come back mean and angry. You won't fade away like your sister."

"No," I stammer, "please, don't -"

I scream again as he drives the knife into my shoulder. I try to pull away, but he quickly pulls the knife out again and steps around to my other side. Letting out a pained cry, I hold my hands up, trying to protect myself from another strike, but this only makes him laugh.

"The ghosts of Lakeforth Hotel are going to make me millions," he continues. "I'm going to succeed where Jobard Nash failed. His ghost has been helping me a little, but most of the work has been mine!"

I reach forward, trying to pull myself toward the door, but suddenly I freeze as I see a figure up ahead. I stare, barely believing that it can be true, and a moment later Steve steps around me and stops just in front of my hand, staring down at me.

"Ruth," I whisper.

"She'll still be the main attraction," he mutters, "but you'll be a decent number two."

"Ruth," I gasp, pointing past his legs and toward the cage, where the rotten, decomposing corpse of the little girl has begun to rise from the plinth. "She... She's there..."

He turns, and we both watch as the dead girl

stands. It's impossible to make out her features in the darkened room, but she's silhouetted against the cracked plaster wall and I can tell she's looking this way as fluid and chunks of rotten flesh fall from her body.

"Well, it's about time she was reunited with her bones," Steve says, stepping toward her, almost as if she's no longer interest in me at all. "You wanted your body hauled up from the depths, little girl, and I was only too pleased to oblige. Do you remember me? Do you remember that night you freaked me out on the jetty? I bet you never thought that one day I'd be in charge of the place, huh?"

I watch in horror as he walks all the way to the cage, and it's clear that he's not scared at all. He's still holding the knife, and he seems genuinely fascinated by the girl's appearance. A moment later, he heads over to the reception desk and grabs a set of candles, lighting them with matches so that finally we can both see the girl's rotten face.

Her eyes are black pits, with flakes of desiccated flesh at the edges, while part of her cheek has been worn away to reveal her teeth. Most of her flesh is covered by the fabric of her muddy dress, but her face and hands are bloated and swollen, with patches where gray bones have already worn through. After a moment, she opens her mouth, letting out a faint, growling gasp.

"What's that?" Steve asks, cupping a hand against his ear. "You'll have to speak up!"

The gasp continues, and I hear a creaking sound as Steve walks past the front of the cage and the dead girl's head turns to watch. Clearly, he has her attention.

"Look at you," he says, tapping the bars of the cage. "You don't have to be in there, you know. You can haunt the corridors all you want, you don't *need* to be in that rotten old sack of a body. I hope you'll shake things up a little from time to time. I don't even know why you've been so desperate to get your body back, it's just a pile of putrefied meat and bone and hair, there's nothing really important there. I suppose you're just sentimental."

"You're torturing her," I gasp, trying but failing to get up.

"By all accounts, she was a lovely young girl," he replies, as I start dragging myself toward the door. "Amazing how death changes a person."

He taps the bars again.

"Isn't that right, Ruth?"

Suddenly the girl lunges at him, snarling and grabbing the bars of the cage. He doesn't pull back, he just smiles as she stares out at him, and as she slowly reaches a rotten hand toward his face.

"She's so beautiful," he says softly, as that bloated, decomposing hand brushes against his cheek. "So cold, so -"

She tries to grab his throat, but he pulls back and smiles. After a moment, he leans just a little closer, letting her brush her fingers against his neck.

"It's like putting your head between the lion's jaws," he continues. "So dangerous, but at the same time... How can you resist? She'll soon learn that she can't hurt me. Maybe she'll even come to see me as her master, as -"

Suddenly she grabs him again, and this time she manages to take hold of his collar and pull him closer to the cage. He lets out a startled cry, and it takes a moment before he's able to pull himself free and step back.

"Nice try," he says, clearly a little shocked. "Obviously you can't be trusted just yet."

The girl pulls back from the bars, still staring at him with pure hatred in her eyes.

"It's fascinating to see these things up close, isn't it?" Steve continues, turning to me. "The anger is truly impressive. Then again, I suppose I'd be an angry ghost, if I'd been killed the way *she* was killed. She's faced with a dilemma, isn't she? Haunt the hotel as a horrifying vision, or inhabit her body and stay caged like this. I suppose I'll be able to advertise a two-for-one show."

He taps the bars again, before turning and coming toward me I drag myself closer to the doors. As he walks away from the cage, the little girl's rotten face turns to watch him.

"I've been trying to understand ghosts," he explains, "and it seems that very few people have the necessary anger or sorrow to stick around for very long once they're dead. Most just fade away, but some of them can't let go. I wonder if you'll be a lingerer, Beth. You should be, considering how much I'm making you suffer."

Suddenly he puts his boot on my leg and presses down, and I let out a cry of pain as I feel him pushing on one of the knife wounds. Grabbing my hair, he pulls me head back until I'm looking up at him.

"I see a spark in your eyes," he mutters. "Yeah,

you definitely have potential."

He laughs as he lets go and steps back, and I immediately start dragging myself forward again.

"Where do you think you're going?" he asks. "You've already tried the doors, Beth. Nothing's going to have changed there. I have the only key, and it's around my neck so don't think for one moment that anything's going to happen there. And it's too late for you to beg for my forgiveness, so don't even think about trying that. You must realize what's going to happen. Your spirit will linger after death, so there's no need to be scared. It's just the fleshy, bony sack you call a body that's going to die."

"Go to hell!" I hiss, turning and looking up at him.

"What was that?" Again, he cups a hand around his ear. "I didn't quite hear."

"Go to hell!" I stammer, although I'm starting to shudder now as the air cools all around me. I feel as if only pure anger is keeping me going. At any moment, I could slump to the ground and lose consciousness. "Go to hell, Steve. That's where you belong."

"But I've got plans, Beth. Big, big plans."

Turning to look up at him, I feel for a moment as if the whole world is spinning around me. As the dizziness settles, however, I look past Steve and see that suddenly the cage is empty. There's no sign of the rotten little girl at all, although a moment later I realize I can see something stepping up behind him.

"The more I understand the rules about how ghosts work," Steve continues, coming closer, "the more

I realize that this hotel is going to be a massive money-spinner. I don't want fame, that's not what this is about. The last thing I'm after is masses of penniless yokels queuing up outside, wanting to pay ten quid a pop to see a real ghost. This place is going to be exclusive. A well-kept secret. Maybe even millionaires won't cut it, I might restrict the experience to billionaires. A billion pounds a night to stay here. How does that sound?"

I open my mouth to tell him that Ruth Maywhistle is right behind him and getting closer, but somehow the words catch in my throat.

"Your preserved corpse will go on display, of course," he adds, as if I'm supposed to be proud of that fact. "Part of the lobby exhibition that welcomes people before they get ready to spend a night here. I need to remember the importance of showmanship, don't I?"

"You're..."

Struggling for breath, I can't get any more words out.

"I'm what?" he asks with a smile. "Brilliant? Impressive? On the verge of being the richest man alive?"

"You're..."

He waits, clearly keen to hear how I finish that sentence.

"Tell me," he continues, as the rotten girl steps closer and closer behind him. "What am I, Beth? How do you see me?"

"You're..."

I pause, before taking a slow, deep breath.

Reaching down, Steve grabs my collar and hauls

me up, while grinning wildly. A moment later, he slashes the knife against my cheek, causing me to let out a gasp of pain.

"What am I?" he asks with a laugh.

I try to open my mouth, but he cuts me again, this time across the forehead.

"A genius?" he continues.

I flinch as he slices the knife down my other cheek and onto my neck. The pain is intense, but I'm too weak to cry out.

"A pioneer?" he adds, as he runs the blade onto my collarbone. "A showman?"

"You're oblivious," I stammer finally. "You haven't even noticed she's out of her cage, have you?"

"Don't try that one," he replies. "She *can't* get out, she's my -"

He stops suddenly, and I see a flicker of fear in his eyes, as if he's finally heard the faint creaking sound that's coming from just over his shoulder. He seems hesitant, almost as if he doesn't quite believe it could be true, and then finally he starts to turn.

Letting out a horrific scream, the rotten corpse of Ruth Maywhistle lunges at him, pushing him back and landing on his chest as he slams down against the marble floor just a few feet from me. At the same time, Steve lets go of my collar and I crash against the wall before slipping down.

Turning, I immediately start crawling away, but I can already hear the girl's scream getting louder.

"Stop!" Steve yells, his voice filled with panic. "You can't do this! You can't hurt me! You can't even get out of the cage! It's impossible! I know the rules, how did you -"

Suddenly his scream replaces hers, and I turn just in time to see that Ruth has bitten hard on his neck. Blood erupts from the wound, and I watch in horror as Steve tries desperately to push her away. Her teeth tear through his flesh, finally ripping thick strips away as more and more blood pumps out from the wound and splatters against the floor.

"Beth!" he gasps, spraying blood from his mouth now too. "Help me. This isn't possible! How did you get the key?"

Reaching up with bloodied hands, he checks the thread around his neck, and he seems shocked as he finds that the key is gone. A moment later, as if to show him how she escaped from the cage, Ruth holds up the key and then lets it drop to the floor.

"Oh, you clever thing," Steve continues, staring up at her rotten face. "And there I was, thinking you'd just tried to grab my throat so you could choke me. I should -"

Before he can finish, the girl reaches down again and bites his cheek, causing him to scream as she tears away another strip of flesh. At the same time, she places a rotten hand on the other side of his face and starts digging her fingertips into his cheek, scraping the meat from the bone.

"I'll let them go!" he shouts, his voice filled with panic. "I'll let all of you go! I'll bury you properly, in a proper graveyard. I'm not the one you should hate! I'm just trying to help you and -"

He stops suddenly, staring at her ghostly face.

"It wasn't Jobard Nash," he whispers finally. "The voice, guiding me here all these years... It was you! But why would -"

Letting out an ear-piercing scream, Ruth bites down hard on his neck once more, this time tearing away enough flesh to silence him. Although he manages a few more choking gasps, Steve seems unable to fight back now, and he keeps his eyes fixed on me as slowly his body falls still. Ruth doesn't stop yet, instead using her teeth and hands to rip more and more meat from his bones. She seems frantic, filled with pure anger.

Steve's mouth shudders slightly, but Ruth's fingers are buried deep in the bloody pulp of his neck. She must know that he's dead now, but apparently even this isn't enough to satisfy her need for revenge. I watch, horrified but unable to pull away, as Ruth digs her bony fingers into his throat. At the same time, she lets out a snarl as she starts pushing her fingertips under the flesh around his jaw and then up onto his cheekbones. I can see the outline of her fingers bulging beneath the flesh of his face, followed by a horrific scratching sound as she digs her bony fingertips against his skull. Finally, she rips her hands out, tearing his face open and sending fresh blood dribbling down onto the marble floor.

And still she lets out a faint, gurgled hissing sound, as she stares down at his corpse. Silhouetted against the flickering candles, she slowly starts dribbling some kind of pale brown liquid from her lips, and finally the hissing stops.

I think she's done.

I don't dare move. Not yet. I simply stay where I am, scared in case I attract her attention. She seems to be still watching Steve's body, looking for any hint that he might still be alive.

Finally, I realize I have to get out of here.

Turning, I crawl away on my elbows, struggling against the pain in my belly and chest. I don't know how much blood I've lost, but I know I feel weak and light-headed. As I crawl toward the door, I figure I'll have to find some way to force it open, and then a moment later I remember the key that Ruth Maywhistle stole from around Steve's neck. I glance over my shoulder and see the key resting on the blood-spattered floor, a few feet from where Ruth is still staring down at his dead, torn face.

I watch for a moment, horrified by the sight, before turning and crawling to the door. Reaching up, I grab the handle and pull, hoping against hope that by some miracle I might be able to get out. When that doesn't work, I haul myself up and lean against the door, before trying the handle a couple more times.

There has to be a way out of here.

"Please," I whisper, as I feel myself already losing consciousness. "I don't want to die here. Please..."

I hesitate for a moment, and then suddenly I realize that my eyes have slipped shut. I force them open, but the lids feel so heavy and they immediately start closing again.

"Hey loser," Annie's voice whispers suddenly. "Are you gonna get that key, or what?"

My eyes flick open and I look around, feeling a

rush of hope at the thought that maybe – somehow, against all the odds – Annie is still alive.

"Where are you?" I whisper, but there's no sign of her.

Still, I know she'd hate to see me give up, so I turn and look over toward the key. Ruth Maywhistle is still picking flesh from Steve's dead body, and I think perhaps her rage has passed. I tell myself that she probably won't even notice if I go and take the key, so I force myself to start crawling across the floor. Every reach of my hands, even breath I take, is agony, but somehow I manage to keep going. Ruth Maywhistle still isn't looking at me, and finally I get close enough to reach out and take the key from where it's resting in a puddle of blood.

And then, slowly, I become aware of a creaking, crunching sound from nearby.

Looking up, I see to my horror that the rotten figure of Ruth Maywhistle has finally turned to look at me with those dead, decayed eyes.

"I just want to get out of here," I whisper, barely even daring to get the words out.

I wait, but she's still just staring at me.

"I'm sorry," I add, closing my fist around the key. "If I could do anything for you, I would. I just want to leave this place and never come back. Why did you want to bring Steve back here, anyway? What did you want from him?"

Again I wait, but her dark, soulless eyes are fixed on me. One of her eyeballs has partially decayed, but the crumbling mess still twitches in its socket. Pale, yellowish liquid is oozing from her mouth and running down her chin, and more is seeping from a hole in the side of her neck. The stench is unbearable, and after a moment I realize that small hook-headed worms seem to be burrowing through some exposed flesh just above the collar of her dress. Her gaze is penetrating, almost as if she's looking straight into my soul, and I don't even dare start crawling away.

"I know you're not evil," I say finally. "I know you just... You wanted revenge, and you got it. The people who hurt you are dead. That's all you wanted, isn't it? They're all dead!"

When she still fails to reply, I realize that maybe it's okay for me to leave. I hesitate for a moment longer, and then I start struggling to my feet.

"I'll tell people," I stammer. "I'll make sure that everyone knows what was done to you."

Turning, I start limping across the lobby, with only the light from the candles to guide my way. The pain in my legs and chest is excruciating, but I can see the door ahead and I still have the key in my right hand. When I finally get to the lobby's far side, I reach out with a trembling hand and slide the key into the lock. To my relief, I find that it fits perfectly, which I guess means that Steve had one master-key for the whole place. My hand is shaking so hard, I struggle for a moment to turn the key, but finally -

Suddenly I hear a faint clicking sound over my shoulder.

I freeze, and then I hear the sound again.

Slowly, I turn and find that Ruth Maywhistle's

rotting corpse is standing right behind me, staring up at me with those rotten, dead eyes. I can see gray bones poking through putrid flesh, and she's dribbling more worms and foul water from several holes in her torso. Her dead eyes are still watching me, as some kind of black, bloodied liquid dribbles down her chin.

"Please," I stammer, feeling a rush of fear, "it's over. Just let me -"

Before I can finish, she lunges at me, hissing loudly and biting down hard on my shoulder. I cry out in pain as I feel her rotten teeth digging deep, scraping against my collarbone. Desperately trying to get away, I reach for the door-handle, but Ruth places her cold, clammy hands on my face and keeps her teeth embedded in my flesh.

"Please!" I gasp, as the pain shudders through my chest. "Don't do this! Everyone who hurt you is dead! You can't -"

Suddenly an unseen force rips me from the floor and sends me clattering across the room until I slam into the wall. I feel a set of sharp snapping pains low down on the left side of my ribs, and by the time I slither to the floor I'm already struggling to breathe properly.

"No!" I gasp, feeling a ripping pain every time I try to inhale. I manage to force air into my lungs somehow, but the pain is so strong, I think I might be about to pass out. Looking around, I try to spot the little girl, but my vision is starting to become blurry. "Why are you doing this to me? I'm not the one who -"

Before I can finish, the same unseen force sends me crashing over toward the stairs, slamming me into the bottom step. The pain in my chest is immense, and I take several deep, agonizing breaths as I roll away and look back across the dark lobby. The candles are flickering on the main desk, casting vast, dancing patterns of light and shadow, but I still can't see properly, not even after blinking several times. All I can really see is Steve's corpse over on the far side of the room, near the main door. The door's unlocked now, so I tell myself that all I have to do is get over there and run outside, and then get away from the hotel.

"I'm not the one you're after," I whisper, just in case the little girl can hear me. "The people who hurt you are all dead now. Please, let me go. You have no reason to hate me I can't do anything for you!"

I hesitate for a moment longer, before starting to limp forward. Every step is agony, and I swear I can feel several broken ribs digging deep into my chest, but I know I have to keep going.

"You're just a little girl," I stammer. "You don't hate me. You're not a monster. You got your -"

Suddenly something rushes past me, flashing inches from my face. All I really make out is a blur of darkness, but it's enough to make me stop for a moment. Swallowing hard, I figure I should just start walking again, but now I feel as if something is watching me. Staring ahead across the lobby, I can't *see* anyone, but I'm certain that there's a figure standing right in front of me. It's as if two dark, angry eyes are making a tunnel through the air to my own, and I feel almost paralyzed by a growing sense of fear. The candles Steve lit earlier are still flickering on the reception desk, but they don't bring much light.

She's here.

She's right in front of me.

I can't see her, but I know I'm right.

"Please," I continue, my voice tense now with pain. "I didn't even want to be here. I was tricked. I just want to leave."

I wait, but there's no reply.

"I'm going to go to the door," I add, "and I'm going to leave. Is that okay with you? Will you let me do that?"

Again, nothing.

I take a deep breath, despite the pain in my chest, and then I step forward.

Instantly, the ghost of Ruth Maywhistle appears in front of me and screams, lunging at me. I flinch, but I'm too late to pull away and a force lifts me from the floor, sending me crashing across the lobby until I slam hard into one of the cases that Steve put in place. I feel the glass cracking against my shoulder, and I drop to the floor just as a torrent of foul-smelling clear fluid comes rushing down all around me. Something large and heavy falls, too, hitting my arm and then slithering across the floor.

Gasping for breath, I turn and see that I hit the tank containing Annie's body, which is now sprawled on the marble just a few feet away. There's a foul, almost overpowering stench in the air from whatever chemicals Steve was using to preserve my sister. Staggering to my feet, with my drenched clothes soaked in the noxious mixture, I look around the dark lobby but once again the little girl is gone.

So I run.

Almost slipping in the liquid, I race toward Steve's body, only for Ruth to suddenly slam into me from behind. I feel her teeth sinking into my shoulder once again, and this time I scream as she tears a strip of flesh away. Crashing to the ground, I try to reach back and force her away, but she's holding me too tight and she's already started biting into the side of my neck.

Crawling forward, I let out a pained gasp.

"What do you want from me?" I stammer, but deep down I already realize the truth. Whatever Ruth Maywhistle might have been like when she was alive, she's become a vengeful, monstrous creature in death. She wasn't just out to kill the people who wronged her, she was out to punish any living soul she encountered. She's become this *thing* and there's no way for her to turn back.

I start dragging myself across the lobby yet again, but I can feel the girl's rotten little teeth chewing deeper and deeper into my neck and I'm already starting to slow. The door is so far away, and I know I'll never make it. For a moment, I stop and actually consider accepting my fate, but then I look up at the reception desk and I spot the candles that Steve lit earlier. Their flickering glow is strangely beautiful, although I figure that if I'm going to die here, then at least I'm going to make sure that nobody else ever has to enter this hotel and face the ghost of Ruth Maywhistle. All this horror and pain has to end.

With the last of my strength, I haul myself off

the floor and stagger to the desk. Taking care to keep clear of the candles, since I'm doused in whatever liquid was in the glass case, I limp around the table and look down at the flames. I can still feel Ruth biting into my neck, so I grip the table's edge and use the last of my strength to push it over, sending the candles crashing down until they land in the puddle that has spread across the floor.

I don't even know if the liquid is flammable, but -

Immediately, a roar of flames bursts through the room. Stumbling back, I'm startled to see that not only was the liquid flammable, but even the vapors have started burning. Within just a couple of seconds, the flames have run all the way over to the bottom of the stairs, and I slump down to the floor as I watch the inferno spreading. In fact, I'm so shocked by the sight of the fire, I don't notice at first that I can no longer feel Ruth's teeth in my neck. When I *do* notice that she's no longer attacking me, I feel a faint flutter of relief in my chest.

Despite the pain that's ringing through my body, I start crawling toward the door. The flames are mostly on the other side of the lobby, but I know they'll spread to this side soon, and I'm soaked in the same highly flammable liquid that caused the fire in the first place. I don't have long, but pain and fear keep me going until finally I get close to the door. I can hear the flames burning through the hotel now, and when I look over my shoulder I see that the wallpaper is on fire.

A moment later, I spot the figure of Ruth

Maywhistle standing in the flames, watching me with the same dark expression I saw before. Nearby, the flames have already reached the cases that contain the various sets of bones that Steve gathered. I watch the destruction for a moment, with my hand still resting on the door's handle, before finally I slump down against the marble floor.

I can't do this.

I can't get out of here. Even if I got out the door, I'd still be miles from nowhere.

Too weak to move, I stare up at the ceiling and watch as the flames come closer. The paper and plaster are burning away from the wall, revealing the hotel's brickwork, and a moment later the chandelier comes crashing to the floor, bringing half the ceiling with it and leaving a vast tangle of wires hanging down. Any second now, my body is going to burn, probably while I'm still alive. I can't move, though. I can't even cry out. Finally, as I see flames rippling through the air, and as I feel the immense heat getting closer and closer, I spot a figure stepping into view above me.

It's Ruth Maywhistle, standing in the flames and watching me as I wait to die. A moment later, I feel a warm rushing sensation on the left side of my chest, and I scream as my body starts to burn.

Please, let me not haunt this place once I'm dead. Let me not be like the little girl. Please, just let there be nothing after the pain ends.

EPILOGUE

One year later

THE BELLS OF ST. MARTIN'S sound even louder in the winter air. It's a cold Tuesday morning as I hurry along the pavement and pass throngs of tourists. One or two of them glance at me, and I can see the expressions of shock and pity in their eyes. A child even wrinkles his nose, as if the sight of me is too hideous for him to comprehend, but he can't stop staring.

I guess I don't blame any of them.

Heading around the next corner, I figure that at least they can't see me anymore. Then again, the next street is just as busy. I should be used to the way people look at me by now, but I'm not. I guess that'll come later. It's not their job to get used to my appearance; it's my job to deal with their disgust. And I will get used to it, according to Doctor Wallace. I'll get past my injuries, and I'll stop feeling so sorry for myself. Taking a deep breath, and feeling a flicker of pain in my chest in the process, I force myself to start limping along the pavement again. I hate being out in public like this. I just want to reach the office and get back to work. But first, there's one place I need to see.

Tucked away in a side-street, the old Mecklethorpe funeral home has been left largely untouched since going out of business. The building was apparently purchased by a company that planned to convert it to apartments, but they've struggled to get planning permission, so here it remains in all its glory while the details are sorted out. According to my research, this is where Maurice Mecklethorpe – aka Jobard Nash – was born and raised. This is the home he ran away from, a few years before he made his fortune and established the Lakeforth.

I don't have permission to enter the site, of course, but I *do* have a pair of bolt-cutters. I check to make sure nobody is nearby, and then I cut the chain.

Annie would be so proud of me.

The funeral home looks so ordinary now, as I make my way across the yard. The main building is securely locked, and I don't fancy my padlock-picking skills too much, so all I can do is cup my hands around my eyes and peer through the window. There's some kind of workshop inside, although any equipment was removed a long time ago. Taking a step back, I realize that I don't exactly know why I made the trek out here, except that maybe I felt as if I was somehow coming full circle. After all, this is where the story of Jobard Nash began, and without him there would have been no

Lakeforth Hotel. Without him, maybe Steve would never have lost his mind. In fact, he -

Suddenly I spot a young boy's face reflected in the window, staring straight at me.

I turn around, but there's no sign of him. Looking at the window again, I find that he seems to have vanished, although I know what I saw. Turning, I watch the yard for a moment, just in case he makes another appearance, and I swear my heart is pounding. I don't know whether ghosts get to choose where they haunt, but if they do, Jobard – or Maurice, as he might want to be known once again – could have chosen to come back here. Perhaps ghosts come not only to the places where they have unfinished business, but instead sometimes to the places where they feel most themselves. Or to the places where they left a part of their soul.

At least, they go to those places once they're free. Once they're no longer anchored to wherever they died.

In which case, I think I understand why several patients at a London hospital have reported seeing two ghostly little girls playing in the grounds.

***

"Ms. Hayes?" a voice calls out. "Beth Hayes? Wait, can I have a word?"

Great, another journalist.

I pick up the pace, hoping against hope that I'll reach the office door before this asshole catches up to me. A moment later, however, I hear footsteps getting closer, and I realize that I'm not going to be so lucky. This happens about once a week at the moment, and I'm starting to think that these people are never going to get tired.

"Ms. Hayes, I -"

"I really don't want to talk," I reply, glancing at him and seeing that – sure enough – it's someone I've never met before in my life. "Thanks, but no thanks. I don't talk to the media."

"I'm not from the media. I'm nothing to do with the press. Please, I just want one moment of your time. I have something for you."

Realizing that this guy isn't going to give up easily, I stop and turn to him. He's older than me, in his forties or maybe fifties, with graying hair, and he seems pretty breathless after hurrying to catch up.

"Whoever you are," I tell him, "I'd appreciate it if you'd just leave me alone. I've done nothing to court attention. I just want to get on with my life."

As I say those words, I realize that I've inadvertently reached up and started touching my scar again. I swear, every time I meet someone new, I catch myself scratching at the spot where a ridge of knotted flesh rises up from beneath my collar and runs to the edge of my cheek. Forcing myself to shove both my hands into my pocket, I still can't help thinking that this guy can probably tell that beneath my thick overcoat and the rest of my clothes, the left side of my body is a scarred mess. My face is just about the only part of me that looks even remotely normal, and even *that* is burned in several places. I've had a lot of operations over the past year.

"It's about the Lakeforth," the man says cautiously.

"Of course it is," I mutter. "I can't remember the last time anyone wanted to talk to me about anything else."

"The hotel is -"

"The hotel doesn't exist anymore," I add, cutting him off. "It's gone. There's nothing there except a patch of ashy ground. The entire place burned down a year ago."

"Oh, I know," he replies. "I've been there. To the site of the fire, I mean. I was never fortunate enough to go when the place was still standing. There were always rumors about the place, but it was never high on the list for any paranormal investigator. Not until everything that happened to you, anyway. I've always thought that it must have been such a strange atmosphere at the hotel. From the photographs I've sourced, it's clear that the Lakeforth had a rather unusual style, somewhere between -"

"Do you want something?" I ask, feeling a flutter of irritation in my chest. At the same time, a man and a woman walk past, and the woman glances at me.

Did she see the scars?

Or did she recognize me? After all, my story hit the papers a while back, even though I just wanted to hide away. Some asshole even got a photo of me and put it all over social media.

"My name is Gavin Wallace," the man says, reaching out to shake my hand. "I've read every report about what happened at the Lakeforth, Ms. Hayes. About its past, about the life of Jobard Nash and the lives of the key people who passed through the hotel's doors. About Steve Culshaw, and all the things he did. And about you, about how you still claim not to remember how you escaped the burning building. How you were found outside when the fire crews arrived. They say it's as if somebody carried you out, although obviously there was no sign of anyone else."

Swallowing hard, I realize that I can't tell him what I really think. I can't tell anyone. Deep down, I'm certain that once she saw the hotel was burning, Ruth Maywhistle realized she no longer needed vengeance. I'm certain that, right at the end, she became herself again.

"I should cut to the chase," Mr. Wallace continues, forcing a nervous smile as he fishes a crumpled leaflet from his pocket and hands it to me. "I know this might seem indelicate, but I'm here today to make you an offer. A financial offer, one that I hope might interest you a great deal."

Looking down at the leaflet, I'm shocked to see that it's for a company that organizes ghost tours. I take a look inside and see various weekend trips advertised, including nights in supposedly haunted houses up and down the country. Just as I'm about to ask what this has to do with me, however, I see that on the leaflet's back page there's an advert for a new tour that's set to launch early next year.

"You're taking people to the site of the hotel?" I whisper.

"We're a small company," he replies. "We've been around for a while, but we're not some big global corporation. It's just myself and my wife who run it. We take small parties to various sights of supernatural significance, and we arrange viewings and ghost hunts, and little talks, that sort of thing. Oh, and tea and biscuits are included free of charge in every trip."

"What does this have to do with me?" I ask, feeling faintly disgusted as I hand the leaflet back to him.

"You can keep that."

"I don't want to."

"But -"

"I don't want it!" I say firmly.

He hesitates, before taking the leaflet.

"We're planning our first trip to the site of the former Lakeforth Hotel," he explains, "and, well, we wanted to offer you the chance to come along as a special guest. We'd pay your travel fees and accommodation costs, plus a small fee of five hundred pounds. Five hundred per trip, that is. I know it's not exactly riches, but ideally we'd like to run up to four of these trips each year., maybe even more if there's enough demand. People do so like to visit haunted locations, you see."

"You can't take people there," I reply.

"We have permission from the new owner of the site. He doesn't mind us going up there while he arranges to bulldoze the ruins."

"That's not what I mean," I continue. "You're crazy, you can't..."

My voice trails off.

"We donate 10% of all proceeds to a local animal sanctuary," he replies. "We only charge £70 per trip anyway, so we're not exactly making a big profit. We're mainly interested in the experience. And obviously, if you were to come along and provide expert, on-site commentary, I'm sure our guests would gain a much better understanding of what really happened at the Lakeforth."

I pause for a moment, before shaking my head.

"Ms. Hayes, your presence would really make the trips more instructive for our guests," he continues. "I know you might not like the idea of going back, but we run a very serious, very -"

"I'm not doing this," I tell him, taking a step back. "I don't even want to talk about it. I told the police everything I know about what happened there. About what happened to my sister. I guess I probably can't stop you taking your little tour to the Lakeforth, but there's no way I'm going along with it. If you think I'd ever want to go back to that place, if you think I want to encourage anyone to go there, then obviously you don't really understand what happened." I turn to walk away, before hesitating for a moment. "Besides, it doesn't matter. Do what you want. You won't find any ghosts there."

"We could perhaps stretch to six hundred pounds."

I open my mouth to tell him what I really think, which is that he's wasting his time. With the hotel destroyed and the human remains destroyed in the fire, I'm pretty sure the ghosts have been set free. Then again,

I doubt he'd accept my word for that.

"Goodbye, Mr. Wallace," I say finally. "Please don't contact me again."

"I'm surprised you're so skeptical of our chances," he tells me. "After what you went through, Ms. Hayes, I'd have thought you of all people would believe in ghosts!"

"I didn't say I don't believe in ghosts," I reply, turning and walking away as a cold wind blows along the street. "I said you won't find any in the ruins of Lakeforth Hotel."

Also by Amy Cross

The Curse of Wetherley House

"If you walk through that door, Evil Mary will get you."

When she agrees to visit a supposedly haunted house with an old friend, Rosie assumes she'll encounter nothing more scary than a few creaks and bumps in the night. Even the legend of Evil Mary doesn't put her off. After all, she knows ghosts aren't real. But when Mary makes her first appearance, Rosie realizes she might already be trapped.

For more than a century, Wetherley House has been cursed. A horrific encounter on a remote road in the late 1800's has already caused a chain of misery and pain for all those who live at the house. Wetherley House was abandoned long ago, after a terrible discovery in the basement, something has remained undetected within its room. And even the local children know that Evil Mary waits in the house for anyone foolish enough to walk through the front door.

Before long, Rosie realizes that her entire life has been defined by the spirit of a woman who died in agony. Can she become the first person to escape Evil Mary, or will she fall victim to the same fate as the house's other occupants?

Also by Amy Cross

The Ghosts of Hexley Airport

Ten years ago, more than two hundred people died in a horrific plane crash at Hexley Airport.

Today, some say their ghosts still haunt the terminal building.

When she starts her new job at the airport, working a night shift as part of the security team, Casey assumes the stories about the place can't be true. Even when she has a strange encounter in a deserted part of the departure hall, she's certain that ghosts aren't real.

Soon, however, she's forced to face the truth. Not only is there something haunting the airport's buildings and tarmac, but a sinister force is working behind the scenes to replicate the circumstances of the original accident. And as a snowstorm moves in, Hexley Airport looks set to witness yet another disaster.

Printed in Great Britain
by Amazon